John Ryan

Alan Glynn is a graduate of Trinity College, where he studied English literature. His first novel, *Limitless* (formerly published under the title *The Dark Fields*), has been made into a major motion picture from Relativity Media, directed by Neil Burger. He is married with two children and lives in Dublin.

Also by Alan Glynn

Limitless

(previously published under the title *The Dark Fields*)

WINTERLAND

A NOVEL

ALAN GLYNN

Picador

A Minotaur Book
New York

For Eithne, Rory and Cian

www.picadorusa.com

Picador® is a U.S. registered trademark and is used by St. Martin's Press under license from Pan Books Limited.

For information on Picador Reading Group Guides, please contact Picador.
E-mail: readinggroupguides@picadorusa.com

Excerpt from *Bloodland* copyright © 2011 by Alan Glynn.

The Library of Congress has cataloged the Minotaur Books / St. Martin's edition as follows:

Glynn, Alan, 1960–
    Winterland / Alan Glynn. — 1st ed.
        p. cm.
    ISBN 978-0-312-53922-1
    1. Dublin (Ireland)—Fiction.   2. Murder victims'
families—Fiction.   3. Gangsters—Fiction.   I. Title.
    PR6107.L93W56 2009
    823'.92—dc22

                                        2009012748

Picador ISBN 978-0-312-57299-0

First published in the United States by Minotaur Books,
an imprint of St. Martin's Publishing Group

First Picador Edition: July 2011

10   9   8   7   6   5   4   3   2   1

Prologue

How has it come to this?

Gina doesn't know – but she looks across the warehouse floor at the three men and decides she can't take any more of it. She has to leave. It's just too much.

'I'm . . . I'll be outside,' she says, though it's barely audible.

She turns and walks over to the metal door. Her hand is shaking as she opens it. She steps outside, into the cold night air.

With her back to the closed door, she takes a deep breath and closes her eyes.

After a moment, she opens them again. It's a fairly desolate scene out here. In one direction the floodlit yard of this industrial park leads to a graffiti-covered wall at the back of a housing estate. In the other direction there are more warehouses, and you can just about see the road up ahead – which is dead quiet at the moment. Five minutes west of here there is a major roundabout, and even at this time of night it would be busy with traffic.

Gina can't believe she's feeling lonely for traffic.

She looks up. The sky is clear and the moon is so dazzlingly bright that it's almost pulsating. She stays huddled in the doorway, puts her back to the wind and tries to get one of Fitz's cigarettes going, cupping her hand around it and flicking the Zippo repeatedly until it takes.

Then, inhaling deeply, she steps away from the door. The intense glow from the moon tonight, combined with the orange wash of the floodlights, gives the space out here an air of unreality, the eerie and soulless feel of a virtual environment. She wishes that that's what this whole thing were – a simulation, a game, something she could tinker with and reprogramme. But she knows there is no – can be no – digital equivalent, or even approximation, of anxiety, of guilt, of fear.

This is real and it's happening now.

But what if Terry Stack finds out where Mark Griffin is? Will that mean it's been worth it? Will that mean she did the right thing by calling him?

Or is it all too toxic now for such a clean exchange?

As she takes her next drag on the cigarette, Gina hears a weird sound. It is short and shrill and penetrating. She looks up and remains still for a few seconds, listening.

She really can't be sure that the sound wasn't just some form of distortion carried here from a distance by the wind.

She closes her eyes.

But neither can she be sure that it didn't come from nearby, from directly behind her, and that it wasn't a scream.

One

1

He is sitting in what they now call the beer garden. Before the smoking ban came into force it was a concrete yard, a skanky area at the back of the pub that was all stacked crates and kegs and empty cardboard boxes. But with a little outdoor furniture – decking, benches, tables, pole umbrellas for when it rains – they've transformed it into a 'space', a haven where smokers can congregate, light up their Players or Sweet Afton and complain about the excesses of the nanny state. There has even been some confusion, not to say tension, over etiquette. If a non-smoker occupies the last available seat, as might happen in summer or on an unseasonably balmy evening in winter, is he obliged to give that seat up to the next smoker who comes along?

Well, in this establishment, *yes* actually, because if you don't smoke – the logic runs – what are you doing out here in the first place and what kind of a fucking baby are you anyway?

But tonight the question doesn't arise. It's a cold and drizzly Monday, just right for the season, and only five people, hard-core smokers, have come outside with their cigarettes and lighters (plus pints, vodkas, whatever) and settled themselves under the various umbrellas.

'Poxy night,' he says, and laughs. This fat, pasty-faced twenty-six-year-old then stares across the beer garden at the young couple who are sitting opposite him. After a moment, he stares at the two old-timers sitting next to them.

One of these old-timers, Christy Mullins, nods his head in agreement. He reckons it's better than doing nothing. He reckons that the fat, pasty-faced man in the denim jacket and white shirt over there isn't someone you just ignore. He reckons that life is short enough as it is.

Still grinning, the fat, pasty-faced man nods back. He then takes a long, serious drag from his cigarette, gazing up at the illuminated, slow-falling drizzle as he does so.

He's a regular here, but not everyone knows who he is.

Christy, for example, doesn't know who he is – though he's certainly seen him from time to time, and even remembers, now that he thinks about it, a specific incident that happened some months back. However, he couldn't give you his name or tell you anything about him.

Which is exactly the way the man himself would like to keep it, because he's not into any of this celebrity crap – talking to *Sunday World* journalists or going on *Liveline*. He doesn't consider it good for business.

'Poxy Irish weather,' he then says, half to himself now, and not looking at anyone in particular. 'Poxy Minister for poxy fuckin' Health.'

Christy manages to ignore this, getting lost for a moment in a minor coughing fit. He then raises his pint with one hand and taps his cigarette against the ashtray with the other. That incident he does remember happened late one summer evening out here in the beer garden. The place was crowded, and the fat, pasty-faced man was sitting with a group of other – what were they – twenty-five-, twenty-six-year-olds? They were all drinking pints, smoking, digging each other in the ribs

and laughing. Suddenly, out in the street, a car alarm went off –
a high-pitched, brain-piercing wail. The immediate reaction
around the tables was a collective sigh of exasperation, and
then, as the wail continued, a loud 'Ah Jaysus' from someone
near the door leading into the main part of the pub.

It was obvious that the offending car was parked very close
by, and possibly even right outside the pub. But something else
was becoming obvious, too. As the general hubbub gave way
to the mute frustration of shaking heads, one of the fat,
pasty-faced man's co-drinkers put his pint down and said, in
everyone's hearing, 'Isn't that yours?'

Or –

'Isn't that yours, *Noel*.'

That was it. He called him Noel. Christy remembers now.

'Isn't that yours, Noel?'

At which fat, pasty-faced Noel shrugged his shoulders.
'So?'

'I just –'

'Well, don't fucking *just* anything.'

'But –'

'Shut *up*, right?'

Noel then reached for his glass, and as he took a sip from it,
staring ahead, not saying a word to anyone, an almost
complete silence, icy and incredulous, descended on the beer
garden, with only one sound remaining – the ceaseless,
demented wail of the car alarm.

Christy threw his eyes up. People were obviously afraid of
this young pup, and it sickened him. Who was he anyway, one
of these gangland thugs you read about in the papers?

Noel took another sip from his pint, and a drag from his
cigarette. Minutes passed, or what seemed like minutes.

Eventually an elderly woman at the next table piped up. 'Ah here, love,' she said, 'come on, I'm getting an awful headache.'

It was only then that Noel stubbed out his cigarette and got up from the table to leave. He was huge, Christy saw – not only fat, but tall and broad as well. A barman appeared in the doorway just as Noel was approaching it. The barman's eyebrows were raised, ready for a confrontation.

'All right, all right,' Noel said, strolling past him, 'keep your fucking hair on.'

Less than a minute later, the car alarm stopped. Noel didn't come back, and noise levels in the beer garden gradually returned to normal.

Now, of course, it is much quieter – later in the evening, later in the year. Darker, colder. The young man and woman, huddled close together, are more or less whispering to each other. The two old-timers, in contemplative mode, have barely exchanged a word since they came out here. Noel himself has been the most voluble, finding it unnatural to be sitting alone, not talking to anyone. He would rather annoy strangers, roping them into any conversation at all, than sit in silence.

'I was watching that fucking Discovery Channel the other night,' he says, lighting up a cigarette. 'Apparently there's over *two hundred* types of shark in the sea.'

The young man and woman both look up, startled. Christy glances over as well.

'Tiger sharks, hammerhead sharks, pigeye sharks, Ga-fucking-*lap*agos sharks.'

With his cigarette in one hand, Christy puts his other hand up to his chest and coughs. He is retired now, but for fifty years he worked as a barber, and in that time he had plenty of what you might call 'characters' in his chair. He recognises this Noel across the way as a distinct character type himself.

Unstable, unpredictable, dangerous.

'The great white is the only shark that sticks its head out of the water to look around. Amazing, isn't it?'

Again – though he's barely listening – Christy nods his head in agreement. All he wants is a quiet smoke.

'I love those names,' Noel says, flicking ash to the ground. 'They're mad. Fucking *hammer*head, what?'

The young couple have turned back in towards each other and are whispering again.

'I said they're mad, *aren't they*?' He is staring directly across at the young couple now, but they don't seem to have noticed. Christy rests his cigarette in the ashtray.

'*Love!*' Noel shouts.

The young woman looks up.

'The *names*. I said they're fucking mad, aren't they?'

She doesn't say anything. Christy can't tell if she's nervous or annoyed.

'Well?' Noel says.

'Well *what*?' the young woman says, definitely annoyed. Her boyfriend hasn't looked up yet. He's definitely nervous.

'What do you mean *well what*? Don't fucking *well what?* me, you frigid little bitch.'

Christy throws his eyes up.

The boyfriend exhales loudly and slaps the palm of his hand on the table.

'What's *your* problem?' Noel says. 'You bleedin' ponce.'

'Stop it,' Christy says. 'Enough of that.'

Everyone turns now and looks at Christy.

'Who asked *you*?' Noel says.

'You're nothing but a bowsie,' Christy says. 'Do you know that?'

Noel holds up his cigarette. 'See this? I'll stick it in your fucking eye if you don't shut up.'

There is a long silence.

Christy wants to say *Go ahead, I'd like to see you try*, but when he opens his mouth to speak, nothing happens. He's seventy-three years old after all. He's thin and wiry and actually quite frail. He has more or less permanent bronchitis from decades of smoking unfiltered cigarettes.

So what does he think he's doing?

The man beside Christy, nudging him in the elbow, whispers, 'Leave it, Christy, leave it.'

But with his heart thumping, Christy makes another attempt, and this time he manages to get it out.

'Go ahead, fatso,' he says – the 'fatso' coming out of nowhere – 'I'd like to see you try.'

'Whoa,' Noel says, sliding along the bench to get out from behind the table, '*What did you say?*'

For some reason, as Christy stares over at Noel, all he can think about is the newspaper headline this is going to generate. More specifically, and like a knotted synapse in his brain, it's the wording he can't get past: VICIOUS THUG ASSAULTS PENSIONER. VICIOUS ASSAULT ON PENSIONER BY THUG. THUG IN VICIOUS ASSAULT ON PENSIONER.

Noel gets to the edge of the bench, and pauses. He takes a drag from his cigarette.

The young woman, meanwhile, stubs hers out. She picks up the lighter and pack of Silk Cut from the table and stuffs them into her bag. Slouched next to her, the young man is trying to look casual, unconcerned.

'Come on,' she says to him, 'we're going.'

PENSIONER VICIOUSLY ASSAULTED BY THUG.

With the cigarette now dangling from his lips, Noel glares over at Christy. He brings his hands together, intertwines them, stretches his arms out and then cracks all of his knuckles simultaneously.

As Christy glares back, a part of him doesn't believe this is happening. He glances down at his half-finished pint on the table, and at the pack of Sweet Afton beside it, and at the smoke rising slowly from his cigarette in the ashtray. It's a familiar, comforting scene, almost like a still life, and he doesn't understand how it can be about to change so radically.

But then, unexpected as this whole thing has been, something even more unexpected happens.

Just as the young couple are about to get up from their table, and as Noel is getting up from his, a figure comes rushing through the doorway of the pub and out into the middle of the beer garden. Tall and reedy, he is wearing a dark-coloured anorak and jeans, and – it takes people a second to realise it, to process what they're seeing – he's also wearing a ski mask.

Like with the impact of an explosion, there is a recoil from this around the garden. What follows it, though, isn't panic. Instead, rapid calculations are made, probabilities are looked at, and soon it's clear – at least to four of the five people out here – that all any of them can do now is hold their breath and *watch*.

The young man and woman remain frozen. The man beside Christy remains frozen, and Christy himself, stifling a cough, remains frozen.

Noel certainly isn't resigned to watching this happen, but he remains frozen too, only his eyes darting left and right. There isn't much else he can do in the circumstances.

The tall, reedy man, his anorak glistening in the rain, appears to hesitate. But then he turns a fraction and is suddenly face to face with Noel – four feet away from him, five at most.

Noel shifts his weight to the edge of the bench.

From where Christy is sitting, he can see the man in the anorak raising his right arm and stretching it out. The gun in the man's gloved hand is metal grey, almost black, and looks like an extension of the glove.

Noel is trembling all over now. He feels a sudden stream of warm, beery piss making its way down his leg. He seems to have no muscular control left. All around him he hears a voice, high-pitched and whining, and he even manages to feel contempt for it – before realising it's his own voice.

Then there is a loud crack. It is followed immediately by another one and another one after that.

Christy starts coughing. The air is damp from the rain, but it is smoky and acrid now as well.

The man in the anorak runs to a wall at the rear of the garden and jumps at it. Grabbing hold of the top, he pulls himself up and swings a leg over. In a second, he has disappeared. A few seconds after that, Christy hears a motorcycle revving up and taking off. He looks over at the others. The young woman, only half standing up, is clutching her boyfriend's sleeve. The boyfriend is sitting down again. People have started pouring out from the main area of the pub.

Christy remains seated. He looks over at Noel, who is still at his table, but slumped forward now, his head at an awkward angle. He looks like someone who has drunk too much and passed out. From the angle Christy is at, and before his view is closed off, he is able to make out a bullet hole in Noel's forehead. There is a small trickle of blood coming from it.

Christy looks down at his pint, and at the cigarette in the ashtray. Smoke is still rising from the cigarette. He lifts it up and takes a drag from it. In all his decades as a smoker, no cigarette has ever tasted as good.

PENSIONER'S RACING PULSE RETURNS TO NORMAL.

He glances around. A lot of people are just standing in the rain now. They are in shock, waiting for something to happen. Most of them are talking – to each other or into mobile phones. Some have umbrellas, others are huddled into their jackets.

The man beside Christy nudges him again in the elbow.

'Jesus,' he says, lifting his pint, 'it's all go here tonight, what?'

2

One of the mobile calls made out of the beer garden is to a guy in Dolphin's Barn, a 'business associate' of Noel's. This business associate calls someone who lives in Stonybatter, and the person who lives in Stonybatter calls a cousin of his in Crumlin, who in turn calls someone *he* knows in Dolanstown. Within minutes, everyone in Dublin knows what's happened. Well, not *every*one – that comes with the next news bulletin on the radio at ten or eleven o'clock – but everyone who matters.

Noel's mother, Catherine, hears about it from her brother – who's also called Noel. He's in a hotel bar in the city centre with an associate of his own, Paddy Norton, the chairman of

Winterland Properties. The two men are in the middle of a heated argument when Noel gets the call from Jackie, and though it's awkward he holds a hand up, excuses himself and goes outside. He then gets on the phone to Catherine, breaks the news and tells her he'll be out to her house in twenty minutes. She's hysterical, but what can he do? He's barely able to get his head around the news himself.

He walks to the multilevel car park down the street and takes the elevator up to the top.

The weird thing is, although his nephew was undoubtedly a pain in the arse – unpredictable, hard to get along with, maybe even a little messed up in the head (not unlike his old man, come to think of it) – he wasn't stupid, and by all accounts he was pretty level-headed when it came to business.

So what happened?

Noel can only guess. Most gangland killings, apparently, in the end, come down to one of three things: a turf dispute, someone creaming off the top, or a clash of personalities. All three are possible in this case, he supposes, though knowing his nephew, only the last one seems really likely.

Noel climbs into his SUV and makes his way down the five levels to the entrance as fast as he can, tyres screeching at every turn. But Dublin's nightlife is hopping and when he pulls out onto Drury Street the traffic is practically at a standstill. He hunches over the steering wheel.

He doesn't need this, just as he doesn't need the band of pain that starts throbbing now behind his eyes.

The traffic moves forward, but only a yard or two. It stops again.

Rubbing his eyes, Noel thinks back to what happened in the hotel bar. He didn't need *that* either. He didn't need Paddy

Norton jabbing him in the chest with his finger, and he certainly didn't need another rundown of the arguments – arguments he's been hearing incessantly now for the last two or three days. The timing of Jackie's call didn't help either, of course. Leaving in a hurry like that made it seem as if he were running away. It was –

Noel shakes his head.

What he *does* need here, maybe, is a little perspective. Richmond Plaza, like any big development, is going to have its fair share of problems. All the ones so far have been surmountable, and this one won't be any different.

His nephew, on the other hand, is *dead*.

As they approach George's Street, the traffic loosens up a bit. Noel takes his mobile out again. He needs to talk to someone. He calls Jackie and asks him if he's heard anything else.

'No, and it's a little strange to tell you the truth. I called around, but pretty much hit a brick wall.'

A detective superintendent based in Harcourt Street, Jackie Merrigan is a good friend of Noel's and – important in the construction industry – a valuable source of information inside Garda headquarters. Over the last year or so, as a favour to Noel, he's also been providing updates of a different kind.

'So, what do you think?' Noel asks. 'Was it a professional hit?'

'Oh, I'd say so, yeah.'

'Jesus.'

'It has all the hallmarks.'

Noel pauses, shaking his head. 'I'm still in shock here. I mean, I was having a drink with Paddy Norton and I just walked out on the man, didn't look back.'

'Understandable, Noel.'

'Yeah. Listen. Thanks. Anyway, I'm heading out to my sister's now.'

'Right.' There is a pause. 'Pass on my condolences, will you?'

'Sure. I'll talk to you again.'

Noel hits End. As he holds the phone in his hand, something occurs to him. He left his folder sitting on the hotel bar.

Shit.

What does he do now? Call Norton? Arrange to swing by his house later to pick it up? He'll have to. He's got that conference call in the morning with head office in Paris.

Shit.

But he can't be thinking about this now. He *can't*. He puts the phone back into his pocket.

A couple of minutes later, he's turning off the South Circular, then crossing the canal, and once he's on Clogher Road, at this time of night, it's a straight run all the way out to Dolanstown.

3

Alone in the house, Catherine is reeling from the news. When the phone rang, she was sipping a vodka and Coke, but now she refills the glass with just vodka and takes a long hit from it. She puts the glass down and picks up her mobile. She phones one of her sisters, Yvonne, who lives nearby, and tells her the news. After the initial shock, Yvonne is all business. She says give her fifteen minutes, that she'll call Michelle and Gina and then come over. Catherine also calls Mrs Collins next door, who says she'll come in and sit with her until Yvonne arrives.

The TV is still on. Catherine was watching a rerun of *Friends*, and even though she's not watching it now, she can't bring herself to turn it off – not until someone arrives, it's company, and anyway holding the remote in her hand makes her feel like she's doing something, like *she's* in control. Through all of this – the calls, the standing around, the *Friends* – she continues crying, either in silence, with tears running down her cheeks, or at full tilt – all out and uncontrollable. At one point, she catches sight of herself in the mirror and gets a fright. Is she really that old looking? Is she really that *old*?

This all seems unreal to her, like it's happening to someone else. Given what Noel was involved in, though, it's not as if she hasn't already pictured the scene a hundred times, on a hundred other nights. It's just that the reality of it is, well . . . different.

When Mrs Collins arrives Catherine immediately regrets having phoned her. The woman is kind, but *too* kind, you know, she'd smother you with kindness, and now five seconds in the door she's already hard at it. After a while Yvonne arrives and takes over, thankfully – even though the first thing she does is whip the glass of vodka away from Catherine, saying a shot or two is fine, for your nerves, but you don't want to overdo it. The cops'll be here soon, she says, and you'll proba-bly have to go somewhere to identify the body, and anyway there'll be plenty of time for drinking later. Then she puts the kettle on – the kettle, the fucking *kettle*.

Catherine hates the kettle.

'Yes, that's it,' Mrs Collins says, looking uneasily into the kitchen after Yvonne, 'a nice cup of tea.'

The 'nice' really grates on Catherine's nerves. To distract herself, she glances over at the framed photographs arranged on shelves in the corner of the lounge. She stands up and walks across the room to get a closer look at them.

She can't believe this. She was eighteen years old when Noel was born, and just *look* at her. She was fucking gorgeous. Every bloke in the area wanted to ride her and wouldn't leave her alone, so it was no surprise when she got pregnant – but of course it *did* have to be with a mad bastard like Jimmy Dempsey. Not that it mattered though. Once she had the baby, she didn't care, and was even relieved when Jimmy fecked off to England. Noel was *her* baby. He wasn't a Dempsey, he was a Rafferty – and a Noel Rafferty at that, just like her brother.

The photos are arranged in order and she gazes at each one of them in turn.

Oh God, she thinks, biting her lip – the little *fella*. Look at him there – as a baby, a boy, a teenager. That's his life . . . *all* of his life now.

Starting to sob again, she turns away. Yvonne approaches her with a cup of tea. Catherine wants to say *Fuck off, would you, I don't want tea,* but she doesn't, she takes it.

The doorbell rings.

Noel.

As he comes in through the hallway, Catherine rushes out from the lounge to meet him. They stand there locked in a tight embrace for up to a minute.

Catherine has always adored her brother, even though in recent years they haven't seen each other as much as they used to, or anyway as much as she'd like. Noel has been up to his eyes with work, spending every waking hour, it seems, locked away in meetings, off on foreign junkets or just stuck on building sites. However, there's more to it than that, and it hits her now, what she's known all along but hasn't ever wanted to admit.

With her son's growing profile, mentions in the paper and so on . . . had he become something of a liability as far as her brother was concerned, a potential embarrassment?

Meaning what?

Catherine doesn't know, but in her confusion she allows the thought a little space to breathe. As she stands there in Noel's arms, stroking the silky texture of his suit and losing herself in the haze of his cologne, she wonders if maybe, at some level, he isn't relieved to have his young nephew permanently out of the picture.

But once the thought is formed, she flinches from it, and confusion quickly gives way to shame.

Noel is the first to extract himself from the embrace. He then holds Catherine's face in his hands and stares into her eyes.

'I'm *so* sorry, Catherine,' he says.

Her face crumples again and they re-embrace for a moment. Yvonne comes out from the kitchen. She and Noel acknowledge each other with silent nods. Somehow, they all move into the lounge and end up sitting on sofas. But it feels weirdly polite, like it's some kind of formal occasion. There's a tension in the room, and no one seems to know what it is.

Then Mrs Collins stands up and it becomes clear.

'I'll just slip away,' she whispers, nodding at Yvonne and then at Noel. She glances at Catherine and cocks her head sideways. But suddenly she's gone and it's just the three of them.

Family.

But this doesn't last very long.

The doorbell rings again and Catherine's heart lurches. She thinks maybe it's Michelle or Gina.

As Yvonne goes out to answer it, Catherine and Noel remain still, looking across the room at each other in silence, listening.

The door opens.

'Good evening, ma'am.'

It's a deep voice, an accent – a fucking culchie.

Noel stands up. 'The guards,' he says quietly.

He goes out.

Catherine listens to the shuffling in the hallway as two or maybe even three of them come in. Not much is being said. She imagines some pointing going on, faces being made, heads nodding. Then comes the moment she dreads. She looks up as two uniformed guards step into the room. Over their uniforms they have on those yellow reflective jackets that make them look like Teletubbies. They both have hangdog expressions on their faces, and are followed by a plainclothes detective, a shorter, older man in a navy suit. This isn't the first time the guards have been to the house, but it's the first time they've ever been let in the door. Catherine feels a flicker of indignation. She knows how Noel would feel about this. But she doesn't say anything. She doesn't have the will. There are too many other things going on in her head, vying for her attention – memories of Noel, images, snatches of things he said. She'd love another hit from that glass of vodka.

Where did Yvonne leave it?

'Mrs Rafferty?'

Mrs? She's not even going to correct them on that one.

She looks up. They're standing around awkwardly. No one tells them to sit down.

'What?' she says.

The detective steps forward. 'I'm afraid we've got some bad news for you, Mrs Rafferty.'

She realises he's only doing his duty, that it's a formality, but she can't help thinking what Noel would be saying if he was here now, he'd be saying, 'Listen, you stupid fucking bogman, tell us something we *don't* know.'

4

On Wicklow Street, parked near Louis Copeland's, Paddy Norton sits slumped in his BMW, staring at his mobile phone. He has just walked back from the hotel, not the better yet of Noel Rafferty's sudden appearance in the bar forty-five minutes earlier.

What in God's name does he do now?

He hesitates, and then places his mobile on top of the folder lying on the passenger seat beside him. He reaches into his pocket and produces a small silver pillbox. He opens it and taps two Narolet tablets out into the palm of his hand. He raises his hand, knocks the two tablets into his mouth and swallows them back dry. With the booze he already has in his system these should kick in pretty soon, help him to calm down.

It's fairly cold outside but he's sweating. He draws the back of his hand across his upper lip.

He shifts his considerable weight in the seat. The car is spacious, roomy, but Norton gives it a run for its money all the same.

He looks down at the phone again.

It was enough of a shock having Noel turn up unexpectedly in the first place, but what was the story then with him rushing off like that – pale all of a sudden, barely a word, no explanation? And who had that been on his mobile? Was it a tip-off of some kind?

Hardly.

There's nothing for it. Norton has to talk to Fitz. The arrangement was no direct contact for at least a week, but clearly that doesn't apply anymore, not in these circumstances.

He picks up his phone again, selects a number and hits Call.

As he is waiting, he feels the first, vague stirrings of the Narolet in his system.

Anticipa-a-tion.

Soon he'll have to keep reminding himself that he is, in fact, extremely angry.

The call is answered with a *'Yep?'*

'What happened?'

Silence at first, then, 'Jesus, I thought –'

'What happened?'

More silence, as well as some eye-rolling probably. Then, 'It went OK.'

'What do you mean? I've just had a fucking *drink* with the guy.'

'What are you talking about? *I've* just had it confirmed.'

Norton says nothing. His breathing pattern is slow, laboured, quite loud. He waits for more.

'It happened an hour ago, less.'

In the silence that follows, Norton struggles to contain himself. He wants to be explicit, but he can't. They're on mobiles here. They have to be discreet.

'Well, I don't understand,' he says eventually, the Narolet all over him now like a heavy blanket of snow. 'Something's gone wrong. Check again. *Christ.* I'll ring you back.'

He puts the phone down, but just as he's about to start the car up, it rings – Vivaldi, one of the seasons.

He grabs the phone again, hoping that it's Ray Sullivan. New York is five hours behind, so Ray Sullivan could easily still be in his office at this time.

Norton looks at the display on the phone.

But it's not Ray Sullivan. It's Noel.

He takes a deep breath.

'What happened to *you*?'

'Listen, Paddy, I'm sorry for skipping off like that, but there's been an emergency, a family thing. It's . . . it's awful.'

'Jesus,' Norton swallows. 'What?'

'My nephew's been shot. In a pub. He's dead.'

Norton closes his eyes and says, '*Oh fuck.*' Then he exhales loudly, deflating like a balloon.

'Yeah,' Noel says, 'I'm out at my sister's house now. She's in bits of course. The cops are here. It's chaos.'

'Well, look, I'm sorry,' Norton says, very quietly. 'Your nephew, wasn't –'

'Yeah, Catherine's lad, Noel. He was into all sorts of shit, so I can't say I'm surprised. But still, it's a shock.'

Norton exhales again. He can barely believe this.

'But anyway, the thing is,' Noel goes on, 'I left that folder on the bar in –'

'Yeah,' Norton says, 'it's OK, I've got it.'

'Well, I'm going to need it. Tonight. There are some things in it I want to check –'

'Look –'

'– for tomorrow morning.'

'Oh come on, Noel, come *on*.'

'*No.*'

'What the fuck am I going to tell Ray Sullivan?'

'I don't know. Tell him the truth.'

'Oh for –'

'Look, Paddy, I'm sorry, but . . . it's just not right.'

Norton stares out across Wicklow Street. On the other side some young women are walking past. Despite the cold, they are all wearing short, skimpy dresses, and despite the acres of flesh on display, thighs, shoulders, backs, there is nothing sexy or attractive about them. They look like a pack of strange animals, roving the plains in search of food and shelter. One of them is lagging behind, weaving drunkenly along the pavement. Norton thinks of his own daughter, pictures her here, like this, and a wave of emotion – unadulterated and operatic – washes over him. The Narolet does this sometimes, makes him a little weepy, leaves him exposed. But that's fine, he likes it, looks forward to it even.

'Paddy?'

Norton shakes his head. He looks at the dashboard, refocusing.

'OK, OK,' he says. 'I'm not going to argue with you any more, Noel. Do what you want. Let's meet someplace and you can pick it up.'

'I can drop out to the house.'

'*No.*' Norton pauses here, closing one eye. 'I'm still in town. We can meet halfway somewhere.'

'Fine.'

They make an arrangement. The car park behind Morahan's. In forty-five minutes.

'See you then.'

'Yeah.'

Norton holds the phone in his hand. It weighs a ton.

He never wanted this.

He's been in the property business for over thirty years – here and in the UK – and during that time he has put up countless hotels, apartment blocks, office complexes and a shopping centre or two. He has made a considerable reputation for himself, as well as a lot of friends, and a lot of money . . . so naturally he's not going to let some self-important little prick like Noel Rafferty flush all of that down the toilet –

Norton shakes his head.

– and especially not over something like *this* . . .

In a reflex movement, Norton brings a hand up to his chest, and winces.

He remains still, letting the seconds roll past – five seconds, ten seconds, fifteen seconds. What's the deal here? Is he just excited or are these actual palpitations? Is this a warning sign or is it the precursor to some kind of massive heart attack?

Who knows?

He waits some more, and it seems to pass.

He looks at his watch, and then back at his mobile. He calls Fitz's number again and waits.

He never wanted this. He really didn't.

'Yep?'

'We need to meet.'

'What? *When*?'

'Right now. In the next twenty minutes.'

5

Coming out of Isosceles, after the gig, after the minimalist repetitions and phase-shifting polyrhythms of Icelandic trio,

Barcode, Gina Rafferty is feeling transported. This is the first proper night out she's had in weeks, and although there is something ironic in the fact that the complex, patterned music actually reminds her of work, of computer code, of the alternating ones and zeroes they all toil so endlessly over in the office, she doesn't feel cheated or shortchanged. It's the same mechanism in each case, for sure – it's the language of order, the language of structure – but the context is quite different. So it'd be like comparing, say, legalese with poetry, the syntax of a contract with the metre of a sonnet . . .

Though the truth is, in *any* case, be it in a legal document or a poem – or a musical composition – Gina likes it, she likes order and structure.

Unapologetically so, in fact.

Which is probably just as well, given the attitude she's already picking up from these two guys she and her friend Sophie came with – not that she's in the least bit concerned about their huffing and sighing. Time was when she would have been mortified and felt she had to explain herself somehow, account for her opinions, even feign opinions she didn't have, but not anymore, not these days, and as they shuffle through the foyer now, she turns to one of them, the tall guy with the beard, and says, 'So, I thought that was pretty cool.'

'What?' the guy says, looking down at her. 'Jesus. No. I thought it was torture.'

The other guy laughs.

Gina rolls her eyes.

Torture? Why is she not surprised? She knew that Barcode wouldn't particularly be Sophie's bag, but she hadn't anticipated that these two guys – colleagues of Sophie's – would be such boneheads.

'You know what it reminded me of?' the guy with the beard is saying. 'Of when I was a kid, at mass, having to sit there. It was fucking awful.'

'Well,' Gina says, not interested in hearing any more of this, and reaching into her pocket for her mobile, '*I* thought it was sublime.'

'Sublime?' the second guy says. 'Come on, it was boring.'

With the music still echoing in her head – the subtle patterns, the mathematical precision, the clarity and grace – what's the point of arguing, Gina thinks. After *awful* and *boring* she's going to counter with words like *clarity* and *grace*?

'Oh, what,' she then says, 'I suppose you'd prefer some boy band in white suits doing cover versions of Perry Como hits?'

'Perry *who*?'

Turning away, Gina sees that she has two texts and a voicemail. The first text is from Beth, 'CU 4 lnch @ 1?', and the second – characteristically unabbreviated and with full punctuation – is from P.J., 'Remember I'm in London tomorrow. Intermetric, at 10.30. I'll call you after.'

When they get out onto Dame Street, the crowd starts breaking up and they're able to move a little faster. Gina switches from holding the phone in front of her, staring at it as she walks, to holding it up to her ear.

The voicemail is from one of her sisters. 'Received at 9.27 p.m.' Pause. 'Gina, it's Yvonne. Oh God. Listen. Ring me back as soon as you can, will you? Something awful's happened.' Gina's heart sinks. 'I suppose I'd better tell you. Young Noel has been shot. He was in a pub somewhere.' She pauses here, almost as if to give Gina a second or two to respond, to say, 'Oh my God', which she does. Yvonne then continues, 'Look, I'd better tell you everything, he's *dead*. It's just . . .

awful. I'm heading over to Catherine's now. Sorry for telling you like this, but what else could I do? Call me.' That's it. When Gina looks up, she realises that she's not moving anymore and that Sophie and the two guys are already ten or fifteen paces ahead of her.

Sophie turns, and sees the shock on Gina's face.

'What's wrong?' She rushes back.

'It's my nephew,' Gina says, putting a hand up to her chest. 'I can't believe this. He's been shot dead.'

Sophie's eyes almost pop. 'What?'

Sophie is from Mount Merrion, not a place where people tend to get shot.

'This is . . . *awful*,' Gina says. 'I have to get out to my sister's.'

She looks around, confused, still in shock.

'There's a taxi rank down here,' Sophie says, taking her by the arm. 'Come on.'

The two guys are waiting, but Sophie disposes of them with a quick remark that Gina doesn't hear.

They then walk in silence for a bit, cross at lights, looking left and right, concentrating on that. Eventually, Sophie asks Gina which sister it is.

'Catherine,' Gina says.

Sophie nods. After a pause she goes on, 'Your nephew? God. How old was he? I have one who's six and another one who's still in nappies.'

'Uh . . .' Gina scrambles in her head for an answer. 'He's only a few years younger than me. Twenty-five, I think, twenty-six.'

'Oh.'

'My sister had him when she was very young. It was . . .' She trails off here.

Gina is the youngest in the family – what used to be called

an afterthought, or even a mistake. She's only thirty-two, ten years younger than the next one up.

All of her siblings are in their forties.

Growing up, Gina could just about relate to Catherine and Michelle as sisters, but with Yvonne and Noel it was a little different. By the time she was only a year or two old they'd already left home and as a result she didn't see them that often, so they were really more like an aunt and an uncle to her. She loves them to bits, of course – but it still feels, even today, like they're from another generation.

'That's so *sad.*' Sophie says as they approach the taxi rank. 'Were you close to him?'

Gina is about to respond to this, but she stops. What does she say? The guy is dead.

She shakes her head.

She opens the back door of the taxi and leans against it. 'OK. Here we are.'

'Gina, do you want me to come along with you? As far as the house even?'

'No, you're grand, Soph. Thanks. I'll call you tomorrow.'

As Gina gets into the taxi, she waves back at Sophie.

'Dolanstown,' she says to the driver, and then gives him the full address.

The car pulls away from the rank, swings around and heads back up Dame Street. In order to avoid conversation with the driver, not that this is likely to work, Gina takes out her mobile and starts texting. She quickly rain-checks lunch with Beth, acknowledges P.J.'s message and then wonders – thumb poised, still staring at the display – if she should call Yvonne or just show up at Catherine's.

She looks out the window.

But what's Yvonne going to tell her on the phone that she didn't say in the message?

'Miserable night.'

See?

Gina turns, glances into the rearview mirror and meets the taxi driver's eyes.

'Yeah,' she says, and looks away.

That's all he's getting.

'You were out for a few jars yourself tonight, yeah?'

Oh God.

'Hhnn.'

She gets this a lot with taxi drivers, especially going home at night, but really, what do they expect her to say? Yeah, bud, I'm well locked, me, no self-control at all, so pull in anywhere that's convenient for you there and off we go?

'Town's fairly busy.'

'Hhnn.'

The taxi driver pauses, regrouping, and then, 'I see on the news there the Taoiseach has put his foot in it again.'

OK, OK, maybe she's wrong. Maybe it's not the erotic charge of her being a young woman on her own, in a short skirt, with drink taken, in *his* cab. Maybe he's just bored and trying to make conversation.

Whatever. But not tonight.

'If you don't mind,' she says, 'I'd prefer not to talk.'

'*Oh*,' he says.

Was that a little huffy? She stares at the back of his head. 'Thanks.'

'No, no,' he says, 'you're fine, you're fine.' But of course that won't do. After a moment, he has to add, 'No problem there, miss. None at all. And no offence taken either. Whatever the customer wants. That's what I always say, always have, and I'm twenty years in this game.'

In order to shut himself up, he reaches down and flicks on his radio. There are speakers behind Gina and the music is quite loud. What's playing is some awful eighties thing she vaguely recognises – it's soft rock, FM, irredeemably lite.

What *did* the Taoiseach say? Suddenly she's curious.

But in the next moment she's back with the immediate reality of what's happened – her nephew, her sister.

For as long as she can remember, Gina's been hearing stories about young Noel, about how he was always getting into trouble and breaking his mother's heart. Catherine raised him on her own (with financial help from their brother), and she did her best in difficult circumstances, but the kid was undeniably a handful. He was hyperactive, rebellious and physically very big – so much so that by the time he hit his teens he was pretty much out of control. He got into all the usual shit, joyriding, shoplifting, burglary and, of course, drugs.

Over the next few years, whenever the sisters met, an increasingly weary Catherine usually went out of her way to avoid the subject, and since Gina herself was pretty busy, doing her diploma in computer programming and then starting work, she hardly ever saw her nephew and heard very little about what he was up to. Though lately his name *has* been cropping up in the papers – and most recently in a *Sunday World* article she saw about the massive profits being made in DVD piracy.

Biting her lower lip, Gina now looks up and around. St Patrick's Cathedral flits past on the left, a new apartment complex on the right.

She's unsure what to think – though really, in Dublin, getting shot in a pub can mean only one thing, can't it?

As if to confirm this, the song on the radio finishes abruptly and a news bulletin comes on.

'All the latest for Dublin at eleven,' the announcer says, sounding as if he's about fifteen and has just drunk a quadruple espresso. 'A man in his mid-twenties has been gunned down in the beer garden of a south-side pub. It happened just before nine o'clock this evening. Witnesses claim the gunman fired three shots into the victim at point-blank range and then made his escape on a motorbike. The incident has all the hallmarks of a gangland killing –'

Gina closes her eyes.

'– and it is believed that the dead man, who hasn't been named yet, was known to the Gardai.'

Oh God. Poor Catherine.

Gina shifts around in the seat and tries to shut out the rest of the bulletin. She'd like to ask the driver to turn the radio off, or at least to turn the volume down, but she feels she's used up any goodwill she might have had with him. She also knows that this is ridiculous. But they're turning at the KCR now and moving pretty fast – so why rock the boat? When she arrives at Catherine's house she's going to need all the composure and self-possession she can muster.

After the sports results, weather report and an ad break the music comes back on, still eighties, but this time a little less grating.

A few minutes later, the cab turns into the road where Catherine lives, a small crescent of semi-detached houses built in the fifties – and barely half a mile from where Gina, her sisters and Noel were all born and grew up. Gina hasn't been out here for a while and she soon remembers why. Despite growing up in Dolanstown, she has always found the design and layout of the place – as with so many of Dublin's suburban housing estates – to be soulless and oppressive.

At night it's not so bad, she thinks. It's dark, street dark, and the atmosphere is a little different.

'This is fine,' she tells the driver, 'just here on the left.'

The cab pulls up.

Gina pays and gets out. It's colder than it seemed earlier, and she's suddenly conscious of what she's wearing – short denim skirt, floral print top and pin-striped jacket – all fine for wandering around town in, but a little bonkers for out here, for this.

There's nothing she can do about it now, though – not that Catherine is going to register what Gina, or anyone else for that matter, is wearing. But Yvonne or Michelle might, and the last thing she wants to see is *them* exchanging glances.

Look at madame.

Is it Gina's fault that they have no social lives anymore? Is it her fault that they are both stuck in a time warp? Is it her fault that they never got out of Dolanstown?

But she's being ridiculous again, and she knows it, and she knows why, too. It's displacement. Because this is going to be really hard. The level of Catherine's grief will be unimaginable. No one will be able to help her. No one will have anything more to offer her than a hug and a few platitudes.

Approaching the house, Gina takes a deep breath.

The first thing she notices is an SUV parked in the driveway. This can only be Noel's.

She rolls her eyes. Every time she sees Noel, which of course isn't that often, he's driving something different.

As she's passing the SUV, she peers into its tinted windows. She sees nothing except her own reflection. Up ahead, the hall door of the house opens and Noel himself comes out. He's wearing a heavy overcoat and appears to be in a hurry. When he spots Gina, he rushes up to her, takes her by the hand and kisses her on the cheek.

'How are you, sweetheart?'

'I'm OK. How's Catherine?'

He makes a face, shakes his head, shrugs his shoulders – each time about to say something, each time about to make an assessment, each time defeated.

Gina nods along.

Eventually, Noel says, 'The Guards have just left. They say she can't go in to identify the body until the morning.'

'Which means it's going to be a long night.'

'Yeah, looks like it.'

They both shake their heads.

Gina then says, 'So what happened? Do we know anything?'

'No. I made a couple of calls a while ago. No one knows a thing.' He pauses. 'You do realise what he's been up to for the last few years?'

'Well yeah, I read the papers,' Gina says. 'But it's not like anyone ever talks about it.'

'No. I suppose. Catherine had a hard time with it, under-standably.' He looks around, shivers from the cold and turns back to face Gina. 'But anyway, from what I've heard it was unexpected.'

'Weird.'

'Yeah.'

Noel then looks Gina up and down. 'Jesus, are you not freezing in that get-up?'

She nods *yes*, then says, 'I was in town at a gig. Going on to a party. What do you want?'

'No, I'm just saying.' He looks at her again. 'Here, do you want my coat?'

He starts taking it off. She puts a hand out to stop him.

'*No*,' she laughs. 'Are you mad?'

This is so Noel.

He shuffles the coat back on.

'Are you sure?'

'Yeah, I'm grand.'

He reaches out and strokes her cheek.

'You're my baby sister,' he says, 'and I love you. I wish I saw you more often. Are you *all right*?'

'Yeah, of course.'

'How's the software business?'

'It's OK,' she says. It feels weird to be talking like this, casually, as if nothing has happened. 'We're under a lot of pressure at the moment.'

'Yeah?'

'Well, with the downturn and all.'

Gina and her business partner, P.J., run Lucius, a small software-development company. They started up with some decent venture capital behind them, but that was back when the economy still seemed unassailable. Now, after two years, they have yet to launch a product on the market, and P.J.'s trip to London is an attempt to drum up some potential customer interest.

'It's a living,' she adds, half defensively. 'Not that my bank manager is too convinced.'

Noel squints his eyes at this.

'*What?*' Gina says.

'Are you all right for money?'

She nods. But that's not enough, apparently. 'Yeah, I am.'

'Are you sure?'

'Noel,' she says, 'that was a *joke*.'

Though actually it wasn't. Since Lucius started up, they've been working on the same software package – a suite of integrated data-management tools – but their burn rate has been pretty startling of late. In fact, the VCs are beginning to get alarmed, which is quite serious, because if they pull the plug now there won't be any salaries at the end of the month. There won't be any jobs.

For anyone.

'Look, I'm *fine*,' she adds. 'I am, really. Thanks.'

Noel shrugs his shoulders.

Gina raps her knuckles gently against the side of the SUV. 'So, where are you off to?'

Noel exhales and looks exasperated all of a sudden. 'Oh, I've got to go and pick something up in town. I'm meeting someone.' He glances at his watch. 'I'll be back, though. Half an hour, forty-five minutes.'

'Whatever happened to office hours?'

He snorts at this. 'You must be joking.'

'I suppose I am. But listen,' she says, 'Richmond Plaza? It's amazing. Really. I look down the quays at it every morning when I come out of my building. It's transforming the skyline.'

'Well, that's the idea,' Noel says. The firm he's a partner in, BCM, are the structural engineers on this docklands development. 'Let's hope we make it to the finishing line.'

Gina furrows her brow. 'Why wouldn't you? Isn't it almost finished?'

'It is, yeah, of course. And we *will*.' He looks out, over her shoulder, hesitating. 'It's just that, well, you know what it's like these days. And you wouldn't believe the headaches involved.' He looks at his watch again, and adds, '*This,* for instance.'

Gina notices for the first time how gaunt Noel looks. He is pale and has bags under his eyes.

'And what *is* this exactly?'

'Oh, you don't want to know, believe me. It's a situation, engineering stuff, an unholy bloody mess.' He waves a hand in the air, as if to magic it all away.

Gina leans forward slightly. 'Noel, are *you* OK?'

He nods vigorously. 'I'm fine, I'm fine, Jesus. Now go on, get inside or you'll catch your death. And I'll see you in a while.'

'OK.'

But neither of them moves.

Noel then reaches out and takes her by the arm. 'I know these are awful circumstances,' he says, staring into her eyes, 'and let's face it, the next couple of days are going to be fairly hectic, but maybe at some point we can sit down and have a really good chat, yeah?'

'Yeah, I'd like that.'

And she would, too. Every time she sees Noel she remembers how much she likes him.

'Great,' Noel says, giving her arm a quick squeeze. 'I'll look forward to it.' He then produces car keys from his pocket. Gina steps back and watches him getting into the SUV. As he pulls out of the driveway, he looks around, beeps the horn and waves.

Gina waves back, turns and heads for the front door.

6

Noel can't help smiling as he cruises along Greenhalgh Road West. He always gets a kick out of seeing Gina. Despite the age gap, he feels connected to her in a way that he doesn't with the others, and it's not some indulgent, avuncular type of thing either – he and she have a lot in common. He and she, as Noel sees it, are the two that got away. Catherine, Michelle and Yvonne all got trapped early – limited exposure to education, maximum exposure to neighbourhood muppets like Jimmy Dempsey. Noel, on the other hand – and with a work ethic inherited from their old man – clawed his way through school and then, as he stacked shelves by day, through an engineering course at night. Maybe Gina didn't have to claw so much, because the times were a little different, but Noel still thinks of her as someone with the drive and ambition to achieve almost anything.

He's helped the others out over the years, paid for things, talked to people, pulled strings, but Gina has always insisted on her independence – which of course Noel loves.

He glances at his watch. As he savours the prospect of seeing her again so soon, his mobile goes off.

He's just passing the Crumlin Shopping Centre.

'Yep?' It's Jackie.

'Look, Noel, I've had a word with a few more people, yeah?'

'Yeah.'

'And it's the same story. No one knows a thing. The other members of the gang are all freaking out apparently.'

Noel taps his fingers up and down on the steering wheel. 'Christ, *someone* must know what happened.'

'You'd think, but the people I spoke to say there was no particular feud going on, no outstanding *thing*, no obvious reason for this.'

Noel exhales. 'Yeah, but I mean look, half of these bastards are going around out of their heads on coke, they're pumped up on steroids and they've got guns they barely know how to use. You told me all this yourself. They don't *need* a reason. You look at them crossways and that's it, you're dead.'

'That's true, but *this* job wasn't like that. It was clean and professional.'

'Jesus, all this gangland shit is –'

'Yeah, but that's just the point, Noel. I don't think it *was* gang-related.'

'What do you mean?'

'I think it's something else, *someone* else, an outsider. Has to be. Whacking Noel Rafferty like this? It makes no sense.'

'Hhnn.' Noel swallows. 'Whacking Noel Rafferty,' he repeats. He knows what Jackie means, but the words leave a strange taste in his mouth. 'OK, Jackie, thanks. Keep me posted, will you?'

Shaking his head, Noel drops the phone onto the passenger seat. His sister, his nephew . . . his nephew, his sister. And now – with Morahan's just up ahead – Paddy Norton, Richmond Plaza, this *bloody* situation . . .

His head is throbbing.

He pulls into the half-empty car park at the back of the pub and crawls along until he spots Paddy Norton's BMW in the corner. He parks a couple of spaces up from it.

He holds the steering wheel with both hands for a second and shuts his eyes. A weird feeling comes over him, a sense that something isn't right. He can't put his finger on it, but it's there, in the back of his mind. It's nagging at him, like a name he's forgotten and is desperately trying to remember.

He opens his eyes and wonders if he has any Advil. He looks in the glove compartment. He finds a box there, but it's empty.

Aware of Paddy Norton getting out of his car, Noel turns and starts getting out of his. He doesn't want any more arguing here. He just wants to get the folder and go. He's scheduled a conference call for tomorrow morning with head office in Paris, and that's all there is to it.

'All right, Noel?' Paddy says.

'Yeah.' Though hardly, given what's happened. He looks at his watch. 'I have to get back out to my sister's. She's distraught.'

'Naturally enough, I suppose.'

The two men stand facing each other. It's cold and quite breezy now. Norton is wearing his Crombie coat, buttoned up, a silk paisley scarf and leather gloves. He's not wearing a hat, and the few wisps of brown-grey hair he has left on his head are being tossed about gently by the breeze. He also has a glazed look in his eyes, a look that Noel has seen before, and dreads. The man is fifty-seven years old, but tonight for some reason he looks a lot more than that, closer to sixty-seven.

'So have you got the folder on you, Paddy?' Noel asks.

'Yeah, I have, yeah.' Norton tips his head back slowly. His eyelids are at half-mast and his voice sounds a little slurred. 'It's in the car.'

'Well, can you give it to me then?'

Norton pauses. 'You haven't mentioned it to anyone yet, have you? Discussed it with anyone? No?'

It's as though his tongue is swollen and the words are having a hard time getting past it and out of his mouth.

'*No*. Of course not. That's what we agreed.'

'OK. Good.'

'So. Come on then, let's have it.'

Norton shakes his head. 'I'm sorry, Noel, no.'

'Why not?'

Noel feels really tired all of a sudden. He still hasn't figured out what is wrong, but the suspicion that *something* is wrong has deepened and is draining him of energy, of resolve.

'Well,' Norton says, raising his eyebrows, 'if you can't figure that one out, you're not *nearly* as smart as I gave you credit for.'

This tone, sarcastic and detached, goes hand in hand with the glazed look and lethargic manner. Noel wonders if Norton isn't on some kind of medication here and if that wouldn't explain the mood swing. He does know from experience that when Norton is in this state you can't reason with him.

'Look,' Noel then says – and of course immediately trying to reason with him, because what else can he do? – 'not giving it back to me won't change anything. I'll just give Dermot a ring.'

'Ah,' Norton says, 'Dermot.' He looks down at the ground, at his shoes, at Noel's shoes, but not at Noel himself. 'Dermot *Flynn*. Now there's an overzealous little cunt if ever there was one.'

'He was just doing his job, Paddy.'

'No he wasn't.' Norton looks up again. 'No one told *him* to stick his nose in. *I* didn't. Did *you*?'

'Look,' Noel says, 'what difference does that make now?' He shakes his head. 'We've been *over* this. We don't have any choice.'

'But there's where you're wrong, Noel. We *do*.' Norton pauses before adding, 'Well, at least *I* do.'

Noel stares at Norton, and that's when it hits him. He

understands now what's wrong and it's confirmed for him when he turns to the right and sees someone approaching from the other side of the car park.

There is light from the street and from the back of the pub, but it takes Noel a moment or two to recognise who this is.

'*Fitz*?'

'How are you, Noel?'

Fitz is a short, muscular man in his late forties. He's wearing jeans and a zipped-up leather jacket. His hair is thinning and he has a round, red, babyish face. He runs a company called High King, which provides on-site security at all of Paddy Norton's construction projects.

'I'm fine,' Noel says, as calmly as he can make it sound, but his head is racing. Who else knows about this? No one. Except for Dermot Flynn of course. Noel got the report from Flynn early last week, looked it over and immediately swore him to secrecy. He then brought it to Paddy Norton – in retrospect, he now sees, probably the last person he should have brought it to. But why *did* he bring it to Norton and not to someone else? Noel doesn't have to think about that for very long. He wanted to impress him – it was that simple, that venal, that stupid. However, instead of the expected pat on the back, what he got was a barrage of abuse, followed by a torrent of arguments for suppressing the report.

And in among these arguments, now that he thinks about it, he also heard a few threats of physical violence.

None of which – even for a second – he took literally.

He looks back at Norton, and then blurts it out, 'You can't be serious, Paddy.'

'Oh, I've never been more serious in my life,' Norton says,

and runs a gloved hand over his head, trying to settle his wispy hair. 'Well, maybe once.'

Noel swallows. He stares at Norton. 'But . . . I mean . . . did . . .'

'What? *What?* Your *nephew?*'

'Yes.'

Norton nods his head in Fitz's direction. 'It was a mistake. This gobshite here. Whoever he outsourced it to was meant to hit *you* and then the spin would be that *that* was the mistake, that it should have been your high-profile bloody nephew. Same name, you know. Comedy of errors kind of thing.' He turns his bulky frame towards Fitz and shakes his head. 'Some bloody comedy, what?'

Fitz shrugs but remains silent.

'It would have been the perfect smoke screen,' Norton goes on. 'Gangland cock-up. But too subtle for some people, it seems.' He shakes his head again. 'If you want something done in this life, am I right?'

Noel is paralysed and can't respond. The notion that this man in front of him is responsible for having his nephew killed is simply grotesque, bizarre, too much to take in. Paddy Norton, Noel finds himself thinking – and as though in some desperate plea to logic – is a pillar of respectability . . . he owns racehorses, he goes to Ascot every year, his wife sits on committees . . .

'Anyway,' Norton says, 'we're now into a damage-limitation phase, I'm afraid.'

Noel just stands there, still processing the information, still incredulous. He and Norton first met professionally about ten years ago – through Larry Bolger. The older man was an industry legend by that stage, a survivor from the eighties – and, it seemed, untouchable, his name never once having come up in evidence given to the tribunal of inquiry into planning irregularities.

'Damage limitation?' Noel suddenly asks, at least *one* part of his brain working at full tilt. 'What does that mean?'

'It means,' Norton says, tipping his head backwards again, 'that I want you to get in the car.'

Noel looks at him. He understands how reluctant Norton must be to let anything jeopardise the project, but . . .

He swallows.

Or maybe he doesn't understand at all. Maybe as an engineer he's been too close to the detail. Maybe he hasn't been seeing the bigger picture. In a sudden rush of clarity he starts to see it now, though. Because the thing is, in relative terms, Ireland itself has seen nothing on the scale of Richmond Plaza since the early sixties. Back then the country was in the throes of a belated industrial revolution, and something like Liberty Hall, an eighteen-storey glass box, was a very big deal indeed. But what's been going on in the country recently, what's been going *up*, is mould-breaking by contrast, and for Paddy Norton, despite the deepening recession, or perhaps even because of it, Richmond Plaza – forty-eight storeys and in with a shout to be one of the tallest buildings in the whole of Europe – is beyond big, beyond important, it's . . . it's to be his legacy.

Noel looks around him. He's boxed in here. A wall to his left, his own car behind him, Norton and *his* car ahead, Fitz to the right.

'Paddy,' he says, a brittle tone entering his voice, a tone he hates, 'why don't you just try and, I don't know, *bribe* me or something?'

'Oh, that's a good idea,' Norton says, and laughs. 'Hadn't thought of that. But you know what? You're too much of a self-righteous prick to take a bribe.'

Noel starts to feel dizzy.

'And besides, no matter how much I paid you, the problem wouldn't go away. I couldn't trust you to leave it alone.' He taps the side of his head with his forefinger. 'It's peace of mind I'm looking for here.'

Then something occurs to Noel. 'What about Dermot Flynn?'

As soon as he says the name, he regrets it – not that he believes there's even the slightest chance that Norton hasn't already thought of this.

Fitz, in any case, pipes up from the right. 'We had a word with him this afternoon.'

Noel looks around. A *word*? What is this, some kind of sick euphemism? 'What do you mean, a *word*?'

'We spoke to him. Gave him a few bob and a couple of Polaroids. It's sorted.'

Noel doesn't know what this means. He's confused. He turns back to Norton. 'For God's sake, Paddy, maybe I could –'

'Noel, listen to me,' Norton says, and then pauses, looking down at the ground again.

'What?' Noel says. He takes a step forward. '*What?*'

Norton exhales, his mood visibly changing. '*Look*, it's too late. We both know that.'

Noel sees the dots joining up properly for the first time. His stomach starts jumping. He can taste something in the back of his throat. It feels like he's been standing here for a hundred years.

'*Because my nephew's dead, right?*' he says, almost in a whisper.

Norton nods. 'Yeah. Obviously.' He exhales again. 'Now. Get in the *fucking* car.'

7

The house is quiet, at last. Everything is still. The girls are asleep. Claire has just gone up. The TV is turned off and the phone is unlikely to ring. Dermot Flynn gets off the sofa and goes into the kitchen. He opens the fridge and takes a bottle of vodka out of the freezer. He pours a large measure from the bottle into the nearest glass he can find. Standing at the counter, he raises the glass to his lips and knocks the clear, filmy liquid back in three quick gulps.

He looks out the window, into what should be the garden, but it's late, and dark, and all he can see is his own reflection staring back in at him.

His heart is pounding.

After a few seconds, the vodka burns a welcome hole through his stomach – and his fear. Pretty soon it's in his bloodstream, shooting warm, happy signals to his brain.

He never thought this moment would come.

He's been looking forward to it for hours, since the middle of the afternoon in fact.

Which was when it happened. Out of the blue. On the street in front of where he works. As he was coming back to the office. With a can of Diet Coke in his hand.

Flynn pours another large measure of vodka and replaces

the bottle in the freezer. He knocks the vodka back, two gulps this time, and puts the glass into the sink.

He wanders into the living room again.

Not saying anything to Claire all evening was hard, but he did need some time to think – and needs *this* time now to work out what they're going to do. He could have had a drink earlier, but he didn't want to get sloppy and stupid and maybe blurt something out.

He only hopes he didn't transmit his panic to the girls.

He looks around. The place is a mess. Normally, he would tidy it up – the crayons and colouring books, the Barbies, the discarded items of clothing, the empty *Shrek* and *Wizard of Oz* DVD boxes – but tonight he just leaves it all and goes through the double doors into what is rather grandly called the dining room. You couldn't fit a proper dining table in here, but it's perfect for what they've done with it, which is convert it into a study.

Closing the doors behind him, he goes over to the desk and sits down. When he got home earlier, he came straight in here and put his briefcase under the desk. Now he reaches down and retrieves it. He elbows the laptop aside and places the briefcase in the middle of the desk.

His heart is still pounding.

After downing five shots of vodka in the space of two or three minutes he should be well on, no question, but apparently the alcohol and adrenaline in his system haven't finished slugging it out yet for pole position.

He holds the briefcase, ready to click it open, and takes a deep breath. But he hesitates. He looks up, and around. On the wall above his desk is a framed poster for a design exhibition. Bookshelves cover the remaining three walls. On the floor there are magazines and periodicals stacked precariously high. Ninety per cent of what's in here is engineering and architectural stuff – manuals on technical drawing, books on skyscraper construction, copies of *American Architect* and *Advanced Structural Review*.

He clicks the briefcase open.

The man who came up to him in the street this afternoon was pale and thin. He wore a denim jacket and had small, beady eyes.

'Dermot Flynn?' he said.

Flynn nodded. The man had an air of menace about him, but when he spoke he was disconcertingly soft-spoken and polite. He smiled as he handed over the thick brown envelope.

'This is for you, boss,' he said. 'A little something.'

Flynn took the envelope in one hand and fumbled with it as he used his other hand to put the can of Diet Coke into his jacket pocket.

'What's this?' he asked, puzzled. 'Who are *you*?'

'I'm a messenger,' the man said. 'And here's the message. That report, yeah? You know the one I mean. Destroy it. Delete any files you have relating to it. Never talk about it again, to anyone, ever.'

Flynn stared at him in disbelief.

The man nodded at the envelope. 'There's two things in there,' he went on. 'One to show you we can be generous, and the other to show you we can be seriously, and I mean *seriously*, unpleasant.' He smiled again, but this time it was thinner, less convincing. 'So. That's all clear then, yeah?'

Flynn swallowed. He was still in shock, still puzzled. He said nothing.

'That's all *clear* then I said, yeah boss?'

'Look, I don't know –'

The man lunged forward. 'No fuckin' "looks", he said, 'or "I don't knows", all right?'

Flynn recoiled at this sudden change in tack.

Had the guy actually been about to *headbutt* him?

'Yeah, it's clear,' he said, holding up his free hand, 'it's clear.' He wanted to add 'take it easy' or 'back off, pal', or something even stronger – but nothing came out.

'The envelope,' the man said. 'It's all there in the bleedin' envelope.'

He then turned and walked away.

Up in his office, at his desk, Flynn opened the envelope and looked inside.

His heart has been pounding ever since.

He lifts the briefcase open now and takes another look. Earlier, in his office, he emptied the contents of the envelope into the briefcase – so there it all is, right in front of him: the sheet of paper with the two Polaroids taped to it and the solid bricks of cash.

Given how thick each brick is, and the fact that they're in fifties – he reckons there's probably about a hundred thousand euro here.

But of course that's not why his heart is pounding.

He lifts up the sheet of paper with the Polaroids on it.

The top one shows Orla. She's coming out the main gate of St Teresa's. She's in her green and grey uniform and is carrying her school bag. There are other kids in the background. The second photo shows Niamh, also in uniform, but she's alone, walking – *skipping* – along what looks like Ashleaf Avenue.

Flynn takes another deep breath and lets it out slowly.

He stares at what is written on the white border below the photographs. It is a spidery scrawl, done in black ink – the same three letters on each.

R.I.P.

Two

1

After twenty minutes on the treadmill, flicking between Sky News and CNN, Mark Griffin decides he's had enough and heads into the bathroom. He takes a shower and shaves. Back in the bedroom he chooses the charcoal grey suit, the pale blue tie and a white shirt. He gets dressed, occasionally glancing over at the bed. He goes down to the kitchen. He puts on coffee, stands at the breakfast bar and slices a grapefruit into neat segments. To the right, his laptop is open. He looks through his schedule for the day.

Mark runs a small company, Tesoro, that imports hand-made stone and ceramic tiles from Italy. It started out as an excuse to make regular trips to places such as Brescia, Gubbio and Pesaro, but it soon took on a life of its own. As recession in Ireland gave way to boom, so linoleum and thick shag gave way to travertine and terra-cotta, and it wasn't long before Mark found himself supplying high-end product to the high end of the residential property market.

After secondary school, and mainly at the insistence of his uncle Des, Mark did a business degree at Trinity College. The prospect of becoming an executive or an entrepreneur was always something he'd viewed with dread, but running Tesoro has never really felt like that, like a business. How could it? He travels to Italy and watches dedicated artisans at work. He deals in the aesthetics of tone, in the endless harmonies of colour, form and design.

Behind him, he hears Susan coming into the kitchen.

'Morning,' she says, in her sleepy drawl.

'Hi. There'll be coffee in a minute.'

He doesn't turn around. After a moment, Susan appears behind the breakfast bar. As she passes on her way to the fridge, she swipes a segment of his grapefruit, upsetting the formation he's made on the plate. Then she goes to the fridge and stands there, holding the door open, staring into the light, humming.

He looks at her and smiles. She's wearing one of his shirts.

Reaching into the fridge, Susan disappears from view.

Mark pops a segment of grapefruit into his mouth. He rearranges what's left on the plate and turns his attention back to the laptop. He has to swing by the showrooms in Ranelagh to pick something up, and after that he's going out to the warehouse, where he'll be for the rest of the morning. Then at two o'clock he's got an appointment in town. He's chasing a tiling contract from a builder who's just put up a new five-star hotel with 120 bathrooms in it. Single property refurbishments are suddenly a lot harder to come by these days, and a hotel contract, if he can get it, makes good business sense.

He looks over as Susan emerges from the fridge carrying a slab of cheese, some sliced ham and a tub of olives.

As she lays the stuff down on the breakfast bar, she makes a face at him, half apologetically, and says, 'Starving.'

Mark looks at his watch. He clicks his tongue. 'I have to go in a few minutes,' he says, 'but I'll leave you a key and the alarm code.'

Susan looks a little surprised. 'A key? Wow. But . . . I see you've already chosen the curtains.'

Mark snorts at this. He met Susan on a skiing trip last winter, and a few nights ago they bumped into each other again in town.

'Yeah,' he says. 'I went ahead. I didn't think you'd mind.'

'No, go on. Jesus. They're fab.'

She tears a slice of ham in two and puts one of the pieces into her mouth.

'How do you like your coffee?' he says.

'Strong. Black.'

Ten minutes later, getting into his car, Mark glances over his shoulder at the house. It's a weird, unfamiliar feeling to be leaving someone behind like this, inside the house.

He pulls out onto Glanmore Road.

It isn't a bad feeling.

He reaches down, flicks on the radio and tunes it to *Morning Ireland*.

Actually, it's a nice feeling.

But Mark doesn't want to dwell on that, because feelings like these – he knows from experience – tend not to last.

2

Gina opens her eyes.

She rolls over in the bed, onto her back, and stares up at the ceiling.

Something is bothering her. It's not just her nephew, that's a given. It's something else, a separate strain of anxiety.

She looks at the clock on her bedside table: 8.45 a.m.

She got home at around three. Yvonne and Michelle had taken charge of things, so there wasn't much point in her sticking around any longer. Besides, she had to get home and change.

She called a taxi at 2.30.

Her mind freezes for a second. Then she remembers what's bothering her.

Noel.

He'd told her outside the house that he had to go and meet someone and would be gone thirty minutes, forty-five at the most, but by the time Gina was leaving nearly three hours later he still hadn't shown up. Yvonne tried him on his mobile a couple of times, but got through to his voicemail. Catherine really seemed to need Noel and kept asking, in between sobs, where he was, so instead of anyone getting worried about the fact that he hadn't come back, they got increasingly annoyed about it. At one point, out in the kitchen, Gina found herself defending him.

'Look, he had some business thing in town. He's –'

'Oh don't give me *business*,' Michelle said, spitting the word out, 'I'm sick of hearing about business. Everything has to stop for business.' She had tears in her eyes. 'It's the middle of *the fucking night* for God's sake . . .'

Gina slides off the bed and walks over to the en suite bathroom in the corner.

Maybe Michelle was right, but the question remains . . . where *did* Noel get to?

Standing under the jet of hot water, Gina wonders if he turned up later, or at all. She'll call Catherine's in a few minutes and find out – after she gets dressed and puts on some coffee.

Though on reflection, these are serious commitments to being awake – clothes, coffee, a phone call – and she's not quite sure she's ready for them yet. She lingers in the shower, still a little drowsy – turning slowly, arching her back, stretching. Not that there's any plausible route back to sleep at this stage. She's awake, and the new day is already in full swing. A few moments earlier, through the open window in her bedroom, she could hear traffic rumbling and the general din of the streets. In fact, her last hour of sleep, with its busy parade of dreams – by turns scrappy and full-blown, lucid and phantasmagoric – had probably been moulded to some degree by this soundscape of the city coming alive six floors below her.

She is normally out of bed by seven, when the process is just beginning – having breakfast, listening to Newstalk, rallying her senses. But as she turns the water off now, steps out of the shower and reaches over to the radiator for her towel, Gina is struck by how *ab*normal this particular day, even before she's left the apartment or spoken to anyone, is shaping up to be.

She dries herself, standing at the washbasin. The mirror is steamed over, her reflection a grey blur. She lets her towel drop to the floor. Then, as she takes a moisturiser and some cotton discs from the narrow glass shelf above the washbasin, the reality of what has happened hits her again – her nephew's life cut brutally short, her sister's life rendered permanently miserable. With Catherine's anguished face in her mind's eye, Gina stands there for up to a minute, staring into the blur.

Out in the kitchen a while later, wearing jeans and a black T-shirt, she packs the Gaggia, switches it on and then gets her phone from where she left it the night before – on the desk in the corner, beside her computer. She calls Catherine's. When Yvonne answers, she asks straightaway how Catherine is and can't imagine any other answer than the one she gets. She then asks if Noel ever showed up.

'No, he didn't, and we're starting to get worried.'

'Worried?'

'Jenny phoned about an hour ago. He never went home, and she can't reach him on his mobile. It isn't like him, she said.'

'Oh my God.'

'She's actually freaking out.'

'*Oh my God.*'

'When you spoke to him outside the house, did he tell you *where* he was going?'

'No, he just said town.' They went over this last night, more than once. 'He said he was meeting someone. He didn't say who.'

Gina wants to articulate something here, but she can't bring herself to do it. What she wants to say is either too ridiculous or too scary.

Yvonne, who quit smoking a couple of years ago, pulls audibly on a cigarette.

'What about his office?' Gina says.

'Jenny was going to call them. She said she'd call me back if she heard anything. I thought you might be her.'

'OK, look,' Gina says, detecting a slight impatience here, 'I'd better get off, but call me back, will you, if *you* hear anything? Or text me.'

'Yeah.'

Gina goes over to the coffee machine. She pulls down a cup and puts it in position. She presses a button and waits for the coffee to trickle out. But when it's ready, she doesn't move. She stands there, staring at the cup, and all of a sudden, in the emptiness, in the silence, her eyes well up. She steps back and leans against the counter. She puts a hand up to her chest and takes a few deep breaths.

It was hard watching Catherine like that last night. It was hard watching Yvonne and Michelle coping with her, and in such different ways. It was hard not having Noel around to provide some kind of ballast. It was *all* hard, every aspect of it, every passing second. What is hard about now, though, is almost worse, this creeping sense of dread that it's not over yet, that something else is going to happen, or maybe even *has* happened.

Gina wipes her tears away and rubs her eyes. She reaches over to the coffee machine, takes the small cup and looks into it. She swirls the coffee around for a moment and then knocks it back in one go.

She looks at her watch: 9.25.

She picks the phone up again. She calls Siobhan at the office and says she mightn't be coming in today, but Siobhan reminds her that she has an eleven o'clock meeting with Tom Maloney.

Gina rolls her eyes.

Most VC-fuelled start-ups have independent boards of directors. Typically, these will include one or two industry experts, people who can keep an eye on things, give advice and occasionally even get some traction for the company's product. Tom Maloney, the CIO of a financial consultancy firm, is one of these. He's not exactly what you'd call interfering, but he likes to be briefed on a regular basis. Gina meets him now and again for coffee and feeds him a line of bullshit about how things are going.

She looks at her watch again.

But if Lucius is ever to secure a second round of funding,

she knows she'll need to be a bit more rigorous than *that*, a bit more convincing.

'Is P.J. busy this morning?' she asks, suppressing a groan. 'Maybe he could do it. My sister has just . . . I'm . . .'

She doesn't want to get into it. What's the point? Lucius Software has a staff of only eight and operates out of three rooms on the first floor of a Georgian house in the centre of Dublin. Soon enough there'll be no avoiding the subject.

'He's in London today,' Siobhan says, 'and then –'

'Of course, of course, yeah,' Gina says, remembering about London.

'If you'd like I could ask –'

'No, no, leave it. It's OK.' Gina shakes her head. 'I'll do it.'

She changes into something more formal and spends half an hour at the desk in the corner, checking emails and scribbling down a few notes for this meeting.

Before she leaves the apartment, she texts Yvonne:

'Any news?'

She knows she's clutching at straws, but she needs to hear something.

On her way down in the elevator, she holds the phone tightly in her hand. When she comes out of the building, she turns right and keeps walking.

It's a pleasant morning, not quite sunny, but bright and fresh. The flow of traffic along the quays isn't particularly heavy, but as she approaches the IFSC, things in general get busier – more cars, more pedestrians, more noise. When she hasn't heard back from Yvonne by the time she's turning onto Matt Talbot Bridge, she decides to put the phone away. She drops it into her bag.

Up to this point she has kept fairly focused, staring straight ahead, but halfway across the bridge, unable to resist, she glances to her left.

Down in the docklands, Richmond Plaza dominates the horizon. Next to it there are two enormous cranes, which look like mechanical high priests, supplicants kneeling before some holy monolith. On previous occasions, Gina has stared in wonder at this rising structure at Richmond Dock, but today it's a little different. Today her only reaction to it – and this reaction is located in her stomach – is a dull steady thrum of anxiety.

Then she hears a mobile ringing close by and it makes her jump. She glances around. She knows from the tone that it can't be hers and even sees a passing suit raise his arm and bark into *his* – but as she moves off towards George's Quay, she still slips a hand into her bag, pulls her own phone out and checks it.

Just in case.

3

About a mile outside the Wicklow town of Rathcross, retired machine-parts salesman John McNally is walking along a winding tree-lined stretch of road. Since the new section of motorway opened last year these back roads have been quieter and more suitable for walking on. Cars still pass pretty frequently, but pedestrians are not in constant fear of being whooshed into a ditch by the slipstream from an articulated truck.

McNally lives nearby and walks the route as often as he can. His wife isn't well and requires a good deal of around-the-clock care, most of which McNally does himself, but a nurse comes in for a couple of hours three mornings a week and when she's there he makes a point of going for a walk. It gets him out of the house. He can stretch his legs and clear his mind.

During a long career as a salesman McNally travelled the length and breadth of Ireland and was familiar with every road in every county – arterial roads, side roads, ring roads, back roads – all of which he thought of as one continuous road, *his* road. What's left to him these days of the greater whole is just this tiny segment, a meandering mile and a half that runs from the small church outside Rathcross to the Coach Inn at Hannigan's Corner.

McNally begins to slow down now, and deliberately so – because until he gets to the bend a hundred yards up the road and catches an inevitable glimpse, beyond Hannigan's Corner, of that new housing development, of its rooftops and satellite dishes, he knows he will remain protected from any sign of the creeping suburbanisation that is, quite frankly, wrecking this part of Wicklow.

But for the moment it's OK. There are woodlands on either side of him. To his right, the trees rise up on a steep incline. To his left, beyond the ditch and thickets of bush, there is a fairly steep descent to a stream running parallel with the road. Beyond the stream, the area of woodland continues, rising back gradually and evening out, more or less, with the level of the road. McNally glances every now and again into these dark woods and is entranced by their stillness, which seems inviting, dense with mystery, even at times a little menacing.

Some night, when his wife is deep in her medicated sleep, he'd love to come out here to these woods, to the pitch blackness and the silence, and sit for an hour at the foot of a tree.

But he knows he never will. Because wouldn't it be a slightly crazy thing to do? Wouldn't it be dangerous, and irresponsible? How would he find his way? What if someone saw him?

He looks around as a car passes, a Volvo estate. McNally watches it rush forward and disappear at the bend up ahead.

Then, a couple of yards in front of him, he notices something in the road – strange marks, a series of curves. They are interlaced and go left from the centre of the road and disappear into the ditch. He knows that these can only be one thing, tyre marks – the result of severe skidding. As he moves closer to the marks, trying to make sense of what he's seeing, he notices that the thick bush at the side of the road where the skid marks disappear has been disturbed – flattened, in fact – leaving a large gap. He approaches the gap and walks right into it, drawn irresistibly to whatever it is he's going to find. He steps across the ditch and looks down the slope. At first, he sees nothing unusual. There is the line of the stream, the glistening water, an occasional boulder on one side or the other.

Then he sees it, and can't understand how it wasn't the first thing he saw. Forty or fifty feet below, at the bottom of a now obvious track through the grass and bushes, he sees the back end of a vehicle. It is wider than a normal car – like a four-wheel drive, possibly an SUV.

It is sticking up out of the stream, which means its front end is probably submerged in water.

Which means the driver . . .

McNally has taken a few steps down the slope before he knows what he's doing, before he realises it's too steep. If he goes on he'll slip and fall, and maybe break his neck. He turns and struggles back up.

Standing in the ditch again, catching his breath, he looks up and down the road, but it's deserted.

He takes out his mobile phone. He hates this bloody thing and hardly ever uses it. Everyone seems to have one these days, and it's all ringtone this and text message that. He bought his to have in case of an emergency.

His hand is shaking as he prepares to key in 999. He glances back towards the stream.

This isn't exactly the kind of emergency he had in mind.

4

At about 7.30, Paddy Norton gets out of bed and puts on his dressing gown and carpet slippers. Bleary-eyed, unshaven, he wanders downstairs. He goes into the reception room at the rear of the house and starts circling the full-sized snooker table he put in a few years back but has hardly used since. He played a lot when he was a young man, and to this day he still derives visceral pleasure from the memory of a maximum break he once scored against Larry Bolger. It was his first – and only – 147, and it actually ruined the game for him, because unless every frame he played after that was another 147, what was the point? Anything less was a taunt – if you were this good once, type of thing, what the fuck is wrong with you now? He got the table put in imagining he'd be able to just mess around on it and relax, but it never felt right – whereas walking around it does feel right. And it's probably because of the sheer size of the table, not to mention the size of the room, that it feels like he's doing more than just pacing up and down, that it feels, sometimes, like he's in the chariot race from *Ben-Hur*.

This morning, though, as he stops to lean against a corner pocket and catch his breath, it feels a bit more like the Stations of the Cross – so he decides to give it a rest. After a moment, he opens the double doors and goes through into the living room.

When Norton left things with Fitz last night and went home, the first thing he did was to take two more Narolet tablets, but instead of knocking him out they kept him awake. He had a glass of Power's and went to bed, but he couldn't sleep, so he lay there staring up at the ceiling. At one point, he even thought about leaning over to Miriam's night table to get her bottle of sleeping pills, but . . .

No.

He sinks into an armchair now and turns on the TV. He watches Sky News for a while – then some *Dr Phil,* then an episode of *Cheers,* whatever is on, his thumb working the remote control, the rest of him, every other muscle in his body, freeze-frame still.

Miriam comes in shortly after nine, already dressed and with her make-up on. She asks him what he's doing.

He looks up. 'I'm watching TV.'

His mouth feels dry.

'Sweetheart,' she says, walking over to him, 'you know I don't like the TV on in the mornings.' She gently extracts the remote control from his hand and points it at the huge plasma screen on the wall above the fireplace. 'It's unhealthy.'

The screen goes blank. She throws the remote control onto a sofa opposite Norton, out of his reach.

A tall woman, elegant and self-possessed, Miriam is wearing a Paul Costello suit and a string of pearls Norton gave her for their last wedding anniversary. 'I'm going into town for most of the day,' she says. 'Then I have that fund-raiser at six.'

It is only then that Miriam seems to notice the dishevelled, exhausted state her husband is in.

'Darling. Are you all right? You look dreadful.'

'I'm fine. I'm fine. Really.'

'Oh, Paddy, honestly.'

What does this mean? He isn't sure. Her tone is dismissive, but indulgent at the same time. He can't wait for her to leave.

'I'm going upstairs now to have a shower,' he says, but he doesn't move.

Miriam leans down and pecks him on the forehead. As she withdraws, he thinks he sees her wrinkling her nose.

'The sooner the better,' she says, and quickly adds, 'OK, I'll see you later.'

She turns and walks out of the room.

Norton doesn't move. He looks over at the remote control. The obvious thing to do would be to get up, walk across to the sofa and retrieve it, but somehow initiating this simple sequence of physical manoeuvres proves beyond him.

When he eventually does stand up, over forty minutes later, Norton ignores the remote and walks out of the room. He stands in the hallway for a moment, hesitating. Then he wanders across the hallway and into the kitchen, where he puts on the coffeemaker – because that's what he needs to kick-start his day, surely, a good strong dose of coffee.

He sits at the huge rectangular breakfast table and waits. Miriam had the kitchen redone recently and it's a cold, industrial look, all chrome and brushed steel, a bit like a restaurant kitchen – which of course was maybe what she had in mind, seeing as how they do so much entertaining.

He looks up at the clock. It's nearly ten.

He goes back to the coffeemaker and pours himself a cup.

Then he reaches over to the transistor radio beside the toaster and flicks it on to get the news headlines.

He resisted doing this earlier. No one has phoned yet, so he isn't really expecting anything, but he figures he might as well check. The first story is yet another worrying ESRI report on the economy. Then comes the announcement of a new investment in the Waterford area by the electronics giant Paloma. Then the stalled CAP reform talks in Brussels. Then the bit he already knows about, the shooting dead last night of a young man in the beer garden of a Dublin pub. This is followed by a drugs seizure story, a car bomb in Baghdad and a row in London over a security breach at Clarence House.

But that's it.

Norton turns off the radio and takes a sip from his coffee. What was he expecting? Who knows? He remembers another occasion like this – also in a kitchen, and a much more modest one, if memory serves. The kitchen in the house on Griffith Avenue. He'd been up all night, waiting for a phone call, which never came.

Norton drinks the rest of his coffee quickly and then refills his cup.

He can hear the Hoover going upstairs. Mrs Burke has begun her daily round. He'll wait until she has finished the bedrooms before going up. He doesn't want to give her a fright.

As he is pouring a third cup of coffee, his mobile rings. It's in the pocket of his dressing gown. He fishes it out and looks at the display. There is no number, which means that it isn't Fitz and it isn't the office. He quickly moves back to the table with his coffee and sits down.

'Hello.'

'Paddy. Ray Sullivan.'

'*Ray.*' Norton stands up. He glances over at the clock.

'Ray, it's 10.15 – what is it, *5.15* there? Jesus, I thought *I* was bad.'

'I can't sleep, Paddy. Never could. I do my best work at 5 a.m. This new business cycle we have these days? With all the twenty-four-hour non-stop global bullshit? *It's* only just catching up with *me*. But listen, how *are* you?'

'I'm fine, Ray, I'm fine.'

Norton sits down again. He takes a quick sip from his coffee. Ray Sullivan is the CEO of Amcan, a company Norton is hoping to secure as the anchor tenant for Richmond Plaza. But several thorny issues – installation specs and naming rights among them – remain unresolved, and negotiations have been dragging on for months.

'Good. Now. Listen to me.'

Sullivan has a particular style, and you don't have much choice but to go along with it.

'I'm listening, Ray.'

'OK. I had lunch with our friends yesterday, like I told you, yeah?'

'Yeah.'

'And what do you know, they'd like to meet with Larry when he's over next week.'

Norton tightens his fist and gives it a little shake. 'Excellent, Ray. I'll set it up.'

'Good. Good.' He pauses. 'But I want to keep a firm lid on this, agreed?'

'Of course.'

Sullivan clears his throat. 'Because let me make something clear to you, Paddy. These are very private people. They *like* their privacy.' He pauses. 'And they go to great lengths to protect it.'

'I understand that, Ray.'

In addition to being the CEO of Amcan, Sullivan also sits on the board of the Oberon Capital Group, a private-equity firm that has extensive business interests in more than a hundred countries worldwide.

'They just want to meet him, have a talk, get the measure of the man. No press releases or publicity or anything.' He pauses again. 'So we're on the same page here?'

'Absolutely.'

Ray Sullivan leaves that hanging for a moment. 'OK,' he says. 'OK. We'll talk again. Say hi to the lovely Miriam for me.'

'And to the lovely Caroline.'

This way of finishing their telephone conversations has become something of a routine.

Norton puts his mobile down on the table.

After a moment, he stands up. He needs to make another call. He goes and gets the cordless phone from the wall unit beside the fridge. Better to use the landline, he thinks. In case anyone is trying to reach him on the mobile.

Still standing, he bangs out the number and waits.

Voicemail.

He doesn't leave a message. He tries another number. And waits.

'Good morning, the Depart –'

'The Minister, please. It's Paddy Norton.'

'Just a moment, please, Mr Norton.'

With the phone cradled on his shoulder, he reties the belt around his dressing gown.

'Mr Norton? The Minister is unavailable at the moment. Can I –'

'No. It's OK. I'll call again later. Thanks.'

Norton should have known. With that Paloma announcement on the news, there's no way Bolger wasn't going to be tied up.

He puts the phone down, then picks it up again almost immediately. With the Oberon Capital Group now firmly in the picture, Norton is pretty sure negotiations with Amcan will be stepping up a gear or two. There are several people he needs to talk to.

But as he stares at the phone in his hand, he realises he's not in the right frame of mind, that his celebrated ability to compartmentalise has – for the moment at least – deserted him.

A while later, at nearly eleven o'clock – and on the jittery side of four cups of coffee – he grabs his mobile from the table, walks out of the kitchen and wanders down the hallway towards the rear of the house.

Once inside the large reception room, he starts circling the snooker table again. This time he falls into a slow, steady rhythm and tries to empty his mind. What he can't get *out* of his mind, though, is how reckless he has been. The thing is, he panicked last night, he overreacted, he left himself exposed – and that's something he wouldn't have done when he was younger, or even a few years ago. After Rafferty showed up at the hotel, direct involvement of some sort was unavoidable, and he did his best to limit that involvement, but the question remains: How much damage has he done? Has he compromised Richmond Plaza? Has he compromised Winterland Properties?

Or is it even worse than that?

After another lap of the table, Norton finds himself wondering if he shouldn't give in and call Fitz. As before, they agreed no contact, but by this stage of the morning he really needs to know what's going on. Because until he gets word from someone, Fitz or whoever, *or* hears something on the radio, he simply won't be able to shake off the feeling that things are spinning out of control.

He's a few paces into the next lap when his mobile rings.

Spring, winter, whatever.

He stops and fumbles at the pocket of his dressing gown. When he eventually gets the phone out, he stares at the number on the display for a second, then presses Answer.

5

Gina has *her* phone on the table, neatly lined up beside her cappuccino and her notebook. Willing the damn thing to ring, she glares at it every chance she gets. But she's not getting too many chances, because Tom Maloney, sitting opposite her in this small café on Dawson Street, is one of those intense people who insist on maintaining unbroken eye contact as they speak. He also has bad breath and an even worse habit of using it to state the obvious.

'Look, it's OK if your version one point zero is a little rough around the edges: what's crucial is to get it out there, get it launched, get it known –'

How could he think she doesn't know this?

'– and *then* you can work on landing the marquee customers.'

Gina realises that what they're talking about – strategy, the future of the company – *is* important, but at the moment she couldn't care less about any of it.

'And of course,' Maloney is saying, 'it may even turn out that your best customers aren't the ones you expect them to be –'

Her phone rings. She whips it off the table. It's P.J. She's disappointed, but doesn't show it. She looks at the time: 11.25.

Short meeting.

'Hi, P., listen –'

'Hey, Gina, so that was pretty useless, and I –'

'Can't talk now, P.'

She says it so firmly that P.J. stops in his tracks. 'OK.' He then says, 'You all right?'

'Yeah. I'll talk to you later.'

'OK.'

She puts the phone down, aware that Maloney is probably flattering himself about how riveted she is to what he's been saying. But what she's actually thinking is *Get me out of here.* Because if she's not going to talk to P.J. –

Her phone rings again.

As before, she whips it off the table, but this time she stands up, having seen from the display that it's Yvonne.

She turns away from the table, doesn't indicate anything to Maloney and heads for the door.

'*Yvonne?*'

It's noisy out on Dawson Street, with traffic, tourists, a plane passing overhead.

'*Gina?*'

'Yes.' She stares at the pavement. 'I'm here.'

'OK, Gina, listen to me.'

'*Yvonne, what's wrong?*'

Gina presses the phone to her ear. Oh God, here it comes.

'It's Noel.' Yvonne pauses. '*Our* Noel.' Gina closes her eyes. 'He was killed last night. His car ran off the road.'

'*Oh God.*'

'Somewhere in Wicklow.'

'*Wicklow?*'

Yvonne is sobbing now, and Gina can't make out what she's saying, or even if she's saying anything at all.

A dozen questions occur to Gina, and as quickly it occurs to her that none of them matters.

'Oh Jesus,' she whispers, 'poor Jenny.'

'I know, I know.'

'Where —'

'They brought the body to Tallaght Hospital. Jenny's on her way out there now.' Yvonne then says something incoherent about 'the two Noels' and starts sobbing again.

Gina nods along. She doesn't know what Yvonne has said exactly, but the impact of putting these three words together is as much as she can deal with.

She swallows. A raw, uncomfortable lump has formed in her throat.

After a long and painful silence, the sisters somehow manage to get practical for a few seconds and make an arrangement. Yvonne says that because Catherine has just come back from identifying young Noel's body and is naturally inconsolable she and Michelle will stay with her for the time being. Gina says that she'll go out to Tallaght. They can talk later on the phone, or text.

As her arm drops to her side, Gina realises that she won't be having that chat with Noel over the next couple of days, the one he seemed so anxious to have. She realises that she won't be *seeing* Noel again, ever.

She looks around. The sun is shining now. Dawson Street looks beautiful, as it always does in the sunshine, and she wonders what is to stop him from just showing up *here*? What is to stop him from appearing, this minute, on the pavement in front of her, striding down from St Stephen's Green, say, or up from Trinity College?

She shakes her head, slowly, as the lump in her throat approaches critical mass.

Where *is* he?

Gina walks back into the café. She retrieves her notebook from the table and her bag from the floor.

'Have to go,' she says, not looking at Maloney.

Outside again, she turns right and heads in the direction of the taxi rank halfway up the street, her eyes filling with tears.

6

'Joining me now from our Dáil studio is the Minister for Enterprise, Trade and Employment, Larry Bolger. Good afternoon, Minister.'

'Sean.'

Waiting for his first question, Bolger stares at a point on the wall directly opposite him.

'Minister, a four-hundred-million-euro investment package, over three hundred and fifty new jobs. In these straitened times it doesn't get much better than that, does it?'

'No, indeed, Sean, it certainly doesn't,' Bolger says, taking off like a greyhound, 'and days like today make *my* job worth doing, I can tell you. Paloma Electronics is a global player, and the fact that they've chosen to invest here, in the current economic climate, is a vote of confidence in our skilled workforce. But you must bear in mind, too – and it's always the case in these matters, be it HP, Intel, Eiben-Chemcorp, Pfizer, Amcan, whoever – that we did face stiff competition for this, both from other locations in Europe and from further afield.'

Bolger shifts in his seat and at the same time adjusts his headphones slightly. He's done countless radio interviews over the years, but he's never liked them. He gets restless and fidgety. TV is better, he thinks, because it's more of a full-on performance. Besides, radio presenters tend to grill you a little harder.

'In your view, Minister, what does today's announcement mean for the Waterford area?'

Though some interviews, like this one, he could do in his sleep.

'Well, Sean, I don't think it's overstating it to say that the investment we've just announced will go a long way towards mitigating the fallout from recent job losses in the south and south-east. Paloma is going to employ upwards of four hundred people at the plant, but many more jobs will be created in surrounding communities. So there's no doubt about it, this is win-win economics.'

And win-win press coverage, too, Bolger thinks.

'OK, we'll leave it there, Minister,' the interviewer says after a few more questions. 'Thank you for joining us.'

Bolger takes off the headphones, nods at the production

assistant who's working the console to his left and gets up from the table.

He needs to take a leak. He leaves the little studio and makes straight for the men's room down the corridor. He had a press conference before this radio slot, and after lunch he has a couple of newspaper interviews to do. Then he leaves for an appointment in Athlone and a reception this evening in Tuam. His PA, advisers and media handlers will all want a piece of him, and at every stage, even as he gets something to eat, so taking a leak – or even better, a crap – is about the only way he can find a moment to himself these days.

Not that he's complaining. He loves this. The last time he was in the cabinet, over five years ago, he practically had a nervous breakdown. He couldn't take the pressure, the hours, the constant infighting, and besides, he was still drinking back then, and carrying on with your woman, what was her name, Avril, *his bookie's wife . . .*

He finishes, and does up his zip.

It was a miracle that he survived that period of his life, politically let alone any other way. This time around he's sober, celibate and extremely focused, and the weird thing is, not only does *he* have his sights set on the leadership of the party, but it seems to be what a few other people want for him as well.

At fifty-three, he feels that his time has come.

As he washes his hands, he glances at himself in the mirror. He's better-looking now, too – that distinguished grey fleck in his hair, laser surgery taking care of the glasses, the sharper suits.

Fuck it, he positively *exudes* gravitas.

Bolger comes out of the men's room and stands in the corridor. He'll get a quick call in to Paddy Norton before the vultures descend on him again. He only heard the news about Noel Rafferty as he was going on air, and he wants to check that there isn't anything about the story he needs to be up to speed on.

But as he's getting the phone out of his pocket, it rings.

'Larry, Paddy.'

'Oh, I was just about to –'

'Listen, I was on to our friend in New York earlier, and you remember that thing we talked about? Well, it seems they want to go ahead with it.'

'Right. Jesus. Good.' He pauses. 'That's *great*.'

'Yeah, but keep it under wraps, OK? Don't go around mouthing off about it to anyone.'

'Paddy, give me a *little* credit, would you?'

'No, I'm just *saying*. I mean, you know what this town is like.'

'OK, OK, whatever.'

'But anyway, I'll get back to you later with the details.'

'Fine.'

'Right.'

There is a pause.

'Listen,' Bolger then says, 'I was going to ask you about this Noel Rafferty thing.'

'Oh? What about it?'

'I was wondering, you know, what's the story?'

Bolger knew Noel Rafferty fairly well and had professional dealings with him on a number of occasions – most recently, of course, in relation to Richmond Plaza.

'There's no story. What do you mean what's the story?'

'No, I just . . . I thought I'd check that –'

'Look, he was over the limit, well over, and shouldn't have been behind the wheel of a car, OK? That's the story. You won't read it in the papers, but believe me, I have it on good authority.'

'Oh.'

'I had a drink with him earlier, in town, and he was well on at *that* stage. The other thing is, you know that shooting last night in the pub? The guy who got shot was his nephew.'

'*What?*'

'Yeah, but that won't be in the papers either. The Guards aren't releasing his name yet, not for a day or two anyway. Out of sensitivity to the family.' Norton pauses. 'Look, I don't know, I suppose he'd just heard the news about his nephew, he was upset, he'd had too much to drink, and boom, he loses control at the wheel. Before you know it he's brown bread. Fucking tragic, but *that's* the story.'

'Jesus,' Bolger says, subdued now. 'Poor bastard.'

Maybe it's a bit of a stretch to say that he'd had actual 'dealings' with Rafferty in relation to Richmond Plaza, but their paths *had* crossed many times over the years. There'd been a few foreign trips back in the nineties – those trade delegations to Shanghai. And he'd often met him at the races or at Lansdowne Road. They'd even played cards a few times.

'But anyway,' he says, 'tell us, is this going to delay things at all?'

'No, of course not. Everything's in place. It's like clockwork at this stage.'

'OK.'

Clearly thinking this over, Norton then adds, 'And again, don't you go around mouthing off about it, saying there *will* be delays, or anything like it, do you hear me?'

Bolger can't believe what he's hearing. 'Jesus, *Paddy* –'

'Because we're at a very delicate stage in negotiations at the moment, with Amcan. If we lose *them* we're fucked.'

'I know, I know.'

'So, let's stay on the same page here.'

'Right, right, whatever. Look, I'll talk to you again.'

'OK.'

Bolger puts his phone away.

Bad-tempered prick.

Now, as he heads back along the corridor to face his assistants and handlers, *he's* in a bad mood as well.

But wasn't the concern he expressed entirely legitimate? Because take a key player out of *any* team and who knows what the consequences will be? The thing is, already – months before completion – Richmond Plaza has achieved brand recognition, iconic status even, and with his own name firmly linked to it in the public's mind, Bolger feels he has an awful lot to lose if anything goes wrong.

Initially, of course – because there was so much opposition to the project – nothing seemed to go right. There was widespread concern about the visual impact a high-rise development would have on the city's skyline. The number of appeals lodged against it with An Bord Pleanála was unprecedented. Submissions came from An Taisce, the Green Party, the Irish Georgian Society, community groups, local councillors, activists, grey-haired hippies, crusties, every toerag in a beard and a woolly jumper.

But when it came to putting a case for the defence, Bolger

was indefatigable. He was also passionate – and never more so than one Monday evening on RTÉ's *Questions and Answers* programme. A speaker on the panel was making some laboured, predictable point about tall buildings and phallic symbolism when Bolger cut in saying that Richmond Plaza wasn't even going to *be* particularly tall, not by global standards. OK, it was probably going to be one of the tallest buildings in Europe, but so what? With the growth of the new service-based economies, Europe was going to have to get its act together anyway and reform its planning regulations, because ten years down the line, cities like Frankfurt and Brussels, The Hague and Berlin, these would all be just like American and Asian cities, just like Houston and Kuala Lumpur ... a process that we in this country – he said, banging his fist on the table – that we in this *city*, had the unique chance to kick-start, *right* here, *right* now ...

It was one of his more full-on performances.

But he also did a lot behind the scenes. He persuaded, cajoled, used his charm, *and* took a lot of flak – so all in all it's not as if he hasn't played his part. And what? The thanks he gets for his loyalty is to be talked to like he's one of the fucking hired help?

Bolger spots his press secretary, Paula, and one of his advisers standing by a pillar in the reception area. They're both on their mobiles. Paula holds up a hand to indicate that she'll be with him in a second.

He waits.

Bolger has known Paddy Norton for many, many years and is beholden to him in ways he'd rather not think about. In fact, he can't really imagine his career without him – but still, there are times, like today, when he wishes to God he'd never met the man.

7

It is just as Mark Griffin is approaching the roundabout that he hears it, and his grip on the steering wheel tightens. '. . . *joining me now from our Dáil studio . . . Larry Bolger . . .*'

At that point, Mark would normally be reaching for the dial to switch the radio off, but with an articulated truck on his tail and the meat grinder of the Cherryvale roundabout directly ahead of him, it is several seconds before this can happen.

'. . . *no, indeed, Sean, it certainly doesn't, and days like today make* my *job –*'

Then, silence.

When Mark replaces his hand on the steering wheel, it tightens again, automatically.

That velvety, media-trained voice, both obsequious *and* arrogant, never fails to unnerve him.

He comes off the roundabout.

It's also becoming a lot harder to avoid. Bolger seems to be everywhere these days – in the papers, on radio, on TV.

He looks in the rearview mirror, indicates and gets into the left lane.

Though in one way or another this *is* something Mark has been dealing with for years. When he was a business student (and way before Bolger had anything like the high profile he has today), hearing that voice on the radio, or even the name, would have been enough to floor him. It would have triggered all manner of weird behaviour – depressive, destructive behaviour like not getting out of bed for days, not taking a shower, drinking himself stupid, arguing incessantly, and with everyone, his girlfriend, his lecturers, his uncle Des.

Mark takes the next exit. He has that meeting in town, in the Westbury, with the building contractor.

But these days, it must be said, things are different. He showers regularly, doesn't drink anymore and is a lot less combative. If he comes across Larry Bolger's name, he'll still react, but more or less the way he's reacting now – in a measured way, nothing extreme. Besides, *these* days, he has responsibilities. He has clients and contracts, and employs three people full-time at the showrooms in Ranelagh.

It's all very grown-up.

So much so, in fact, that on occasion Mark has a hard time believing the whole thing is for real. It's as if he expects an official with a clipboard to tap him on the shoulder one day and announce, politely, that it's all been a mistake, that his company is to be dissolved, that his house and his car are to be repossessed.

Stopping at traffic lights, Mark closes his eyes for a moment. Then he opens them again and bangs on the steering wheel.

Shit.

Now he's all anxious.

Shit, shit, shit.

Twenty minutes later, on his way into the Westbury, he gets a call on his mobile. It's from the contractor saying he'll be a few minutes late.

As he waits on his own in the lounge, Mark toys with the idea of ordering a gin and tonic.

Just one, he thinks, a quickie.

The waiter approaches. Mark clears his throat. He asks for a black coffee.

Then he turns back and glances at the table in front of him. There is a newspaper on it. After a moment, he lifts the paper up, leans over and tosses it onto the next table along.

Three

1

The removal to the church of young Noel's remains takes place at 5.30 the following afternoon. The Gardaí have released his name by that stage, and the story is all over the front page of the *Evening Herald* – SHOCK DOUBLE TRAGEDY FOR FAMILY. Inside, on page 4, a piece is headed THE TWO NOELS. It's obvious when you read it that they're straining to make a connection, to join up the dots, but they can't, and the two stories remain stubbornly separate. Something else they can't do is print what's already been widely rumoured around town – that the older Noel had been drinking heavily before his car ran off the road.

Over a two-page spread, the paper's crime correspondent concentrates on the nephew. Known locally as 'Grassy' Noel – on account of his preference for marijuana over hash – the twenty-six-year-old belonged to a Dublin gang with strong links to drug suppliers operating out of the Netherlands. The gang's other activities include prostitution, mainly involving foreign nationals, and an elaborate piracy operation – involving anything from DVDs and computer software to Gucci handbags and Manchester United jerseys.

The gang leader is forty-two-year-old Terry 'the Electrician' Stack, and it is believed that Noel Rafferty was one of his trusted lieutenants.

The article goes on to say that usually within hours of a

gangland killing, detectives know why the victim was killed and who pulled the trigger, but that apparently in this case everyone is baffled. However, one thing various sources say you *can* be sure of is that sooner or later, knowing Terry Stack, an act of reprisal will take place.

The Electrician, it seems, is not happy and won't be sleeping until someone pays a price for this.

The *Herald*'s coverage is exhaustive. Another article reports how the beer garden of the pub was cordoned off so that members of the Garda technical bureau could carry out a complete forensic examination of the crime scene. According to Superintendent Frankie Deeghan, who is leading the inquiry, the State Pathologist then arrived to carry out a preliminary examination of the body, after which the remains were transferred to the city morgue for a full post-mortem.

Yet another report describes the kind of gun used in the shooting, and gives details about ballistics and fragmentation. It mentions wound cavities, torn muscle tissue and severed blood vessels.

No one who arrives for the removal – at the Church of Our Lady Queen of Heaven in Dolanstown – is seen holding a copy of the *Evening Herald*.

From about five o'clock on, mourners start drifting into the church. There are a lot of people from the area: friends and neighbours of Catherine's; friends and 'associates' of Noel's; Terry Stack, naturally; his entourage; friends of Yvonne's and Michelle's; friends of Gina's. There are onlookers (friends of no one's in particular), as well as a local councillor, a few journalists, a few photographers, and maybe one or two plainclothes detectives.

Our Lady Queen of Heaven, built in the early fifties, is

enormous, a brick and granite echo chamber that can hold up to fifteen hundred people. When the ceremony starts, it is almost a quarter full. Sitting in the front pew, next to the coffin, are Catherine and her three sisters. In the couple of pews behind them are immediate family – Yvonne's husband and their three kids, Michelle's partner and their two, plus other family members, cousins, two aunts, an uncle.

Behind them is everyone else, the congregation thinning out farther back in the church.

Catherine is staring at the altar. She took a Xanax before coming out, and feels numb. Her mouth is dry. Every few minutes – literally, since Monday night – it's been hitting her, the news, what happened . . . and each time it's as though she's hearing it for the first time. Her mind goes blank and then it hits her. Her mind goes blank and then it hits her *again*. But at least now it's like someone hitting her with the cardboard tube from a roll of kitchen paper. Before it was like someone hitting her with a baseball bat.

The news about her brother, on the other hand, has barely sunk in at all.

It has for Yvonne, Michelle and Gina, though. They are grieving for Catherine and her loss, but also for their brother, Noel, and it's pretty much unbearable. One day you're going about your business, everything is normal, and the next you're plunged into an abyss of anguish and pain.

Who could make sense of *that*?

Certainly not this Father Kerrigan, it occurs to Gina. As the priest walks out of the sacristy and onto the altar, she feels a mild hostility rippling across the surface of her grief. Everyone stands up, and the sound of a few hundred people collectively shuffling to their feet reverberates throughout the church.

Father Kerrigan positions himself at the lectern and leans towards the microphone. He is a portly man in his fifties. He has receding hair and is wearing glasses. He makes the sign of the cross.

'In the name of the Father,' he says, leading the congregation, 'and of the Son –'

Gina doesn't move or say anything.

'– and of the Holy Spirit.'

Father Kerrigan's amplified voice and the voices of the crowd echo loudly. It is such a familiar sound, a sound from her childhood. Gina hasn't been inside this church for at least ten years, not since her mother died. She looks around. She looks at the marble pillars, the confession boxes, the statues of Our Lady, the Stations of the Cross represented in paintings that line the walls on either side.

She really can't believe this is happening.

Back at the house someone offered her a Xanax, but she refused it. She knows that Yvonne and Michelle took a half one each, and already, coming from the funeral parlour to the church, she could see the medication taking effect, could see her sisters retreating into its quiet, chilly cocoon.

Gina can understand the attraction here. Her own mind is a riot of thoughts and emotions, and she'd love to put it temporarily out of commission, or even calm it down – but not at the expense of clarity, or of rawness, or of anger.

Most of what she's feeling makes a kind of sense to her, and she doesn't want to lose that. The rawness certainly makes sense. She has cried a lot over these past couple of days and has felt a depth of sorrow she hadn't previously known was possible.

But she's been angry a lot of the time, too, and although that makes sense to a degree, it doesn't make sense entirely. Her anger at the seeming randomness of what happened makes sense. Her anger at what she's learned about her nephew's activities makes sense, as does her anger at what's been suggested might have caused her brother's accident – but she's angry about something else as well, and she doesn't know what that is.

It's below the surface. It's like a scrambled password, a piece of code.

It's what *doesn't* make sense.

It's the two Noels.

As Gina listens to the liturgy, and to the readings, and to the extravagant promises about souls reposing in the afterlife, she strains to see a pattern in events, something that might explain what happened. She's sure there is one, because randomness only goes so far – it's an easy way out, shorthand for *I give up*, for defeat, for what her mother's generation would have called God's will. But for Gina that's not enough. For Gina, what happened on Monday night is simply *too* random.

There has to be a more satisfactory explanation.

As Father Kerrigan steps forward to say a few words, Gina braces herself, expecting the worst, platitudes, condescension. Soon, though, she has to admit that he's doing a pretty good job in the circumstances. Young Noel isn't exactly a shoo-in for Paradise and yet the priest manages to say some simple, affecting things about life – regardless of how it is lived – and about death.

But it is when the ceremony ends and the members of the congregation file past the front pew that Gina wishes she'd taken a tranquilliser after all. Because this most public part of the ordeal is very intense. It's exhausting, and emotionally draining. Knowing that they have to go through it again tomorrow doesn't exactly help either.

Every once in a while Gina glances to her left to see how the others are coping. Of course it's a lot harder for Catherine, who not unreasonably breaks down several times, the sudden appearance of a familiar face triggering fresh waves of tears and sobbing.

For her part, Gina doesn't recognise many of the faces at all. Sophie passes, as does P.J., and a couple of others from work. She recognises a few of the neighbours from when she was a kid. She thinks she recognises one or two of Noel's associates. She's seen their photos in the papers.

She definitely recognises Terry Stack.

He has an unmistakable air about him, of arrogance, of self-regard. He's quite short and lean and rugged-looking. When he reaches out to shake her hand, Gina notices a flicker of interest in his eyes.

Who's your one?

He nods. She nods back but keeps her head down. The line shuffles on.

Afterwards, on the steps of the church and in the car park, people mingle and things loosen up a bit. Sophie comes up to Gina and they hug. P.J. comes up to her as well. They haven't spoken since the other day on the phone, and they clearly need to talk, but – equally clearly – that's not going to happen now. At one point, Father Kerrigan is passing. Gina stops him, shakes his hand and thanks him. Yvonne sticks close by Catherine, holding her arm, as they move slowly through the crowd. Michelle stands at the side with Dan, her partner, and her two kids. She's clutching an unlit cigarette in one hand, a lighter in the other, and looks lost.

People are invited back to the house for something to drink, or at least that was the idea before it became clear how many people this might involve. But then word quickly gets around that Terry Stack is taking over Kennedy's pub down the road, and that tea, coffee, sandwiches and drink are available for anyone who wants to come along, all taken care of, all in honour of Noel.

Gina sees Stack over with Catherine now, arms around her for a second, then looking into her eyes, *talking* to her – Noel this, she imagines, Noel that. Catherine was always ambivalent about Noel's association with Stack, but she's vulnerable at the moment and he's probably laying it on with a trowel.

At one point Stack looks over in Gina's direction, and their eyes meet. That's when she knows he'll be coming up to her, sooner or later, to introduce himself.

It happens about ten minutes later. Having shared a few words with a neighbour of Catherine's, Gina turns around and there he is.

'Howa'ya,' he says, holding out his hand. 'I'm Terry Stack. Gina, right?'

He's already done his homework.

'Yes.'

They shake.

'I'm sorry for your troubles.'

'Thanks.'

Stack is flanked by two younger guys. He's wearing a suit. They're in jeans and hoodies. He looks like he could be a businessman, or a teacher, or even a priest in civvies. They look like drug dealers.

'Noel was a sound bloke,' Stack says, 'and a good earner. He didn't deserve this.'

'No.'

Gina isn't being tight-lipped here. She wants to say something, but just isn't sure what, exactly.

'Listen, love, I'd like you and your sisters to know something. I'm not going to let this rest.'

'No?'

'No.' Stack shakes his head. 'Whoever done this is going to fucking *pay,* believe me.' His face contorts with the emphasis he places on the word *pay.* Normally, Gina would be freaked out by this – boys in hoodies, threats, lingo – but what's normal here?

'Excuse my French,' Stack then adds, a gentlemanly afterthought.

Gina notices one of the hoodies eyeing her up. He has a tattoo on his neck. She *is* freaked out.

'Look, Mr Stack,' she says, 'I suppose –'

'Call me Terry.'

'OK. *Terry.* I suppose you know that my brother died on Monday night as well?'

'Yeah, terrible,' he says, nodding.

'Well, what I want to know is ... could there be any connection between the two deaths? It seems weird that –'

'I doubt that very much, love. Your brother had a car accident. It's terrible, it's awful, but ... it's a coincidence.'

Gina exhales. 'I don't believe in coincidence.'

She turns directly to the hoodie who's been eyeing her up and holds his gaze until he looks away.

She then turns back to Stack and waits for a response.

'I don't either,' he says eventually, and a little uncomfortably, 'but I don't see what connection there *could* be, because I mean –'

'Yeah, yeah,' Gina goes on, 'but am I right in thinking that you don't have any idea *why* my nephew was killed?'

'No.' He shakes his head.

'Or who did it?'

He pauses. 'No.'

'Or who was *behind* it even?'

'No.' He swallows, and pauses again, clearly uneasy at the way this is going. 'No, not yet, but –'

'So it's wide open. Anything is possible.'

Now it's Stack's turn to exhale.

'I . . . suppose.'

Gina can see him thinking, *What's this mad bitch on about?* But she doesn't care. She mightn't get the chance again.

'OK, so Terry, let me ask you another question. Do you people have any links maybe with the building trade? With suppliers? Unions? Could there –'

'Ah, hold on here, love. For Jaysus' sake. You're losing the run of yourself.' Half turning back to one of his hoodies, he says, with a smirk, '*You people.* I like that.'

'I'm sorry, I didn't –'

'Don't worry about it.' Stack looks at his watch. 'Anyway, listen,' he says, 'are you coming down to Kennedy's? We can continue this little chat over a drink.'

Gina hesitates, and closes her eyes. What is she doing? What does she expect here? Some kind of revelation? Hardly. In the following few seconds it all breaks up anyway. When she opens her eyes, someone has approached Stack and is asking him a question. The tattooed hoodie is gazing down at her legs again. The other hoodie is texting.

She stands there for a moment, but then just walks off. She goes over to Sophie and throws her eyes up.

'Who was that?' Sophie asks.

'Terry Stack.'

'Oh my God.' She puts a hand up to her mouth. 'I'm sorry, but this is *very* weird.'

'Yeah.' Gina nods. 'Tell me about it.'

'I was just *reading* about him,' Sophie says, 'before I came here, in the paper. They call him the Electrician. Apparently because he *is* one, or trained as one, but it's more because he uses electric shock as a –' she stops suddenly, and looks at Gina, not knowing where to go with this, '– form of . . .'

'Thanks, Soph. I really needed to know that.'

'Oh God. Sorry.'

As they stand there for a while, not speaking, Gina trawls back through everything in her mind – everything that happened the other night. She thinks about the conversation she had with her brother outside Catherine's house. Noel said he was going into town, so how did he end up out in Wicklow? He was tired and maybe a bit stressed, but he certainly wasn't – as some people seem to be suggesting – *drunk*. Besides, Noel wouldn't drive a car if he was drunk. Noel was one of the straightest and most responsible people she's ever known.

Gina feels dizzy. It's as if she's standing on the edge of a cliff, fighting the impulse to jump.

She swallows, and looks over at Terry Stack again. He's talking into his mobile. She can't help wondering if he avoided her question just now, or *evaded* it? Was he being honest, or was he lying through his teeth? The thing is, she has no way of knowing. Her instincts aren't telling her anything. Except that what happened to her brother – what is supposed to have happened to her brother – *makes absolutely no sense at all . . .*

2

Miriam chooses his tie, as usual – burgundy, to go with his dark suit. Years ago, Norton used to have a weakness for garish ties – multicoloured, psychedelic affairs, ones depicting cartoon characters even – but Miriam eventually put a stop to that.

'If you want to dress like a *politician*,' she said with contempt, 'go up for election.'

Norton sees the sense in this now. Larry Bolger still wears a Homer Simpson tie occasionally and he looks like a fool in it. But it gets him noticed.

Norton has no interest in being noticed. It took him years to understand this about himself. Politicians live to be noticed, it's like photosynthesis to them, attention is their light – and that's why they're so easy to manipulate. Take it away and they're fucked. Give it to them, a steady supply, and they'll do anything for you.

Men like Norton, on the other hand, thrive in the shadows. Miriam – with her background – understood this instinctively, and it was she who steered him in the right direction. It was she who taught him what to wear, and how to present himself. It was she who made him realise that being rich meant never having to smile for the cameras.

Shaved and fully dressed now, Norton stands in front of the mirror in his bathroom and puts on some cologne.

So is that what drove him earlier in the week? Not just a dread of negative publicity, but a dread of any publicity at all? Maybe. In part. But he's not an idiot. He knows, for instance, that the official opening of Richmond Plaza is going to involve *some* exposure, that he might have to appear in a few press photos or on the six o'clock news. But so what. He'll be anonymous, just another suit in the background. The real focus will be on the architect, on Ray Sullivan's people, on Larry Bolger.

Norton stares at himself in the mirror.

In terms of publicity, however, the alternative scenario doesn't even bear thinking about. He'd get caught up in it personally. He'd be fodder for the tabloids and for the radio talk shows. They'd run an identifying clip of him on the TV news, and repeat it night after night as they spun the story to death – maybe a shot of him walking along a street, looking shifty, or struggling to get out of a car.

The idea horrifies him.

Exposure like that, of course, would be the least of his worries – because there'd also be protracted litigation, followed, almost certainly, by bankruptcy, disgrace, ruin.

Norton straightens his jacket and runs a hand across his hair.

Definitely, on reflection, he did the right thing.

He goes through the bedroom and out onto the landing. He looks at his watch: 4.45.

'Miriam!'

'Yes, yes, I'm coming.'

Miriam appears from her bedroom. She is wearing a navy suit, navy shoes and a navy pillbox hat. She looks elegant and appropriately sombre.

'Which church is it?' she says, adjusting one of her earrings.

'Donnybrook.'

Miriam stands in front of the full-length mirror on the landing and repositions her hat. 'Do you think there'll be many people there?'

'I'd say so, yeah,' Norton replies. 'Actually, I wouldn't be surprised if it's packed to the rafters.'

'Really?'

'Yeah. He was very popular.'

'How well did *you* know him?'

'Not very. I had dealings with him the odd time.'

Most recently, of course – Norton thinks – in the last week or so. And given what he soon found himself contemplating, that fact had naturally raised something of a red flag in his mind. But then he also remembered reading about Rafferty's nephew in the paper, in a report about local gangs and DVD piracy.

'Come on, Mo. There'll be traffic.'

'I'm *coming*.'

She finishes at the mirror and they both head downstairs.

It had seemed like a good plan – a few words in the back of his car with Fitz and that should have been more or less the size of it, at least as far as his own involvement was concerned.

But then look what happened.

They leave the house and get in the car. As he drives slowly across the gravel to the gates, Norton runs it through his mind once again. Monday night, the panic, the sleeplessness, the hours of waiting – how *close* he came to self-destructing. Then, on Tuesday morning, the phone call. It took him a long time to calm down after that, but as the day progressed, and he spoke to different people, the story *did* gel into place. He nevertheless found it hard to shake his sense of unease. It had been a very close thing.

Now though, on Thursday afternoon, as he drives to the church for the removal – where he will sit and pray in front of Noel Rafferty's earthly remains – Norton feels calm again, and secure.

The panic is gone. The threat has been lifted.

It's almost five o'clock and Larry Bolger is on the plinth outside Leinster House. He is looking over at Buswell's. He has just left the chamber after a debate on stamp-duty reform and is waiting for his car. He knows that a group of four or five backbenchers is meeting in the hotel to discuss what are euphemistically called 'developments' and he wonders how they're getting on.

The weirdest thing about this stage of a leadership challenge is that all you are required to do is behave as if it isn't happening. Other people do the important stuff for you – the mobilising, the lobbying, the whispering.

'Er . . . Larry, can I have a word?'

Bolger looks around and releases a low groan. '*A* word? There's no such thing, Ken, not where *you're* concerned, so no –'

'Yeah, but this is –'

'Look, I've no time at the moment.' Miraculously, the car pulls up. 'I'm on my way to a removal. Tomorrow maybe, or when I get back from the States.'

Bolger hurries down the steps and opens the back door of the car.

'Larry, you're going to *want* to hear this, believe me, because it's –'

'Some other time, *OK*? I'm busy.'

He gets in the car and bangs the door shut behind him.

The driver knows enough not to delay. 'Good evening, Minister,' he says, pulling away. 'Where are we off to?'

Bolger takes a deep breath.

'Er . . . Donnybrook, Billy. The church there on the corner. Thanks.'

Billy nods. They go out the main gates and turn left onto Kildare Street.

Bolger then leans back in his seat and exhales. Is he alone in finding the chief political correspondent of the *Irish Independent* an epic pain in the arse? Like one or two of the other hacks in the press gallery, Ken Murphy is never off the radio talk shows and seems to claim ownership of practically every story that makes it into the news.

But at the same time, if this leadership bid is to succeed, Bolger realises – be it a messy heave, or a bloodless coup – he *is* going to have to be . . . well, a little more accommodating, and play the game.

He closes his eyes, luxuriating in a kind of steely clear-headedness – something he associates these days with not drinking.

The choreography of the next few months is going to be crucial, of course. The Paloma announcement the other day, his upcoming trade mission to the States, the opening of Richmond Plaza in the new year . . . each of these, incrementally, will ratchet up his profile – in the party, with the media, with the public at large.

Bolger opens his eyes again. They're almost at Leeson Street Bridge.

It's certainly been a long time coming. He entered politics in the mid-eighties – though as far as he remembers, and it's all a bit vague now, standing for election hadn't even been *his* idea. Frank, his brother, had held the seat originally but died, and then somehow Larry was persuaded to come back from Boston and contest it in the ensuing by-election. With plenty of backing from within the party, and much to his own surprise, he won the seat. What followed was a blur that has lasted two and a half decades, a blur of clinics, funerals, functions, branch meetings, Oireachtas committees and, every few years or so, like a recurring anxiety dream, the curious sensation of being raised shoulder-high by screaming mobs of your own supporters at a count centre. Eventually, a junior ministry materialised, along with a little national exposure – on *Morning Ireland*, on *Questions and Answers*, on *Tonight with Vincent Browne*. Other junior portfolios came along, and then, at last, his first full seat at the cabinet table.

After that it was all very serious and grown-up – access, privilege, power.

Compromise.

He opens his eyes. They're on Morehampton Road now, passing the old Sach's Hotel.

But all of a sudden, for some reason, his mood has shifted. He feels anxious. He feels that familiar jumping in the pit of his stomach.

Then, as the car approaches the gates of the church, and he sees a big silver BMW pulling in just ahead of them, he realises why.

It's because no matter how he looks at it, no matter from what angle, there is one constant in all of this, in his career, in his life, stretching right back to that surprise by-election of nineteen eighty whenever-it-was, and stretching right into his future, too, inescapable, looming like an Atlantic weather front. And that constant – over there now, struggling to climb out of his BMW – is, of course, Paddy Norton.

3

Despite her exhaustion (she didn't get any sleep last night, and young Noel's funeral was this morning), Gina immediately registers the contrast between yesterday's removal in Dolanstown and the one today here in Donnybrook. Passing through the gates on the way in, she can't help noticing all the BMWs, Mercs, Saabs and Jags. The church is smaller, too, but the crowd seems to be bigger. As she and Jennifer and her sisters (except for Catherine, who is at home, in bed, unconscious) get out of the funeral car and follow the coffin into the church and up the aisle towards the altar, Gina glances left and right at this congregation of what appear to be well-groomed middle-aged men and their brittle, pampered wives. There isn't a hoodie or a tracksuit in sight. Instead, she sees silk suits, cashmere overcoats, fur coats – and *hats*, dozens of them (how many women yesterday were wearing hats?). And is it her imagination or is there something in the air, a certain pungency – a subtle fusion, perhaps, of incense, cologne and expensive perfume?

The ceremony passes quickly. It is dreamlike – the same words as yesterday, the same sentiments, the same skewed sense that none of this can possibly be for real. The hardest part – again, like yesterday – is when the members of the congregation file past the front pew to express their condolences. Although a form of torture, this also happens to be when Gina realises for the first time just how far Noel travelled in his life. She always knew that he was successful, but she is surprised to see certain people file past here, people he must have known, people whose circles he must have moved in – politicians, businessmen, sports stars, TV personalities. She realises how little she really knew him, and this adds to her heartache.

Afterwards, outside the church, the mood is sombre, but there is still an air of conviviality, as people greet each other, shake hands, slap shoulders and talk.

Jenny is very dignified, but she is frozen in her grief, moving slowly and saying almost nothing. Yvonne and Michelle, who are as tired as Gina, also find it hard to speak.

Gina, though, forces herself. She doesn't know where to begin, or who to talk to, but she moves around, introducing herself to people, determined to get *some* kind of a fix on Monday night. It seems obvious to her that the sequence of events, at the very least, needs to be established. What she finds hard to take, however, is that no one else is asking any questions. An official version of Noel's accident very quickly fell into place, and was accepted, but hasn't it occurred to anyone that what happened was, well ... *strange*? There is the supposed coincidence of the two deaths, Noel's unaccounted-for trip into Wicklow and the downright *un*acceptable notion that he was drunk behind the wheel.

But it's not that easy. Actually, it's very awkward. How do you quiz people without coming across as abrupt, or rude, or possibly even – given how exhausted she is and must *look* – unhinged? Perhaps now is not the most suitable time for this. But when is? When else does she find practically everyone Noel knew herded together in the one location?

She talks, then, to people who knew Noel through work but didn't really *know* him. She talks to people who knew him well but hadn't seen him for ages. She talks to someone who regales her with anecdotes about Noel's capacity for work, his dedication, his legendary perfectionism. She introduces herself to a TV presenter who apparently played a lot of poker with Noel.

As things break up and people begin leaving, Gina feels frustrated, as if she's blown her one chance at this. But trying to get someone's life into focus, trying to square up different people's perspectives on the same person, is difficult. More than difficult. It's like trying to pick mercury up with a fork. How do private investigators do it? How do biographers do it? Although she's only starting, she already has a nagging sense of how futile this might prove to be.

There is a general invitation to come back to the house – Noel and Jenny's new spread on Clyde Road. Despite how tired she is, Gina decides to go, and accepts a lift from Jenny's brother, Harry. Yvonne and Michelle have to get back to Catherine's and they leave. Goodbyes are said and very quickly the crowd disperses – cars inching towards the gates and feeding out into the evening traffic.

In the house people are received, coats are taken, drinks are served. Jenny sits in the main reception room, in an armchair, sipping a cup of tea. The room gradually fills up, as does the hallway outside, as well as a large kitchen area at the back. Gina hasn't been here before and is amazed at how grand the place is. Noel and Jenny only moved into it from their place in Kilmacud a few weeks back and had been meaning to have family over. Gina stands with a glass of wine at the bay window in the main reception room – which is more like a ballroom – and looks out onto the floodlit front lawn.

She is alone, and her will has flagged, but when someone approaches her she musters energy from somewhere and introduces herself. She quickly finds that she is talking to a Detective Superintendent Jackie Merrigan. He is the first person she has met today who it turns out actually *spoke* to Noel on Monday night, and this fact animates her further. He tells her that he was a friend of Noel's from years back and that it was he who informed Noel about their nephew's murder.

'You phoned him?'

'Yes.'

Gina latches on to this and tries to find out as much as she can about the conversation. Merrigan is tall and slightly stooped. He's in his fifties and has a shock of silvery white hair. He seems to understand Gina's desperate need for information, that it's part of the grieving process, and she, in turn, seems to understand that he is indulging her in this, and is grateful.

One fact that comes out of their exchange is that when Merrigan made the call, Noel was having a drink somewhere with Paddy Norton, the developer.

Gina nods along at this. 'I see.'

Merrigan then turns to his left and looks around the room. 'In fact,' he says, pointing, 'that's him over there, in that group. The one in the dark red tie.'

Gina scans the room and zeroes in on the red tie.

She takes a sip from her wine. 'Thanks,' she says, almost in a whisper.

The room is full. Most people are in clusters of two or three, but standing in front of the fireplace (a huge marble affair, the fire roaring), and in a rough circle, are five men in suits. They are holding glasses of wine or whiskey, and two of them are smoking cigars. One of them is young, twenty-four or twenty-five, but the rest of them look older, mid-fifties maybe, or late fifties. The man wearing the dark red tie is holding forth about something. The others are listening.

Alan Glynn

As she makes her way across the room towards the group, Gina recognises one of them, and then another. The young guy, tall and thickset, is the captain of the Ireland rugby team. The man on Norton's right, standing with his back to the fire, is a cabinet minister, Larry Bolger. The other two she doesn't recognise, but they look generic – they could be barristers, solicitors, accountants, *anything*, bank executives, equity-fund managers.

She reaches the edge of the circle and stops, uncertain how to proceed. She can't just break in here – though she *could*.

Jenny's brother passes with a bottle of wine and offers her a refill.

She holds up her glass. 'Thanks. How's Jen?'

'She's OK. Well. I don't think it's really hit her yet.'

'No, me neither.'

'It's sad, you know,' Harry goes on. 'She keeps looking around this place in disbelief. There are still a few boxes upstairs they haven't unpacked yet.'

This hits Gina hard, and she groans, 'Oh *God*.' It's another unexpected little window into her brother's life.

Then, as Harry turns one way to refill someone else's glass, Gina turns the other, and finds herself looking directly at Paddy Norton. He's not speaking now, but is listening to one of the barristers or equity-fund managers and staring down at the carpet. After a moment, he lifts his head and looks in Gina's direction. Their eyes meet. Gina instinctively raises her eyebrows and gestures to him, pointing to the side. Surprised, Norton immediately moves, mumbling a word of excuse to no one in particular, and exits the circle. Gina moves around it and they meet head on.

'Excuse me, Mr Norton,' she says, extending a hand. 'I didn't mean to interrupt, but my name is Gina. I'm one of Noel's sisters.'

'My *dear*,' Norton says, shaking her hand vigorously, 'my dear. Of course. *Gina*. How are you? I'm very sorry. You have my deepest sympathies.'

'Thank you.'

'How *are* you?'

People keep asking her this – how *are* you? – as if they really want to know, but it's just a formula.

'I'm fine.' She pauses. 'I suppose.'

'Of course. It's . . . it's very hard on all of you.'

She nods. Norton is holding a glass of whiskey. As he speaks, he looks into it and swirls the whiskey around. Up close, he is quite portly, but his tailored charcoal grey suit does a lot to disguise this. He has chubby manicured hands and beads of sweat on his upper lip. His eyes are blue and very intense.

'How well did you know my brother?'

Here she goes.

'Not very well, I'm afraid. We liaised, of course, on the project.'

'On Richmond Plaza?'

'Yes. Which, incidentally, you know, will be a tremendous tribute to your brother when it's finished.'

'I'm sure it will, yes.' She pauses. 'But you didn't know him socially.'

'Not really, no.' Norton takes a sip of whiskey from his glass.

'Because, I was just wondering –' she half turns here, vaguely indicating behind her, 'you see, I was talking a minute ago to a Detective Superintendent . . . Merrigan I think it was, and he says that you had a drink with Noel on Monday night. Is that correct?'

She doesn't mean this to sound quite so inquisitorial. But she's *very* tired and it's weird standing here. It's almost surreal. She's aware of the government minister a few feet away from her, and the rugby captain, and she's just spotted – over Norton's shoulder – the presenter of a popular new reality TV show.

'Well, yes,' Norton says. 'There's social, I suppose, and social. If a quick drink after work to go over some notes qualifies as social, then yes.'

What she really wants to ask him is the question she asked Terry Stack, only in reverse – because it seems to her, on reflection, that Stack *was* lying. But she has to build up to it.

'I see,' she says, 'and what . . . notes were these?'

'Just, you know . . . work-related stuff.'

'Right.' She nods. 'When I saw Noel later he did seem fairly stressed all right.'

'Stressed?'

'Yes, *very*, in fact, I'd say. About work.'

She keeps glancing over his shoulder. How does she phrase this without putting him off the way she put Terry Stack off?

'What did he say?'

'What did he *say*?' She looks at him now, directly. 'Um, he . . .' She goes on staring into his eyes, as she struggles to recall what Noel said, to summon up his words – even though she's tired, even though time seems elastic . . . but eventually something comes to her. 'He mentioned *the situation* . . . he said it was an unholy mess.'

Norton nods. 'I see.' He continues nodding, and Gina feels compelled to nod along with him. She also feels that the wine she's been drinking has kicked in and that she needs to be a little more focused here.

'I see,' Norton says again.

Maybe she should start by asking him out straight if he knows who Terry Stack is. Take it from there.

'Mr Norton, do –'

'Look, Gina –'

Just then the government minister appears behind Norton and slaps him on the back.

'I've got to be pushing on, Paddy,' Bolger says. He smiles at Gina, and then, as if remembering he's a politician, stretches out his hand. 'Larry Bolger,' he says. 'Deepest sympathies. Your brother was a fine man.'

'Thank you,' Gina says, shaking his hand. 'You knew him?'

'Oh indeed, quite well. Noel beat me at poker on more than one occasion – humiliated me, you might say.'

'Really?'

'Oh yes. He was a quite serious card player, your brother.'

Gina wants to pursue this, but just then a tall woman in a navy suit appears and Bolger takes a couple of steps back. The woman says to Norton, 'Sweetheart, we should be leaving, too.' She reaches out to take the glass from his hand.

Norton, who looks a little pale now, lets her.

Gina sees her chance slipping away here. But Norton leans towards her and whispers, 'We should talk about this again.'

She can smell the whiskey on his breath.

'Yes,' she says.

Someone with an empty tray is passing, and the woman in the navy suit puts Norton's glass onto it.

'Phone my office in Baggot Street,' Norton says, handing her a business card, 'and we can arrange to meet, or . . . if you could just come *there*?'

'Yes,' Gina says, nodding. 'The funeral's tomorrow, so – I don't know – Monday?'

'Yes, fine. Absolutely.'

'Er . . .'

'Ten o'clock?'

She nods again. 'OK.'

The woman in the navy suit, Norton's wife presumably, tugs at his sleeve and leads him away.

Larry Bolger moves away as well. The captain of the Ireland team and the two solicitors – or fund managers, or whatever they are – continue talking by the fire.

Gina turns and walks back across the room to the bay window. She glances at Norton's business card and then slips it into her pocket. What just happened there? She's not quite sure. He seemed eager to meet – which might mean something, or it might not. At least in the privacy of an office, and when she's not so tired, she'll have a better chance of assessing what Norton has to say – and she'll ask him then, out straight, if he or anyone in his organisation has links with Terry Stack.

Once a couple of people have left, others start leaving as well, and the room quickly thins out.

After a while, Gina gathers her strength and goes over to have a few words with Jenny.

4

'You drive.'

'What?'

'*You* drive. I don't feel well.'

'Oh for goodness' sake, Paddy. Give me the keys.'

Norton hands Miriam the keys and goes around to the passenger side. He gets in and immediately fumbles in his jacket pocket for his silver pillbox. As Miriam is putting on her seatbelt she looks at what he's doing and says, 'You're not still taking *those,* are you?'

He pops two of the tablets into his mouth and turns to her. 'What do *you* think?'

'Oh, Paddy. On top of . . . what were you drinking in there, whiskey?'

'Just drive, would you? *Jesus.*'

Norton swallows the pills. He can still see those eyes, staring at him accusingly. He's assuming accusingly. The thing he *can't* believe is that Noel Rafferty blabbered about this to his kid sister. But how much did he tell her? How much does she know? Maybe he should have stayed and had it out with her, but he felt weak standing there, like he was going to faint. He needed to get away and was glad when Bolger and Miriam appeared.

His mind is racing. He goes back over the conversation. First she wouldn't look him in the eye and then she wouldn't look away, taking ages over it, going for maximum effect – *the situation . . . he mentioned the situation . . .*

Jesus Christ.

And what was that about a detective superintendent knowing where he was on Monday night?

This is too much.

'Are you feeling ill?'

'What?'

Miriam is tapping her fingers on the steering wheel. 'Are you feeling *ill*?'

'Yes.'

'Those pills won't help, you know.'

'Yes they will.'

They already are.

'You're not in *pain*, are you?'

'No.'

'Then how can they help? They're meant to be pain*killers*, aren't they?'

'There are different kinds of pain, Miriam.'

'Oh for goodness' sake.'

'Yeah, well.' He pauses, regroups. 'Anyway, look who's talking.'

'What's that supposed to mean?'

'Oh come on, the sleeping pills? You've been taking those for as long as I've known you. So don't talk to me about –'

'That's entirely different. They're for a diagnosed, clinical condition.'

'Hhnm.'

They drive in silence for a while along the Dual Carriageway.

'Look,' Miriam says, 'do you want me to stop off at Dr Walsh's?'

'No. I'm fine. I'm just a bit stressed at the moment.'

'But –'

'All I need is some peace and quiet.'

'Yes, but –'

'Oh for *fuck's* sake, Miriam –'

There is a pause.

'Don't you dare speak to me like that. I don't care how you feel, there's no call for *language*.'

She reaches down and aggressively flicks on the CD player. Lush sounds fill the car. *Adagios to Die For, Volume 3*.

Norton sits back and exhales.

What is he going to do? Should he call Fitz? Should he wait? He has to do something. He's too deep into this to let it unravel now. But what does Gina want? Is she going to blackmail him? Is she linking what she knows – or thinks she knows – with her brother's death? Is she as much of a threat as *he* was?

Norton closes his eyes. He sees drizzle falling in a beer garden and a young man slumped over a wooden table. He sees an SUV skidding off the road and hurtling down a ravine. He sees a Merc and a Toyota, one concertinaed into a tree, the other merged with an old brick wall. Through a pervasive rain-drenched orange glow, he sees speckles of red – everywhere – and a continuous rotating blue light. He sees carnage, one body in the Merc, three in the Toyota, mangled, misshapen. He sees a little boy, his face streaked with blood, eyes vacant, but *walking* somehow – walking across shattered glass and strips of metal towards the flashing blue light and his own mangled, misshapen future. He sees a catalogue of panic, of fuck-ups, of near misses – and he's tired of it, tired of having to piece together in his mind what he was never there to see, tired of having to confront these dark shards of imagining, these little glimpses into hell.

The Narolet has been building steadily, and now, like the music coming from the speakers – aching strings, sweet, swirling woodwinds – it reaches a crescendo, rises up in a tide of emotion and washes over him.

As it ebbs away, he opens his eyes – drained, spent. He glances to the right.

It takes him a moment to refocus.

He has always liked the way Miriam drives – fast, but very

controlled. She really concentrates. She changes gears with the determination of a Formula One driver.

He's such a fool.

'I'm sorry, darling.'

They're speeding down through the underpass.

'When we get home, you should go to bed,' Miriam says, after an appropriate pause. 'Or at least,' she goes on, more tenderly, 'at a decent hour. For once.'

'You're right. I will.'

They remain silent for a while. The sound of a single violin, lonely and resonant, carries them forward.

Fifty yards ahead, the traffic light turns and they come gliding to a halt.

'Who was that girl you were talking to?'

'Gina Rafferty. One of the sisters.'

'She seems young.'

'Yeah. Big family apparently. She must be the youngest. She was quite upset, of course. She wanted to talk about her brother.' He stares at the dashboard. 'About what he did, and the building and stuff.'

'Poor thing.'

'I've asked her to come and see me at the office.'

The light turns green and they surge forward – as does Norton's stomach. He detects a slight chemical shift, somewhere deep inside the dense, woolly fug of the Narolet.

'You should take her to see it,' Miriam says. 'If she's so interested.'

'See what?'

'The building. Give her a tour. Bring her up to the top. Show her the view.'

'Hmm,' Norton says, feeling a bit queasy now. 'Maybe.'

He closes his eyes, and a rapid sequence of images flashes by, like frames of celluloid spooling to the end of a reel: the top floor of Richmond Plaza ... howling winds, tarpaulin sheets flapping, sunlight flickering through the grid of interlocking steel girders. The scene is spectacular, with the city spread out below – Liberty Hall, the Central Bank, the spire of Christ Church Cathedral, and then, farther out, the parks and green-belt areas, the housing estates that look like electronic circuit-boards, the gigantic shopping centres, the new ring roads and motorway extensions, languid and serpentine, laid out in every direction ...

The new city.

His city.

'Yes.' He nods, opening his eyes again and placing a firm, steadying hand on his stomach. 'Maybe that's what I'll do.'

Four

1

As Mark is letting himself in the front door, he calls out his aunt's name. He does this so that she won't get a fright when he suddenly appears in the kitchen or the living room. She isn't used to being alone yet and the least thing seems to spook her. Of course, it's been only six months since Uncle Des died, which is nothing, Mark supposes – especially if you've been married to someone for more than forty years.

He takes a few steps along the hallway and calls her name out again. 'Aunt Lilly?'

From behind the kitchen door, he hears a sharp, panicky intake of breath.

Shit.

'It's only me, Aunt Lilly. It's *Mark.*'

'Oh. Oh.' Then, 'I'm in here.'

Mark opens the door and walks into the kitchen. His aunt is sitting at the table. There are piles of documents spread out in front of her. Through a door on the left he can see into the living room. The TV is on, but the sound is down.

His aunt looks up at him and smiles nervously.

'Thanks for coming, Mark. I don't know what I'd do without you.'

'Oh, you'd be fine, Aunt Lilly, believe me.'

He goes over and kisses her on the forehead. He then pulls out a chair next to hers. He sits on the edge of the chair and leans forward, hands together, like a doctor about to begin a consultation. He even says, 'Now, what seems to be the problem?'

Aunt Lilly is in her late sixties but looks older. Her hair is grey and she is small and bony. Mark can see that the last few months have taken a lot out of her.

'It's these Eircom bills,' she says, pointing to the pile directly in front of her. 'I don't understand them, and they seem so *high*.'

'I barely understand mine, Aunt Lilly. I think you'd need a degree in accountancy to understand the average Eircom bill.'

He takes a page from the top of the pile and examines it. After his uncle Des died, it quickly became apparent that Aunt Lilly had no idea about money or bills – 'that was always *his* department,' she said – so Mark ended up dealing with the solicitors and processing all of the necessary paperwork. He's been helping her out ever since, with little things: setting up standing orders at the bank, cancelling subscriptions to magazines and, not least, interpreting the runic complexities of her utility bills.

'That's a lovely suit,' Aunt Lilly says, reaching over and stroking the sleeve of his jacket.

'Yeah, it's Italian,' he says, not looking up from the Eircom bill. 'Surprise, surprise.'

'And the shoes?'

'Yeah. You have to make an impression. That's what it's all about these days.'

'*La bella figura.*'

'Well, they invented it.'

Mark half suspects that these emergency calls of his aunt's are as much about the company as anything else – which is fine. It's a bit like having the TV on, unwatched, in another room. He does see her regularly, at least once a week, but if she needs an extra visit now and again, he's more than willing to oblige. She's certainly done enough for *him*.

'Erm, did Uncle Des have broadband?'

Aunt Lilly looks slightly pained, as though he's just asked her to explain the general theory of relativity. 'Broad – ?'

'Broadband. On his computer. There's a monthly charge here for it.'

'He did use the computer quite a bit.'

'Well, I'm sure that's it then. I'll get them to cancel it. Don't worry about it. I'll take care of everything.'

He replaces the Eircom bill.

From where he's sitting Mark can see the TV flickering in the next room. He shifts his chair slightly so that the TV is no longer in his direct line of vision.

'You're very good,' Aunt Lilly says. 'Would you like a cup of tea?'

Mark looks at his watch. It's just after nine. He's meeting that builder again in town, but not until eleven.

'Yeah, why not? Thanks.'

It was a more convoluted process than he'd imagined, but he's pretty confident now about securing the contract.

Aunt Lilly gets up and busies herself with the kettle.

Mark flicks a tiny piece of lint from his trouser leg.

Then he turns his attention to the documents spread out on the table. Besides the pile of Eircom bills, there are ESB bills, NTL bills, bank statements, share certificates, tax-relief certificates, P60 forms. They go back over what must be years, and in some cases possibly even decades.

He feels a sudden ripple of anxiety.

'Aunt Lilly?'

'Yes?'

'Why do you keep all of this stuff?'

She's standing at the counter, and turns around. He sees that she's slicing what looks like a Madeira cake.

'I . . . don't know. Des was very conscientious about paperwork and things like that. Why?'

'It isn't necessary, that's all. Going back a few years maybe, but this seems a bit extreme. I mean, these days, with identity theft and all, you can't be too careful.'

The second he says that he wishes he'd kept his mouth shut.

'Identity *what*?'

He explains briefly, doing his best to make it sound as innocuous as possible. She is, nevertheless, appalled.

He knows that his aunt is trying to keep herself busy here, organising all of this paperwork, but he resolves to bring a small office shredder with him the next time he comes, and with her permission he'll destroy most of it.

She arrives carrying a tray. Mark makes some space on the table by picking up a thick wad of old bank statements, and as Aunt Lilly settles the tray and starts fussing with the tea things, he idly flicks through them.

Some of these statements are more than twenty years old.

Uncle Des . . .

Mark gives a little shake of his head.

The man was so fastidious, so hardworking, so morally upstanding. OK, he was also introspective and moody, and seemed, on a permanent basis, to be *angry* about something – but he managed to keep that to himself. He never took it out on anyone. He never lost his temper.

He was a good man, a good father, and Mark misses him.

He rests the wad of bank statements in his lap.

This isn't easy. Mark has only the vaguest memories of his natural father – his parents died when he was five – but whenever he does think of him, of *Tony*, he gets this weird feeling in his head, or maybe it's in his heart . . . a plunging, plummeting rush of confusion, of longing, and of course – *Jesus* – of guilt. It's intangible and unquantifiable, but the feeling is as real to him as a migraine headache, or a malignant tumour.

With his uncle, on the other hand, things were always a good deal simpler. Despite the moodiness, Des was a father figure who didn't come with any real baggage.

Looking around the room now, at all the documents on the table, up at Aunt Lilly, Mark wonders – and quite possibly for the first time – what it was that his uncle ever had to be so angry about. He also wonders – and most definitely for the first time – if any of it had to do with *him*, if any of it might somehow have been *his* fault . . .

2

When she gets up, Gina has a splitting headache. She did have a few glasses of wine last night, finally – but this isn't a hangover. She hopes that taking a shower will ease the pounding in her head. When it doesn't, she takes two Panadol. She puts on coffee and goes to the bedroom to get dressed.

She's glad the weekend is over. As it was happening, it felt endless, and desolate, and empty. Now that it's Monday morning, though, she's not sure how much any of that is going to change.

After the funeral on Friday, there was a big catered thing

back at the house on Clyde Road. With her three sisters there, and various relatives, and old friends from Dolanstown – all of them clearly uncomfortable – Gina came to appreciate for the first time the divide that existed in Noel's life between where he came from and where he ended up. Later on, out in Yvonne's house, there was a lot of reminiscing, vodka-fuelled for the most part, and sitting there listening to it Gina also came to realise that there was a good twenty years of Noel's life – the first twenty – that she had no knowledge or memory of at all.

Saturday was spent mainly at Catherine's. Various people stopped by, but there was no real structure to it anymore. The formal side of things was over, and as the day progressed there was an awful sense of not wanting to let go – coupled with a growing realisation that everyone else, the rest of the world, already had. On Sunday morning, lying in bed, Gina thought obsessively about the previous weekend. She was tormented by its innocence and abandon, by its blind ignorance of what lay ahead. She spent most of the day alone, curled up on the sofa, unable to face any of the usual Sunday stuff – the papers, the eggs, the laundry.

She managed to rouse herself from this torpor towards evening time. Then at around seven, P.J. phoned, and she agreed to meet him for a drink. They met in Kehoe's and had a fairly depressing conversation about the future of Lucius Software. They skirted around it but eventually had to admit that with no production date in sight, and the economy heading into recession, the chances of a second round of VC funding were looking increasingly slim.

Sitting at her kitchen table now, Gina sips coffee, unconcerned about the location of keys, mobile phone, earrings, her Monday morning drained of its urgency.

She'll go into the office all right – there's plenty to do – but not until later. In the meantime, she has that appointment in Baggot Street at ten o'clock.

As Gina leaves her building, walks along the quays and makes her way over to Pearse Street, she thinks about Paddy Norton and what she's going to say to him. She also thinks about her sisters, none of whom seems to share her concerns about the way their brother died. When she brought it up on Saturday, for the second or third time, Michelle even snapped at her and told her to *stop it*.

Which, in fairness, she did.

Gina's concerns are real, but she also knows that people grieve in different ways, and that maybe this is just *her* way. If so, she doesn't want to impose that on anyone else – at least not for the moment.

Halfway along Baggot Street, Gina takes Norton's business card out of her bag and looks at it.

After another few minutes, she finds the address.

It's a modern office building, an International Style glass box, but at only six storeys a little odd-looking – like a skyscraper in miniature, something squeezed down in scale to fit into its more elegant, Georgian surroundings. Put up sometime in the late seventies, she guesses, or early eighties, the building is quite ugly, and already appears dilapidated, streaked on the outside, as if it's been dipped in some sort of corrosive chemical.

Gina goes into the lobby and glances around. Straight ahead, there is an unoccupied marble reception desk. Hanging above it there is a huge frameless painting – thick yellow stripes against a grainy bluish background. Next to this there is a directory, which Gina consults. She sees that Winterland Properties is on the third floor.

She takes the elevator up, and Norton's secretary shows her into his office. Gina is surprised by the decor. Like the fittings and corporate artwork in the lobby, it has quite a dated feel to it. Norton's desk is a huge mahogany affair, and in front of it there are two red leather sofas with a glass coffee table between them. The table is scattered with magazines. On the wall facing the desk, there is a mahogany cabinet with a large TV set in the middle of it.

'Gina . . . *Gina.*'

Norton comes out from behind his desk and extends his hand. He's wearing a grey suit with a powder-blue shirt and a slightly darker blue tie. Gina steps forward.

'Hi, Mr Norton.'

'Paddy. Jesus. Call me Paddy.'

They shake hands.

'OK . . . *Paddy,* thanks.'

'How *are* you?'

'I'm all right. You know.' The face Gina makes here – half pained, half resigned – is meant to express a keen desire to move on. But before she can say anything more, Norton claps his hands together.

'Gina,' he says, 'I was going to propose something to you this morning. I was going to ask if you'd like to come and have a look at Richmond Plaza, let me give you a tour, show you the view from the top.'

Gina stares at him for a moment in surprise, as though he has just spoken to her in Chinese.

'In Noel's honour sort of thing.' He pauses. 'I mean, we both know how dedicated he was to the project, right?'

Gina certainly wasn't expecting this, but after a pause she nods her head and says, 'Yes, yes, I'd really like that.'

'Good,' Norton says, 'good.'

There is a coat draped on one of the leather sofas. He reaches over and picks it up. He puts it on and holds a hand out, indicating the door. 'OK then,' he says, 'let's go.'

In the mid-morning traffic, it takes them about twenty minutes to get to Richmond Dock. Norton's car is spacious and very comfortable, but with its sickly beige leather uphol-stery and pine air freshener dangling from the rearview mirror, Gina ends up feeling a little queasy and doesn't say much. Norton, in any case, talks non-stop and goes into a level of technical detail about the project that she quickly finds incomprehensible.

At the site, Norton parks on the street, and they get out of the car. There is a wide paved concourse in front of Richmond Plaza, and as they walk across it, Gina leans backwards and looks up. Most of the building has external cladding in place and looks finished. The very top levels, though, seem more exposed, and dissolve into a blur. At the base of the building there is an arched glass entranceway, with space on either side for what will probably be large retail units.

Leading the way, Norton goes left across the concourse towards a sectioned-off area. Here, behind the wooden hoard-ing, it looks like a proper building site, with mud and cables and diggers and Portakabin huts. There is a gigantic tower crane on its concrete base. There are construction workers everywhere. Norton and Gina make their way to a row of prefab structures, one of which is an office. Norton signs in and introduces Gina to the project manager, a thin, earnest man in his late forties. They don hard hats and safety jackets, and the project manager then takes up where Norton left off – rolling out specs and statistics.

They go back across the concourse and enter the building proper. It takes Gina a moment to realise, as she looks up and around her, that what they are standing in here is a colossal atrium. It must extend to at least ten levels above them. Through the scaffolding and hanging power cables she can see that it's going to have galleried floors on three sides, with Plexiglas elevators, probably, on the fourth. On one of the sides, reaching up diagonally to the next level, there is an esca-lator frame, not quite locked into place, that looks like a huge dinosaur skeleton in a natural-history museum.

They cross the atrium, passing a bank of six more elevators over to the right, and walk along a dimly lit corridor, eventu-ally coming out at a large service elevator next to a loading dock. When they get into the elevator car, the project manager hits an unmarked switch. The car lurches slightly, starts moving and then picks up speed.

A few moments later, the door opens and they step out. 'Level 48' is painted on a partition directly in front of them. To the left there are five or six construction workers standing around and next to them on the floor are some loose sections of what look like air-conditioning ducts.

The project manager leads the way, taking Gina and Norton around the partition. Except for the core section and a grid of supporting steel columns, Level 48 is an open space. Its left and right sides have wall units and glazing frames already fitted, but the far end, with only a few interlocking steel girders and protective barriers, looks very exposed.

'It's not safe to go up on the roof,' Norton says, 'but I think you'll get the picture from here.'

The project manager is about to say something when his mobile goes off. He answers it, listens, nods. After a moment, he gestures at Norton, pointing downwards. He turns to Gina, shakes his head apologetically and then scuttles back towards the elevator, the phone still at his ear.

'Impressed?' Norton says.

'Yes. Yes. It's . . . amazing.'

'Of course, a project of this sort is all about teamwork and collaboration, that goes without saying – but don't be in any doubt, Gina, your brother made his contribution here, and you should be proud of him.'

As Gina turns to look at Norton, her eyes well up. 'I am,' she says in a whisper.

Norton puts a hand out to her, but Gina moves away. She quickly regains her composure, takes a paper tissue from her pocket and blows her nose. 'Sorry.'

'Jesus,' Norton says. 'For what?'

'Oh, you know. I suppose. I don't know. Look, er . . .' She hesitates, dabbing her nose with the tissue.

'Yes?'

'We were . . . talking on Thursday evening –'

'Yes.' Norton straightens up. 'Yes indeed we were.'

'So I just wanted to ask you –'

'Yes?'

'Well, the thing is, you see, I'm finding it hard to accept that the two deaths . . . well, that they were entirely unconnected.'

'Oh?'

'Yes. I mean, you know what kind of activity my nephew was involved in, right?'

Norton nods.

'Well, I can't help feeling that *his* killing may in some way have led to, or caused, my brother's death.'

'Oh. Oh. I see.' Norton appears to relax a bit. 'But what are you basing this on? I mean, Noel's death was an accident, surely?'

'Yes, but . . . I don't know. What I wanted to ask you was – and maybe this is totally out of order, please tell me if it is – but . . . could there be any links between the building trade and gangland crime . . . I don't know, with *unions*, or suppliers, or . . .'

She feels totally out on a limb with this, even more so than when she put the same question to Terry Stack.

'*Gina*,' Norton then says, indulgently, not quite smiling, 'maybe that's the image you have of the building trade from TV and movies, but let me tell you, the reality is quite different. These days it's a *very* regulated industry. The contractors I use are *crucified* with regulations and directives and what have you.'

Gina nods along.

'So really,' he goes on, 'I think what you're suggesting is . . .' He decides to leave it unsaid.

Gina continues nodding.

'Look,' Norton then says, 'I know it's hard to accept, but this was a *road accident*. Noel was tired, he was stressed out. You said so yourself.' He pauses. 'Didn't you?'

'Yes.'

'Stressed out about work, you said.'

'Yes.'

Norton stares at Gina. Is he waiting for her to expand on this? He seems to be.

'Well,' she says eventually, 'there was that problem, that . . . situation, some engineering thing he said . . . he didn't go into it, but –'

'Yes, yes.' Norton looks down at the floor. 'That was sorted out. It was just a minor hitch, one of *many* along the way, believe me.'

'Anyway,' Gina goes on, 'what's really bugging me is this idea that he was drunk. The Noel I knew wouldn't drive –'

Norton looks up again. 'Listen Gina,' he says quite firmly, 'all *I* know is – and this may not be easy to accept either – all *I* know is . . . I was with him in town earlier, and he *did* have a couple of drinks.'

'Yeah, but –'

'And the police have said that he was over the limit.'

'But –'

She stops there. What's the point? Noel wasn't even remotely drunk when she spoke to him outside Catherine's house. So what does she do now? Call Norton a liar? Or a fool? Call the *police* fools?

After a moment, another question occurs to her. 'When Noel left you, he went out to my sister's house, yeah?'

Norton nods.

'But then he went back into town. He told me he had to pick up something. Do you have any idea where he might have gone . . . or who he might have seen?'

Norton shakes his head. 'No. I'm sorry. I have no idea.'

Gina's eyes plead for more.

'I *am* sorry,' he says, 'really. But I'm afraid something you can't discount, Gina, is the possibility that wherever Noel *did* go –'

'– that he had more to drink there?'

'Yes,' Norton says, and shrugs.

Stung by this, Gina doesn't know what to say next. Her stomach is churning. Also, in her skirt and jacket she's not exactly dressed for the occasion – it's windy up here and very cold. Not about to give in, though, she points at the far end of Level 48 and says, 'Can we take a closer look?'

'Of course.'

They walk the length of this huge space in silence. As they get nearer to the south-facing end, the view rises up to meet them. They stop in front of the protective barrier, with about a yard to spare, which is plenty, because spread out below them – half framed by the crane's tower and jib sections – is the whole of Dublin city. It is spectacular, and Gina begins to feel a little overwhelmed. Visible everywhere are landmark buildings, church spires, parks, squares, housing estates – with the river, like a deep, irregular gash, dividing it all in two.

She looks for her apartment building along the quays. She then locates where Dolanstown should be, and stares at it in amazement. Unreal, dreamlike, this is an entirely new perspective on where she grew up.

'It's incredible,' she says.

'Yes, it is. But it's only the start, you know.'

Gina turns to look at him. 'The start? What is?'

'*This*,' Norton says, 'Richmond Plaza. I see it as the first in a cluster of riverfront skyscrapers.' He raises his arm in a grand gesture to indicate the entire docklands area. 'I see all of this being developed. I see it becoming a sort of new Hong Kong on Europe's Atlantic rim.'

Gina nods. Her expression is neutral.

'This downturn won't last,' he goes on. 'It can't. There's too much left to do. And besides, development like this will stimulate a new wave of inward investment from the US. So we *can* do it. I mean, look at what they did in Shanghai ten years ago.

It was phenomenal.' He pauses, as something seems to occur to him. Then he says, 'Of course, Noel was there, *he* saw it, back in the late nineties –'

'Really?'

'Yeah, on trade delegations, with Larry Bolger . . . it was in some sort of advisory capacity, I think. Anyway, he said that across from the Bund you used to see only fields and maybe a warehouse or two. Then suddenly it was all bamboo scaffolding and green safety nets. Then before you knew it, wham, they had a skyline.'

Gina remembers these trips now, but only vaguely – because what would she have been doing at the time? Studying for her diploma? Starting her first job? Glued to a computer terminal in some windowless office? She didn't see Noel very often back then.

'Or look at Dubai,' Norton is saying. 'There's no reason why we can't do *that* in this country, if we hold our nerve, no reason at all. And Noel saw these possibilities too, you know. It's just . . .' He pauses, shaking his head in what seems to be exasperation. 'It's just that a grand-scale project like this requires *more* than vision. It requires, if you'll excuse the expression, balls of steel –'

Gina gets the feeling he's no longer talking about her brother.

'– because you can't let anything get in your way, you can't let any*one* get in your way . . .'

Norton is interrupted here by a sudden burst of baroque concerto music. Gina is startled and it takes her a moment to realise that it's a mobile ringtone.

She watches as Norton pulls his phone out and checks the incoming number on the display.

'Sorry,' he says, holding up a finger. 'I'll ... just a moment.' He turns away and cuts the Vivaldi off. 'Larry, what is it?'

Gina turns in the opposite direction. She takes a couple of steps closer to the protective barrier – which hardly comes up to her waist – and looks down. Far below she can see tiny cars streaming along the quays.

Behind her, she can hear Norton talking.

To Larry *Bolger*?

'. . . yeah the Wilson, it's up on Madison Avenue, in the low seventies I think . . .'

Gina was surprised to find out the other night that Larry Bolger and her brother knew each other so well. She is surprised to find out today that they went on trade delegations together to Shanghai.

'. . . and remember he's an old man, he's been around a long time . . .'

Gina is beginning to realise just how many things there are about Noel that she doesn't know.

'. . . look, meet him tomorrow and we'll talk afterwards, OK?'

She turns around. Norton is putting his phone away.

'Who was that?' she says. 'Larry Bolger?'

Norton looks surprised. 'Yes, it was, as a matter of fact.'

'Oh.'

'He's at the airport.'

'I see.'

'Heading off to the States, on a junket. It's another one of those trade delegations, actually.'

Gina nods. 'So he and Noel knew each other pretty well?'

'They did, yes.'

'When I spoke to him on Thursday, he said they played poker together. Is that right?'

'Yeah, Noel ran rings around him, I'm afraid. Took him to the cleaners. Poor Larry's probably going to be the next taoiseach and the man is an alcoholic and a compulsive gambler. God help us all.' He stops suddenly and stares at Gina. 'I didn't say that . . . you didn't hear that from me.'

Gina gives her head a quick shake, as if to say, *Don't worry about it.*

'I'm sorry,' Norton says, 'I'm sorry. Larry's a good friend of mine, I've known him for twenty-five years. It's just that, well, impulse control wouldn't be his strongest suit.'

Gina nods along.

'But he's on the straight and narrow these days. He really is. He's doing well. He's sober and . . . whatever. Why are we talking about Larry Bolger?'

Gina doesn't know. She shakes her head.

Norton glances at his watch. 'Listen, I've got a meeting with some letting agents, so . . .'

'Of course,' Gina says.

He starts to move.

But she can feel another opportunity slipping away here. If she's going to persist in this, she needs to be more focused, more direct.

'Er . . . Paddy,' she says, 'you worked with Noel, you knew him, or at least *talked* with him, right?'

Norton stops, tensing a little, and turns back. 'Yes.'

Gina takes a deep breath. 'Did he ever mention . . . *our nephew*?'

Norton puts on a pained expression. 'Look, Gina –'

'Or Terry Stack, or . . .'

'No, he didn't.'

There is a shift in his tone here.

'Well,' Gina says, pushing on, 'I don't know, can you think of a reason, any reason at all, why –'

Norton throws his eyes up. 'Why *what*?'

'– why anyone might want to kill him?'

'*Gina*,' Norton says, openly impatient now, 'for God's sake, no one wanted to *kill* your brother, and no one *did* kill him. It was an accident.'

Gina swallows. 'I'm afraid I just don't accept that.'

Norton takes a couple of steps towards her. 'Well, you're going to *have* to accept it. People die on our roads every day of the week.'

When he's standing directly in front of her, he reaches out and takes a firm grip on her arm. He stares into her eyes. Gina isn't comfortable with this and would like to move. But it's awkward. She'd have to pull away and step around him.

Because she can't very well step backwards.

He tightens his grip. '*Do you hear me?*'

Gina meets his stare.

Up close like this, there's something a little unsettling about the way Norton looks. She's only noticing it now. His fleshy face has a pale, almost greyish, complexion. The pupils of his eyes are like pins, and seem to be dilating. She is also surprised – despite the cold – to see a bead of sweat on his upper lip.

And she can smell him.

It's a pungent mixture, though of what she's not sure – cologne anyway, cigar smoke probably . . . and something else, mouthwash possibly, or mints.

'*Gina?*'

She nods. 'Yes, I hear you, but I don't – I *can't* – accept it.'

'*Jesus,*' Norton says, close to shouting now, 'why does every-thing have to be a bloody conspiracy these days? The man was *drunk,* behind the wheel of his *car.* Isn't that *enough*?'

Gina stares at him.

Enough for what?

Her arm is starting to hurt.

She can feel the barrier pressing against the back of her legs.

Another couple of seconds pass and then Norton steps away suddenly, pulling her towards him. 'It's dangerous there,' he says, releasing her roughly. 'You were too close to the barrier.'

He turns and walks off.

Gina looks over her shoulder, heart pounding, and catches a glimpse of the city below. The view is shifting, almost kaleido-scopic, and it makes her feel a little dizzy. For the first time up here she can actually imagine losing her balance.

When she looks back, Norton is already halfway to the service elevator at the other end.

She follows him.

On the way down neither of them says a word.

Gina closes her eyes.

What is it, she wonders . . . with Norton, with her sisters? Everyone seems to be pissed off at her. Yvonne and Michelle she can understand, in a way – they're not ready to face this yet, and that's fine. But Norton? What's *he* afraid of? Some perceived threat to his precious business interests? The nega-tive publicity that a possible link with a gangland killing might generate?

As the elevator comes to a halt, Gina opens her eyes.

But what if her suspicion – or theory, or whatever she wants to call it – is confirmed?

What if there *is* a link?

They walk in silence through the atrium and out of the building.

But then again, what if there isn't?

They go back to the prefab office, where they hand in their hard hats and protective jackets.

Out on the street, Gina does her best to ignore the shift in mood and thanks Norton for the tour of the building.

He grunts something in reply.

When they get to his car, he asks – staring at the pavement – if he can drop her off anywhere, but she says she's OK. She lives on the quays, up towards town, and will walk.

Norton hesitates. 'I'm sorry about before,' he says. 'It's just . . . this is all very upsetting.'

'I know. I know.'

'I just . . . I think the man should be allowed to rest in peace.'

'I know.'

He then nods at her and gets into his car. Gina watches as he speeds off towards the East Link toll bridge.

She bites her lower lip.

People die on our roads every day of the week.

So is that it? Is he right after all?

Maybe.

She crosses to the other side of the street and heads up the quays. She holds her jacket closed against the wind.

But maybe – and just to see it through – she should have one more little chat with Terry Stack.

Even though the prospect doesn't exactly appeal to her.

As she walks along, Gina glances every now and again to the left, into the dark-flowing Liffey – but this only adds to her anxiety. It's as though the river might somehow have a surprise in store, as though it wouldn't be at all inconceivable for the murky water itself to rise up suddenly and reach out from between the stone banks in a great whoosh to engulf her.

Soon after he gets across the East Link toll bridge, Norton pulls in at the side of the road. He puts a hand up to his chest and takes a few deep breaths.

'Oh my God,' he says out loud.

He fumbles in his jacket pocket for his pillbox. When he finally gets it out, he knocks back two Narolet tablets.

'Oh my God.'

He cannot believe how close he came to pushing that girl over the barrier, to giving her a quick shove and . . .

He shakes his head.

He has never committed an act of violence in his life, not directly . . . but *Jesus* . . .

It would have been so easy.

And, of course, for a variety of reasons, *insane*. Because someone would have seen him doing it, one of the construction workers behind them, or one of the crane operators maybe. And in the unlikely event of no one seeing it, there'd be the sheer coincidence of another death in the same family, and the awkward questions *that* would raise. Not to mention the negative impact of all the publicity.

But apart from anything else, it was the feeling – for the two or three seconds he was holding her by the arm – the *feeling*, the urge to do it.

Like electricity in his veins.

Jesus.

Talk about fucking impulse control.

Norton's hands are shaking.

He had no real intention of doing it, clearly, it would have been madness, it's just that . . . *she was being so stubborn.*

He rubs his chest. He's still breathing heavily.

Could he actually have done it?

He thinks of his daughter, Patricia, who lives in Chicago and would be the same age, more or less, as Gina. He tries to picture her standing there, in Gina's place. He tries to drum up the appropriate level of emotion.

But it doesn't come.

He feels flushed. He looks at himself in the rearview mirror.

He starts the car again.

By the time he's on Strand Road, and the Narolet is kicking in, he begins to calm down, and to realise that the issue here isn't whether or not he is capable, or was capable, of pushing Gina to her death; the issue is how close he came, *again,* to self-destructing.

But he has to think now, and be logical. Because Gina doesn't actually know anything. She's just speculating, and not even in any focused way. She's looking for answers. She's upset. She's grieving.

Norton reaches down and turns on the CD player.

She seems to think that there's some link between her brother's death and the gangland killing of her nephew – but she isn't going to find one. She also seems to think that her brother wouldn't have driven his car if he was drunk – but the alcohol level in his bloodstream is on record, and is irrefutable.

So sooner or later, and despite an obvious – and obviously congenital – stubborn streak, she'll have to come to her senses.

Norton goes through the junction at Merrion Gates. He turns right and heads back towards town.

But still – and just to be on the safe side – he wonders if he shouldn't arrange to have Fitz keep an eye on her.

He relaxes his grip on the steering wheel.

The track that's playing at the moment on the stereo is gorgeous – it's the intermezzo from . . .

He can't remember what it's called. It was in an ad.

He'll phone Fitz later on.

As he's passing the RDS, Patricia comes back into his mind. She's working as an administrator, or a curator, in a museum, or a gallery, or something – he isn't quite sure what it is. She doesn't come home very often. She and her mother had a falling out a few years ago. It was over . . . again, *something* – he isn't clear on the details.

He pictures her once more – he can't help it – pictures her where Gina was standing, directly in front of him, ready to be shoved, to fall backwards into the howling wind, into the abyss.

As the music gently climaxes, he feels a lump forming in his throat. When the music stops, he glances into the rearview mirror.

He has tears in his eyes.

3

It is a crisp and sunny morning in Manhattan and Larry Bolger is walking north along Madison Avenue. Every half block or so he looks to the right and catches a glimpse of himself reflected in a store window. Over the coming week – here in New York, in Boston, in Chicago – this figure he sees floating beside him will be meeting the top management teams of twenty major companies. He'll be addressing chambers of commerce and Irish-American community groups. He'll be visiting factories and business parks. He'll be attending power breakfasts.

He'll be talking himself blue in the face.

But for the moment at least, and for the next hour or two, he is off the radar, a fugitive from this intense, punishing schedule, as well as from the other people on the delegation – his private secretary, his handlers, the IDA executives, the journalists.

Twenty minutes ago, Bolger slipped out through a side entrance of the hotel on 57th Street where they're all staying and headed up here on foot. He could have used a town car or taken a cab, but he decided to walk instead. After sending a quick text to Paula, he even switched off his mobile phone.

Because the truth is, he's actually a little nervous about this.

He crosses at 71st Street.

Up ahead, on the sidewalk, a uniformed porter is chatting with the driver of a parked limousine. The granite-clad building the two men are standing in front of is imposing but fairly anonymous. The only thing that tells you it's the Wilson Hotel is an oval plaque on the wall next to the entrance.

Bolger strolls past a second porter. He goes through a set of revolving doors and into the lobby. He is immediately struck by how sumptuous the place is inside – with its crystal chandeliers, enormous gilt mirrors and Louis XVI-style furniture.

He heads for the desk, but before he reaches it he spots Ray Sullivan approaching from the other side of the lobby.

'Larry, good to see you,' Sullivan says, arm outstretched. 'Glad you could make it.'

They shake hands vigorously.

Bolger last met Sullivan a couple of years back, in Dublin, when Amcan was opening its new plant in one of the industrial estates.

'We have a suite upstairs,' Sullivan says, 'so let's just go on up, OK?'

'Fine.'

Bolger loves the understatement.

We have a suite upstairs.

He knows that the Oberon Capital Group not only has a suite upstairs, it actually owns the whole hotel – along with about ten billion dollars' worth of other stuff around the globe.

'We'll meet some people,' Sullivan says as they're getting into the elevator, 'and then Mr Vaughan will join us for lunch.'

Mr Vaughan – James Vaughan, the old man – is a co-founder of Oberon. He's also a Wall Street legend, a former deputy director of the CIA and a veteran of the Kennedy administration.

They get out on the fifth floor and walk along a wide, empty corridor. At the very end they arrive at a door, and Sullivan raps on it lightly.

Bolger's stomach is jumping.

The door is opened by a young man, who nods at Sullivan and then stands aside. They pass through a sort of vestibule and emerge into a large reception room. At a quick glance Bolger counts six people – two standing, four sitting. They are all men. The ones who are sitting immediately stand up and there is a general hubbub of welcome. Moving around, Bolger shakes hands with each of them in turn. One is shortish and rotund, and Bolger recognises his name – he's a Nobel prize-winning economist. The rest of them are tall and chiselled, each with the appearance and demeanour of a five-star general in civilian clothes, or of a presidential candidate. One of them, a senator, actually *was* a presidential candidate a few years ago. Another one is a former defence secretary. Then there is the CEO of Gideon Global, Don Ribcoff, whom Bolger has met before. The other two he's not sure about.

'Sit down, Larry,' Ray Sullivan says, ushering him over to a sofa. 'Can I get you something to drink?'

'Er . . .' Bolger would kill for a large whiskey.

'Water's fine,' he says. 'Sparkling, thanks.'

He lowers himself onto the sofa. The senator, the former defence secretary and the economist all sit down as well – but on the sofa opposite.

'So, Larry,' the senator says, 'until a while ago, it looked like you guys over there in Ireland had pretty much rewritten the rule book on how to run a successful economy.'

'Yeah,' Bolger says, 'it seems we were doing *something* right, I suppose.'

Hearing himself here, Bolger is suddenly appalled. This is *America* he's in. They don't *do* self-deprecation. He has to play it up.

'Well, the thing is,' he goes on quickly, 'we've structured a corporate tax environment that allows enterprise to breathe, to really grow, so as long as we can resist harmonisation from Brussels and get out of this slump we all seem to be in at present, I don't see why it shouldn't continue to go our way.'

Over the years, Bolger has never been fazed by anything he's ever had to do in his capacity as a public representative – but this feels different. This feels like a job interview.

'Ah, Brussels,' the former defence secretary says, and with more than a hint of sarcasm. 'Our friends in the Commission.'

The young man who opened the door earlier appears from Bolger's left and presents him with a glass of water. The glass, which is on a silver tray, looks like Waterford cut crystal. Bolger takes it and raises it to the three men opposite. This feels like a foolish gesture as he's doing it, and it is, but he can't help himself.

He takes a sip from the glass.

'Look,' he says, 'Brussels is still reeling from our rejection of Lisbon, but whatever way it plays out, whether the Treaty eventually passes or not, one thing you can be sure about, and probably for decades to come, is that tax-based competition between member states *will* continue – which of course is great for *us,* because attracting inward investment is exactly where our tax regime is so strong.'

The economist takes up this point and they tease it out for a few minutes before moving on to other topics. After about half an hour, someone's mobile phone rings. Five minutes after that the door leading to the vestibule opens and a burly man wearing dark glasses comes in. He is followed by another man, who is much older and walking very slowly.

This is James Vaughan.

Everyone stands up.

Throughout his years as a politician, and especially since being appointed to the cabinet, Bolger has met a lot of people – dignitaries, the occasional head of state, showbiz celebrities – but this is of a different order of magnitude.

He steps forward and extends his hand. 'It's an honour to meet you, sir.'

Vaughan, who must be in his mid- to late seventies, is a small man, stooped and quite frail-looking. But his eyes are astonishing – blue, bright, very alert.

'So,' he says, shaking Bolger's hand, 'how is the next prime minister of Ireland?'

'Oh, well, let's not –'

Bolger stops himself. His impulse is to dismiss this, but he holds back. He bows in acknowledgement of the question, and smiles.

'Or what is it you guys call it again?' Vaughan says. 'Tee something . . . Tee –'

'Taoiseach.'

'That's it. Means chieftain, right?'

'Yes. Leader. It's –'

'Chieftain. I like that,' Vaughan says, looking around at the others. 'Maybe we should use that from now on, chieftain executive officer.'

Everyone laughs.

'OK, Phil,' Vaughan then says, turning to the burly man he came in with. 'I think we're all set.' Phil nods silently and retreats. Vaughan moves over towards the sofa, but he doesn't sit down.

'So, Ray,' he says, 'what's the deal here, we're going to eat something?'

'Yes,' Ray Sullivan says, turning backwards and clicking his fingers. The young man walks over to a set of double doors on the far side of the room and opens them.

Through the doors Bolger sees what looks like a full-sized dining room. The table is set and uniformed servers are hovering about, adjusting cutlery and repositioning glasses.

'Larry,' Vaughan says to Bolger, beckoning him over with an outstretched arm, 'come, come, sit with me.'

The next hour passes very quickly for Bolger. He listens with great attention as Vaughan talks – and exclusively to *him* – on a wide range of subjects, including his time as Assistant Secretary at the Treasury Department under Jack Kennedy, his famous run-in with LBJ, and how he was told on good authority *over thirty years ago* that Mark Felt was Deep Throat. One story Bolger particularly likes is about Vaughan using the expression 'irrational exuberance' in a private conversation with Alan Greenspan two days before the Fed Chairman used it himself in a black-tie dinner speech and caused a worldwide wobble in the markets.

As coffee is being served, Vaughan suddenly turns the conversation around. 'So tell me, Larry. How are things down on Richmond Dock? I hear we're making quite an impression on your skyline over there.'

'Yes, Mr Vaughan, indeed.' The 'we' isn't lost on Bolger. With a 15 per cent stake in the building, and Amcan, which it owns, set to be the anchor tenant, Oberon – he supposes – *is* a key player in the project. 'Aside from the usual objections about height,' he says, 'everything has gone pretty smoothly. I think the city is ready for this.'

'Sure it is,' Vaughan says, '*sure* it is, a city needs its symbols. And what's so awful about height anyway? I mean, it's just a basic expression of . . . ambition. It's in the DNA. I know it's in *my* DNA.' He waves a hand in the air. 'Look, for an earlier generation the big idea was frontier expansion – go west, young man, that kind of thing – but for us it was go *up,* it was the great land grab in the sky.'

Bolger nods along at this, engrossed, barely aware of anyone else around the table.

'And back then,' Vaughan continues, 'size mattered, too. That's what it was about in the end, really, scale. It was all get a load of this, and get a load of that . . . I don't know, *eight* miles of elevator shafts, *three thousand* tons of marble, *two and a half million* feet of electrical cable, *ten* million bricks . . .'

He follows this with a story about how in the late fifties, when he was East Coast Vice-President of Wolper & Stone, he personally oversaw the construction of the firm's new corporate headquarters in midtown Manhattan. After that, he somehow loops back to the present and to the strategic importance for Oberon of establishing a high-profile base in Europe. In the space of about five minutes, he manages to use the words 'bridgehead', 'gateway' and 'portal'.

But then, at around 2.30, and out of the blue, he announces that he has to go and lie down. 'It's been a pleasure, Larry,' he says, 'but I've got this blood condition. Doctor's orders.'

'Of course, please, please.'

As Vaughan gets up, everyone else at the table gets up, too. Ray Sullivan confers with the young man, who immediately takes out his mobile phone and starts making a call.

'Walk me to the door, Larry,' Vaughan says to Bolger, taking him by the arm.

'I can't tell you what an honour this has been for me, Mr Vaughan, really.'

'Well thank you, Larry, nice of you to say so.' He applies a little pressure to Bolger's arm. 'And let me just add something.'

'Of course.'

'No one ever knows what's going to happen in politics, am I right?'

Bolger nods.

'These are democratic times we live in.'

'Indeed.'

'It's the people who decide.'

'Hhmm.'

'But from what *I'm* told, in Ireland right now, *you're* the man to watch, so I want you to know something.' Vaughan lowers his voice here, almost to a whisper. '*We're behind you all the way.*'

'Well, thank *you.*'

'*And if there's anything we can do to help . . .*'

'*Thank* you.'

When they get to the door – where the burly Phil is waiting – Vaughan releases Bolger's arm. He turns and extends his hand. 'Larry,' he says, 'it was nice meeting you.'

They shake.

'And remember what I said.'

'I will.'

Vaughan turns again and leaves.

Twenty minutes later, after more arm-squeezing, more handshakes, more urgent, whispered assurances of support, Bolger leaves, too. Ray Sullivan takes him back downstairs, where a car is waiting.

The driver slips across to 72nd Street and then turns left onto Fifth Avenue.

With his head still reeling, Bolger tries to interpret what has just happened.

It was an endorsement – plain and simple. Bolger is primed to take over his party. The party is a shoo-in at the next election. The Oberon Capital Group needs to maintain a US-friendly European base for its biotech, aerospace and defence contractors.

It isn't exactly rocket science.

Nor is he under any illusions about what might be required

of him. *Or* about how easily an endorsement from Oberon could be withdrawn.

But still, he enjoyed what just happened, and would like more of it . . . the naked flattery, the attention, the *access*.

He places his hand on the shiny black surface of the leather car seat and strokes it. He's enjoying this, too – being driven at speed through the city, invisible behind the tinted windows of a limousine. On the outside, people flicker past, heads occasionally turning, but never close enough to see in any detail. Buildings, storefronts, façades – these are all insubstantial, one-dimensional, the city reduced to a celluloid, hallucinogenic rush. What it would be like to have a police escort, or to be at the head of a full motorcade – open top, waving at crowds, engines roaring all around you, *in the line of fire* – he doesn't even want to think about, because the whole thing gives him such a tingling sense of urgency, of power, that it's almost unbearable . . .

The car pulls up outside his hotel. As he waits for the driver to open the door, he takes out his mobile phone and switches it back on.

Crossing the sidewalk, he glances left at the dark windblown canyon that is 57th Street, and feels a sudden chill.

On his way into the lobby, holding his mobile out in front of him, he sees that he has six voice messages and seven texts. That volume of traffic over only a couple of hours is just a *little* heavy, even for him – so before he spots Paula approaching from the other side of the lobby, ashen-faced, shaking her head, Bolger knows that something is wrong.

'What is it?' he says.

Paula is still shaking her head when she speaks. 'Ken Murphy.'

'Jesus,' Bolger says, 'what?'

'He's working on a story for tomorrow.'

'About *me*?'

'Yes.'

He swallows.

Paula seems reluctant to go on. She also seems angry, or disgusted, or just weary – he isn't sure which.

'*And*?'

'Well,' she says, not looking him in the eye, 'apparently it's something about an affair and . . . unpaid gambling debts?'

4

'How's it going, love?'

Gina turns around. She's startled but tries not to show it. She arrived early and sat in a booth opposite the bar, with a clear view of the entrance. She ordered a bottle of Corona. She waited.

Now, unexpectedly, Terry Stack has appeared from behind her.

She looks up at him. 'Fine.'

She wonders if he was already here. She doesn't think so, because she looked the place over before sitting down. Does that mean he has special privileges? He's allowed to come in by the back door?

Maybe he actually owns Kennedy's now.

Stack slides into the booth opposite Gina. He nods at the bottle of Corona in front of her and says, 'Get us a pint there, would you?'

For a second Gina thinks he's talking to her, but then she sees one of his hoodies sloping over to the bar. She doesn't want to look around again, but she also suspects that the previously unoccupied booth behind her is now occupied.

More boys in hoodies?

His security detail.

'Thanks for agreeing to meet me,' she says.

Gina is determined to be civil with Stack – and neutral, as neutral as she *can* be.

'The pleasure's all mine, love.'

But straightaway she's wondering how civil or neutral it would be to tell him that her name isn't *love*.

'Whatever,' she says, studying the label on her Corona bottle.

'Anyway, I'm glad you've kept in touch, because –'

'I wasn't *keeping in touch,*' she interrupts. 'Jesus. I just have a few questions I want to ask you.'

'Right, right. Yeah. Anyway, I was going to contact *you.*'

'Why?'

'We'll get to that.'

The hoodie returns. He places a pint of stout in front of Stack and then, glancing at Gina, disappears. Stack takes a sip from the pint and clears the foam from his upper lip.

'So,' he says, 'how *are* you?'

'I'm fine.'

She has no intention of elaborating. It's none of Terry Stack's business how she *is*.

'I knew Noel's ma had a few sisters,' Stack then says, 'but I didn't realise –'

He stops here, searching for the right words.

'What?'

'That one of them'd be so young and . . . gorgeous-looking.'

Jesus. 'Well, there you go.'

She takes a sip from her bottle. He takes another sip from his pint.

'So what do you do?'

Gina wants to scream. Is this a *date* she's on? 'I work in software.'

'Oh?'

Not exactly the opening he was looking for, she expects, because what's he going to say now? *That's funny, I dabble in software, too – the piracy end of things.*

'What area?' he says.

'Data recovery. I work for a development company.'

'That's interesting.'

'No, it isn't.' She leans forward. 'Look, Terry, I don't want to talk about my job or about how I fucking *am* – I just want to talk about my brother and my nephew, OK?'

Civil, neutral. Nice going.

Stack smiles. He looks less like a priest in civvies today. He's wearing a jacket and shirt but no tie. He has thick greying hair and tired brown eyes, and there's a weird twist to his mouth when he speaks.

'OK,' he says, 'fine.'

'Right. OK.'

'I told you I wasn't going to let this rest, and I'm not. I've been making, er . . . let's call them *enquiries.*'

He pauses for effect.

Eventually, Gina says, 'And?'

'You're in a real fucking hurry, aren't you?'

'Aren't *you*? I thought you said whoever did this was going to pay.'

'I did. I did. And they will.'

'*So?*'

Gina can't believe the tack she's adopting here. Is it nerves? Is she compensating for the fact that she's actually terrified? Because the thing is, she got Stack's number from Catherine, but before she rang him she trawled through a few newspaper archives on the Web, and it turns out that Stack's gang not only infringe the Copyright Act to the tune of millions of euro every year, not only deal heroin, cocaine, ecstasy and cannabis, not only traffic young girls in from Eastern Europe, but they are widely believed to be responsible for – and she can't discount, she supposes, possible involvement in this by young Noel – three recent and particularly vicious murders.

She's also aware of the unorthodox uses to which Stack himself sometimes puts his training as an electrician.

So just what is it, she wonders – given that she's pretty much spent the last ten years of her own life sitting in front of a computer screen – what is it that qualifies *her* to be so pushy and aggressive with *him*?

Stack shakes his head. 'I'm *getting* to it. Jesus. OK, first up, there *are* feuds going on out there, right? Fuckers blowing each other away because one of them has a lip on him, or he gave the other one's girlfriend a dart, or *whatever,* but *I* run a tight ship.'

She nods.

'The lads I have working for me are focused, you know what I mean?'

Gina wants to say, *Yeah, yeah, get on with it.*

'So there was no reason for anyone to do Noel, no reason *I* know of, no reason at all in fact.'

Gina swallows. 'What does that mean?'

Alan Glynn

'Well, like I said, I talked to some people and . . . I'm getting some fairly fucking strange reports back. There's rumours going around.'

'What kind of rumours?'

'Well.' He takes a deep breath. 'I heard this from a couple of different people. They're saying that the hit was really meant for your brother, that there was a mix-up –'

'*What?*'

'– with the names being the same and all. The whole thing was arranged in a big rush, apparently –'

Gina leans forward.

'– and wires got crossed. It was just assumed that a hit on Noel Rafferty had to be, well, a hit on *our* Noel.'

Gina feels like she's been punched in the stomach.

'Now whoever done the job was a pro,' Stack goes on. 'There's no denying that, but they could only act on the basis of information they were given, and that information –'

'No, no, *wait* –' Gina is shaking her head at this, and vigorously, as though trying to brush aside anything that isn't one hundred per cent relevant. 'I don't understand –'

'What?'

'*Who would want to kill my brother?*'

Stack pauses and grunts.

'You tell me. I don't fucking know.'

'I don't know either. How would *I* know?'

'He was *your* brother.'

'Yeah, but –'

Gina is lost here. For a week she's been contending that there was more to what happened than met the eye – and now, faced with a possible confirmation of this, she finds herself unable to accept it. She assumed there was some connection

148

between the two deaths, a causal link – but in her mind it all remained vague and non-specific.

What Stack has just posited, by contrast, is shockingly specific.

'I mean . . .' She doesn't know what to say. 'It was still an accident, the way *he* died, wasn't it?'

'I don't know,' Stack says. 'Maybe.'

'*Maybe?* What are you saying?'

'I'm not saying anything. Just that this . . . well, it changes things.'

'Are you saying that maybe it *wasn't* an accident?'

'I don't know. It still could have been, I suppose. But not necessarily.'

'*How?* He was over the limit, that's in the autopsy. His car ran off the road. Everyone *says* it was an accident.'

'Gina, love, you can *fake* an accident. You can hold someone down and reef a naggin of Power's down their throat. You can fiddle with the brakes of their car. There's a million different things you can do.'

'I don't believe this.'

'Look, if your brother was the target of the original hit and they fucked *that* up, then it makes sense that they'd try again.'

'But do it differently.'

'Yeah. Probably. Chances are there was a bit of panic in the air.' He takes a sip from his pint. 'Of course, there's no way of proving any of this now. Because he's gone, he's buried, and the forensics are gone, too. Not that anyone would believe it in the first place.'

'Oh God.' She lowers her head.

'Listen to me, Gina,' Stack says. 'This is still only speculation. No one knows who the shooter was, not yet anyway. So what *you* should be doing is trying to find out if anyone had it in for your brother.'

She looks up. 'But he was . . . he was an *engineer*.'

'Ah go on, would you. These professional cunts are no different from anyone else.' He pauses. 'Think. Did he owe money to anyone? Did anyone owe *him* money?'

Gina shakes her head. 'How would I know?'

'Believe me,' Stack says, lifting his pint again, 'with this kind of thing it's nearly always about money.'

Gina looks around her in exasperation.

The place is almost empty. Two old-timers are sitting at the bar, and there's a group of middle-aged women in the far corner.

It's early, though.

This is the second time in a week that Gina has been in Kennedy's, and she's finding the experience unutterably weird. It's a quiet suburban pub now, carpets and dark wood everywhere, at least four TV screens that she can see, and a blackboard menu with stuff on it like seafood chowder and toasted paninis. But when she was growing up, Kennedy's was a very different place. What it *was*, in fact, was an awful dive.

Guinness, Harp, Woodbines, King crisps.

Spit, piss, vomit.

Her father used to drink here.

Gina remembers coming in as a kid – being *sent* in – to get him or to give him a message.

Her mother used to drink at home.

'And if it isn't about money,' Stack is saying, 'chances are it's about sex.'

Gina looks at him. He has what could develop into a smirk on his face.

'Noel was a happily married man,' she says, immediately realising that to someone like Stack this might sound naive.

'But sure they're the worst,' he says on cue. 'I see blokes like that all the time, gagging for it.'

Gina doesn't want to get into this. Taking a sip from her Corona, she tries to think of a neutral response. But then, luckily, Stack's mobile phone goes off.

He takes the phone out of his pocket and puts it up to his ear. 'Yeah?'

Gina looks away – over at the bar. She's still in shock and feels a little sick. She turns back and stares down at the table.

'When did he ask?' Stack is saying, and in a loud whisper. 'Was it this morning?'

Up to now Gina's been assuming that her brother's death was some form of collateral damage, a messy, possibly unintended consequence of her nephew's murder. But now she has to deal with the fact that maybe the reverse is true: that her nephew's death was the unintended consequence of her brother's murder.

She lifts her head again. Stack is tapping his fingers against the side of his pint. His brow is furrowed. He is listening intently.

To avoid looking at him, she glances around.

Three of the TV screens are showing snooker. The fourth screen, mounted above an alcove near the door, is showing the six o'clock news. The sound is down, but Gina watches it anyway. After a few seconds it cuts from the newsreader in the studio to a reporter outside. Talking directly to camera, the reporter is across the street from a large hotel in what looks like Manhattan. Gina can't hear him, but she senses an urgency in the way he's speaking. Then it cuts to another man entering an office, sitting at a desk and picking up a pen to sign a document. This is one of those staged and fairly stilted archive clips they use to identify government ministers.

In this particular instance the government minister is Larry Bolger.

Gina finds this a little strange. Not strange that he's in the news – Larry Bolger is frequently in the news – but strange because she actually had a brief conversation with the man only last week.

'He's a little prick.'

Startled, Gina turns back and looks across the table at Stack.

'I gave him the details yesterday,' he's saying into his phone, 'so he knows what the story is. He's a scabby *bollocks*. Look, don't let him leave. Keep him talking. I'll be there in ten minutes.'

He closes the phone and puts it away.

Gina wishes she hadn't heard that.

'Have to go,' Stack says. 'Sorry.'

'Er . . . that's OK. Thanks for the information.'

'No problem.'

Gina takes a Lucius business card out of her wallet and hands it to him. 'If you hear anything else, will you let me know? My mobile number is on there.'

'Sure. Yeah. Of course.'

As he gets out of the booth, Stack produces a business card of his own and places it on the table. Without picking it up Gina can see what's printed on it.

Terry Stack, Electrical Contractor.

'Feel free,' he says, 'if *you* ever want to contact *me*.'

She nods, but doesn't say anything.

'Any time of the day or night,' he adds. 'It's a twenty-four-hour service.' He winks at her. 'Emergency call-out.'

She nods again and says, 'OK. Whatever. Thanks.'

Then she slides his card off the table and puts it into her wallet.

Stack picks up his pint and drains it. 'Right, love,' he says, putting the glass back down. 'Take it easy.'

He walks off. He nods at the barman as he passes. Three guys in hoodies follow him out.

Gina's stomach is jumping. She wants to leave now, too, but decides to hang on for a couple of minutes.

She takes a sip from her Corona.

She rubs her eyes and wonders if she shouldn't go back and speak to everyone again. If so, who does she start with?

Eventually she puts her wallet away and slides out of the booth. On her way over to the door, she glances up at the TV screen above the alcove.

The news is still on. The German Chancellor is standing at a podium, addressing a press conference.

As Gina opens the door, she braces herself for the cold night air.

5

Mark is *that* close to calling the waiter over and ordering a drink.

Just to make this bearable.

The atmosphere tonight at Roscoe's is lively – but not at this table. At *this* table, to put it mildly, things are a little strained.

Mark picks at his rocket salad. The building contractor, a

small, muscular Corkman in his early sixties, moves asparagus tips around on his plate and tells a rambling story about his early days in London. The fat accountant concentrates on his fish cakes in blue-cheese sauce.

There is a bottle of San Pellegrino mineral water in the centre of the table and Mark stares at the label on it.

How could he have been so naive?

It has taken him until this, his third meeting with the building contractor, to realise that the elaborate dance of negotiations they've been involved in so far has really been about getting Mark to pay some money up front before any agreement can be reached. The builder hasn't said anything explicit, but with one of his accountants sitting beside him this evening it's clear he wants to take the matter to the next level.

He probably assumes that Mark has been playing some kind of hardball. It won't have occurred to him that Mark is actually an *idiot*. In fact, it's only when the figure of twenty thousand euro is mentioned – albeit in a suitably ambiguous context – that it dawns on Mark what is actually happening. He can't believe he didn't see it coming.

And they're only on their starters.

Which is why he'd kill for some neat gin – and served, preferably, in a pint glass. But the builder and the accountant aren't drinking, so Mark isn't going to risk it.

He concentrates on his salad, the fat accountant mops up what's left of his blue-cheese sauce and the builder goes on talking. It soon becomes obvious, however, that the builder is one of those people who can't rein in irrelevant detail when telling a story, because he's now caught up in establishing exactly when in 1969, *to the week,* some event – which is unrelated to the main part of the story – occurred.

Mark goes on staring at the bottle of San Pellegrino.

He doesn't know what kind of signals he's sending out here, but he's pretty sure they're mixed. Given that he really wants this contract but appears unwilling to pay for it, you'd think he'd be a little more concerned.

But the truth is Mark has been distracted of late.

He looks up.

The builder's story is drawing to a close. Then the waiter appears and starts clearing away their plates.

'Are you all right there, Mark?' the accountant says. 'You're very quiet this evening.'

'Yeah, no, I'm . . . I'm fine.'

An awkward silence follows. Sensing Mark's apparent unwillingness to engage with the substantive issue, the accountant clears his throat and says, 'So, did you see that about Larry Bolger?'

Mark tenses.

The builder whistles and says, 'Yeah, Jesus, I reckon it's going to be wall-to-wall fucking Larry for the next week at least.'

Mark is aware that *something* happened today, but he isn't sure what.

'They're already calling for his resignation,' the accountant says, 'but I can't see him giving in that easily, can you?'

'No,' the builder says, 'especially as I'd say the leak came from within the party.'

'Would you?'

'Oh God yeah.' He waits for the waiter to move off before he continues. 'There's an element in HQ trying to undermine him. It's this crack he's taking at the leadership. I'd lay even money on it.'

Mark's impulse here is to remain silent. But he doesn't. 'What happened?' he asks. 'I missed it.'

'It was in the *Independent* this morning,' the builder says. 'Ken Murphy is claiming that Bolger owes some bookie ten grand. Now he could probably get around that, but he was apparently having it off with the bookie's *wife* as well.'

'He's a gouger,' the accountant says. 'He always was.'

'Well, he's had his fair share of controversies down through the years, that's for sure.'

Mark's pulse quickens. 'What controversies?'

'Oh, different things, gaffes, putting his foot in it, a fondness for the gargle, nothing major.' He pauses. 'Though it really goes back to the beginning, I suppose, the *whiff* does – if you know what I mean.'

'No,' Mark says, shaking his head, 'I don't.'

The builder clicks his tongue. 'Well . . .' He draws the word out. 'Neither of you would remember it, but when Larry was first elected there was quite a bit of . . . *talk.*'

He stops and looks around, as though to check if anyone behind them or next to them is listening. Then he looks at Mark, and perhaps in that moment realises they don't know each other well enough to be having this kind of conversation.

But Mark isn't going to let it go. He leans forward, and says, *'What kind of talk?'*

The builder hesitates, alarmed suddenly at the urgency in Mark's voice. 'Look, to be honest,' he says, 'I don't really know. It was just talk, and anyway –'

'Didn't Bolger contest the seat,' the accountant cuts in, 'after his brother died?'

'Yeah, he did,' the builder says. 'Yeah.'

'So what happened? How did the brother die?'

'Well, that's just it . . . he died in a car crash.'

Mark feels flushed all of a sudden. He thought he could handle this, but now he isn't sure.

The builder exhales loudly. 'It was *horrendous* . . . three or four people were killed.' He shakes his head. 'It was *awful*.'

The accountant nods along. 'And?'

'There were questions about how it happened, apparently. At the time. Anomalies. But with old man Bolger around, and the likes of Romy Mulcahy, that all got hushed up pretty quickly. Or maybe there was nothing *to* hush up, I don't know. I was talking to Paddy Norton about it once and he said it was all nonsense.'

Anomalies?

That's the only word Mark hears and it cuts into him like a knife. 'What anomalies?' he whispers.

The builder turns to him but again seems reluctant to continue.

Mark leans forward even more. 'I *asked* you . . . what anomalies?'

'Look, you know what,' the builder says, 'forget about it. There are strict libel laws in this country and I'm not –'

Mark bangs his fist on the table. '*What anomalies?*'

The builder is stunned.

'Ah, now hold on here,' the accountant says. 'Take it easy.'

There is a long silence as Mark and the builder stare at each other.

What Mark really wants to do is reach across the table and grab this burly Corkman by the throat.

What he does instead is get up from the table and walk out of the restaurant.

6

By the following morning, the story has gone nuclear. It's on all the front pages, broadsheet and tabloid, and on all the radio breakfast shows. Given the essential ingredients – gambling, sex and, according to one editorial, 'a little bit of politics thrown in to spice things up' – interest in the story is overwhelming. Opinion is divided, though. Some people think Larry Bolger is just what the country needs, a colourful character, a man with flaws like the rest of us; others think he is a degenerate and should be hounded from office. Pundits and punters alike have their say, and the issue is debated endlessly in op-ed columns, on panel discussions and on radio phone-ins.

In the main, Bolger's government colleagues are supportive. An emerging line of defence seems to be that the minister did nothing illegal, and there is much semantic hand-wringing over the difference between an 'unpaid' debt and an 'outstanding' debt. We are also declared to have matured as a nation and talk of the extramarital affair is dismissed as unseemly and prurient.

But with Bolger still in the US and pressure growing for some kind of official statement, cracks begin to appear. When asked about the matter during an interview on *Morning Ireland* the Minister for Health displays a studied ambivalence. On *Today with Pat Kenny* a backbencher makes the first public reference to Bolger's leadership ambitions, and a collective *swish* is almost immediately heard from Leinster House as knives are drawn and then sharpened. On the *News at One* opposition leaders call for the minister's resignation, and by *Liveline*, members of the public, supporters and detractors, are shouting at each other live on air.

This is at two o'clock in the afternoon.

But in Boston – where Bolger is attending a breakfast of business leaders in the Signature Room of the John Hancock Conference Center – it is nine o'clock in the morning, and news of these developments is only just beginning to filter through.

So far, Bolger has frozen journalists out and apart from an initial and hastily formulated non-denial denial has refused to answer any questions. Being three thousand miles away, it is difficult to appreciate the level of engagement this whole thing is causing at home, but as Bolger addresses the business leaders over ham and eggs, Paula is outside in the lobby with her laptop listening to *Liveline* on the Web – and growing paler with each new contribution.

After the breakfast, she fills Bolger in and recommends that they either issue a new statement or do some interviews. They trawl through the Irish papers online looking for an angle. They discuss the possibility of Bolger's cutting short his trip and flying home.

A little later, in one of the hotel restrooms, Bolger locks himself into a cubicle and buries his head in his hands. He can't believe this is happening. The allegations are true of course, but they refer to a period in his life he's always felt he'd successfully compartmentalised and moved on from. He certainly never imagined he'd be revisiting it like this.

Bolger knows that the timing of the story is no accident. And there is little doubt in his mind as to who leaked it – someone inside his own party. But the real question is, can he brazen it out? Can he contain the damage? Can he ring-fence it, or even turn it to his advantage?

As he raises his head wearily and stares at the shiny,

lacquered cubicle door, his mobile phone rings. He takes it out of his jacket pocket and looks at the display.

He groans.

It's Paddy Norton.

He lets it ring out and go into message.

'. . . so, er, I'll be in and out of the office for the next few hours. Or you can just get me on the mobile. Right? OK . . . Jesus, this is a *disaster*. I'll talk to you later.'

Norton presses End and throws his mobile onto the desk.

He sits back in his chair and glances at his watch. He hasn't heard from Ray Sullivan yet, but he *will* – that's for sure. Amcan's occupancy of more than forty floors of the building is not contingent upon Larry Bolger becoming Taoiseach, but it'd help. It's definitely there in the background, part of the mood music – so there's going to be a lot of explaining to do if Bolger's prospects go belly-up.

Norton seems to spend most of his time these days putting out fires, and he's getting sick of it.

Which reminds him.

He reaches forward and picks up his mobile again. He selects a number and waits.

'Yeah?'

'Fitz, Paddy.'

'How's it going?'

'All right. Any developments?'

'Er . . . let me put you on hold there for a second, Paddy, will you, and I'll just check my notes, see what I've got for you.'

'Right.'

Norton clicks his tongue.

Notes.

These days Fitz may be calling himself a private security consultant, but coming as he does from a heavy-duty paramilitary background, it's far from fucking *notes* that he was raised.

Norton glances out of the window. From the sixth floor of this building there's a view of Richmond Plaza – but there isn't one from here, from the third floor. Which is annoying. He's been trying to get the people on six, a firm of solicitors, to move out. But so far without success.

He hasn't been trying hard enough.

'Paddy?'

In a few months, though, he'll be moving *into* Richmond Plaza, so it doesn't really matter.

'Yeah.'

'OK. She met Terry Stack yesterday evening for about twenty minutes. Other than that she's either been at work, which is an office in Harcourt Street, or at her place, which is an apartment building on the quays. But that's it. Back and forth. No visitors. She doesn't have a car. She buys her food in Marks & Spencer. She reads . . . I think it's *What Hi-Fi?* magazine, or *What Camera?*, or what fucking *something*, computers, juicers, I don't know.' He coughs. 'I'm working on getting access to her email and stuff, but that takes time.'

'How about her mobile?'

'Give me a day or two. I'm waiting on a delivery. It's a new scanner that should do the job.'

'Right.' Norton pauses. 'What does she work at, by the way?'

'Software. It's a small company, a start-up. From what I can gather they're not in great shape, though.'

'What do you mean?'

'They're struggling. Financially. Victims of the downturn, whatever. So I'm told anyway.'

'Right. And Terry Stack?'

'I wouldn't worry about him, he's a fucking muppet.'

Norton doesn't say anything to this.

'Look, he *is*, believe me.'

'Fine, fine. OK.' He pauses again. 'And how about our other friend?'

Fitz has been keeping an eye on Dermot Flynn as well.

'He's behaving himself. Nothing to worry about there.'

'Right. OK.'

Norton stares at the floor. Does he find any of this convincing? Reassuring? Yes? No? Maybe? He can't tell. He's still in shock about the Larry Bolger situation.

He gets off the phone and tosses it back onto his desk.

Ten *bloody* grand. Why didn't he just ask for it? *Jesus.*

It wouldn't have been the first time. The man is a liability and has been since the day he got elected. But you can only work with what you've got, and back then Larry was all *he'd* got.

Frank, as it turned out, was no use to anyone – so Larry was it.

Norton buzzes out to his secretary and tells her to bring him in a double espresso. In a few minutes he has a meeting with the directors of a UK investment company who are developing a chain of health centres in a joint venture with Winterland, and Norton needs to go over some figures with them.

But he needs some caffeine first.

Because he hasn't been sleeping too well of late.

The Bolger story calms down considerably on Friday and Saturday, but no one involved takes any consolation from this, or – depending on where they're coming from – is disappointed. Everyone knows it's how the Sunday papers play it that will determine if the story has legs or not.

As it turns out, none of the papers on Sunday comes up with a killer blow – it's more like a thousand little ones, with each paper taking a different angle, each headline a different tone, sanctimonious, analytical, trashy. The effect of this is not to confuse people, however, or to turn them off, but to pique their interest.

Gina, for example, who would normally buy just one paper, ends up buying three. She's not sure how much of this stuff she'll actually read, but having a thick bundle of newspapers under her arm as she walks along the quays gives her a vague sense of security, of comfort even.

She's out early.

It's a bright morning, cold and windy, and the gusts coming in from the bay are bracing, but that's exactly what Gina wants. She doesn't want mild and dull and overcast, she wants fresh, clear, *invigorating*. She still feels raw from the last two weeks, and her grief, ever present, is like a thumping sensation in her chest.

It's relentless – like an echo of her heartbeat.

But she's determined not to let it overwhelm her.

She wanders past her apartment building and walks on for another hundred yards or so. She stops and looks downriver, at Richmond Plaza.

Paddy Norton was adamant that Noel's death was an accident – caused by stress and too much alcohol. It's the official view and it's a fairly convincing one. It's supported by logic, by common sense and, crucially, by evidence. It's a view that Gina was on the point of accepting herself.

Until she spoke with Terry Stack on Wednesday evening.

She turns around and heads back to her apartment building.

Since that conversation she has been haunted by the image, conjured up so casually by Stack, of someone forcing whiskey down Noel's throat.

It's a horrible idea, but it's also the only way of explaining the level of alcohol in his bloodstream. Because the simple fact is, Noel wasn't a heavy drinker. He liked a pint now and again, he drank wine at dinner, but that was as far as it went.

Back up in her apartment, Gina throws the papers onto the sofa and goes over to the kitchen to put on some coffee.

She sorts through her laundry and fills the washing machine.

When she eventually sits down to tackle the papers, she finds herself skipping the Larry Bolger stuff at first. She's really tired and not in the right frame of mind. Instead, she reads a few book reviews, flicks through a colour supplement, reads a recipe for moussaka, scans the international pages.

But then she gives in.

The first piece she reads calls Bolger gaffe-prone and goes through a series of incidents where he displayed, to say the least, questionable judgement – such as the classic time when as junior minister at the Department of Transport in charge of road-safety initiatives he was conducting a live radio interview on his mobile phone and it became apparent *on air* that he was driving his car at the same time.

She reads a detailed account of how at the taxpayers' expense some woman called Avril Byrne accompanied Bolger on various foreign junkets – or 'fact-finding missions' – and how the pair routinely stayed in lavish hotel suites. On one occasion Bolger used a departmental credit card to charge

€ 2,400 for a meal at an exclusive restaurant in Singapore. It is also alleged that when Ms Byrne needed a pricey dental procedure Bolger diverted party funds to pay for it.

Simultaneously, it seems, the minister was running up a huge tab – as yet unsettled – at a bookmaker's owned by Ms Byrne's estranged husband.

In another paper Gina reads an analysis of Bolger's career in politics: his voting record, the various issues he has supported, the crucial role he played in an earlier leadership heave. It also explains how he came to win his Dáil seat in the first place. Gina didn't know this, but Bolger only decided – or was persuaded – to enter politics after his older brother Frank, the sitting TD, was killed in a car crash.

Gina lowers the paper onto her lap. She stares out across the room for a moment.

People die on our roads every day of the week.

Then she picks up the *Sunday World* and flicks through it until she finds a two-page spread that she previously only glanced at. At the bottom of the first page there is a small black-and-white photograph of a wrecked Mercedes. The caption reads: FRANK BOLGER IN ROAD CARNAGE.

She scans the accompanying article, but it contains only a brief reference to the crash.

. . . outside Dublin . . . two cars . . . four people killed . . .

Gina takes a deep breath.

. . . including a little girl.

She stares at the photograph for a while.

Then she puts the paper down, adding it to the pile she already has beside her on the sofa. She glances out of the window. The day has become overcast, but it's still windy. Clouds roll by.

She thinks of Noel's SUV skidding off a country road, swerving, plunging . . . then the impact, then Noel crushed and battered inside, surrounded by fumes and burning smells, oil, blood, rubber. She thinks of him lying there half conscious, groaning, *dying* . . .

What went through his head in those last few moments?

Tears come into her eyes. She rolls sideways, onto the pile of newspapers, and starts to sob.

After a few minutes, the tears subside. Using her sleeve, she wipes her eyes. She curls up. She gets drowsy. She falls asleep.

About an hour later – in the middle of a confused dream – she wakes up, startled.

The phone is ringing.

She rubs her eyes.

She gets up from the sofa. The phone is on the desk in the corner, next to the computer. She goes over and picks it up. She pulls the chair out and sits down. 'Hello?' she says, sniffing.

'Hello, Gina, it's Jackie Merrigan.'

Gina furrows her brow. She is puzzled. Does she know any Jackie Merrigan?

But after a second it hits her.

That old friend of Noel's she met at the removal. The detective superintendent.

'Oh. Hello. How are *you*?'

'I'm fine. I'm fine. I was just ringing to check in and see how you are. I hope you don't mind.'

'No, no, not at all. Thank you.'

'I was thinking about Noel today and . . . he was very fond of you, you know. He often mentioned you.' He pauses. 'It's still only sinking in, isn't it?'

'Yes. It's hard to believe.'

Gina pictures Merrigan – tall and stooped, silver hair, distinguished-looking. He seemed quite gentle, not at all the ·stock image of a detective superintendent.

'And how are your sisters?' he asks.

'They're OK,' Gina says. 'Catherine isn't, of course. She couldn't be, really.'

'No, I suppose not.'

As they chat about Catherine and then Noel, Gina has a growing urge to put a few direct questions to Merrigan, to air her theories, but something holds her back. She doesn't want to be patronised. She doesn't want to be told, yet again, that there's nothing mysterious here, that it was just a tragic accident.

'Strange about Larry Bolger,' she eventually says, for want of something else to say. 'I've just been reading about him in the papers.'

'Yes,' Merrigan says. 'It looks pretty serious for him all right. I don't see how he can wriggle out of this one.'

'No,' Gina says. She stares at her reflection in the blank computer screen. 'Though one thing I didn't know about was his brother being killed in a road accident. Did you?'

'Oh God, I did, yeah. I remember that well. It was awful. I was actually stationed in Swords at the time. I was still in uniform.'

'Really?'

'Yeah.'

She hesitates, but then says, 'How did it happen?'

He sighs. 'Well, it was a quiet stretch of road, as I remember. It wasn't late, eight or nine in the evening. There were two cars and they swerved to avoid each other . . . but one of them hit a wall and the other one hit a tree. There were four people killed. *Awful.*'

Gina nods along, biting her lip.

'Anyway,' Merrigan says, 'two or three months later Larry Bolger wins the by-election, and the rest, as they say, is history. But I'll tell you one thing.' He laughs. 'Frank Bolger was a very different kettle of fish from his brother.'

Gina refocuses. 'What do you mean?'

'Ach . . . he was a bit of an idealist. Always getting people's hackles up. He'd object to everything. There was never any question of a compromise with Frank, or of being pragmatic. I'm not sure he'd have lasted as long as Larry.'

'He didn't, though,' Gina says, 'did he?'

'No, I suppose you're right, he didn't.'

There is a pause.

Then Gina says, 'But getting back to the accident. Whose fault was it? Do they know?'

'That's an interesting one,' Merrigan says, 'because there was quite a bit of talk at the time.'

'Talk?'

'Yeah, there were conflicting . . . opinions, let's say, about what caused it. The official story was that the driver of the other car was seriously tanked up, the usual bloody story.' He pauses. 'But then claims were made that maybe this guy hadn't been drinking after all, that he was a teetotaller in fact, and that maybe Frank Bolger was the one who'd been drinking and that there was a campaign on to protect his reputation.'

'And?'

'It blew over. These things usually do.'

'*Jesus.*'

'Of course none of it was in the papers, or in the public domain, as they say. It was all just rumour and speculation. I mean, God, you know what this town is like.'

'Sure.'

'There was even a suggestion at the time that it might have been convenient for certain people to have Frank Bolger out of the way.'

Gina is stunned at this. She waits for Merrigan to say more, to elaborate, to go further and join up the dots.

She's ready to do it for him.

'But you know what?' he then says. 'Whenever a public figure dies in an accident you *always* get this kind of crackpot nonsense. It's typical.'

'Hmm.' Gina looks down at the floor.

'Today, I suppose,' Merrigan goes on, with contempt, 'you'd call it a conspiracy theory.'

'Yes.'

'But the sad fact is —'

'I know,' Gina says, swallowing. 'I know. People die on our roads every day of the week.'

'Exactly, Gina, exactly. I mean, take —'

He stops here. Gina is pretty sure he has just looped back in his mind to Noel and to what happened and that he feels a sudden awkwardness.

'Well anyway,' Gina says to fill the space, 'it's still awful, no matter what caused it. I mean, Bolger died, this other guy died, his wife died.' She pauses here and closes her eyes. 'And their little girl died . . .'

'Yes, that's right,' Merrigan says. 'It *was* awful. Absolutely tragic.'

They both remain silent for a moment. An articulated truck

rumbles past outside, along the quays. Somewhere in the distance an alarm is ringing.

'But then of course,' Merrigan says, 'there was the little boy.'

Gina opens her eyes. 'The *what?*'

'Yes,' Merrigan goes on, 'there was a little boy, too. The second car had four people in it. The father, the mother and *two* kids. The girl died, but the little boy survived. And with nothing more than a few scratches. It was a miracle. They reckon it was the side of the car he was in, and the angle, in relation to the impact.'

'My God.'

'But he more or less got up and walked away. They kind of played it down afterwards. Again, the tabloids would be all over a story like that today, but back then they were a little more circumspect. I mean, the kid would have been only what, five, six years old.'

Gina sits up. 'And what happened to him?'

'As far as I remember someone in the family took him in, adopted him.'

They both go silent again. All Gina can do is shake her head in disbelief.

Eventually she reaches forward, across the desk, and grabs a pen. 'Jackie,' she says, holding the pen poised over a piece of paper, 'I don't suppose you can remember the name of the little boy, can you?'

'As a matter of fact I can,' he says. 'I remember it very well. His name was Mark Griffin.'

7

'*Australia?*'

'Yes.'

'I don't think so.'

'Why not?'

'Dermot, people in their twenties go to Australia. I don't know, they get drunk and go surfing and stuff.'

Claire holds her wine-glass up and studies her husband.

He can see that she's struggling to take this seriously.

'The girls would love it,' he says.

'What? The beer and the surfing?'

'No, the –'

'Dermot, what *is* this? I thought –'

'OK, not Australia, somewhere else, the States, Canada.'

He looks around. Being Sunday evening, the place is not that busy. It's also the first time he's been in a restaurant where the tables are so far apart you'd have to shout to be overheard.

But he likes it. He likes the privacy.

'I don't understand where this is coming from,' Claire says. 'I thought the job –'

'Look, BCM have offices all over the world.'

'Oh God.' She's on the point of getting annoyed.

'*What?*' he says, taking a mouthful of risotto and hoping they don't end up being overheard after all.

'You want to know *what?*' She leans forward. 'I'll *tell* you what. The girls are settled in school. They have friends. You can't just yank them out of that for six months or a year. And besides.' She skewers a scallop with her fork. 'Mum and Dad aren't getting any younger. I don't want to be thousands of miles away.'

Which is precisely where Dermot wants to be.

But he nods in agreement. She's right and he knows it. They can't just take off the way he's proposing. It's not that they're trapped here exactly, but *they're* settled too, they have responsibilities.

He just thought . . .

'Well?'

He looks up. Claire is nodding at his risotto.

'The truffle,' she says, an edge in her voice. 'Can you taste it?'

'Yeah. It's amazing.'

She does a quick thing with her eyebrows, a non-verbal *It'd bloody better be, at forty euro a plate.*

Dermot pushes the risotto in her direction. 'Try it.'

She reaches across with her fork and scoops a bit up.

What he hasn't been able to tell Claire, of course, is that for the last couple of weeks he has been under constant surveillance. That's the working assumption, at any rate. These people know where his office is and where the kids go to school. He takes it they're watching the house as well, and logging his every move – where he goes, who he talks to. And maybe there's more to it than that. He doesn't know. Are they recording his phone calls, for instance, and intercepting his emails? Are they tracking his internet use?

Are they filming his life – twenty-four hours a day, seven days a week?

Obviously not. That'd be absurd.

But the thing is, *they may as well be.*

Because Dermot is now painfully self-conscious about every single thing he does. He can't move or speak without feeling ill at ease. It's as though he's been cast against his will in some nightmarish reality TV show – but no one has explained to him what the rules are or who's producing it.

Nevertheless, he's been playing along. He drops Orla and Niamh off at school every morning. He goes into the office. He works. He comes home. He hasn't uttered a word to anyone about the report – which he has also deleted, along with an early draft of it and any relevant emails. He hasn't got into a conversation with anyone about Noel Rafferty. Nor does he have any intention of doing so. Because these fuckers have his balls in a vice grip and he's not going to give them the slightest excuse to tighten it.

'Oh my God,' Claire says, 'that *is* delicious.'

He looks across at what she is having. 'How are the scallops?'

'Yeah,' she says, 'they're fine.'

Fine? Whatever.

Dermot smiles thinly across the table at his wife. He has told her more lies in the past two weeks than in all the rest of the time they've known each other, which is the best part of twelve years. He has lied about work, about money, about his state of mind.

He lied to her earlier today about why he wanted to take her out to this overpriced two-star Michelin restaurant. He said he wanted to make it up to her for being so moody and hard to live with recently. But the real reason was that he wanted to send *them* a coded message. Originally, he'd had a grander gesture in mind – he wanted to go straight out and blow all the cash on a new car, a Mercedes SL or a Jaguar, something that screamed, *Hey, I'm not shy about spending your money, I'm not conflicted, I'm in.* But he couldn't have explained it to Claire. The bonus he'd lied about getting at work wasn't *that* big.

So he figured, in the meantime . . . dinner at Cinq.

And some jewellery.

He bought her an expensive pair of earrings and a chain the other day – mainly to be *seen* buying them – but he hasn't had the nerve to give them to her yet.

He nods at her plate again. 'Well, they *look* nice.'

'They *are*. Jesus. I didn't say they weren't. Here.' She skewers a scallop up and holds it out to him. It's almost like a challenge. 'Try one.'

With both forks held high, they make the transfer. It's an awkward manoeuvre, and slightly combative-looking. Dermot places the scallop at the side of his plate.

A waiter then glides up to the table and asks them if everything is all right.

'Yes,' Dermot says, smiling up at him, 'wonderful, everything, thank you.'

'Yes,' Claire says, '*thank* you.'

After the waiter has gone, Dermot says, 'The service here is great, isn't it?'

'Yeah.'

It's the more abstract lies that he hates, though – the emotional lies, trying to pass his fear off as despondency, trying to make it seem as if he's burned out and needs a change of scene.

That stuff is really hard to maintain.

Because Claire isn't stupid. Far from it. In fact, from the look she's giving him right now, he even thinks she might have her suspicions about what's going on.

At *some* level, anyway.

'Dermot,' she says, and shrugs, 'I'm not sure what's happening here, the weird behaviour . . . Australia, *this*.' She spirals a forefinger in the air to indicate their immediate surroundings. 'I'm really not, but –'

'Yeah?'

Now he *hopes* she has her suspicions, and that she's smart enough to work it out, because he's getting desperate here. He needs to be able to share this. He looks her in the eye, willing her to see, to understand.

'– the *thing* is,' she says, and hesitates.

'Yeah . . . *yeah*?'

It's almost as if he's panting.

'Look, I hate myself for even asking you the question,' she goes on finally – and all of a sudden his heart sinks – 'but, I don't know . . . are you having an *affair* or something?'

Five

1

On the way into town from Dublin Airport the next morning Larry Bolger skims through the statement he's going to be making at a press conference in twenty minutes.

Paula is slumped in the seat next to him. She has fallen asleep and is snoring lightly. Bolger himself hasn't slept in over thirty-six hours and probably won't for at least another twelve.

On the plane, he revised the statement endlessly, each time making amendments, but now he's more or less satisfied with it. On Saturday he issued a bald statement from Chicago denying all of the charges. This is merely a clarification of that denial with some specifics thrown in.

But it's the Q&A part of the press conference that he's dreading.

It's not that he'll have a problem answering any of the questions they throw at him – he won't – but getting tied up in Jesuitical knots over his personal finances, justifying expense sheets and unauthorised credit-card use – it *looks* bad. It's undignified and will dent his credibility.

Of course, he'll do his level best to turn things around by focusing on what the trade mission accomplished and by constant use of the phrase 'going forward', but they, the media, will drag it *back* – inevitably, inexorably – to the race meetings and the assignations, to what he ordered from room service on such and such a date . . . to the betting slips and the Cristal and the lobster and the porcelain veneers.

It will be a war of attrition.

He looks out of the window to the left. They pass the Bishop's Palace and approach Binn's Bridge.

He hates the media. Some of the stuff they dug up in the papers yesterday was despicable. Two of the articles he saw online went as far back as Frank's accident and even included archive photos of the crash scene.

He shakes his head.

They're a shower of bastards.

Because of them, as well, he now has to explain to his wife and daughters what he was doing five years ago with some woman they'd never heard of until last week. He has to work on convincing the party that he's not a loose cannon. He has to maintain his composure and pretend to his supporters that his chances of taking over as leader haven't been seriously compromised.

He can't *begin* to imagine how all of this is looking from the fifth floor of the Wilson Hotel. According to Paddy Norton, who phoned again yesterday evening, no one's been in touch about it yet – though of course they will be.

Bolger looks down and straightens his tie.

It has certainly raised his profile *here*, though. Nationally. Bolger is in the cabinet and gets interviewed a lot, he's well known, but *this* level of name recognition is something else again. It's the kind most politicians only ever dream about.

That is, of course, if you accept that there's no such thing as bad publicity.

They take a left at Gardiner Street.

Beside him, Paula is muttering something. He turns to look at her. She's still asleep.

'. . . but my phone isn't charged . . . yes, I know . . . nine point seven . . .'

Different parts of her are twitching. It's as though she has a low-level electrical current running through her body.

Deciding not to wake her up just yet, Bolger turns away again. He glances out of the window, at Mountjoy Square.

He wonders what Frank would have made of all this – or, if he wasn't so unwell, the old man? What would *he* make of it? Politics was big in their house when they were kids. Liam Bolger was a local councillor for many years, and two of his brothers – Larry's uncles – were in the trade-union movement. All of them were fierce party loyalists. Frank showed an interest from the beginning, and the old man encouraged him, took him to meetings, got him involved. Larry showed little interest, and if he wasn't a disappointment to the old man, it was never exactly clear what he was. Frank, in any case, was the golden boy, and all of the family's hopes for a successful political career – all of the old man's hopes – were pinned on him. But then came that awful night . . . the trauma and grief of a fatal car crash, the horror of losing a son, the crushing blow of seeing your dreams die. Afterwards, in a desperate attempt to regroup – and with unyielding determination – the old man turned the spotlight onto his next son down.

Bolger closes his eyes.

There was a touch of that whole Kennedy thing to it, the royal succession, the passing on of the baton, of the *flame* –

though over the years Larry has never been able to figure out if his relationship to Frank was more like Jack's relationship to Joe Jr., or Bobby's to Jack, or maybe even, and most likely, Teddy's to Bobby.

He opens his eyes.

Just ahead is the Carlton Hotel, where he's giving the press conference. He nudges Paula awake.

'Oh . . . oh shit. Where are we?'

'At the gates of hell,' he says. 'Look.'

She leans forward.

Dozens of reporters and photographers, jostling for position, are gathered at the entrance to the hotel.

Paula whips a compact out of her pocket, flicks it open and examines herself.

'Oh God,' she says, making a lame attempt to adjust her hair. 'Look at the state of me.'

'I wouldn't worry about it,' Bolger says. 'I don't think you're the one they're interested in.'

As the car pulls up at the hotel, the photographers and reporters surge forward.

'Remember,' Paula says, like a ringside coach slipping in his plastic mouthpiece, 'you're indignant about all of this, you're bewildered, you're *hurt*.'

'Yes,' Bolger says, nodding his head.

He takes a deep breath and reaches for the door. Then, as he steps out of the car and into a hail of clicks, whirrs and flashes, he repeats to himself, over and over, mantra-like, *indignant, bewildered, hurt . . . indignant, bewildered, hurt . . .*

2

It takes Gina no more than ten minutes to locate Mark Griffin. When she gets into the office that morning she sits at her desk, pulls out the phone book and simply looks up his name. There are six Mark Griffins and over twenty M. Griffins. She starts with the Marks. Most of the previous night she lay awake thinking about how hard this would be, anticipating all sorts of obstacles, dead ends, trails gone cold – but now she's surprised at how easy, and obvious, it is.

With the first and second Marks she's a little awkward in her approach, a little too direct, but by the third one she's got it right.

'Hello, may I speak to Mark Griffin please?'

'Speaking.'

'Hello. I hope I'm on to the right person. I'm, I'm looking for a Mark Griffin who lost family members many years ago in a road accident, I –'

'No, no,' comes the immediate response, 'no, no, sorry . . . you must be looking for someone else.'

The next response, number four, is very different – a silence that goes on so long Gina eventually has to interrupt it.

'Hello?'

'Yes,' the voice says, 'I'm here.'

Gina swallows.

This is him. She can tell. She glances at her watch.

Ten minutes.

She didn't think it would happen so fast, and now she's not prepared. What does she say next?

'Thank you.'

Thank you?

'Look, who is this? Are you a journalist?'

'No, no, of course not. My name is Gina Rafferty and I . . . I lost someone myself, two weeks ago, a brother, in a road accident, I . . .'

She doesn't know how to proceed.

Then it's Mark Griffin's turn to interrupt the silence.

'You have my condolences,' he says, 'really, but listen, I'm not a grief counsellor, I –'

'I know, I know, and I'm sorry, but I do have a specific reason for calling you.' She pauses. 'I wonder if we could meet somewhere and talk.'

He exhales loudly and then says, 'How did you get my name? How do you know about me?'

'Can I explain all of that when we meet?'

Somewhat reluctantly he agrees, at first saying he's busy and that it'll have to be sometime later in the week. But then, as he flicks through what Gina imagines to be a diary or a notebook, his attitude seems to shift.

'Look,' he says, 'what are you doing now?'

'*Now?* This morning?'

'Yeah.' There is a new urgency in his voice. 'In the next hour or two.'

'Well . . . nothing, I suppose.'

'OK then.'

They arrange to meet in a café on South Anne Street at eleven.

Before he leaves the house, Mark stops for a moment in front of the hall mirror. He looks awful. He didn't shave this morning and his eyes are puffy. If it wasn't for the Italian suit he's wearing, he'd probably look more of a shambles. He doesn't care, though.

He gets in the car and pulls out onto Glanmore Road.

It's just after ten o'clock. Rush hour in Dublin never really ends, but if he's lucky he should be able to make it into town in twenty-five, thirty minutes, get parking and be at the café on South Anne Street just before eleven.

He needs a little time to get his head together.

Mark has no idea who Gina Rafferty is or what she wants, but in the half hour since she called he's come as close to having a panic attack as it's possible to get without actually, technically, having one – the only thing holding it in abeyance, in fact, being a blind and unreasonable expectation that this woman, whoever she is, is going to be able to *tell* him something.

The traffic through Drumcondra is light enough, and once he crosses Tolka Bridge it loosens up even more.

Mark looks in the rearview mirror – at himself. His eyes are still puffy . . . and red and rheumy. This is the first hangover he's had in a very long time. It was the first *drink*.

Half a bottle of Bombay Sapphire.

He'd resisted for days. But eventually there didn't seem to be much point. It'd been so long since he'd had to confront head-on the reality of the accident – and it turned out to be more of a strain than he could bear, sifting through his memory like that . . .

The thing is, Mark *thinks* he can remember the crash happening, but the truth is he probably can't. No doubt, in retrospect, his imagination has filled in a lot of the detail – provided colour, splashes of red, a wash of orange, a rotating blue light, as well as sound effects, screeches, screams, groans – but the reality of it all, buried deep somewhere in his subconscious and effectively inaccessible to him now, may have been quite different. What he can picture in his head, and what shows up unbidden every once in a while in dreams, is a serviceable version of the event. It may not be an accurate representation of what actually happened, but this 'memory' accords with the facts as they've been handed down to him, and anyway, it's all he's got.

He finds a parking space on Nassau Street.

But what is really strange here is that the subject has come up twice, and separately, in the space of a few days.

Is that just a coincidence, or is there something going on?

Mark doesn't know. But either way, this is the single most formative event of his life, and never once – it occurs to him – never once has he had a proper conversation about it, *ever* . . . with anyone.

He looks at his watch and wonders now, nervously, as he walks back towards Dawson Street, if that isn't about to change.

Gina leaves the office and walks along Harcourt Street. As she's approaching the junction with St Stephen's Green, a silver Luas, bell ringing, glides by. She crosses at the lights after the tram and enters the Green.

So much about Dublin has changed in recent years, but this great garden square with its winding pathways and formal flower beds isn't one of them. In fact, if it weren't for people's clothes – Gina thinks – and their mobile phones, this could be twenty-five, fifty, even a hundred years ago. There's something reassuring about that – even if it doesn't make today, or what she's about to do, any less real.

Not that she's at all clear in her mind what that is.

A lot will depend on Mark Griffin. He was a kid when the accident – the *crash* – happened, so how much does he know about it? How much was he told when he was growing up? Is he aware that at the time there was lots of what Jackie Merrigan called 'talk'? Griffin sounded relatively normal on the phone, but how will he respond to the fact that Gina's theory, pretty shaky to start with, is not backed up by a single shred of evidence?

The thing is, for her theory to come into any kind of focus, for a discernible pattern to emerge, there needs to be a stronger connection between her brother and Larry Bolger. What she has is that they played poker sometimes, and apparently weren't evenly matched. Meaning what? Bolger owed Noel money? He couldn't pay it back?

Gina groans.

That's pretty weak.

But then she remembers what Terry Stack had to say and it makes her want to scream.

She crosses the stone bridge over the pond and heads for the Dawson Street exit.

There's something else, too, not a connection exactly, not anything she can use – but a memory . . . from when she was a kid. It came to her last night after she got off the phone with Jackie Merrigan and was on the sofa taking another look at that two-page spread in the *Sunday World*.

It was of the house in Dolanstown . . . the front room with its old wallpaper, thick carpet and ornaments on the mantelpiece. The TV was on and her mother was in the armchair, cigarette dangling, glass in hand. Gina herself was playing on the floor when out of the blue – and almost shouting – her mother said, 'Ah Jesus, Mary and Joseph, *no.*'

Gina turned around. Her mother was pointing at the TV screen.

'*Look* at that. Oh *God* isn't it awful.'

Gina looked.

What she remembers now is more like an abstract image than anything else, because how was she supposed to make sense of what she was seeing – of what must have been a close-up shot of the second car, mangled and crushed out of all recognition? She didn't understand what she was hearing either, though one thing she does remember is a man in uniform saying, 'tragic altogether, the mother and father, and their little girl . . .'

What sticks in Gina's mind the most, however, is her mother saying over and over again, 'That poor little boy, that *poor* little boy . . . my Jesus, that poor *unfortunate* little boy.' Gina was puzzled at this and wanted to say, *No, no, Mammy, it was their little girl, it was their little* girl, *Mammy . . . the man* said . . .

But she remained silent.

In time, Gina learned how to handle her mother when drink was involved, but back then she just used to keep her head down and stay quiet. Besides, she was the only one left in the house at that stage – all of the others had gone, even Catherine and the baby.

Or was Catherine still there? Was little *Noel* still there? Upstairs asleep in his cot maybe?

The memory doesn't stretch to that kind of detail, but what seems pretty certain now – as Gina crosses at the light and heads down Dawson Street – is that when she was a kid, six or seven years old, she saw a report on TV of the car crash that killed both Larry Bolger's brother and the parents and sister of the man she's about to meet.

Already scanning the room as she walks through the door, Gina identifies Mark Griffin more or less immediately. He's sitting alone in a corner. The place is quite busy, but he's the only person she can see who fits the age profile.

She goes straight over to him.

'Mark?'

'Yeah. Gina?' He half stands up and puts out his hand.

They shake and Gina sits down, her back to the room.

'So,' she says, feeling horribly awkward.

Their eyes meet for a second. Then he looks over her shoulder.

'What would you like?' he asks, raising a finger. 'Coffee, tea, juice?'

Gina glances down at what he's having. It seems to be a large black coffee.

'Er . . .'

A young Chinese guy appears at her side and says, 'Hi, good morning. What would you like?'

'Er . . . I'll have a double espresso, please.'

The Chinese guy takes a moment to write this down and then goes away.

Thankful for that little breather, but sorry now it's over, Gina looks up and smiles.

Mark Griffin is dark. He has dark hair, dark eyes and a dark complexion. He's wearing a *very* nice dark suit and a plain dark tie. But he's also unshaven and looks somewhat the worse for wear. Gina doesn't know what she was expecting – although a small, irrational part of her was expecting a five-year-old boy in short grey trousers and a V-necked jumper.

'Thank you for agreeing to meet me,' she says. 'I realise this must be difficult for you, but I just wanted to, er . . .' She hasn't really worked out how to put this. 'I just wanted . . .'

'Look,' Mark Griffin says, leaning forward, 'it *isn't* easy for me, that's true, but from what you said on the phone I'm sure it isn't easy for *you* either.' He pauses. 'Why don't you start by telling me what happened to your brother?'

Gina nods and says, 'OK.'

She intends to go for a slow build, with plenty of context and detail, but by the time the waiter arrives back with her double espresso a couple of minutes later, she finds she's already blurted most of it out – even to the extent of using phrases like 'faked accident' and 'professional hit'.

She does stop short, though, of mentioning Larry Bolger.

She leans forward and takes a sip from the espresso. She looks at Griffin for a reaction, but there isn't one.

After a moment he reaches out and takes a sip from his own cup.

What is he thinking?

Gina doesn't know, but it would seem reasonable to assume that he's torn between wanting to hear more of her theory and wanting to be told what the *fuck* any of this has to do with him.

He looks at her. 'You didn't say why you think anyone would want to kill your brother.'

'Well, I don't really *know* why. That's what I'm trying to find out. But the thing is' – here goes, she looks into his eyes – 'the thing is, he did some work over the years with Larry Bolger . . . and I –'

Griffin blanches. 'Sorry . . . *Larry Bolger?*'

'Yes.'

'That's what this is about? Something to do with Larry Bolger?'

'Well maybe. I don't know.'

'Jesus.' He exhales. '*Jesus.*'

'I'm sorry. I didn't mean to –'

'No . . . it's OK.' He exhales again. 'But I don't understand. What are you trying to say?'

Gina feels her stomach sinking. How coherent an answer to this question can she give?

'Look,' she says, 'I'm probably on shaky ground here, and I don't want to stir up any bad memories or upset you in any way, but I was talking to someone last night, someone who remembers the crash from twenty-five years ago, a cop, and he was saying that the official story was that your father –' she pauses, swallows, 'that your father caused the accident. Because he'd been drinking. But that . . . maybe things weren't so clear-cut. This guy said that at the time there was a question mark over whether your father even drank at all, and that maybe it was Frank Bolger who was drunk. He said there could well have been a cover-up to protect his reputation . . . and that Larry Bolger was the one person who had the most to gain from . . .'

Gina has never had anyone look at her the way Griffin is looking at her now. It's a queasy kaleidoscope of disbelief, hurt, confusion, fury. He puts a hand on the edge of the table to steady himself.

'This is insane,' he whispers.

'Oh God,' Gina says, 'I'm sorry.'

He's looking away now, over her shoulder, and shaking his head.

Does she go on or shut up?

'I don't know,' she says after a moment, the silence unbearable, 'it just seemed to be a pattern . . . accusations of drunk driving used deliberately and maliciously to . . .'

Her voice trails off.

Twenty-five years apart, different circumstances, the link

with Bolger tenuous at best and probably just a coincidence – is that a pattern? Gina has a sudden sense of how flimsy all of this is, and of how irresponsible she's being in presenting it to someone who has such a profound emotional involvement in what she's talking about.

'All my life,' Griffin says, still whispering, still staring into the distance, 'all the time I was growing up and in all the years since, I have lived with the horror, with the *shame,* of knowing that my father was responsible for that crash, and for the deaths of four people . . . including my sister and my *mother . . .*' He looks directly at Gina now. 'It was like some sort of black creation myth. And I never talked about it to anyone, I never discussed it with anyone . . . but it was always *there.*'

Gina swallows again. She wants to retract and apologise. She wants to get up and leave. She wants to reverse time.

'And now,' Griffin goes on, 'after all these years, out of the blue, I'm faced with the possibility that maybe it *wasn't* his fault? That it could have been someone *else's* fault? That there was . . . that there was even some uncertainty *at the time*? Jesus Christ.'

The edge in his voice unnerves Gina. The thing is, this is only a theory, and her impulse now is to play it down a little.

'Mark,' she says softly, 'I can't prove any of this.'

But he doesn't seem to be listening anymore. She's about to elaborate on her point when he suddenly stands up and shuffles out from behind the table.

'Mark, please, listen –'

He holds a hand up to silence her. There are tears in his eyes. He walks off.

Gina swivels around and watches as he goes out the door of

the café. He turns right, passes along by the window and quickly disappears from view.

3

Norton looks at his watch. It's almost midday. He picks up the remote from his desk and flicks on the TV.

Sky News.

He leaves it on mute. Then he slumps back in his ergonomic swivel chair and glances around. He doesn't like this office anymore. He has set aside an entire floor of the new building for Winterland Properties and can't wait until it's ready.

That's assuming, of course, that everything goes smoothly. Because there are plenty of people out there who'd love to see Norton fall flat on his face, people who said at the outset that the project wasn't financially viable, that Richmond Plaza would lie vacant for years.

Well, they don't have much longer to wait.

Norton reaches for the remote again and switches over to RTÉ. On the bulletin at midday there should be some mention of the press conference at the Carlton.

As he waits, he goes over some paperwork relating to the agreement-for-lease of one of the smaller tenants moving into Richmond Plaza. There's been some dispute over the net lettable area – which bits, exactly, they will or won't be renting – and he needs to be on top of this before a meeting with their agent at two o'clock.

After a while, he glances over and sees that the news bulletin is starting. He picks up the remote and turns on the sound. The press conference is the lead story.

Norton shakes his head. Is there nothing else happening in the world? No earthquake or hostage crisis? No development in the Middle East? No further slump in the housing market or surge in inflation? Is there nothing to deflect attention from Larry *fucking* Bolger?

Norton couldn't believe the coverage in the papers yesterday. It was savage, with the rushed and giddy feel of a premature obituary. What he's increasingly afraid of, however, is that if they push it and finish him off, Bolger mightn't be the only one who gets buried.

On screen, it cuts from the studio to the press conference. The minister is sitting at a table in front of a bank of microphones.

'. . . and I want to reassure people,' he's saying, 'that I have the full support, the full backing, of my family, my friends and my colleagues.' He hunches forward. 'But look, I want people to see this for what it is, which is a witch hunt, pure and simple . . . it's a sinister attempt to undermine . . .'

Norton's mobile phone goes off. He whips it up and looks at the display. No number. He hesitates, then answers it. 'Yeah?'

'Paddy, Ray Sullivan.'

Closing his eyes, Norton emits a low groan. Then he says, 'Ray, listen, can I put you on hold for a second?'

'Er . . . sure.'

Norton lowers his arm and dangles the phone by the side of his chair. He refocuses his attention on the press conference.

'. . . and on the other hand accountability, so that I as a public representative, going forward, can get on with the job I was first elected to do as an ambitious young man more than twenty-five years ago.'

Abruptly, the clip ends, and they cut back to the newsreader in the studio. Norton presses the Mute button on the remote. He raises his arm and puts the phone up to his ear again. 'Ray?'

He's been dreading this call.

'Paddy. What the hell is going on over there? I thought you might have gotten in touch by now.'

Norton squirms. 'I know, I know. I was just waiting to see if it'd blow over.'

'But . . . it hasn't.'

'Not as yet.'

'Not as yet.' Sullivan clears his throat. 'So let me ask, how's your boy doing?'

Norton is irritated by the phrasing. 'He's OK. He's stone-walling. Which he's pretty good at. He's a politician.'

'Fine, Paddy, but get this, the story has just come up on the old man's radar screen, and I have to tell you, he's pretty pissed. I wasn't going to mention it to him, at least not yet, but it turns out he's no stranger to the blogosphere.'

'What?'

'Yeah, I know, at *his* age.' Sullivan clicks his tongue. 'But anyway, the thing is, he feels let down. Oberon's put a lot into this and let's just say that Mr V. thinks any scandal or unpleasantness should have been flagged *way* in advance.'

'Ray, believe me,' Norton says, 'this *will* blow over. It's just . . . it's part of the process. Larry's getting himself into position and . . . the gloves are off. Don't tell me shit like this doesn't happen all the time up on the Hill.'

'It *does*, but people get screwed, Paddy, they get indicted, they go to fucking prison.'

Norton remains silent.

'Here's the thing, OK? Mr V. doesn't want to shake this guy's hand one week and then have to watch him doing a perp walk on TV the next.'

'I know.'

'It'd look bad.'

'Yeah. I know.'

Norton chews on his lower lip.

As a possible future prime minister of the only English-speaking country in the Eurozone, and with a six-month stint as EU Council President also in prospect, Larry Bolger would undoubtedly be useful to the Oberon Capital Group – he'd be a handy point man to have in terms of regulatory influence and the awarding of contracts.

'And he *liked* him,' Sullivan is saying. 'He did. So let's hope you're right. Let's hope it *is* going to blow over.'

'It is, Ray, trust me.'

'OK,' Sullivan then says. 'Where are we on naming rights?'

'Ah, yes,' Norton says, thinking, sly move. 'I'm glad you brought that up.'

'So?'

Naming rights is an inexact science if ever there was one, and very easy to get wrong. The future marketability of a building, for example, will often hinge on how its original name resonates. In this case, the Docklands Regeneration Commission has pretty much decided that the neutral-sounding, location-specific Richmond Plaza works best in the context of urban renewal. Ray Sullivan, on the other hand, has been arguing that Amcan, as anchor tenant, should have exclusive rights in the naming of its shiny new European head-quarters.

So . . . the Amcan Building.

It's not how Norton imagined it, and certainly the last thing he needs right now is another protracted tussle with the Docklands Regeneration Commission, but the smart move here is probably just to cave in to Sullivan's demands and bring the negotiations to a head.

Besides, given the current economic uncertainty, locking them in like this mightn't be such a bad idea.

'Very well,' he says. 'Let's put some numbers together. And talk later.'

'OK, Paddy, excellent.'

After the call, Norton sits in silence, staring across at a weather update on the TV.

He shakes his head. How and when – he wonders – did Larry Bolger become central to all of this? How and when did he go from being a sweetener, the icing on the cake, to a *deal point*?

When ads come on, Norton flicks the TV off with the remote.

So perhaps he should be maintaining a closer watch on Bolger. He seemed fairly composed at the press conference there, but he *is* under a lot of pressure, and anything could happen. Norton knows how *that* works after all – how the tipping point can just creep up on you.

He picks his mobile phone up again. With his other hand he reaches into his jacket pocket, leans a little to the side and rummages around for his silver pillbox.

4

'Mark, you look dreadful. What's . . . what's the matter?'

'Nothing.'

As he strides across the kitchen, Mark can see the alarm in Aunt Lilly's eyes. When he gets to where she's standing, over by the sink, he doesn't do what he usually does, which is bend down and peck her on the cheek.

He just stands there.

Driving out here from town Mark rehearsed what he was going to say. Out loud. These days, of course, you can do that and not have to worry about seeming deranged. You can be alone in your car, even stopped at traffic lights, and talk, shout, make hand gestures, wave your arms about – because for all the guy in the next car knows, you could be barking at your stockbroker or on a conference call to head office in Tokyo.

Or blubbering to your analyst.

But looking into his aunt Lilly's eyes now, Mark feels the rage and indignation draining out of him. Suddenly, it doesn't seem fair, or appropriate, to subject her to what would be, in effect, an interrogation.

'What is it, Mark?'

At the same time, he can't let it go. He has to ask her something.

'Aunt Lilly, did . . . er . . .'

As he was flying out along the coast road, this was the one question that he held in reserve, that remained in his head, unrehearsed and unarticulated.

'Yes?'

'Did . . . Dad . . .'

But he doesn't get beyond that second syllable, which is not a syllable he has used – on its own, out loud – in as long as he can remember. Using it now finishes him off. His eyes well up again.

'Oh Mark . . . *Mark* . . .'

He turns away. Through the door leading into the living room he can see that the TV is on. As usual, the sound is either off or pitched so low that he can't hear it.

'Aunt Lilly,' he says, 'are we really . . .' There is an ad on for mobile phones. He stares at it. 'Are we really sure that Dad . . . that the accident was *his* fault?'

He turns back and looks at her.

She is ashen.

Mark has never talked to Aunt Lilly about this before. When his uncle Des was alive, he never talked about it to him either. Any time Mark's circumstances were alluded to over the years, which was usually for practical reasons, it was in a kind of code, it was hushed and hurried, as though mere contemplation of what had happened might be perilous to mental, even physical, health. Mark's own understanding of what had happened derived mainly from conversations he overheard in the days and weeks following the crash. Some of these, even at that early stage, were hushed and hurried. Others – looking back on them now – were pretty careless, and really shouldn't have been conducted in his presence. It was as though people thought that because Mark was so small he wouldn't understand what they were saying, or take anything in, or *remember*.

But he was five; he wasn't stupid.

He recalls, for instance – it was in a crowded sitting room or a kitchen – one man loudly whispering to another, 'I hear poor Tony had drink taken.' Now Mark may not have grasped the full import of these words at the time, but he certainly took them in and he certainly remembered them. In fact, he will never forget the day some years later – and it was seemingly out of the blue – when the phrase came into proper focus for him, when sufficient context had accrued around it for its meaning to light up suddenly and explode inside his head.

Tony had drink taken.

He recalls hearing the word *Bolger,* too – from the days right after the crash – hearing it repeatedly, incessantly, until it took on an obscure, elusive kind of significance for him. Much later, there was a moment when the context around *that* word clicked into place as well.

The thing is, when Mark was growing up, his adoptive parents never told him anything about what was, up to that point, undeniably, the central event of his life, and he, in turn – assuming there was a good reason for their silence – never asked. He did feel that *some* attempt at a conversation about it was inevitable though, and as a confused, solipsistic kid he often tried to imagine this. It was something he looked forward to, craved even, but as he got into his teens, and as the silence deepened and thickened, it dawned on him that no such conversation was probably ever going to take place. Then, as he got older – and as his retrospective impressions coalesced into a kind of horrifying revelation – he started to dread that one still might, and he did all in his power to demonstrate to his aunt and uncle that he neither needed nor wanted one.

Mark knew what had happened, he believed – and *they* knew – so what was there to say about it? Why subject themselves to the embarrassment and the shame?

It was the perfect conspiracy of silence.

Looking at his aunt Lilly now, at the confusion in her eyes, Mark sees the breadth and reach of that conspiracy, and is prepared to bet that she has nothing useful to tell him, not because she chooses *not* to remember, or because she *doesn't* remember, but because she doesn't *know*, not anymore.

'Mark . . . I . . .'

And perhaps she never did.

'It's all right,' Mark says, turning away again, unable to face her. 'I was just –'

'We always meant, your uncle Des and I, we . . .'

She trails off here, and Mark is relieved. The person he should probably be talking to, in any case, isn't in the room. He's been dead for six months.

Standing in the doorway, Mark looks at the TV and sees that a news bulletin is starting up. He lowers his head and closes his eyes.

But if Uncle Des *were* still alive, he wonders, and here in the room today, what questions would he put to him?

Uncle Des . . . what really happened that night? Do you remember? Do you know? Were you told? Did you believe what you were told? Did it make sense to you? Did you ask questions? Did you get answers? Were you bullied? Were you coerced into silence? Did that silence last the rest of your life?

He opens his eyes again.

Was my father wrongly accused? Was he made into a scapegoat to protect someone else's reputation?

Uncle Des may be gone, Mark realises, but *someone* still needs to answer these questions.

He raises his head. He looks at the TV.

A man is sitting hunched forward at a table in front of some microphones.

It takes Mark a second or two to recognise who it is.

He goes over and grabs the remote from the arm of the sofa. He fumbles for the button and raises the volume.

But all he catches are the final few words.

'. . . *the job I was first elected to do as an ambitious young man more than twenty-five years ago . . .*'

5

After she leaves the café, Gina walks around for a while, aimlessly – down Grafton Street, along Wicklow Street. On the phone earlier Mark Griffin had asked if she was a journalist and she'd said no, of course not. But now she *feels* like one, feels like the worst tabloid hack – someone who thinks nothing of exploiting someone else's grief for a story.

She turns left onto Drury Street and then right at Claudio's Wines. She walks through the old South City Markets and comes out onto George's Street.

She should have left him alone. It was unfair of her to plant a doubt in his mind like that and then have nothing to back it up. It was irresponsible and selfish.

She has a knot in her stomach now, and a headache.

She walks on a bit and stops at a corner. But when she looks across the street, the knot in her stomach tightens.

Because the building directly opposite is where Noel used to work. It's where BCM has its offices.

She looks around her for a moment, and then back across the street. Gina has passed this building many times but has never been inside. On the rare occasions that Noel took her out to lunch, they met nearby, in the Long Hall or in Grogan's.

So what is she doing here now? It's not as if she came this way deliberately. It wasn't anything conscious.

Seeing as how she *is* here, though . . .

She crosses the street.

Inside the building, the lobby is all granite and tinted glass, with leather banquettes and discreetly placed artworks. BCM is on the fourth floor.

She goes up in the elevator.

The receptionist, when she realises who Gina is, gets quite emotional, and Gina has to struggle to maintain her own composure. After a few moments, she asks to see a particular colleague of Noel's, a Leo Spillane, someone she met at the funeral.

'Oh my *dear,*' the receptionist says, making it sound as if this might be the last straw for Gina, 'I'm afraid he's out sick today.'

'That's OK,' Gina says. Then, not really knowing why she's here but still feeling a need to explain herself, she adds, 'I just wanted to talk to someone. You know. Someone who worked with Noel.'

The receptionist nods her head vigorously and says, 'I understand, I understand. I know there's a meeting going on, but look, take a seat and I'll check who's back there.'

Two or three minutes later a pale young man about Gina's age, or maybe a bit older, emerges from a corridor to the right of the reception desk. He's quite thin and is wearing a suit that looks at least a size too big for him. He approaches Gina with his hand extended.

'Er, hello,' he says. 'Pleased to meet you. I'm . . . I'm Dermot Flynn.'

He's floating through this – and through everything these days really – as though in a dream, and of course this *could* be a dream, because it's got all the elements of a dream: anxiety, tranquillity, perplexity, guilt, more anxiety, and now, bizarrely, Noel Rafferty's kid sister . . .

He sits down beside her in reception. He offers his condolences.

'So tell me,' she then says, 'you worked with my brother, is that right?'

The tranquillity part – due to the medication his doctor prescribed him last week – is already feeling a little diluted.

'Yes,' he says, 'I worked under him. I was, *am,* a member of the team.'

As he describes his job and his place in the company, Dermot Flynn looks closely at Gina. He sees the resemblance all right – Noel's angular, drawn features reflected in this younger, fresher, more attractive face.

Up to now he hasn't allowed himself to think about Noel – and for good reason. Clearly the man was put under the same kind of pressure as Dermot himself was, but whether he skidded off that road by accident or did it deliberately is immaterial – in the end *that* wasn't what killed him.

'On that last day,' Gina says, 'the Monday, did he seem particularly tense for any reason?'

'No, I don't think so. I'm not even sure I saw him that day.'

He didn't, in fact – but he's still lying. He looks around reception. He's not happy being interrogated like this.

'Do you want to go outside,' he says, 'get a coffee somewhere?'

'Yeah, sure.'

It's only when they're in the elevator on the way down that it occurs to him.

I can't be seen talking to this woman.

But it's too late.

Out on the street, he feels exposed, and horribly self-conscious. He tries to hurry things along. They go to a small café around the corner and Dermot sits with his back to the window.

'So how is Richmond Plaza coming along?' she asks.

'Fine,' he says, 'yeah, fine.' He feels like adding, *Why?*

'I was up there last week,' she says, 'with Paddy Norton. He showed me around.'

Dermot swallows. What's he supposed to say to that? It's like she's teasing him.

'Yeah . . . it's nearly finished, couple of months to go,' he says, and clears his throat. He can't bring himself to say anything more on the subject.

She then asks him a few questions about what Noel was like to work with. It's neutral enough territory and he answers as best he can. He actually talks for quite a while – though at one point he finds himself in the middle of a long sentence and realises he has no idea how he got there. He also has a headache. He starts massaging his temples.

After a few moments of this, Gina says, 'Dermot, are you OK?'

He looks up. 'Yes.' He puts his hands down on the table. 'I'm fine.'

But the truth is he isn't. He hasn't been sleeping lately, or eating, and he's lost a lot of weight. He's also been bickering constantly with Claire, something they never used to do, and he isn't able to look either of his girls in the eye anymore without having his own eyes well up with tears.

He starts massaging his temples again.

Then he looks at Gina.

'I have to go,' he says.

6

Mark throws the remote onto the sofa, turns away from the TV and goes back into the kitchen. It doesn't surprise him that Aunt Lilly is busy – that she's over at the counter sieving flour into a bowl. Without saying a word, he walks right past her. He goes out the front door, pulls it behind him and heads straight for his car. As he's backing out of the driveway, he puts on his seat belt.

He checks the rearview mirror, but the front door of the house remains closed.

Driving along the coast road, he glances left, at the sea, and across the bay to the mountains. It's cloudy, but the sun is beginning to break through in patches.

He doesn't have a specific destination in mind, but he's feeling a gravitational pull towards the city centre.

He turns back to face the traffic. His heart is pounding.

So what *did* happen?

Mark doesn't know, but the questions are multiplying in his head. Was Frank Bolger the one who got into his car that night with a few too many pints on him? Was he the one who lost control at the wheel and ended up killing himself and three other people? Was talk of drunk driving causing multiple fatalities considered too damaging, too toxic, for such a high-profile TD? In such a key constituency? With a brother waiting in the wings to take the seat? If so, were certain measures then taken? Was the 'talk' hushed up? Was evidence suppressed? Were new rumours – this time concerning the driver of the other car – put into circulation?

And what happened next?

Mark's head is spinning.

Did Des Griffin start voicing objections, saying they had it all wrong, that his brother didn't even drink? Was he told to shut up – for the sake of the boy? Was he intimidated, threatened, informed he might lose his job in the civil service, or be transferred – or *worse*? Is that why he was always so . . . ?

Mark passes through Fairview and onto the North Strand Road.

Is this really how it all happened?

Jesus.

If it is – and increasingly it makes sense to him – then surely Gina Rafferty is right. The one person who had anything, indeed *everything*, to gain from this cover-up . . . was Larry Bolger.

Gina is reluctant to let Dermot Flynn go, but she can't very well stop him.

When he stands up to leave, he fumbles for his wallet.

Gina waves him away. 'It's OK,' she says. 'I've got it.'

He doesn't argue.

She watches him go out the door and into the street.

When he's gone, she takes a deep breath. She stares into space and tries to reconstruct the last twenty minutes in her head.

For some reason Flynn was deeply uncomfortable. He was nervous and jittery. He was evasive. He kept staring at other people in the café. He kept interrupting himself, hesitating, not finishing his sentences.

But why was he like this?

Was it something to do with Noel?

That's the first thing Gina thinks of, not surprisingly – but maybe she's got it wrong. Maybe Flynn is a nervous *type*. Maybe he's bipolar and forgot to take his meds. Maybe she caught him on a bad day.

She can only speculate.

On the short walk back to her own office, she chides herself for not being more aggressive, for not putting Flynn more on the spot.

But she's tired, she's confused, and it was such a painful interlude that she just wanted it to end.

As she goes in the door and walks up the stairs, Gina finds herself wishing this whole *thing* would end – the way sometimes, half consciously, in the middle of one, you want a dream to end.

Mark finds a parking space on Merrion Square. As he walks up towards Baggot Street he makes a couple of calls on his mobile. The first is to directory enquiries and the second is to the press office of the Department of Enterprise, Trade and Employment.

The minister, it seems – not that Mark asked – has made his statement and isn't available for further comment. In any case, he will be busy all afternoon in the Dáil, and later he'll be –

'That's fine,' Mark says, 'thank you.'

He puts away his phone. He walks by the Shelbourne and turns right onto Kildare Street. In less than a minute he is standing in front of Leinster House. He looks in through the tall railings of this Georgian mansion that was originally built as a town house for the Earl of Kildare and is now the seat of both houses of the Oireachtas. There are two gardaí standing sentry at the gates, but they seem to be spending a lot of their time redirecting tourists to the National Library or the National Museum, which are located on either side of the parliament building.

Mark looks at his watch. He wonders what Larry Bolger is going to be so busy with all afternoon. An urgent debate on some vital piece of legislation? Leaders' Questions? But then he remembers it's Monday and that when the Dáil is in session they don't commence business until Tuesday. So what's Bolger doing in there? Hiding from the media after his press conference? Trying to make himself look busy?

Mark would like to find out, but you can't just swan in through the gates here. You need clearance or a visitor's pass. He looks up and down the street. Apart from pedestrians and tourists, there is a bedraggled man with a placard pacing back and forth in front of the sentry box and another man circling idly on the pavement, talking into his mobile.

Farther up the street, people are waiting at a bus stop.

Inside the gates there is an occasional flurry of activity as someone comes or goes or a car passes in or out. It's not busy though, and after a while Mark begins to feel self-conscious. One of the guards in the sentry box has glanced over at him a couple of times, and it can't be long, he supposes, before an approach is made.

Eventually he moves away. He wanders up the street a bit, towards the bus stop.

He doesn't know why he came here. It just seemed like his only option.

But about twenty minutes later – and as though to dispel any doubts he might have had – three men walk out through the gates of Leinster House. They wait to let traffic pass and then cross the street. They enter Buswell's Hotel on the corner of Molesworth Street.

Mark is pretty sure, even from this distance, that one of the men is Larry Bolger.

Back in the office, Gina sits and stares at her screensaver. There is plenty of work she could be doing, but her heart isn't in it, not least because she knows the company's days are numbered. P.J., by contrast, is a lot more positive and talks up the company's prospects every chance he gets. Siobhan in reception is playing her part as well – though in the room at the back, where the designers and programmers operate, you could cut the atmosphere with a knife.

Gina rubs her eyes.

Either way, *she's* been out of the equation since her brother died, and no one is expecting anything of her just yet. P.J. could do with the support, but he also knows her well enough not to push it. In any case, it doesn't take Gina long to realise that sitting around the office in a trance isn't much of a help to anyone.

She gets up from her desk again. As she's walking towards the door, she looks over at Siobhan. 'I'm just . . .'

'Yes?'

'I'm . . .'

But that's it. That's all there is.

On the way down the stairs she wonders how unhinged that must've seemed – how unhinged *she* must seem.

Even though, actually, it isn't how she feels at all.

Outside, she looks down the gentle curve of Harcourt Street towards the Green, and hears the bell of an approaching tram. There is a slight breeze blowing.

Actually, she thinks, if anyone is unhinged here it's surely the two men she met this morning, both of whom seemed to be under a great deal of pressure.

Though presumably for different reasons.

Or maybe not.

She starts walking.

If there *is* a connection between them, it's not as easy to see right now as the contrast. Because Dermot Flynn – she's pretty sure – was afraid of something or someone, and seemed vulnerable, whereas Mark Griffin was more like a wounded animal, and seemed, quite frankly, a little dangerous.

He waits for a van to pass, and then a bus, before striding across the street himself. It may be a stroke of luck that Bolger appeared when he did, but that's certainly not how it feels. Walking down to the corner, heart pounding, Mark feels a keen sense of inevitability about what's happening. It's as though the confrontation ahead could no more be avoided than the setting of the sun.

He turns the corner and goes up the steps of the hotel. Before going inside he takes out his mobile phone and switches it off. He enters the lobby and immediately spots Larry Bolger, who is over to the left, standing at the entrance to the bar with the two men he came in with. It strikes Mark how amazingly informal all of this is. Bolger is a government minister, and yet he doesn't seem to have any security around him, or an entourage.

Maybe it's the place. This small hotel opposite Leinster House does have that kind of reputation. It's known to be a sort of home away from home for politicians.

Mark walks across the lobby, and as he does so Bolger and

the two men he's with separate. The two men turn towards the bar, and Bolger heads for a corridor to the right of the reception desk.

Mark follows him – and continues to follow him, seconds later, into the men's room.

Which is empty.

'Er . . . Mr Bolger, can I have a word?'

Mark's voice is quite shaky and even in danger of sounding a little hysterical.

Two feet away from the urinal, hands already working his fly, Bolger stops and turns around. He looks alarmed. 'What?'

'I want to ask you a question.'

'Hold on a second . . . who are you?'

Bolger looks smaller than he does on TV. He's quite a dapper little man, all groomed and primped. He's wearing a silk suit, cuff links, a gold watch. Even from across the room Mark can smell his cologne.

'The crash,' Mark then says, 'the one . . . the one your brother was killed in, did you –'

'*Jesus*,' Bolger interrupts. 'Are you fucking serious? In *here*? Get the –'

Mark holds a hand up. 'No, no, simple question. Did you cover it up? Did –'

'Cover *what* up? I don't –'

'The fact that *he* was the one who was drunk, *he* was the one who caused the accident, your brother, and not –'

'That's outrageous. Jesus Christ. That's the most outrageous thing I've ever –'

'Is it? Things worked out pretty well for *you* though, didn't they?'

'How *dare* you. I –'

Sensing movement from behind, Mark spins around.

A young guy in uniform – a hotel staff-member pre-sumably, a bellhop or a porter – is coming through the door.

Mark freezes.

The guy in uniform stops and looks around for a moment. 'Mr Bolger,' he says, a little suspiciously, 'are you –'

'I'm grand, Tim,' Bolger says. 'But I think this gentleman here might have lost his way looking for the exit.'

Mark turns back to Bolger. 'Well, did you?'

'Did I *what*?' Bolger snaps. Then he shakes his head. 'You fucking journalists are a breed apart.'

'I'm not a journalist, I'm –'

'I don't give a shite *what* you are, you're only a scumbag as far as I'm concerned.'

'Come on, sir,' the bellhop says, '*this* way.'

As Mark turns again, he glances into the large mirror above the row of washbasins. All of a sudden the room seems crowded, and the situation a little trickier than he'd imagined. At the same time, Mark can't believe who he's standing next to. This man's name – the word, the very *sound* of it – is something he has lived with all his life, as he has lived with ambivalence, confusion, shame . . .

And anger.

'Sir.'

An emotion he has always managed to repress.

'*Sir.*'

Mark holds a hand up, a warning hand.

But he hesitates.

This isn't the time or the place.

210

He steps around the bellhop and quickly makes it over to the door. Avoiding eye contact with Bolger, he leaves.

Less than an hour later, he is pulling into his driveway on Glanmore Road.

In the hall he sees that there's a message on his answering machine. It's from Susan. She wants to know if he's on for tonight. They had a semi-arrangement to go for dinner.

'. . . so anyway, Mark, call me when you get this. I did try you on your mobile, but it was —'

Before the message ends, he reaches down and presses the Erase button.

He takes out his mobile and throws it down, along with his keys, onto the hall table.

He goes into the living room and looks around. The bottle of Bombay is still on the coffee table from the night before. He goes over, picks it up and takes a slug — neat, straight from the bottle. Then he holds the bottle up and examines it.

There's only half of it left, less even — which is not going to be enough.

He lowers his arm and thinks for a moment.

There's red wine in the house. Somewhere. A bottle of Barolo one of his suppliers gave him. He's pretty sure it's in the kitchen, in one of the cupboards.

That'll do.

Then he raises his arm again, slowly, deliberately, and as the bottle makes contact with his lips, he closes his eyes.

'. . . he was a young fella, I don't know, late twenties, early thirties, *Jesus* —'

'Calm down, Larry, would you?'

'No, Paddy, I'm *very* upset. I mean, Christ, I'm under enough pressure as it is, with all this crap in the papers.'

Norton has come outside to take the call. The French doors are open behind him, and he can hear Miriam inside going on about the nation's obsession with reality TV and how *vulgar* it all is.

'What did he say exactly?'

'He asked me about the accident. I don't know. He seemed to be implying that it was *Frank* who caused it.'

It may be chilly out here in the moonlight, but it's nothing compared to the more abstract chill that Norton feels creeping up on him.

'I see.' This comes out almost in a whisper. 'What else did he say?'

'He accused me of covering it up.'

'What did *you* say?'

'I said that that was outrageous. I mean, what else —'

'How did he react?'

'I'm not sure. It all happened very fast. Tim came in, and then he left. He just walked out. We were in the fucking *jacks*, for Christ's sake.'

Norton stares out across the floodlit lawn. 'What did he look like?'

'Well not like a journalist, that's for —'

'Hold on, did he *say* he was a journalist?'

'No, he actually said he wasn't one, but sure what else could he be?'

'Hmm.'

Norton turns, the gravel crunching under his feet. He glances in through the French doors at everyone gathered around the dining table – at the Doyles, the Shanahans, the Gallaghers.

Miriam is still holding forth.

'I don't know, Larry, he probably *was* a journalist. From one of the tabloids. It's the only explanation.' He pauses. 'I mean, Jesus, you're a sitting duck at the moment.'

'Yeah, but this is below the belt.'

'Below the belt is their m.o., it's what they do. They're obviously digging up any old shit they can think of.'

Norton wants this phone call to end.

'The other stuff I can take,' Bolger goes on, 'it's par for the course, but not *this* . . . this is painful. I haven't thought about Frank in a long time, you know.'

'Hmm.'

'I mean . . . he was my *brother* –'

When Norton hears the emotion in Bolger's voice he winces.

'Of course he was, Larry, of course he was.'

'– so I don't know what this sick bastard was mouthing on about.'

'Look,' Norton says, 'you can't let this derail you.'

'No.'

'That's what they want. They're trying to come at you from every angle.' Norton turns again to face the garden. 'Anyway, you did well at the press conference this morning.'

'Yeah? You saw it?'

'Of course.'

Norton proceeds to butter him up over this and then gets off the phone as quickly as he can. But instead of heading straight back in to the dinner party he walks across the gravel and onto the lawn. He wanders down as far as the tennis court.

He stands at the wire fence.

They've had the house for ten years and he's never once been inside the perimeter here, never once set foot on this all-weather acrylic surface.

Because what's a fat fuck like him going to do with a tennis racquet in his hand? That's one thing Miriam has never had her way on. Going to the races he took to like a duck to water. Wine, bridge, paintings, antique fucking furniture, whatever. But not tennis.

He takes a couple of deep breaths. The churning in his stomach hasn't stopped and he can't be sure he isn't going to throw up.

He turns around, leans back against the wire fence and looks up at the moon.

It's him, isn't it?

It has to be.

For the first time Norton has a real sense of how out of control this situation is getting – and it *is* all the same situation, he has no doubt about that.

He holds up his phone, scrolls down to Fitz's number and calls it.

It goes straight into message.

He rolls his eyes. After the tone, he says, 'It's Paddy. Call me in the morning.'

He puts the phone away and walks back up towards the

house – towards the French doors, where from this angle he can see Miriam neatly framed at the head of the table.

He steps onto the gravel.

The men's room in a city-centre hotel?

A *toilet*?

That's not how he ever imagined it happening – not that it necessarily had to happen at all. It didn't.

He walks in through the French doors and smiles at his guests.

Miriam nods at someone over by the entrance to the kitchen.

But if it *did* – Norton continues, a little wistfully, finishing the thought – he had always imagined it happening, somehow, to *him*.

It can't hurt, Gina decides.

She dials Mark Griffin's number and flops down onto the sofa. With her free hand she picks up the remote and flicks off the TV.

She needs to talk to him again. She needs to be blunt. She needs to know if he can help her out or not.

There's always the possibility, of course, that after talking to *her* today, *he's* the one who needs help.

She needs to know that, too.

It's ringing.

With the TV off, the room is dark – city dark, electric dark, light shimmering in from adjoining buildings, from the street below, from traffic – a wash of sombre golds, reds and blues.

The ringing stops and there's a click.

Damn.

Then, 'Sorry I'm not here at the moment, but please leave your name and number after the tone and I'll get back to you.'

Beeeep.

'Er . . . yes, hi, this is Gina Rafferty. From this morning? I just wanted to apologise for –'

Another click.

'*Gina?*'

'Oh. Mark.' She swallows. 'You're there. Hello.'

'Hello.'

'Look, I was saying, I'm . . . I'm sorry about earlier. I didn't mean to upset you or anything, I –'

'It's OK.'

'I felt awful, but the thing is –'

'No, no, don't apologise. You actually . . . you did me a favour.'

'What?'

'A favour . . . you did me a favour.'

Gina presses the phone against her ear. It's hard to tell, but he sounds a little . . . *weird*?

'How did I do that?'

'You opened my eyes. You made me *see.*'

She says nothing to this.

'Really, you did. But you know what? I don't understand how I could have been so *bloody* stupid, and for so *bloody* long.'

It's clear to her now that he has probably – and very understandably – had a few drinks. He's not slurring his words exactly, but there's something different-sounding about him. It's an easy familiarity, a looseness, that wasn't there before.

'Mark, I don't think –'

'I went to see him, this afternoon.'

'You what . . . *who?*'

'Larry Bolger. I went to Leinster House. I didn't go in, but I hung around outside, near the entrance, and after about twenty minutes he and these two other guys came out.'

'Oh my God.'

'And I followed them into Buswell's.'

'Did you *talk* to him?'

'Yeah, I did, and I'll tell you what, he's a smug little bastard, because he just stood there with this *look* on his face . . .'

Sitting in the half-light of her apartment, staring at the blank TV screen, Gina struggles to take this in. 'What did you say to him?'

'I put it to him directly . . . what *you* said this morning.'

'What *I* said?'

'Yeah, I accused him –'

'But, Mark,' she interrupts, suddenly feeling out of her depth here, '*Mark,* Jesus, I didn't say . . .' She hesitates. What exactly *did* she say? 'I didn't . . . look, I didn't tell you this morning that I had evidence, or proof, or anything *like* it. I –'

'Gina?'

'I didn't claim . . . I mean I was just –'

'*Gina?*'

She stops. 'What?'

'*I* have proof.'

She shuffles into an upright position on the sofa, unable to believe what she's just heard. '*What* proof?'

He hesitates. 'Well . . . not *proof* exactly . . .'

Gina groans.

'. . . but I *believe* it, your theory. It explains a lot . . . about Des. You see I . . . I think he knew, or suspected, or . . .'

Gina stares across the room. Who is he talking about? *What* is he talking about?

'. . . but then he didn't, or wasn't able to . . . oh *fuck* it.'

'Mark, are you OK?'

'No. Not really, no.'

Gina gets up off the sofa. As she walks over to the window, she whispers, 'Do you want me to –'

'You know what?' he interrupts. 'You know what I should have done? I should have gone for him while I had the chance. I should have tackled him to the floor . . .'

Gina squeezes her eyes shut.

'. . . and kicked his *fucking* head in.'

What has she unleashed here?

She opens her eyes again and looks down at the river.

'It's just –' he hesitates, but then pushes on, clearly unable to help himself, 'it's just that this all makes perfect sense to me, because it *fits* . . . it fits with the way my uncle was for the last twenty-five years, it fits with the way my aunt is now, it fits with how that smarmy fucker today *looked* at me . . . I . . . I *know* it.'

'OK, OK, *whoa*.' Gina holds a hand up. It's as though he's there in the room, standing right in front of her. 'Please, Mark, listen to me. Don't do anything rash. *Please*.'

He doesn't answer, but she can hear him breathing. She walks back to the sofa and sits down.

His uncle? Is that the Des he mentioned?

'*Mark?*' she says eventually. 'Are you there?'

'Yeah.'

'Can we meet again some time? To *talk* about this?'

'OK.' He pauses. 'Give me your number and *I'll* call *you*. I need time to think.'

She gives him her mobile number.

'And *call* me, OK? Don't leave it too long.'

'OK.'

When she puts the phone down, she rolls sideways and stretches out on the sofa.

What if he's right?

She looks up at the ceiling.

Shit.

Then that means *she* was right.

Six

1

Norton has put his phone on vibrate, but the noise it's now making as it rattles on the glass table in front of him is almost as much of an intrusion as any ringtone would be.

He picks it up and looks at the display.

Fitz.

'I have to take this,' he says and stands up. There are six people sitting around the table – three tax advisers, two lawyers and a management consultant. As Norton turns away, there is a general redeployment of energy in the room, papers get shuffled, throats cleared, water sipped.

Norton says, 'Yeah?'

'How's it going?'

'OK.'

He steps out into reception.

'I got your message,' Fitz says. 'Sorry I couldn't take the call. I was swamped.'

'Right. Anyway, er ... I need –' Norton glances over at the receptionist. 'I need to talk to you about something.'

'OK. But listen, I have an update for you.'

'Oh?' Norton crosses reception and stands at a window looking down onto Baggot Street. It's raining. Traffic is at a standstill. 'What is it?'

'The skinny fella, yeah? He went for coffee yesterday with your one, the sister.'

'*What?*'

'Yeah, she went to the office and then they came out. Went to a coffee shop. About twenty-five minutes in total.'

'You're only fucking telling me this *now*?'

'Look, I just got the report myself.'

'*Fuck.*'

Gina Rafferty talking to Dermot Flynn? Jesus. What is the bitch *up* to?

'Anything else?'

'Yeah, she met some other bloke for coffee as well, earlier, but we don't know who he is.'

Norton swallows and runs his free hand over his head. 'A young guy? Old? What?'

'Thirtyish. Tall, dark. In a suit.'

Feeling as if the room is about to detach itself from under his feet and start spinning, Norton reaches out and leans against the sash of the window. 'We can't talk about this on the phone. Meet me down in the car park.' He looks at his watch. 'In an hour.'

'But –'

'*Don't* fucking start with me, Fitz.'

'Right. Right. OK.'

Norton puts his phone away and walks back towards the boardroom. Since he likes to stay as clearheaded as possible for these financial meetings he didn't take any Narolet this morning as he normally would have. And now he needs some.

Badly.

Standing at the door, he reaches into his pocket for his pillbox. But it's not there. Which means he must have left it at home, on the bedside table maybe, or in his bathroom.

Damn, he thinks, totally distracted now as he re-enters the boardroom.

An hour later he's down in the building's small underground car park. Fitz is sitting next to him.

They sit in silence for a while.

Over the fifteen years that these two men have known each other they have become mutually dependent in ways neither of them is keen to dwell on. Not long after they met, and with Norton's financial backing, Fitz set up High King Security and emerged from his pre-ceasefire chrysalis of republican activism into the open air of so-called legitimate business. The firm specialised in on-site security for the construction industry, and Norton quickly became its principal client. But when new developments in technology nudged High King in the direction of private investigations and electronic surveillance, Norton found himself relying on the company quite a lot, and on Fitz in particular.

Lately, of course, things have moved to another level. They both know this but have yet to have a proper discussion about it. Nevertheless, the two men *do* understand each other: Fitz is no choirboy and still has his connections from the old days; Norton is a hard-nosed pragmatist and not someone to let fools stand in his way.

A vehicle passes behind them, and the interior of the car darkens over momentarily.

All the same, it *is* a little awkward sitting here like this. Because the most glaring aspect of what they haven't discussed yet, and very pointedly, is the terrible fuck-up that led to things getting so complicated in the first place. OK, it was rushed and frantic, no one's arguing with that, and it was Norton who came up with the idea originally – so he's prepared to accept *some* of the blame at least . . .

But my Christ.

There was serious money involved as well.

He stares straight ahead at the dull concrete wall in front of them.

Now isn't the time, though. He needs Fitz. He can't just replace him.

'OK,' he says, 'first the skinny lad, Flynn.'

'Yeah,' Fitz says, shifting his weight in the seat. 'Do you want me to have another word with him? From what I understand he's been acting up a bit lately. Maybe he needs a stronger message. We could take one of his kids for a couple of hours, go for a drive sort of thing, up the Dublin Mountains. *That'd* scare the shit out of him.'

'I don't know.'

Left on his own, Norton thinks, Flynn would probably be safe enough, but with Gina Rafferty *at* him, asking questions, probing, he could easily crack.

She's the problem.

'Leave the kids alone,' he says after a long pause. 'It'd be messy. You'd only be asking for trouble.'

'Right.'

'Keep it simple. But have a word with him all the same.'

'Right.'

'So.' He exhales. 'The sister. What's the story there? Any joy with the mobile calls?'

'Yeah, I finally got this new piece of kit I was telling you about, it's amazing, about the size of a laptop. You target someone's phone, right? Then you can listen in, record calls, download texts and emails. It's fucking brilliant.'

'How does it work?'

Fitz shrugs his shoulders. 'I dunno. How does anything work these days? You install the software and that's it, off you go.'

'Yeah, but . . . do you have to insert anything in *her* phone, or get –'

'Ah, Jaysus no, no. It's all remote. It picks up the signal. It's got this sniper antenna thing on it. For long-distance use. So you can be anything up to seven or eight hundred yards away.'

'OK. Good.'

Norton is still annoyed about the Narolet, and as a result is feeling massively irritated by everything – by Fitz here beside him, by the texture of his own suit, by the colour of the car's leather upholstery, by the fact that it's Tuesday. He *needs* his pills. As soon as he has a chance, he thinks, he's going to have to drive out home and get them.

'Anyway,' he goes on, still looking straight ahead, 'I want you to keep a *very* close eye on her from now on.'

'Yeah. No problem.'

'And listen. There's someone else I want you to keep an eye on. I think it might be that other fella you mentioned, the one she met earlier.'

Norton's voice has a slight tremor in it. He finds this, in equal measure, embarrassing and annoying.

He's not sure how noticeable it is.

'Right,' Fitz says, seemingly oblivious, and taking a small notebook out of his pocket. 'What can you tell me about him? Shoot.'

2

The Dáil chamber is packed for Leaders' Questions, and there's an air of excitement about the place that you normally wouldn't get unless something major was in the offing. In the front row of the government benches, three seats along from the Taoiseach, Larry Bolger sits stony-faced, keenly aware of the cameras, keenly aware that he'll be in frame whenever the Taoiseach is speaking. On the other side of the chamber, opposition party leaders limber up, consult their notes, confer with colleagues.

These will be key exchanges this afternoon and may even have a bearing on the outcome of the next election. They'll certainly have a bearing on Bolger's future. A lot will depend, of course, on how the Taoiseach chooses to play it. Most commentators agree he's in a very difficult position and has only two options. In the first, he comes on strong and hangs the minister out to dry. This addresses the issue at hand *and* sees off a challenger, making him look strong and decisive. But it's also quite risky because what if he comes on *too* strong? What if he appears disloyal or even vindictive? As well as bringing Bolger down, he could very well take a serious hit himself. In the second option – the path of least resistance – he gives his unequivocal support to the minister. But this is also inherently risky for the Taoiseach because it means he'd be throwing a lifeline to someone who everyone knows has been plotting against *him* for months. And that would only make him look weak.

Clearly, this second option is what Bolger wants, and needs – though there isn't much he can do to bring it about now. Apart, that is, from sitting there with a serious look on his face.

And regardless of how he does *that*, he'll still be perceived in a variety of different ways – as defiant, or contrite, or reflective, or baffled, or bored even.

All of which, in a sense, he is.

Not to mention exhausted, and anxious, and *angry*.

As the leader of the main opposition party gets to his feet and starts framing a predictably labyrinthine question for the Taoiseach, Bolger fixes his gaze on a section of carpet in the middle of the floor. To look at him you would think he was concentrating hard on the question being asked, analysing and parsing it, but in fact his thoughts are elsewhere. What he's doing – and has been doing all day – is analysing and parsing the brief, cryptic conversation he had the previous evening in Buswell's Hotel.

Because he's extremely upset about it. It's not the fact of being accosted in a toilet that's troubling him; it's the shocking and downright scandalous reference to his brother. Initially, and after speaking to Paddy Norton, he dismissed it as a tabloid hack's calculated attempt to provoke him. But later on he wasn't so sure. On reflection, the young man didn't seem like a hack at all. There was something odd about him, something tentative, a nervousness that didn't square with the lizardlike weariness you get with most working journalists.

Later still, when he was in bed and unable to sleep, Bolger gave some thought to the charge itself. Once again, he dismissed it out of hand – but as he lay there in the dark, as he tossed and turned, it kept re-forming in his mind.

Inevitably, it gained a certain traction.

The thing is, Bolger's recollection of that whole period is patchy at best. He wasn't even around when the accident took place – he was a junior associate for a legal firm in Boston, a

job he'd got through a cousin of his mother's a couple of years
earlier – so his take on the event is the received one, i.e. what
happened was a simple road accident, a tragedy, a statistic. He
was very upset of course, but by the time he got back from the
States pretty much everything had been settled and it was
straight into the funeral. Almost immediately after that, he was
taken in hand by the party, and the grooming process began.

At the time, Bolger had a sense that he was being shielded
from certain things, that information was being carefully
managed, not to say manipulated. Nevertheless, he does have a
vague recollection of someone mentioning alcohol, and in
reference to the driver of the other car.

But then last night in the toilet of a hotel, and according to
this total stranger . . . it was *Frank* all of a sudden? *Frank* was
the one who was drunk? The one who caused the accident?

It was certainly the first time Bolger had ever heard this.
Even though the idea, if he thinks about it, is hardly out-
landish. Back in those days it was common practice for people
to drink and drive – three, four, five pints, whatever – it was
almost expected, and Frank, like anyone, was fond of a jar,
so . . .

Bolger stops.

He knows full well what's at work here. It's the insidious
nature of rumour and hearsay. It's the impulse to believe, the
instinctive rush to judgement, the feeling that if someone says
something to your face, and with conviction . . . then it *must* be
true.

It's a dynamic, after all, that on a professional level Bolger is
familiar with.

He glances around the chamber. The opposition leader is
shaking a finger in the direction of the government benches.

'And *furthermore,* let me put *this* to the Taoiseach . . .'

Bolger can see the sprays of spittle from here.

His own mouth feels thick and grainy. He didn't get much sleep last night, and he's been drinking coffee non-stop since he got up.

He shifts his weight in the seat.

In any case, if it *is* true about Frank, he can understand why they kept quiet about it, at least on one level – because *he* wouldn't be sitting here in this chamber today if they hadn't.

But what if the story gets resurrected now? It would be awful, a PR disaster. Even though it'd be impossible to prove, a story like this, a sort of Chappaquiddick by proxy, would in all likelihood scupper any chances Bolger had of bouncing back from the current crisis.

But what he *really* can't get his head around – and it's been working on him like a slow burn since late the previous evening – is how this rewrites everything, and not just the facts, the circumstances surrounding a terrible tragedy; it rewrites his own personal history, his reasons for going into politics in the first place.

Actually, talk about a slow burn.

That one's been working on him for the best part of twenty-five years – resentment of his father for putting so much pressure on him, frustration at a career he never truly 'owned', a sense of loss for the life he could have led, and in fact *had* been leading, over there in Boston.

It pains him to think of it even now, of how young he was, and idealistic, and of how *stimulated* by everything he was: the summer heat, the atmosphere around Cambridge, the exotic fare on offer at Faneuil Hall (exotic back then, to *him*), his apartment on Comm Ave, his colleagues at the law firm, the conversations, the women he met.

To say nothing of the money he could have earned.

Larry really wanted to stay, and if he had known the truth, the alleged truth at any rate, about Frank – that he got into his car that night drunk as a fucking lord and killed all those people as well as himself, he *would have* stayed. He would have had the moral advantage, the leverage to resist, the courage to stand up to his old man.

It could all have been so different. So is it any wonder that along the way he went off the rails a bit?

Across the chamber, the opposition leader concludes what one editorial will later call 'not so much a question as a Kalashnikov-hail of bullet points'.

He sits down. The Taoiseach gets up.

In a reflex reaction, Bolger and others around him adjust themselves in their seats.

The Taoiseach clears his throat.

Bolger braces himself.

Regardless of which way it goes for him here today, he intends to follow this other business up. He intends to make discreet enquiries. Look at the records. Talk to people. Maybe he'll even go out to Wicklow, to the nursing home, and talk to the old man.

He needs to know the truth.

He turns his head slightly to the right and refocuses.

'Before I answer your, er, question, Deputy,' the Taoiseach begins, 'I'd like to state for the record that Laurence D. Bolger is a public servant of the highest calibre, a man of integrity and an esteemed colleague . . .'

3

He sees them approaching from the other end of Ashleaf Avenue and his heart starts pounding. It's nearly nine o'clock and already quite dark, but it's the suburbs, and in the orange glow of the streetlights the two figures are clearly visible.

Dermot slows down and swallows.

Something like this was inevitable, and in a weird, alternative-universe kind of way he almost welcomes it. He recognises the guy on the left. He's the one with the small beady eyes and the denim jacket – except he's not wearing the denim jacket this evening, he's wearing an overcoat. The guy on the right is tall and is wearing a tracksuit.

Dermot is walking home, briefcase in hand, up the few hundred yards from the DART station. These days he leaves work as late as he can to minimise contact time with Claire and the girls – which he knows is ridiculous, and unsustainable, but it's a survival mechanism.

He quickly looks behind him, and then around. The road is quiet. Leafy. Deserted.

Oh God.

Just up ahead there is a right turn off Ashleaf Avenue – onto Ashleaf Drive – where Dermot lives, halfway down, on the left.

He can't believe this. If he maintains his current pace, they're all going to converge on the corner.

So . . . should he turn around? Should he head back towards the train station?

He feels sick.

'*Dermot?*'

And what do they want? Is it because they saw him talking to Gina Rafferty? It has to be.

The guy with the beady eyes – a few paces ahead of his partner now – is strutting towards the opposite corner.

Dermot gulps and swallows back some vomit.

He's a fucking coward and he hates himself for it. In fact, over the last few weeks he has experienced the emotion of self-hatred more intensely, more completely, than he's ever experienced any other emotion in his entire life – more so even than his grief at the death of his mother, or his love for Claire, or his exhilaration at the births of his two daughters.

Which strikes him as pathetic, not to say unforgivable.

Nevertheless, as the guy with beady eyes steps off the pavement and onto the road, something unexpected kicks in.

Dermot realises that there is no way he is going to allow either of these two guys onto Ashleaf Drive, let alone anywhere *near* his family.

He looks to his left.

Across the road, between two large semi-detached houses there is a narrow walled laneway that leads out onto Bristol Terrace.

He makes a run for it, knowing they will follow him.

Within seconds he is in the laneway, sprinting, panting, resisting the urge to look around.

'Hey! Stop! *HEY!*'

Unable to gauge from this how far behind him they are, Dermot gives in for a split second – but as he's turning he puts all his weight into flinging the briefcase in his hand backwards and hopefully right into the path of the two men. As he withdraws his arm, he catches a glimpse of the guy in the overcoat. He then hears a *thwack* and takes it to be the briefcase making contact with the chest or shoulder of the guy in the tracksuit. It is followed by a loud, '*Ow . . . bollocks.*'

Seconds later Dermot emerges from the dim laneway, but he's going so fast that he can't make a smooth turn and is forced, in a wide arc, out onto the road.

There is a roaring in his eardrums. Which is what? The rush of blood to his head? Maybe, he doesn't know, but through it, in the middle of it, he hears a voice, 'Wait . . . wait . . . *WAIT*.'

He hears another sound, too, in the background, like some kind of overlay, but he never gets to identify it as the hum of an engine because he slips in a streak of oil on the road and falls sideways, his head colliding with the polished chrome bull bars of an oncoming SUV.

4

The next morning, just before twelve, Mark Griffin arrives at his aunt Lilly's, but instead of pulling into her driveway, as he normally would, he parks out on the street – a few houses down and on the opposite side. He remains in the car. He has a clear view of the front door. He waits. It's a bright, chilly morning and everything on this tree-lined suburban street is dappled in sunlight. Mark is relieved not to be hungover, as he was the previous day, but he still feels awful – sick, anxious, barely human.

After a while, Aunt Lilly emerges from the house. She shuts the door behind her and walks down the driveway. She's wearing her navy overcoat and a paisley headscarf. She has a carrier bag folded under her arm. She turns left at the gate and heads in the direction of the shops, which are about a fifteen-minute walk away.

Mark stares across at her as she passes. He then looks in the wing mirror and tracks her until she disappears from view.

A couple of minutes after that, he lets himself into the house. He goes upstairs and straight into the small room at the back that his uncle used as an office. There is a table with a PC on it, a chair, a filing cabinet, a wardrobe and a stack of boxes – some of which are the ones Aunt Lilly had been going through that day down in the kitchen.

He opens the first drawer of the filing cabinet and starts flicking through it. He knows vaguely what he's looking for. It's something he remembered yesterday, out of the blue – something he overheard his uncle referring to once, many years ago. Mark was curious at the time but he never gave it much thought afterwards. The occasion was a Christmas party or a birthday celebration, and his uncle was talking to . . . someone. In the living room. Mark doesn't recall exactly. All he remembers is him saying, 'No, no, me and Tony were very different. He was the good-looking one.' This got a laugh, and then his uncle added, 'I have a bunch of old photos upstairs. I must dig them out sometime.'

These words came back to Mark yesterday in the middle of what was a searing hangover, so it took him a while to process them. But when he did, finally, it was like waking up from an oppressive dream, and one that had lasted for years.

He opens the second drawer of the filing cabinet.

He never wanted to see the photos before, and maybe for good reason. Fine. But now he does. *Now* he's excited at the prospect, feverish almost.

When the third drawer yields nothing, he moves on to the wardrobe. As he opens it, he glances at his watch and tries to calculate how much time he's got. There's no reason why he couldn't be doing this with Aunt Lilly in the house, downstairs, working in the kitchen – she wouldn't object to anything he wanted to do, and he wouldn't have to explain himself – but he's so agitated at the moment that he doesn't think he'd be able to deal with her, talk to her, *look* at her even.

At the bottom of the wardrobe there are some old shoe boxes. He lifts these up and places them on the table. He removes the lid from the first one.

Photographs.

There are hundreds of them, some loose, some in packets. Most of them are of places in Italy: the Pantheon, the Colosseum, Mount Vesuvius, the Grand Canal, churches, palazzos, piazzas, vineyards. Uncle Des and Aunt Lilly feature in a lot of them, separately and together. Mark himself is in some of them, pale and gawpy-looking. The second box is the same. In the third box he finds a plastic bag, folded over and sealed with tape. He peels off the tape and opens the bag. Inside it is a padded brown envelope. Inside the envelope are more loose photos, dozens of them.

Upending the envelope, Mark pours the photos out onto the table and sees at once that these are what he came for. Using his arm, he shoves the keyboard of the computer as well as the three shoe boxes sideways and onto the floor. He spreads the photos out, face up, as many as he can fit on the surface of the table. His hands are shaking. These photos are older than the Italian ones. The colour in a lot of them has faded. Some are in black and white.

Most of them are of his father.

Tony Griffin.

Some of them – colour ones – feature his mother, Marie,

and his sister, Lucy. He's even in some of them himself – as a very small child.

Mark steps back and gazes down at this random collage – at his father, pencil thin in a suit and tie, standing outside the old Adelphi Cinema on Abbey Street; at the whole family on a beach, blue skies in the background, towels and sandcastles in the foreground; at his parents in a gaudy seventies-style living room, holding hands and smiling; at himself and Lucy, both impossibly small, enfolded in their father's arms . . . the three of them on a lawn somewhere, in a garden . . .

A garden? *Their* garden?

Mark takes another step backwards.

He doesn't remember any of this, any of these places. Jesus, he doesn't even really *recognise* his mother. He knows it's her, because . . . it can *only* be her, it –

He takes in a gulp of air. This becomes a sob, a loud one, and then a series of them . . .

He puts his hands up to his head.

This is his family. These are people whose very existence he's been more or less denying for years, out of an irrational and misplaced sense of shame. But now, through a film of tears, he *looks* at them, goes from the first photo here to the last – and each one, in its own way, is a shock, each one a revelation.

He looks at his sister, a spindly young girl bristling with energy and intelligence; he looks at his mother, a woman who seems to be at just that point in her life when the early flush of having kids has caught up on her, and suddenly she's weary . . . but still glamorous, still holding on . . .

Above all, though, he looks at his father – younger in most of these photos than Mark himself is now, yet somehow older-looking, more grown-up – and it just hits him in the gut . . .

he's known it for days, but he feels it now . . . this man was wronged, he *was* made into a scapegoat. Mark isn't being naive here, he realises values were different back then, attitudes were different, but at the same time not everyone was reckless and irresponsible, not everyone was capable of putting their family in mortal danger for the sake of a lousy few pints.

This man wasn't.

Mark is sure of it. But his name was blackened nonetheless . . . in order to protect someone else's reputation. And as a result Mark's own life – slowly, relentlessly – was contaminated as well . . . polluted with lies, and with toxic silence, and with guilt . . .

He walks out of the room, crosses the hall and goes into the bathroom.

He lunges at the toilet bowl and throws up.

Gina's not used to being at home like this on a weekday morning. It feels strange. She's sitting at the breakfast bar in her kitchen, dressed for work but with no intention of going to work, or even of leaving the apartment. What she's doing is waiting for the phone to ring, and has been since Monday night – since her conversation with Mark Griffin.

It was her mobile number she gave him, so there's nothing keeping her in the apartment. But this morning, for some reason, she dreads the thought of going out, of having to negotiate crowded streets, and traffic, and people . . .

She looks around. Objects in the living room that should be familiar to her seem slightly alien, even a little threatening. The light coming in from outside, a muted, late-autumnal grey, feels uncommonly bleak.

Nothing seems to be in proportion.

Gina thinks she might be on the cusp of a nervous break-down – or would be, if she weren't so *bloody* self-aware. Because she knows exactly what's going on here. She has deferred the grieving process – parked it, but left the motor running. And in the absence of any conclusive evidence about what actually happened to Noel she's had to suppress a whole range of emotions, especially anger. Throw a little denial into the mix, about the future of Lucius Software say, and you have the ingredients for a panic attack.

But her heart isn't racing, she isn't dizzy, she doesn't have a dry mouth.

Not yet, anyway.

She reaches across the counter for her phone.

The thing is, either she succumbs to this incipient . . . what-ever it is, breakdown, depression, collapse, or she just keeps pushing and doesn't give in. She does whatever it takes to move on from this. Because Gina *would* like to move on. She'd like to grieve. She'd like to come to terms with the loss of her only brother. She'd like to stop having to ask all these questions. She'd like to look in the mirror and recognise the person she sees there.

She'd also like to meet Sophie for lunch and talk about movies, talk about *shoes*.

But none of that, she knows, is going to happen for some time.

Gina flicks open the phone and calls Mark Griffin's home number. Once more she gets through to his answering machine. Once more she rings off without leaving a message.

She'll try again later.

Because if they're both right about this, then they really need to talk.

Next, she scrolls down through her phone list. She has three numbers entered for Noel – home, mobile and work. She calls the third one.

This has been nagging at her since the other day. It doesn't really fit in with the Larry Bolger scenario, but the more she thinks about it, the more it needs to be explained. Neurotic behavior is one thing. This was different. This was off the charts.

'Good morning, BCM, can I help you?'

'Yes, good morning,' Gina says, adopting her no-nonsense office voice. 'Can you put me through to Dermot Flynn, please?'

When Mark has finished throwing up, he staggers over to the washbasin and turns on the cold tap. He rinses his mouth out and splashes water on his face.

When he looks up and meets his reflection in the mirror, something occurs to him.

Why *was* Uncle Des always so angry? Up to now the working assumption has been that he never forgave himself for something that happened in the days following the crash. It was put about that Tony had been drunk at the wheel, which Des must have known to be highly unlikely, so either he said nothing at all, or he raised objections . . . but was told to shut up.

And did. For the rest of his life.

Why, though? Was he threatened, intimidated? Did he not have the balls to stand up to them?

Or maybe it was something else.

Again – like the rest of it – this is only speculation. But the more Mark thinks about it, the more it makes sense. Because Uncle Des's anger wasn't directed at other people – it was directed at himself. In fact, there was probably quite a thin line, where Des was concerned, between anger and self-reproach, between anger and self-*loathing*.

Mark goes back into the little office room. He turns to the stack of boxes containing the documents Aunt Lilly was sorting through the other week. He opens the first one and pulls out a thick wad of ESB and Bord Gáis bills, hundreds of them. After a moment he drops these back in the box, pushes the box aside and opens the next one down. It contains miscellaneous papers, tax certificates, letters, God knows what. The third box contains the bank statements.

Standing there, Mark thumbs through wads and wads of these, going back ten, fifteen, twenty years. He doesn't know what he's looking for, and he certainly doesn't come across anything that jumps out at him – no large, unexplained deposits, for example. But is that really what he thinks? That they paid him off, that they bought his silence? That he accepted their offer . . . both of the money *and* of the life sentence that came with it – twenty-five years of silence, of bitterness, of corrosive guilt?

Maybe – except there's nothing here to back this up. And would he find it anyway? Would that kind of payment show up on a normal bank statement?

Mark doesn't have a clue.

Probably not, he thinks.

And that's when he spots it.

The address. It changes. On the bank statements. From one month to the next. In April, Des and Lilly are at an address in Broadstone – and then suddenly in May they're living here in Clontarf.

The accident happened in January.

Of the same year.

Mark looks around. He looks through the door and along the hallway. He's always taken it for granted, this place where he grew up. It's a large, detached redbrick Victorian house. It has four bedrooms, off-street parking, rear access and a substantial back garden. It's ordinary enough, but twenty-five years ago it would have been a *very* dramatic trade-up from what had probably been a pokey little terraced house in Broadstone.

Mark feels his stomach lurch again.

There could be a hundred explanations for this, but –

He lets the wad of statements he's holding slip from his hands. Loose pages fan out and glide, landing everywhere.

Uncle Des was a low-ranking civil servant on a very modest income. So how could he possibly have afforded to buy a house like this?

What happened?

Mark bends down and retrieves a few of the pages. Then he picks up a few more. He examines these closely, looking from one to the next, flicking them back and forth.

He swallows, feeling an uncomfortable lump in his throat.

Before May there were monthly mortgage repayments, presumably on the property in Broadstone. After May – it appears – these just stopped.

Mark lets go of the pages and stands up again.

They could easily have inherited the house from a relative and then sold the other one.

But no. Mark shakes his head. The timing is too much of a coincidence.

They fucking *bought* his silence.

Come on, Des, they probably said, *stop this, would you? Leave it alone. There's no point. And anyway, think of the boy, think of his future . . . we could maybe help you out there, you know . . .*

Mark turns to face the window. He stares out at the long garden and thinks back to when he was a kid. He never really wanted for anything, did he? His uncle and aunt sent him to good schools. They took him on all those trips to Italy. Later, when he was at college, they bought him his first car.

He swallows again.

They helped him out when he was setting up his business.

They *gave* him the deposit on his house.

He closes his eyes.

Jesus Christ.

It was blood money. And they used *him* as a bargaining chip. Which means that his whole life, his education, his career, everything . . . it's all been based on lies, on blood, on his own *family's* blood.

He takes out his mobile phone.

And when Mark thinks *they,* of course he means *him.* He means Larry Bolger . . .

Standing there but looking out the window, he calls the number he got the other day from directory enquiries. When he gets through to the department press office he asks – politely, in a controlled voice – if someone could tell him what public engagements the minister has on for the rest of the day.

Then he turns back around and looks down. He selects three of the photos from the table and puts them into his jacket pocket. He walks out of the room and goes downstairs. But instead of leaving straightaway, he hesitates. He stands on the bottom step, with his hand on the banister.

Please, Mark, listen to me. Don't do anything rash.

After a moment, he turns and goes into the kitchen. Over by

the cooker, he pulls open a drawer that contains various trays of cutlery. He rummages around and selects a knife, a big one. It has a laminated wood handle, a long, narrow stainless-steel blade and a curved tip.

It is used – he thinks – for filleting fish.

He opens his jacket, but there isn't anywhere for him to put it.

Using the blade of the knife, he makes a rip in the jacket's silk lining. He slips the knife inside and then lets the jacket hang loosely to see how it feels.

It feels fine.

On his way out, he glances at himself in the hall mirror to see how it looks.

It looks fine, too.

'Oh my God.'

Gina is off the stool now, her free hand flat on the counter, pressing down.

'Yes, we're all in shock here,' the BCM receptionist is saying. 'I mean, it's just awful. No one can believe it.'

Gina doesn't know what to say.

'And of course, as well,' the receptionist continues, 'coming so soon after your brother.'

Gina winces. She turns around and leans back against the counter. 'So . . . you're saying it was an *accident*?'

'Yeah, he stepped out onto the road, near where he lives apparently, and didn't see the car coming.'

People die on our roads every day of the week.

Gina closes her eyes. 'And did, er . . .' This isn't the first question that occurs to her, but she asks it anyway. 'Did he have any family?'

'Yes. A wife and two little girls.'

'Jesus.'

'Yeah, I know.'

'*Jesus.*'

Gina doesn't ask any more questions.

When she gets off the phone, she walks over to the window and looks out. There's been a break in the cloud cover. Crisp sunlight has replaced the grey of a few minutes earlier. But it's not going to last.

It never does.

Gina shakes her head.

Another accident. What are the odds? Way too long for comfort. Which means that she *was* right before – this doesn't fit in with the Larry Bolger scenario. Her whole thing with him was based on . . . what? Very little really. It was supposition. It was tenuous and fanciful. It was wishful thinking. *This* is still supposition, but it makes a lot more sense. The two men worked in the same office, they worked on the same projects and they both died a couple of weeks apart in what appeared to be road accidents. There is good reason to believe, however, that Noel was actually murdered. And it also seems clear to Gina – in retrospect anyway, from the little she saw of him the other day – that Dermot Flynn was walking around in fear for his life.

She turns away from the window.

So there must have been something going on at BCM. Big international firm? Contracts worth billions every year? *They'd* go to any lengths to protect their interests, wouldn't they?

She holds her breath. The idea is simultaneously horrifying and exciting.

But then, letting go, she deflates.

Because . . .

What? Sensitive information got leaked? By accident? Deliberately? There was an 'impropriety' – something financial, something personal even? The scandal had to be covered up, and not everyone was prepared to cooperate?

Gina groans.

Whatever it might be, what chance does someone like her, a complete outsider, have of finding out? Who does she talk to? How does she even broach the subject? What kind of attitude does she adopt? What kind of vocabulary does she use?

And how soon, in the face of implacable corporate self-preservation, does she fold?

It occurs to Gina that maybe what's required here is a countervailing force – someone with the authority to ask awkward questions and demand answers, someone with a ready-made attitude and vocabulary of their own.

Jackie Merrigan?

Although the detective superintendent wasn't exactly sympathetic to the idea that Noel's death was anything other than an accident, maybe when he factors in Dermot Flynn's untimely passing, Gina thinks, *then* he'll –

But before she can complete the thought, something else occurs to her.

Where does all of this leave Mark Griffin?

She rushes over to the counter and picks up her mobile. She calls his number again, and waits.

As before, the answering machine comes on.

Damn.

'Mark, hi,' she says. 'It's Gina Rafferty. Please call me.' She repeats her own mobile number. 'Please. It's urgent. I think I might be wrong about . . . you know, what we were saying the other night. So call me, OK?' She pauses. 'And listen, whatever you do, don't . . . don't . . . just *call* me, OK?'

It takes Mark just under an hour to get to the Garryowen Business Institute in Terenure. Set in old church grounds – half of which have been redeveloped for residential use – the Institute consists of three single-storey modern buildings. There is a parking area to the front and a large playing field to the side. The parking area is more than half full, and Mark finds a space not too far from the main gates. He stays in the car after he has parked it, and looks around. This campus may be fairly nondescript, but the Institute has a reputation for churning out successful young entrepreneurs and future business leaders. Today it is hosting an IT conference, and the minister is due to address the delegates at half past two.

Mark looks at his watch.

It's 2.17.

He shifts in the seat.

Driving out here he was aware all the time of the knife concealed in the lining of his jacket – he could feel it pressing against his side. He can feel it now.

He looks around again.

There are a few people gathered at the entrance to the largest of the three buildings. They could be a reception committee. Or smokers. Mark can't quite see from this distance.

Another car – the second or third since he arrived – comes through the gates behind him and cruises around looking for a parking space.

Mark glances at his watch again: 2.21.

He puts his hand into his jacket pocket and takes out the

three photographs. He glances at each of them in turn, but tentatively, as though afraid he'll *react* again. But he doesn't feel anything – except a curious sense that his emotions, as well as his reason, have been fast-tracked, heightened to a pitch where he's no longer conscious of them. He feels that he's now operating without any guidance system, that his internal GPS has been deactivated.

In the distance he hears seagulls squawking.

He puts the photographs back into his pocket. He opens the door of the car and gets out. He straightens up and automatically buttons his jacket – then remembers, and unbuttons it again.

He glances around. There is no one nearby. He reaches into the slit in the lining of his jacket, takes the knife by the handle and partially withdraws it.

He looks down. He tests his grip on the handle. When he's satisfied, he eases it back in.

He starts walking very slowly towards the main building.

Thick grey clouds are gathering, and it seems as if it could rain at any second. The trees along the far side of the playing field – a straight line of tall evergreens – are swaying in the wind.

Mark doesn't look back, but he's aware of another car – or cars, maybe – coming in through the gates behind him. A moment later, a black Mercedes glides by on the driveway. It is followed by another car, a silver Opel. The two cars pull up at the main building, the ministerial car flush with the entrance.

More people have gathered, and as Mark gets closer he sees that it *is* a reception committee – made up, no doubt, of students, lecturers, administrative staff and conference delegates.

Two men get out of the second car first. They are in their late thirties or early forties, and are obviously Special Branch. One of them, medium height, thin, and with a moustache, walks forward and opens the back door of the Merc. The other one, tall and burly, goes straight inside the building.

The minister gets out and is greeted by a man in glasses and a grey suit – the Director of the Institute presumably.

Mark has walked to the edge of the parking area and approaches the little gathering from behind. He moves through it and within seconds is at the front – barely three yards away from the minister, who is standing with his arms folded, nodding, listening to the Director of the Institute.

Mark studies the Special Branch detective. He is standing next to the minister, and is doubtless armed – but Mark has the advantage here because no one will be expecting anything . . . because no one, surely, looks on this as any kind of a security risk. The scene, in any case, is informal, it's relaxed, with the minister and the director – clearly for the benefit of those gathered around – engaging in some good-natured banter.

'That's right, the Venture Capital Symposium. Yes, I remember now. Lord, that must be, what –'

'Two years ago.'

'*Two?*'

Mark closes his eyes.

'I'm afraid so, Minister. *Tempus fugit,* as the man said.'

'Well, let me tell you, if greying hair and stomach ulcers are any index to go by, it feels a lot longer than *that.*'

This gets a generous laugh, and as Mark lets the sound of it wash over him he tries to visualise the next twenty seconds – to see himself pulling out the knife and lunging forward, driving the blade into the minister's side, twisting it, shoving it up as far as it will go. Then releasing it and withdrawing. Then bedlam, maybe a gunshot or two, the minister falling forward into the arms of the director, both of them staggering sideways for a moment before falling over. Then the Special Branch man and others grabbing Mark, like in a loose scrum, forcing him down, pinning him to the ground.

Screams, groans, chaos.

Blood.

Mark opens his eyes. Now is the time to move. But his arm feels leaden all of a sudden. *He* feels leaden. It's like an anaesthetic taking effect . . . those final few moments before you go under.

As he stares at the minister, in profile, Mark realises that this isn't going to happen – that he can't do it. So he just stands there, paralysed, disorientated, watching the next twenty seconds unfold for real – though in slow motion it seems, in silence: the director raising an arm and mouthing *Shall we?* at the minister, then guiding him towards the entrance to the building . . . the Special Branch man following close behind, the small crowd moving forward as well, people shuffling through the door, disappearing in twos and threes.

Then, from one second to the next, everyone has gone, and Mark is standing alone, out in the open.

Holding his breath.

Eventually, he exhales. His whole body is trembling. The anger is still there, still raging inside him, but its power has been undercut by an awful, creeping, undeniable sense of relief.

After a few more seconds, he puts a hand out to feel the first, tentative drops of rain, and turns to go – at which point he sees that he's *not* alone.

Standing a couple of yards away, and looking directly at him, is a tall man in jeans and a green parka. 'Have a word there, boss?'

Mark looks at him, confused. 'Sorry . . . what?'

'I need to have a *word* with you.' The man then indicates to the right, with his hand, as though inviting Mark into an office.

Mark shakes his head. He moves away, and quickly, to the left, towards the parking area. The raindrops are more persistent now and he can feel them on his face.

The man follows him.

Mark thinks rapidly. He's done nothing wrong here. He's got a knife concealed in his jacket, but that's just what it is, *concealed* – no one knows it's there. Besides, this man doesn't look like . . . anything. He doesn't look like a security guard, and he certainly doesn't look like a cop.

So who is he, and what does he want?

'Hold on there,' the man says. 'Slow the fuck down, would you?'

'Look,' Mark shouts over his shoulder, 'what do you want?'

'Just stop for a bleedin' second and I'll tell you.'

Mark reaches the last row of cars before the playing field begins. He turns left. His own car is parked at the end.

The man is right behind him now.

Half glancing back, Mark says, 'Get away . . . get *away* from me.'

Then his right foot catches on something, and he stumbles forward. He reaches out to try and keep his balance, but there isn't anything there to hold on to. He falls to the ground, careful as he lands to sweep his jacket back. He then rolls sideways and just about manages to sit up. But the tall man is standing there, towering over him. Mark leans back on one hand and holds his other hand out in front of him.

'*Jesus,*' he says, and glances over his shoulder. There's no one around. All he can see is parked cars. It's also raining properly now, and getting heavier by the second.

'OK,' the tall man says, 'you fucking keep away from *him*, right?' He points in the direction of the buildings they've just come from. '*Right?*'

'Yeah, yeah.' Mark's head is spinning. He attempts to get to his feet, holding one hand out to protect himself. 'Just let me get up.' But the man steps forward and in a quick, efficient manoeuvre tackles him back to the ground.

On his knees now, Mark leans forward and groans.

'You don't approach him,' the man is saying, 'you don't talk to him, you don't *contact* him. That clear?'

Mark stays hunched forward, covering his stomach with both arms.

'You *got* that, prickface?'

Mark looks up and makes eye contact. He opens his mouth as though he's about to say something, but in that same moment – and still on his knees – he draws the knife from the lining of his jacket and lunges forward, aiming at the man's thigh. He sticks the knife in and pushes it hard. Then, using the handle of the knife for leverage, he pulls himself up. As he does so he feels the blade tearing deeper into flesh. The man screams out in agony. Mark lets go of the knife and stands back.

The man staggers sideways and slumps against the nearest car. He clutches the knife with his left hand and bangs on the roof of the car with his right. This triggers the alarm. He slides his hand off the roof and brings it down to his side.

Mark turns and runs towards his own car. A couple of seconds before he reaches it, he hears a sound – it's loud and sharp, but with the pounding in his ears, and the adrenaline pumping, and the wind, and the alarm, not easy to identify. At the same time, from behind – but without making the obvious connection – he *feels* something . . . an aggressive dig in the back, like the sensation of being shoved forward in a crowd. As a result of this, he stumbles and falls to his knees, but he immediately struggles up again and lunges for the car door. He opens it, gets in and looks back.

The man is glaring at him. 'Bastard!' he shouts. 'You're bleedin' dead!'

He then hops forward on one leg and raises his right arm.

There seems to be something in his hand.

In a blind rush, Mark pulls the door shut, starts the car, backs onto the driveway, turns and accelerates. As he approaches the main gates, he slows down and looks in the rearview mirror – but with the rain pelting down now he isn't able to see anything clearly.

A few seconds later, in any case, he's out on the main road, heading towards Terenure. It's only then, as he tries to get his breathing under control, that he gives it any consideration – this sudden, intense throbbing in his side, this *pain* – and that it dawns on him what is causing it.

'Hold please.'

Gina watches the first raindrops hit the windowpane. She can actually see the shower approaching, almost in its entirety, sweeping in from the other side of the city. In five or ten minutes it will have passed and it might even be sunny again.

This is no climate for a sane person to live in. Which maybe explains a lot.

'Hello?'

'Yes?'

'I'm afraid Detective Superintendent Merrigan is away for the day.'

'Oh.'

'He's due back tomorrow. But if you'd like to leave a message?'

Gina considers this. 'No, that's OK,' she says. 'Thanks.'

She places the phone on the window ledge and walks over to the sofa. She picks up one of the newspapers that has been lying there since Sunday. She looks through it, page by page, until she finds what she's looking for. At the bottom of the editorial page there is a small box with the paper's contact details in it.

She goes back over to the window. Sheets of rain are now pelting against it, and the city below is little more than a kinetic, impressionistic blur.

She picks up the phone. She's never done this before, spoken to a journalist, not in this way, and she isn't clear in her mind how she should approach it.

When she gets through, she asks to speak to John O'Driscoll.

'Please hold.'

There is a click and then an electronic version of 'Summertime' comes on.

Gina is nervous. She takes a deep breath.

O'Driscoll is a political reporter. She's read his stuff over the years. He's seems reasonable enough, objective, sane even.

But who knows?

As she waits, the sound of the driving rain merges in her mind with the desecrated Gershwin coming down the phone line.

Eventually, after what seems like ages, O'Driscoll comes on. 'Yep?'

5

As Paddy Norton walks out of the pharmacy, he feels he has a true understanding of what it is to be schizophrenic. OK, not in the strict clinical sense – he knows that schizophrenia is a complex disorder – but rather in the popular-misconception sense . . . of being schizo, schizoid, a split personality, two people at the same time sort of thing. Because right now that's the deal. Right now – at the same time, in the same skin – Norton is giddy with relief *and* incandescent with rage.

He glances around.

The rain has stopped and the sun has broken through the clouds.

Again.

It's been like this all day, unsettled – showers, sunshine, overcast, more rain. But for the time being at least, everything is still, and wet . . . glistening, luminous – this little block of shops, the pavement slabs at his feet, the neat row of boxed shrubs at the kerb. The neat row of houses opposite. The passing traffic.

His own car.

He gets into it and settles himself. He rips open the paper bag from the pharmacy. He takes out the packet and opens that. He slides the top blister of twenty pills out and pops two of them into his cupped hand. He breathes in deeply and swallows the pills back dry.

He looks down at the packet.

He's used to getting them in a bottle, and from Dr Walsh. These are a different brand – Nalprox – but it's the same stuff. When he got home on Monday he couldn't find his Narolet anywhere, and it transpired that Miriam had flushed them down the toilet. Then he went to Dr Walsh, and it transpired that she'd more or less flushed *him* down the toilet, too – scaring the man off with talk of overprescribing and of possible complaints to the HSE.

Norton didn't argue with him – though he did argue with Miriam later, when he got home.

They haven't spoken since.

Which is a major pain in the arse. Plus it's taken him all day, and endless phone calls here, there and everywhere, to organise *this*.

But now that he has it, a fresh supply, he is walking on air.

He checks the box again. Three blisters, sixty pills, minus the two he's just taken, that's fifty-eight. Four a day, give or take.

So two weeks. More maybe. Or less.

OK.

He puts the packet away, into his pocket, and then looks at his watch: 4.15.

By the time he meets Fitz – in about twenty minutes, down on Strand Road – the tablets will have kicked in, and his rage will have subsided somewhat. So he'll have to . . . well, act it, he supposes. Put it on. From memory.

Not that it'll be any less authentic for that.

*

Mark turns left off the Cherryvale roundabout and heads for the industrial estate. He's been driving for more than an hour now, aimlessly – south-side, north-side, the M50 – sitting in traffic for most of it. The pain in his side is intense, but steady. If he sits in a particular position *and* keeps a very tight grip on the steering wheel, it's just about bearable. He should really head for the nearest A&E, or see a doctor – but he's not going to. Because without having examined the wound or even looked at it properly, he knows what it is. It's a bullet wound, and how's he supposed to explain *that*? Or the fact, which would inevitably surface, that before getting shot, *he* stabbed the other guy with a kitchen knife – an action he's been replaying over and over in his head as he cruises around . . . the split second of contact, the pressure he applied, the resistance he can still feel in the form of tiny spasms, like nerve ends twitching in his hand and wrist . . .

Mark doesn't know how this stuff works, the neurology of it, but it's giving him something to focus on when the broader picture gets too chaotic, when the questions start multiplying, and the answers mutating – like, for instance, where does he go? Where is it *safe* to go?

He exhales.

Not home, certainly, and not the showrooms. But *why* not? Because they know where he lives? Where he works? Is that it?

Multiply, mutate.

Because maybe Bolger had him followed the other night from Buswell's? And now realises who he is? Or maybe knew him anyway? Realised who he was straight off? Recognised him somehow? Had been expecting this for years *and isn't going to stand for it*?

Stopped at a red light, Mark leans sideways, puts a hand inside his jacket and dabs at the wound as gently as he can.

Then he withdraws his hand and holds it up to look at. His fingertips are smeared with blood – though it doesn't seem *too* bad. Maybe the bullet just grazed him, and the wound is superficial. Or maybe there's an actual bullet lodged in there, and most of the bleeding is internal. But what does he know?

The light changes.

So. Where does he go? Where is it safe to go?

Eventually, because he can't drive around for ever, he decides on the warehouse – his unit at the Cherryvale Industrial Estate. It's down the road here, and is anonymous, unmarked, safe as anywhere. Most of Tesoro's business is conducted from the showrooms in Ranelagh, and Mark comes out this way only a couple of times a week, whenever there's a shipment in or a delivery to be organised.

He comes to the estate and drives into the yard. He turns right and then takes the third left. He goes past several of the larger units – past busy loading docks, freight trucks, forklifts – and arrives at his own unit, about halfway down. He parks in front of a rolling steel shutter.

When he gets out of the car – which ends up being quite a struggle – he immediately feels dizzy. It also seems really cold. But at least the rain has stopped.

Holding the car door open, shivering now, he looks down at the seat and sees that it's smeared with blood. He looks away.

Was it this cold earlier?

He pushes the car door shut and locks it. He glances around the yard. A few units back, towards the entrance, a freight truck is reversing and pulling away. At the far end of the yard there is a graffiti-covered wall, and beyond that is Cherryvale Downs, an irregular grid of nearly four hundred identical houses.

At his feet there is a pool of rainwater. Scraps of cloud drift across it. For some reason looking at this makes him feel vaguely hysterical. At the same time, he feels weak, and wonders if he wasn't better off driving around – though all of a sudden the notion of being at the wheel of a car and negotiating traffic seems implausible to him, remote in its complexity and danger.

Moving slowly, he makes his way over to the black metal door next to the rolling steel shutter. He pulls a bunch of keys out of his jacket pocket and holds them up.

It takes him a while, but he eventually manages to get the door open. Inside, he clicks the door shut again and reaches out for a switch on the wall. A second after that fluorescent tube lights flicker and stutter into life overhead. He looks around. On one side of the warehouse there are rows of wrapped pallets stacked on raised wooden platforms, as well as some loose boxes and crates and a small forklift truck. On the other side, there is an area of unused floor space, and in the far corner there is a modular office unit.

Mark goes over to the office, which is bare and strictly functional. There is a small bathroom to the left and a kitchenette to the right. He eases himself onto the hard plastic chair behind the metal desk in the middle. He leans forward for a moment and rubs the back of his neck. His skin feels clammy even though he's cold.

His heart is thumping. His mouth is dry.

He sits up and holds his jacket back to feel the wound again. It seems to have stopped bleeding.

Is that good or bad? He isn't sure.

It hurts like fuck, though.

He works to get his shivering under control. He stares at an irregular mark scratched onto the surface of the metal desk.

Alan Glynn

What happened this afternoon?

He finds it hard to believe. Quite clearly, his intention had been to attack, to lash out, to exact some form of revenge – and who could blame him for that – but *he* hadn't acted, *they* had.

He shakes his head.

They attacked *him*. They intimidated him, provoked him, and when he finally tried to defend himself, *they fucking shot him in the back* . . .

And clearly by *they* he still means Larry Bolger. The Bolger family. Someone *in* the Bolger family. Up to now – at least since he spoke to Gina – that's been the working assumption.

Jesus.

He gets up from behind the desk. He limps out of the office, looks around and picks up the nearest object that catches his eye – a crowbar lying on a wooden crate. He holds it up and imagines what he could do with this, imagines how much more satisfying it would be to use than a knife . . . imagines the whoosh of air, the solid . . . *contact*, the sinew and muscle, the brain tissue and bone . . . blood spurting . . .

As he walks across the warehouse floor, swinging the crowbar, Mark feels a rush of energy. But this lasts only a few seconds.

It is followed by a blinding wave of dizziness.

He staggers forward, losing his footing. He reaches out to grab on to something and finds the side of the small forklift truck. After he regains his balance and catches his breath, he looks at the crowbar again, examines it.

Who does he think he's kidding?

Where? When? *How?*

He tosses the crowbar onto the plastic seat of the forklift truck and takes a few more tentative steps forward, each one causing him to wince. He stops at the first row of stacked pallets. Next to them is another wooden crate. He leans his back against the pallets, puts a hand onto the crate for support, and slides down into a sitting position on the floor.

In his mind's eye, he tries again to picture what happened earlier, to retrace his steps, but it's all out of sync now and won't settle down. There's a feverish, shape-shifting quality to it, the quality of a nightmare.

A while later, he reaches into his jacket pocket and takes out the three photographs. He lays them side by side on the cold concrete, next to the wooden crate. He passes his eye over each one of them in turn, does this again and again, quickly at first, but then less so, lingering a bit longer each time – a few seconds, then more – on the faces of his father, his mother and his sister . . .

The tide is out and it's very cold, but the sky is spectacular – red, painterly streaks of cloud are all that is left of the day's storms.

It's going to be a clear night.

Norton is sitting on a wooden bench, legs crossed, hunched into his overcoat. A few isolated figures are visible out on the strand, people with dogs, throwing sticks. Behind him is a small parking area. Directly behind him is his own car. He hears another car pulling up beside it.

A minute later, Fitz appears from the right. He sits down next to Norton and grunts.

Norton pauses and then takes a deep breath. 'What the fuck is going on, Fitz? I mean, sweet holy suffering mother of *Jaysus*.'

'I know, I know. But let's face it, Paddy, this isn't exactly everyday stuff we're dealing with here, is it? I mean, High King is more used to –'

'Oh, what, all of a sudden this isn't your . . . your métier? Is that it?'

'What?'

'Because that's not what you told me before. Piece of piss you said.'

'Yeah, but –'

'And it's not like you were shy about taking my fucking money –'

'Ah, Paddy, come on, would you?'

'No, *you* come on. *You* come on. For *fuck's* sake.'

The first of the three calls that day came early in the morning. Norton was at home, in the kitchen, fighting to keep down dry toast. He was also shivering, and not just because of the arctic chill that had developed between himself and Miriam. When the second call came, much later, he was in the middle of his frantic search for a new, more pliant GP. Then, not too long after that – about an hour ago now – the third call came. He was in his car at the time, driving out to a doctor's surgery in Milltown.

But it was only as he was leaving the surgery – scrip safely in hand at last – that the gravity of the day's developments hit home, and that he found any space in his head to think about them.

Taking a deep breath, Norton fills his lungs with healthy sea air. In front of them, two seagulls flap past, squawking. Out on the horizon there is a ship, a tiny dot, one of the ferries.

Anyway.

About Dermot Flynn, he's ambivalent. What happened was a mess and should have been avoided – though in the heel of the hunt no real harm was done, and in a way they're lucky to have him out of the picture.

But as for the second situation, Norton is barely able to get his head around it. Mark Griffin stalking Larry Bolger with a kitchen knife? Going around stabbing people in the *leg* with it?

It's not an image he can dwell on for too long.

Eventually, and as calmly as possible, he says, 'Look, there's nothing we can do about Flynn now, but this other guy . . . you're going to have to find him. You're going to have to *stop* him.'

'Stop him? Jesus, Paddy, I don't know. This is all getting –'

'What? Out of hand? And whose fault is that?'

Fitz doesn't answer.

There is a long silence. An elderly couple stroll past. The man nods at the two gents on the bench and says, 'Grand evening.'

The two gents nod back.

'None of this would have happened,' Norton then says, 'if the original hit on Noel had gone according to plan. All the focus now would be on gangland crime, and how *it's* getting out of hand. Your one Gina wouldn't be going around asking awkward questions.'

Fitz grunts again but doesn't speak.

'Right,' Norton goes on. 'The phone call. What did she say exactly?'

This was arguably even more serious than the Mark Griffin situation. Because it was clear that Mark Griffin was trauma-tised, disturbed, whatever. He was weak, and wounded. He could be dealt with.

But Gina Rafferty?

No.

Leaving messages on Mark Griffin's answering machine?

Putting a call through to Harcourt Street? *Talking to a journalist?*

No fucking way.

Fitz exhales. 'Well,' he says, his voice thick with reluctance, 'basically she asked him if they could meet. He asked why. She said she had a story. He asked what it was and she said she didn't want to go into it over the phone. Then he said he was busy and did she know how many calls like this he got in a week, that she'd have to give him *something*. So then she went on for a bit about the two Noels, but by this stage she was sort of rambling, and I don't think your man was too impressed.'

'Did she mention any other names?' Norton says. 'Terry Stack? Larry Bolger?'

'No. I think she was going out of her way to be, what's it, circumspect?'

'Right.'

Norton swallows. He feels a sudden tightness in his chest. This Nalprox stuff is supposed to be the same as the Narolet, but he's not so sure – he's detecting subtle variations, little wrinkles in the texture of it.

'So, how did it finish up?'

'O'Driscoll said that unless she could come up with some hard evidence she was wasting her time. *And* his. Then your one went all quiet. And that was it.'

That's *not* it, of course, Norton thinks. He looks at his watch.

'Something has to be done,' he says. 'Tonight. This can't be allowed to spill into another day.'

'Jesus, Paddy.'

'*What?*'

'I don't know, I mean . . . another two –'

'What's the *alternative*, Fitz?' This comes out in a loud, desperate whisper. 'Tell me. Because it's only a matter of time. A few more *bloody* questions from her, to the wrong person, and we're at the tipping point. This could all fall apart.'

After a long pause, Norton then says, 'Look, Fitz, things have got out of control here, I know that. And I take some of the blame. I do. But if you can contain this tonight, *end* it . . . on top of what I owe you already I'll give you five hundred grand. Offshore account. No traceability.'

Fitz turns to look at Norton. He makes a whistling sound. 'You serious?'

'Absolutely.'

'Fuck's sake.'

Norton stares out at the horizon, waiting.

Fitz runs a hand through his hair. Eventually he says, 'Yeah. Fair enough.'

'Do it any way you want, just take care of it. And *you* do it, do you hear me?'

'Yeah.'

'No operatives, no outsourcing. *You* do it.'

Fitz nods.

After another long pause, Norton says, 'Where is she? At the moment?'

'Er . . . at home. In her apartment. She's been there all day.'

Norton stands up. It's darker than when he sat down, and chillier. City lights are shimmering now along the bay.

He looks at Fitz. 'Well, what the fuck are you waiting for? Get back there. Stay on top of her. Maybe she'll phone Griffin again. Maybe *he'll* phone *her.*'

6

Gina's mobile rings at a quarter to eight. She's on the sofa watching an old episode of *Seinfeld*. Half watching it. Not really watching it at all. She presses Mute on the remote and looks over at the desk, at her phone, stares at it – disinclined, though, to get up and answer it. She's not in the mood for dealing with anyone.

Earlier in the day her incipient panic gave way to despondency, then torpor. After a brief but humiliating conversation with that journalist she threw her mobile on the desk, went into the bedroom – still dressed for work – and lay down. She was fuming.

But she knew he was right.

If she'd been more explicit and mentioned people by name, he still would have said what he said, which was, 'Yeah, fine, great, but where's the evidence?'

Later, in the afternoon, she changed into jeans and a T-shirt. She made coffee, sat at her desk and went online in the vague hope of . . . she didn't really know what. She googled BCM and found out as much as she could about the company her brother worked for. She followed links to other engineering companies. She read an official report on an EU website about corporate malfeasance. She read an article somewhere else about a recent scandal in Greece involving bribery, blackmail and a couple of supposedly accidental deaths – which, when she first came across it, sent a little pulse of excitement through her system, as though the story might actually provide her with some sort of corroboration. But the excitement didn't last, because none of it was relevant. It wasn't evidence of anything. It was stuff on the Internet. It was stuff she'd have to be out of her mind to imagine could have any bearing on anything.

And as she waits now for the phone to ring out – hours later, slumped on the sofa – she thinks, Yes, out of my mind, *that* feels about right. Eventually, though, when the phone does stop, she can't help getting up off the sofa and going over to it.

One missed call. New number.

She presses Reply. She stands there, waiting. She *is* out of her mind.

It answers. 'Gina?'

She recognises the voice straightaway. *'Mark?'*

'Yeah.'

'Are you OK? Where are you? Did you get my message?'

'No, I'm . . . *message?*'

'I left a message on your home phone this morning, I didn't have your mobile number.'

'I –'

'It's just, I was saying . . . I think I'm maybe on the wrong track, about Bolger. I mean, it doesn't seem –'

'I went . . . after him today –'

'What?'

'At least tried to. I didn't come close.'

'What do you mean *went after him*?'

Silence.

'Mark?'

'I tried to . . . *attack* him.'

'Jesus.'

'I really wanted to, but . . . I didn't even . . .' He stops here, struggling, it seems, to get the words out.

Gina turns and looks at the TV, as though for assistance on this, as though it should be running a news flash or something, a crawl, *anything*. What she sees instead is Kramer hurtling through the door of Jerry's apartment.

She looks away again.

'You didn't even *what*?'

'I had a knife. I —'

'Oh God.'

'I didn't even take it out. I couldn't. I was just standing there, looking at him, and —'

'Where *was* this?'

He explains, but his voice is shaky, and he pauses constantly to take deep breaths. When he gets to the part about sticking the knife in the guy's leg, Gina flinches.

'Oh my God,' she says. 'What happened then? Did *you* get hurt? You sound —'

'No,' he says quickly. 'I didn't. I'm . . . I'm fine.'

'Well, you don't *sound* fine. At all.' She waits, but he doesn't respond. 'You actually sound awful, Mark. Spacy. Are you OK? Where *are* you?'

He still doesn't answer.

'Mark?'

'Listen,' he then says. 'I . . . I finally saw them. Today. For the first time in . . . I *saw* them. Saw what they looked like.'

Gina closes her eyes. 'Who?' she whispers.

'My family.' He pauses. 'I'm looking at them now. Lucy was so small, she . . .'

'Mark?'

'. . . she was *tiny*, but the funny thing is . . . what I remember is . . . how *big* she was, I remember her hands, her —'

'*Mark,*' Gina pleads.

'What?'

'Where *are* you?'

He tells her. But he says he can't move. He's afraid to move. He's been sitting here for ages, maybe hours – he doesn't know. His heart is pounding, he says, like it's about to explode. He feels sick.

'That's . . . that's anxiety,' Gina says, 'trauma . . . it's post, er . . .' She doesn't know what she's saying. 'You're in shock.' She pauses. 'Mark, do you want me to come out there?'

'Yes.' He groans. '*No.*' He groans again. 'Would you mind?'

She takes directions. The Cherryvale Industrial Estate – right at the entrance, third row along, eighth warehouse on the left.

Unit 46.

Norton is standing in the lobby of the Four Seasons Hotel, waiting for Ray Sullivan to appear, when his phone rings. Sullivan has made a surprise stopover on his way to a conference in Vienna and wants to have dinner. Norton didn't mind changing his plans – the opening of a Friel revival at the Gate – but he's agitated about what's going on and isn't exactly in the mood right now for a full, high-energy dose of Ray Sullivan. He'd much prefer to be sitting in a theatre, constrained to silence, letting his mind wander.

He looks at the display. It's Fitz, which is good. Maybe. Hopefully.

He presses Answer and holds the phone up to his ear. 'Yeah?'

'Paddy, listen, I'm in the car. I've located your man.'

Norton is relieved. But what now? And does he *really* want to know? He glances around the lobby. What he said in the carpark – standing there, doors open, wind blowing all around them – was that he didn't want the details, just the broad strokes.

The timeline.

He said he wanted closure.

'Paddy? You there?'

'Yeah.'

'OK. So I'll talk to you in a while then?'

'Yeah. Good. Good man.'

That's it.

As Norton is putting his phone away, he glances across the lobby and sees Ray Sullivan stepping out of an elevator.

Gina puts on a sweater and then her brown leather jacket. On the pavement outside her building, waiting for the taxi, she zips the jacket up. The rain has moved on and the sky is clear, but it's cold.

As she wills the taxi to arrive, her heart is pounding.

She looks up and down the quays, sighs, turns.

The building she lives in is just one of many in this riverside regeneration, but there is a desolate feel to the place at night. At ground level everything is closed, except for the odd Spar, or empty Italian restaurant or theme pub attached to a new hotel. The streets here, between these new hotels and new apartment blocks, lack any atmosphere – they seem forced, a developer's idea of 'new' city living.

Gina still has a hard time thinking of this as town.

The taxi arrives.

The driver appears to be the silent type, which is good, but instead of going back the way he came, *from* town, he heads for the toll bridge. This makes sense – it's just that Gina isn't prepared for the shock of having Richmond Plaza loom up on her so suddenly like that.

But once they get past it and are heading west across the

city, Gina can think of only one thing. What is she letting herself in for here? Since Monday, either face to face or over the phone – and while remaining, effectively, complete strangers – she and Mark Griffin have had this series of intense, urgent, almost intimate conversations. It's been very weird. Actually, in a way, she feels responsible for him – because if she hadn't steered him in the direction of Larry Bolger, would he have . . . ?

But a *knife*?

Her stomach sinks.

He seemed a little dangerous to her the other day, and she was obviously right about that. At the same time he seemed vulnerable.

Gina stares out of the window.

Soon her thoughts are a blur, like the view, which has become this gentle strobe effect, this seemingly endless, self-replicating pattern of semi-detached suburban houses.

After a while, tired, apprehensive, she closes her eyes.

Lucy in the sky . . .

He remembers that now. His father used to say it all the time, and Lucy used to love it, used to pretend that she could fly . . . arms out . . . running . . .

In that garden maybe? The one in the photo?

Mark shifts his position on the floor and winces. The pain is severe and constant, additional shoots of it accompanying even the slightest movement. But that's exactly what he has to do now – move, and all the way over to the door, to open the damn thing, because otherwise how will Lucy get . . . Gina . . . how will *Gina* get in when she arrives?

He hasn't been on his feet in a while and doesn't know if it's going to be possible. He leans back against the wooden crate and manoeuvres himself up, one inch, one searing shock wave of pain, at a time.

Lucy in the sky . . .

It's funny, but his sister today – if she'd lived – would be about the same age as Gina is . . . and might even, he imagines, look a bit like her, too.

Up on his feet, he moves tentatively, shuffles forward, reaches out to the nearest sturdy object for support.

It seems blindingly obvious to him now, but having seen his family, even if only in photographs, having seen their *faces*, he realises what it is that in one form or another he's been experiencing all these years. Loneliness. He's been *missing* them. After all, he was only five at the time. He was happy. They were his entire world, and he loved them, as purely, as unconditionally, as viscerally, as only a small child can love.

And then one night it all came to a dead stop.

So what did he expect?

As he looks over at the door, the throbbing in his heart falls into a sort of rhythm with the throbbing in his side, making each footstep he has to take, each passing second, that shade more bearable.

And then, quite suddenly – grunting, gasping – he's there. He flicks the catch with his hand and pulls the door open slightly, letting in a gust of cold air.

Mark doesn't know why he called Gina. It seemed to make sense, and to be about the only physical action he was capable of taking – picking up his phone, pressing the keys – that wasn't liable to kill him.

But it still felt proactive – contacting the one person with at least *some* understanding of his situation, the one person who could appreciate, for example, how important finding those photographs was for him.

And maybe she has new information.

Because didn't he interrupt her? On the phone? Wasn't she about to say something when he cut across her?

He wonders now what she'd been going to say.

He stares at the door.

In the meantime, though, there's something he needs to do, and urgently – he needs to take a leak, has done for the best part of an hour. Back over there on the floor, he even debated whether or not he shouldn't just surrender to it, and let it happen, let it flow, because what difference would it make?

But then he thought, no . . . not with Gina coming.

He shuffles across the floor towards the office, and when he gets there he stops and presses his forehead against the wooden door frame. He is dizzy and weak, and could easily, almost happily, collapse right here on the floor.

But he's not going to.

He feels his way like a blind man along the wall and goes into the tiny bathroom. He struggles with his zip and eventually manages to get going, but halfway through he hears something outside – a car door being closed.

He groans, half in pain, half in relief. When Gina sees the state he's in, she will insist on calling an ambulance, and he won't be able to stop her. But that will be OK . . . now, at this stage, that will be OK.

He does up his zip with great difficulty and turns around.

When he hears the steel door clicking shut, he tries to call out – something like 'In here' or 'I'm in the bathroom', or just simply 'Gina', but he can't get anything past his lips. His throat is dry as a bone.

Then *he* hears a voice, and freezes – because it isn't Gina's.

'Hello?'

It's a male voice.

'Hello? Mr Griffin?'

Mr? Who *is* this?

Footsteps on the concrete floor.

'Hello? Anyone *here*?'

There's already a hint of impatience in the voice, and Mark feels a rising sense of dread. He doesn't move, just leans against the wall and waits.

The next time he hears the voice it is closer – if not actually inside the office, then at the doorway or just outside it.

'*Griffin?*'

No *Mr* this time.

Mark remains still.

He hears footsteps again, but this time they're on wood – *inside* the office.

The door leading to the toilet is open, and from the angle Mark is standing at, he's –

But then a sound cuts the air. It's a mobile ring tone – the theme tune from some movie. An impatient sigh overlies it. The ring tone stops.

'Yeah?' Silence for a moment. Then, 'There's no sign of him, Shay. There's a fucking car outside all right, but ... I don't know. I'll have a squint around.' The voice moves away. 'Look, I have to go. Your one'll be here any minute. Give us a bell in half an hour if you haven't heard from me, right?'

Footsteps again, back on concrete, receding.

No sign of him? Your one? Here any minute?

How does he know all of this?

Mark pats his jacket pocket for his own mobile, to call Gina, to warn her . . . but *shit,* it's not there. He left it on the floor over by the wooden crate.

Fuck . . . what has he done?

Mark leans back against the wall and slides down into a sitting position on the floor, next to the toilet bowl.

Calling her in the first place was clearly a mistake because . . . because whoever this guy is, *he must have been listening in . . .*

And that guy today, at the Garryowen Institute, how did *he* know that Mark would be there?

They must have been following him all along; there must have been . . . operatives, surveillance, everything . . .

The pain is almost unbearable now, and Mark can feel himself sliding even further, down into an abyss of darkness, but he fights it, pushes himself back up against the wall, off the floor, and into a standing position again.

He can't let this happen.

He *can't . . .*

But what he can't do either is stay here, where he is, in the warehouse, because he wouldn't stand a chance, not if it came to . . .

What he needs is to get away, to raise the alarm, he needs to . . .

Up . . .

He looks up. High above the toilet there is a window. It's small, but . . .

He puts the lid down on the toilet. He clambers onto it and then onto the cistern. He reaches up to the window and nudges it fully open. Cold, invigorating air streams in.

Drawing on some deep reserve of energy, he pulls himself up and wriggles through the opening. When he's more than halfway out, and facing the wall of the next warehouse along, he realises there isn't going to be anything to grab on to for leverage and that he's going to have to drop the six feet or so to the ground.

Which, a second before he's ready to do, he does.

And as much energy as it's taken him to get out here to this dark alleyway, it takes him as much again, if not more, to absorb the pain of the fall *and not to scream* . . .

He rolls over on the cold, wet concrete, clutching his left arm, which he may have broken, and gags into his chest.

After a few moments, he raises his head.

Twenty yards in front of him, at the end of the alleyway, there is a tall coruscating monolith of orange light, and as Mark gazes at it, something flickers past . . . a figure.

He recoils, slams his head back against the wall.

Jesus, who was that?

And how many of them are there?

Is he going to be able to get away from here? He needs to get to that phone box out on the main road. That's where he needs to get to, at the very least.

If not as far as . . .

He tries to move – his right arm, his legs, all of him at once – but he can't, each option a new route back to the same place, to the same blinding core of pain.

Very slowly, he turns his neck, directing his eyes back towards the light.

But his head is spinning now . . . he's seeing double, treble . . . tracers . . .

Who *was* that?

And then, as his head slumps forward, and he slides back helplessly into the abyss of darkness, the horrifying thought occurs to him that maybe it was Gina.

The taxi approaches the Cherryvale roundabout, and a few minutes after that they're approaching the industrial estate. Gina considers asking the driver to hang on, but she decides against it.

She's assuming Griffin has a car.

They stop at the entrance, which is wide open and not very clearly marked. Gina pays and gets out. The taxi turns and leaves.

She looks around. The place is desolate, cold and windswept, with everything washed in an unreal orange glow from the floodlights positioned at various points along the perimeter.

Gina goes in, turns right and walks to the third row of buildings. At the far end she can see a wall covered in graffiti. There are two vans and a large truck parked in front of the first unit. Other than that the yard is practically empty, with only a few cars dotted around the place. One of these is parked in front of what she takes to be Unit 46.

Walking towards it, hugging the buildings on the left, all of which are in complete darkness, she starts to feel nervous.

What is she doing?

High in the sky the moon is shimmering. Little scraps of cloud race by. The wind is whistling in the narrow alleyways between the warehouses. As she approaches Unit 46, she sees from a row of frosted-glass windows along the top that there are lights on inside.

The car, a Saab, is parked directly in front of a steel shutter. Next to this is a black metal door with a bell and an intercom.

How prepared is she?

The truth is, not very. What's driving her forward is this sense of responsibility she's feeling. In addition to which, if she's honest about it, she liked Mark Griffin when they met the other day. He was nice. He was interesting. He was good-looking. OK, unstable and possibly dangerous, too – but that's actually not a state Gina herself feels terribly removed from right now.

She presses the bell.

At least ten seconds pass before she hears anything. Then there is a click and the door opens. At first she doesn't see anyone. It's as if the door has opened automatically, and maybe it has. She is about to call out Mark's name when someone else appears from behind the door, holding it open.

Her heart jumps.

It's a short, stocky man in his late forties.

'Er . . .'

'Are you Gina, are you?'

The man is wearing black jeans and a zipped-up leather jacket – not unlike the one Gina herself is wearing. He has a round, plump face.

Gina doesn't move, or utter a word.

'Because Mark asked me to wait for you,' the man says. 'He had to be taken off to hospital, to St Felim's.'

'Oh *no*.' Gina puts a hand up to her mouth. 'Is he OK?'

'Well, I hope so,' the man says, sighing. 'He called me in a state. I don't live that far from here.' He extends an arm and says, 'Come in for a second and let me explain.'

Gina steps forward, the word *hospital* still resounding in her ears, but she's barely inside the door when it occurs to her . . . Mark had her mobile number, why didn't he just get this guy to phone her, or . . .

She turns.

The man has already closed the door and is leaning back against it.

'Listen,' Gina says, holding a hand up, 'I think I should –'

'No, no, you're grand.' He winks at her. 'But I need to have a word with you.'

Gina doesn't say anything, doesn't react, because there's something quite creepy about this guy. The silence between them thickens, and eventually, in a calm, controlled voice, she says, 'Where's Mark?'

'Well, he's not in the hospital, I can tell you that. *Yet.* He fucking will be though if he doesn't watch it.'

There is a beat, and then Gina deflates.

She walked right into this. How could she have been so stupid? *Jesus.* All of her speculation, all of her doubts, her neurotic need to be circumspect, her fear that she might be deluded.

And now *this*?

She shakes her head. It's her own fault.

'Where *is* he?' she repeats.

'Look, don't . . .' The guy pauses, a smirk rising on his face. 'Don't be worrying that pretty head of yours, not over the likes of him.'

Gina groans. Who *is* this vile little person?

She turns and takes a couple of steps across the floor, but then an even more urgent question occurs to her – are they alone? Is there anyone else here? She doesn't *see* anyone. She sees an office partition in the corner, and rows of stacked pallets on raised wooden platforms to her right. A small fork-lift truck. Loose stuff lying around on the floor. A wooden crate. The place is brightly lit, fluorescent units dangling on chains from the ceiling.

No sign of anyone else, though. No sign of Mark.

She turns back and looks at the man again, studies him. He's doing the same, eyeing her up and down.

He has a round face, with a florid, unhealthy complexion. His features are small and mean – his mouth hardly more than a slit, his eyes tiny and dark.

He has the face of an overfed rat.

Ratface.

He is still leaning back against the door.

Gina realises that she's actually quite nervous now. But she's also determined not to show it.

'And who the hell are *you*?' she asks.

'I'm . . . I've been asked to deliver a message,' he says.

'Well. Let's hear it then, and I'll be on my way.'

'Not so quick, love.' He steps forward, away from the door. 'I mean, what's your hurry?'

Gina swallows.

Maybe to deflect attention from herself, maybe because it's the one thing she actually wants to hear, she repeats her question from earlier. 'Is Mark OK?'

Ratface cracks a smile. 'Well, you know how it is with the old post-traumatic stress. It's never easy.'

Gina stares at him in disbelief. He was listening in on Mark's *phone*? He overheard their *conversation*? Well, of course. Isn't it obvious? That's why he's here.

But who is he? Who is he working for?

Isn't that obvious, too?

On Monday evening Mark said he approached Larry Bolger, and just a while ago he said he actually tried to attack him – so even though Gina's own suspicions have moved on from Bolger, Mark's clearly haven't, and must be the source of all this unwelcome attention he's receiving.

But how does that explain Ratface here? There's no way he's . . . official. In *any* capacity. Representing a government minister?

Look at him.

Gina is confused.

'So who are you working for?' she asks. 'Whose message are you supposed to be delivering?'

'*Supposed* to be? We'll see about that.' He steps farther away from the door.

'It's Larry Bolger, isn't it?' Gina says. 'You're working for Larry Bolger.'

Ratface laughs at this and says, 'You haven't a fuckin' clue, love, have you?'

He starts walking around her, slowly, in a wide arc, never taking his eyes off her.

Gina glances over at the door but doesn't move. Did he lock it?

She turns back.

'I wouldn't bother,' he says, 'You wouldn't get very far.'

She swallows again.

She's definitely uneasy now – OK, scared – but her need to understand what is going on seems to be even greater. Because she keeps wondering . . . if this guy doesn't work for Bolger, then who *does* he work for?

It's frustrating.

'OK, look,' she says, fishing now for some hard information, 'this *message* of yours. What is it?'

Ratface grunts. 'The message? You want the message?'

'Yes. Of course I do.'

'All right.'

He puts a hand into the pocket of his leather jacket and slowly withdraws something.

Gina's heart stops.

It's a gun.

Oh *fuck*.

'So, I was going to just *give* you the message,' he says. 'If you know what I mean.' He waves the gun in the air between them. 'Get it over with. But now I don't know. I might give you something else first. Because you're not being very nice, are you? I think you need some manners put on you.'

Gina watches in horror as he then brings his free hand around to his crotch, applies a little pressure to it and breathes in sharply.

'Right, come on,' he says, nodding at her, almost in distaste. 'Get some of that off you. We haven't got all night.'

He puts the gun back into his jacket pocket and pats it.

'Oh Christ,' Gina says in a barely audible whisper, 'you've *got* to be kidding.'

She steps away, reeling slightly, and turns to the right.

In front of her is the small forklift truck. Feeling weak, she bends forward, arms outstretched, and leans against it, unsure if she isn't going to throw up. Then her eyes focus, and she sees what is lying on the forklift's shiny, worn plastic seat.

'Oh *yeah*,' the man says, from behind her. 'I like that.' There is a slight tremor in his voice now. 'Stay that way . . . in that position.'

Gina listens hard, gauging the man's steps as he approaches. Then she reaches down and grabs the crowbar with both hands. Summoning all her strength, she swings it up and around, keeps it moving and smashes it bang on target into the side of the man's flushed and pudgy face.

'It's all about the optics,' Ray Sullivan is saying. 'It's about *perception*. These days, post-Enron, post-Spitzer, whatever, you just can't afford to dick around.'

Norton looks at his watch. It's too soon, he knows. But he can't help it.

Then he looks at his plate. He has barely touched his chicken livers. Which is another thing. Narolet never used to affect his appetite like this. But maybe it's not the Nalprox. Maybe he wouldn't be hungry anyway.

'What was it Ike said, that phrase he used in relation to Nixon?' Sullivan slices one of his artichoke hearts in two. 'After the funding scandal in fifty-two? "Clean as a hound's tooth?" Even back then, *he* understood. Ike was no idiot, you know.'

Norton shakes his head. 'Look, Ray, if we're talking about Larry here, you've got it out of proportion. The media have already pretty much filed away what happened under peccadillo and consigned it to last week's news. The story *this* week is how Larry has snookered the Taoiseach into supporting him one hundred per cent.' He pauses. 'And on the basis of what doesn't kill you makes you stronger, I'd say Larry is well on course for the top job, and maybe even sooner than we expected.'

Giving this some thought, Sullivan dips and drags one of his pieces of artichoke heart in the sauce, a spoory trail, running around the plate, of Marsala and honey. 'I like that,' he says, the fork poised at his mouth. 'What doesn't kill you makes you stronger.'

'I know, I know. Who said *that*?'

As Norton laughs, leaning back, he steals another glance at his watch.

For Gina, each passing second now is elastic, a nanocentury of experience and sensory overload – the fluorescent lights above her too bright, the air around her too cold, the thumping in her ears and chest too loud, too persistent. She's not sure she's going to be able to cope.

Without taking her eyes off Ratface, however, and still clutching the crowbar, she staggers backwards a few feet and manages to straighten up.

She tries to assess what she has done. Ratface isn't moving. He staggered a little himself as he fell and is now lying on his side, facing away from her – so she can't see where she hit him. Holding the crowbar up, ready to strike again if necessary, she retraces a couple of her steps and takes as close a look as she can bear at the . . .

At the *body*?

She remains still for a moment and stares. There's a slight movement. It's hardly perceptible. But he's definitely breathing.

She pulls back.

Fuck.

She's relieved and not relieved – relieved that she hasn't killed him and not at all relieved because what does she do now?

What if he wakes up?

Fuck.

She looks around. Sticking out from under one of the raised wooden platforms that the pallets are stacked on is a loose, thin strap of plastic. It's the stuff they use for securing industrial loads. She puts down the crowbar, walks over and picks it up. She feels under the wooden platform and finds another one.

She goes back, kneels down beside Ratface and proceeds to tie his ankles together with one of the plastic straps. It's awkward, but she manages to get it done. Then, in order to tie his wrists behind his back with the second strap, she has to shift his weight a bit and pull his right arm out from under him.

When she's satisfied that he has been sufficiently restrained, she puts her hand into his jacket pocket. Very slowly, she pulls out his gun. She holds it between her index finger and thumb. It's solid-feeling and quite heavy. She stands back up, careful to keep it at arm's length. She goes over to the wooden crate next to the first row of stacked pallets and places the gun on top of it.

Then, leaning back against the crate, still in shock, she wonders what to do next. Does she leave? Does she wait to see if he is all right? Does she call the police? Does she call an ambulance? *What?*

As Gina considers these questions, she glances down at the floor and notices in a distracted way that she's standing on something, a piece of paper or card. She bends down to pick it up. Her hand is shaking as she turns it over.

It's a photograph – old, slightly faded, and now slightly smudged as well. It's of a little girl. She's thin, has dark hair and is wearing a blue denim dress. She isn't quite smiling but looks impish, as though she's doing her best to withhold a smile, as though this is a game she's playing.

Puzzled, Gina casts her eye around – down at the floor,

beside the crate, in behind it. She finds two more photos, one of a man, the other of a woman. She also finds a mobile phone, which she puts on the crate beside the gun. She holds the three photos up together and studies each one in turn.

My family . . . I'm looking at them now . . .

Gina slides the photos together and puts them down on the wooden crate. With a sinking feeling, she then reaches into her pocket and pulls out her own mobile. She calls the number for Mark Griffin, waits, and a few seconds later the phone on the crate starts ringing. She presses End and puts the phone back into her pocket.

What does *this* mean?

Before she has time to think about it, however, there is another, more immediate demand on her attention.

Ratface is groaning, and moving – or at least trying to.

Gina walks around him in a wide arc. She keeps her distance but notices something straightaway. It's just beneath his head, on the floor . . . blood, a few crimson drops glistening against the dull grey of the concrete. She hunkers down to see a little better, to see what condition the side of his face is in. There's a nasty gash there, all right – but she's having a hard time connecting it to anything *she* might have done.

Then Ratface opens his eyes, and Gina starts back in fright.

'Jeeeesus,' he groans. 'What the *fuck*?'

Gina keeps her balance. She remains hunkered down and watches as he struggles to move. She watches him squirm and wriggle and slowly realise what's going on.

Up to this point he hasn't looked at her, but now their eyes meet.

'You . . .'

'Where's Mark Griffin?'

'...*cunt*...'

'Where *is* he?'

He groans again and wriggles vigorously for a while. 'Let me go,' he then says, seeming to accept that there's no chance he'll get loose on his own. 'For *Jaysus*' sake.'

Gina stands up. 'Tell me where Mark Griffin is.'

'I don't fucking *know* where he is.'

'Yes you do. You heard him giving me directions on the phone and then you rushed out here before I arrived and you *took* him somewhere, now *where*?'

She feels like punctuating this with a kick to his abdomen, or his crotch, but she resists.

'Fuck off.'

Gina takes a deep breath. She knows that if he keeps stonewalling here she'll start to fall apart. She'll lose the advantage.

'If you won't answer *my* questions,' she says, taking out her mobile again, 'maybe you'll answer a few for the police.'

'Ha.'

What does that mean?

She waits for him to say something else and when he doesn't she holds her phone up and tries to focus.

'Go ahead,' he says. 'Brilliant. Call the cops.'

Gina hesitates. 'I'm going to,' she says.

'Great. Because I'd love to hear how you're going to explain *this*.' He yanks his head sideways at her, exposing his wound. 'I'll have an army of bleedin' lawyers up your arse and down your throat so fast you'll be wishing *I* was the one who fucked you. Which I then *will*, after they let you out on bail.'

He's playing for time here – because why would he try to dissuade her from making the call, if what he says is true?

But then again, what he says probably *is* true. The cops arrive – but who do they arrest? Him? *Why?* What do they charge him with? Being tied up and assaulted? And how does *she* avoid coming across as deranged and hysterical?

She puts the phone down by her side.

'You're right.'

'What?'

'You're right. It's not the Guards I should be calling.'

She puts the phone into her jacket pocket and takes out her wallet. She searches through the wallet and extracts a business card. She puts the wallet away and takes out the phone again. Looking down at him, business card held up in one hand, phone in the other, thumb poised, she says, 'Where is he?'

'Get stuffed, would you?'

Gina keys in the number, spins on her heels and walks away. By the time she's a couple of yards across the warehouse floor the number is ringing. She looks at the business card again, and swallows.

Electrical Contractor.

She waits. There's a click. Then, 'Hello?'

She slips the card into the back pocket of her jeans.

'Terry? It's Gina Rafferty.'

There is a pause.

'Well, well. How's it going, love?'

'OK.' She closes her eyes. 'Listen, I think I might need your help with something.'

Because of the way he is sitting – fully forward, elbows on the table – Norton can feel his mobile phone pressing against his ribs. It's in the inside breast pocket of his jacket, and he wishes it would ring.

'. . . so we'd like you to consider it,' Sullivan is saying. 'I mean, *we* think in the current climate it makes a lot of sense.'

Sullivan is proposing a last-minute design modification to the lobby of what will soon be called the Amcan Building – the installation of optical turnstiles with infrared sensors.

'Basically, it's an ID-card verification system,' he says, 'but they can also be fitted with barriers, either a steel arm or a retractable wing. The barriers aren't essential, but they do add a measure of psychological, what'll we call it . . . comfort.'

Norton looks across at Sullivan, trying to focus. 'I don't know, Ray. Fine, you're the anchor tenant, but there's at least a dozen others, and I doubt if *any* of them will agree with your assessment of the threat level. They certainly won't want to share the costs.'

'Believe me, Paddy, in the long run this shit *will* be cost-effective. All it takes is one security alert, one nut job, and you're ahead of the game. Back home, since 9/11, installing these things has been standard practice.'

Norton can see a certain logic to this, and how it might work here as a marketing tool to woo US companies jittery about investing in what they perceive as an increasingly vulnerable Europe, but he isn't in the appropriate frame of mind to tease the issue out tonight.

He looks at his watch again, this time openly.

When is Fitz going to call him?

'Paddy?' Ray Sullivan says, leaning forward. 'Are you OK?'

'Yes, yes.'

'Somewhere else you'd rather be?'

'No, of course not.'

Norton busies himself with what's left on his plate, a last piece of monkfish and some fennel.

Should *he* call Fitz?

When Gina comes back and resumes her position at the wooden crate, she is overwhelmed by a sudden wave of exhaustion. She gazes down at Ratface. It's clear that he's in severe pain now, his supply of adrenaline surely, by this stage, pretty much depleted.

'You're in over your head here,' he says after a while, struggling to get the words out. 'I'm telling you. Don't be making things worse for yourself than they already are.'

But not in any mood to be listening to this, Gina looks around, spots something on the floor beside the forklift and goes over to pick it up. Holding it behind her back, she approaches Ratface, hunkers down again and says to him, 'Where is he?'

'Fuck off.'

'You're not going to tell me, no?'

'No.'

'Or who you're working for, no?'

'No.'

'Or who killed my brother, no? No? *NO?*'

'*No, you fuck –*'

In a single swift movement she brings the dirty, oily, bunched-up piece of rag around and stuffs it hard into his mouth. To the sound of him gagging, she stands up again and walks back to the wooden crate.

Over the next few minutes, she looks at her watch several times.

She should have asked Terry Stack if he could bring a couple of Valium with him, or a Xanax, or *something*. She wishes, at the very least, that she had a cigarette. Not that she smokes anymore, but in the last few weeks she's had the old craving more than once, and each time she resisted. If there were a pack in front of her right now though, she wouldn't resist for a second.

Then it occurs to her that maybe *he* has some.

She gets off the crate and walks over to Ratface again. Seeing her coming, he goes rigid. His eyes bulge and he mumbles something through the cloth. It's as if he's expecting her to kick him – which she's still tempted to do, but instead she bends down, holding a hand out in front of her for protection.

He makes a sudden movement and her heart lurches.

But it's not as if he's going anywhere.

The gash on the side of his face is awful-looking. It's deep and messy. But what can she do? Her concern is genuine, just misplaced – because does she really imagine that when Terry Stack arrives he'll be busying himself with washing the wound in warm water and gently applying disinfectant and a bandage?

Avoiding eye contact with him, she reaches down to his other pocket. The first thing she extracts from it is a mobile phone, which she places on the floor beside her. Then she extracts a packet of twenty Major and a Zippo. She'd prefer something milder – in another lifetime she used to smoke Camel Lights – but Major will do.

She puts the cigarettes and lighter into her own pocket and looks down at the mobile phone. She should have thought of this earlier. What if it rings?

Shit.

It'd be liable to give her a heart attack.

She picks up the phone and strides across the warehouse. When she gets to the steel door, she opens it and steps out into the cold air. She raises an arm and flings the phone as far away as she can. She just about hears it land – on the other side of the floodlit yard somewhere.

She turns back.

When she gets inside the door again, she stops for a moment and looks around.

They *are* alone here, aren't they?

On the far side of the warehouse there is another door. She goes over and tries it, but it's locked. Then – and conscious of not letting Ratface out of her sight – she goes over to the office unit and pokes her head around the door.

It's empty.

Walking back towards the wooden crate, she takes the cigarettes out of her pocket and lights one up. Her hands are shaking, but the first drag is exquisite, more than she could reasonably have expected. Her brain chemistry seems to go through a rapid series of changes and her mood elevates.

But this lasts only three or four seconds.

With the next drag, and the one after that, it's business as usual. After another couple, she looks at her watch.

How much longer before Stack gets here? Five minutes? Ten minutes?

And then what?

When she finishes the cigarette, she throws it on the floor and stubs it out with her foot.

She picks up the gun from beside her and examines it. It's the first time she's ever handled a gun and it feels strange. Is it loaded? Is it ready to use? Do you just pull the trigger? What about blowback and recoil? She's not even sure she knows what these terms mean – but then again, does she really want to know?

Isn't that why she called Terry Stack?

She puts the gun down again. She walks over to Ratface.

He turns his head slightly and looks up at her.

'Listen,' she says, 'I'm going to ask you one more time, OK?'

She pauses, waiting for him to indicate that he understands, but he just keeps staring up at her.

'Right. Where is he? What have you done with him?'

Ratface appears to mumble something, but Gina isn't sure if he's answered the question or not. She leans down and pulls the rag out of his mouth.

'*Where is he?*' she says again.

'Get stuffed, you bitch.'

Gina stands back up. 'That call I made a while ago? Do you know who it was to?'

'Phone a fucking friend, was it?'

'Yeah, right. Ever heard of Terry Stack?'

He doesn't react in an obvious way, but Gina can tell from his eyes that he's stunned.

'Yeah.' She nods her head. 'I thought you might have.'

But then she looks up, hearing something outside.

A car.

'That'll be him,' she says, and turns away.

She picks up the gun, the mobile and the photos from the crate and stuffs them into her pockets. She walks over to the steel door, opens it and looks out into the yard.

An unmarked transit van is parked a few spaces along from the Saab. The driver and passenger doors open at the same time and two men get out. As they approach, Gina sees that

one of them is carrying something by his side, a briefcase or –
oh God, of course – a toolbox.

When he gets to the door, Terry Stack smiles and says, 'Gina,
how's it going? I'm glad you called me. You did the right thing.'

Gina shrugs her shoulders. She's cold and tired, and
suddenly feels way out of her depth. What she wants to do
more than anything else right now is cry, break down and sob,
but Terry Stack would love that. He'd love nothing more than
to be putting his arms around her and going, 'Ssshhh, there,
there, love, it's all right.'

She stands back, holding the door open for them, and
points. 'He's over there.'

Wearing an overcoat, Terry Stack struts in, followed by the
other guy, who is younger and wearing the standard-issue grey
hoodie. This younger guy is the one carrying the toolbox.

Terry Stack turns to Gina and says, 'You work in software,
right? That's what you told me, data retrieval?'

She nods but doesn't say anything.

'Well, I'm pretty good at data retrieval myself, so don't
worry love, we'll sort this out.'

Gina wants to stop everything right there, to reverse this,
but –

'I just need to find out –'

'I know, Gina, I *know*. You told me on the phone. It's all
right. It's under control.'

She sighs and then trails behind the two men as they walk
over to where Ratface is lying on the floor.

Terry Stack leans down and takes a look at him.

'Ah, well Jaysus,' he says, half laughing. 'Will you look who it
is?' He straightens up and rubs his hands together. 'Fitz, me
auld flower, *how's* it going?'

Fitz.

They seem to know him. Is that good or bad?

As though in answer to her question, Gina glances over and sees that not only is this Fitz wriggling now, but he's trembling, and has just pissed himself.

Lightning quick, Terry Stack kicks him in the stomach.

Gina gags.

'Open the box up there, Shay, would you?' Terry Stack says. 'And see if you can find the nearest socket for me as well.'

Gina shakes her head and says in a sort of strangled whisper, 'I'm . . . I'll be outside.'

Without looking back, she makes straight for the steel door, opens it and heads out into the cold night air.

Having extracted a promise from Norton that he'll look into the optical-turnstiles thing, Ray Sullivan now embarks on an anecdote about his father, the apparently legendary Madison Avenue advertising executive Dick Sullivan. It's about how some town in California during the sixties decided to change its name for commercial reasons and hired Sullivan Sr., who ended up sketching his ideas out to members of the County Board over lunch on the back of a cocktail napkin.

But Norton has never heard of the veteran adman and is barely listening anyway.

By the time their coffees arrive, Sullivan Jr. has moved on to another story and is getting quite animated. There are gestures involved, and funny voices. For his part, Norton occupies himself with the cream and sugar. At one point, noticing a sudden lull, he looks up. Sullivan is staring at him, and has also – it quickly becomes apparent – asked him a question.

Norton just stares back.

Then he gets up from the table. 'Ray, I'm sorry. I have to go outside for a minute. I'll . . . I'll be back.'

He strides across the dining room. When he gets out to the reception area and is heading for the main exit he reaches into his jacket pocket.

The sound Gina hears as she takes the next drag on her cigarette is short, shrill and penetrating. She looks up and remains still for a few seconds, listening.

She really can't be sure that the sound wasn't just some form of distortion carried here from a distance by the wind.

She closes her eyes.

But neither can she be sure that it didn't come from nearby, from directly behind her, and that it wasn't a scream.

She moves quickly, out into the middle of this windswept, floodlit yard.

The cigarette in her hand is a welcome distraction – though in normal circumstances a second one of these and she'd be on all fours, ready to puke.

After a while, feeling a little too exposed, she heads towards the opposite side of the yard. The units here are larger. They have more elaborate loading docks, with metal awnings and concrete ramps.

She huddles in a corner, by the side of one of these ramps. She stubs the cigarette out, and immediately starts shivering.

How long will this take?

She has no idea. It's not as if she has a frame of reference. But one thing she does know for sure: things are beginning to unravel.

And a couple of seconds later, as though on cue, she hears another weird sound.

She steps forward.

It definitely isn't a scream this time. It's also too close to be coming from the other side of the yard.

So what is it?

The direction of the wind changes. For a second or two the sound becomes clearer.

A bloody *ring tone?*

She looks down and sees it, Fitz's mobile. It's on the ground in front of her, a few yards away, emitting the theme music from a spaghetti western, one of the Clint Eastwood *Dollar* movies.

Rolling her eyes, she walks towards it, this tiny object, its backlight pulsating electric blue.

As she reaches down to pick it up, blood rushing to her head, Gina thinks she sees what is on the display – the caller ID – and her heart stops. She stands up and tries to steady herself. She holds the phone out and looks at it, squinting. But then, in the split second before the phone rings off and goes dark again, it comes into focus for her.

Very clearly.

But not just the two words on the display, not just the name.

Everything does.

He decides not to leave a message. What's the point? He knows it'll come up as a missed call.

Standing under the portico, he gazes out over the hotel's front lawn and beyond it to the hushed suburban tranquillity of Ballsbridge.

Why didn't Fitz answer just now?

Norton turns right and takes a few steps along a manicured pathway.

He really wants to believe it's because Fitz is *busy* – that he's being thorough and scrupulous.

But something won't let him.

An angsty thrumming in the pit of his stomach.

He looks at his watch, and mouths the word *fuck*.

The problem is, there's no one else he can call. He has no choice but to wait.

He turns back towards the portico.

His phone rings.

He freezes, thinking, *Well thank Jesus*. He fumbles in his pocket, but when he gets the phone out he sees at once from the display that it's Miriam.

'*Damn*,' he says, and loud enough to draw a surprised look from the uniformed porter at the entrance to the hotel.

He stares at the display and decides not to answer it. They're still not speaking face to face, so why should they speak on the bloody phone? If he wants a review of the Friel play, can't he read the *Irish* fucking *Times* in the morning?

He puts the phone away and storms back inside.

As Gina is standing there, gazing across at Unit 46, a vertical slit of light appears. It's the steel door opening, a fraction at first, then wide. Terry Stack comes out and looks around.

'Gina?'

She takes a few steps forward. 'I'm here.'

Stack sees her and starts walking across the yard, his shoes click-clacking on the concrete. He huddles into his overcoat and shivers loudly.

Gina stands, waiting. She's still in shock from seeing that name on the caller ID of Fitz's phone.

Paddy Norton?

She'd been so convinced by him that day – by his indignation at what had happened, by his impatience with *her*. He'd
seemed hurt as well, and sad. She tries in vain to remember
if there was anything about him that might have been
suspicious. But she can't.

Terry Stack comes to a stop directly in front of her. 'Right,'
he says.

Gina looks at him, her mind swimming now with other
stuff she *is* remembering – questions about Norton and her
brother, for instance. They had a drink that evening in town.
But where? At what time? And what did they talk about?

'Gina?'

'Yeah.'

'Quick update. Little fucker in there is a former INLA man,
Martin Fitzpatrick, a republican –'

'Republican socialist?'

'Socialist me *hole*, love,' Stack says, laughing. 'He owns about
twenty apartments all over town and runs a private security
outfit. High King. They do construction sites, that sort of stuff.'

'Construction sites?'

'Yeah. Mainly.'

Gina nods along. Sagely. She feels light-headed. She feels
drunk.

'Anyway,' Stack goes on, 'he arranged the job on Noel. I got
that much out of him. *And* he did your brother.'

'Oh my God.'

'Yeah, both of them. He's a cunt.'

'*How?* How did –'

'The brakes. He did something with the brakes in his car.
Got him loaded and then . . .'

'Oh my God.' She takes a deep breath. '*Why?*'

'I don't know yet. I'm working on it. Give us a bit more time.'

'Mark Griffin?' Gina then says, almost in a whisper.

'I haven't got that yet either. He's holding out, says he doesn't know where he is, that no one was here when *he* arrived, but that's bollocks. We'll get it out of him, don't worry. It's all about pacing, this is . . . the build-up –'

Gina swallows.

'– the threshold, if you know what I mean.'

She does, in theory, of course, and wants to tell him *enough*, wants to be the one to end this, even though she's the one who started it. But what she says instead is, 'Get him to tell you about a man called Paddy Norton.'

Stack furrows his brow. 'Paddy Norton? He owns Winterland Properties, doesn't he?'

'Yeah.'

'That's . . . that's the crowd High King does most of its security work for.'

'Yeah well,' Gina says, 'I'm pretty sure you'll find he's also the one Che Guevara in there is answerable to for *this* job.'

'Fuck's sake,' Stack says. 'How do you know that?'

The phone is in Gina's pocket, but she doesn't want to give it to him. She ignores the question. Besides, isn't it obvious now? 'Just get him to tell you the reason for all of this, will you? *Why?* What did Noel ever do?' She pauses, then adds, '*My* Noel,' and gets a stinging sensation behind her eyes as she says it. But now isn't the time. She stares into Terry Stack's eyes. 'Will you do that for me?'

'Of *course* I will, love. Jesus.'

He holds her gaze for a moment. It's a long moment, and

she doesn't look away or even blink. But she feels unreal doing it, numb, like she's on smack.

'Look,' he says eventually, and a little too excitedly, 'I'll be as fast as I can.' He glances at his watch. 'Are you going to wait here?'

She nods.

'Probably just as well.' He clicks his tongue, and winks at her. 'I won't lock it.'

He turns and walks back to the other side. Gina watches him disappear behind the steel door. Then she retreats to the concrete ramp and huddles down into the corner, shivering. After a moment, she takes the packet of Major out of her pocket, looks at it and flings it away. She does the same with the Zippo lighter. Then she takes Fitz's mobile out but doesn't look at it. She wants to throw this away too, but resists. It might contain evidence, numbers, messages.

She tosses it from one hand to the other.

Paddy Norton.

She pictures him – this portly respectable man with his pinprick blue eyes and soft, chubby features, his thin wisps of grey hair, his expensive overcoat. She remembers his smell, too – cologne, mints, cigars, the smell of money. Then she thinks of Martin Fitzpatrick. She looks across at Unit 46. Did this burly, bottom-feeding former INLA piece of *shit* take his orders directly from Norton? Did he carry them out *himself*?

She lowers her head and closes her eyes.

If that turns out to be the case, and she suspects it will, probably already *has* . . . then what happens next?

Here. Tonight.

Terry Stack vowed that whoever killed young Noel would

pay the price. Is *that* what will happen next – and as a direct consequence of *her* actions?

Suddenly she feels sick.

Get him to tell you.

Would you do that for me?

Oh God.

Taking a deep breath, fighting the nausea, she opens her eyes. But the first thing she sees makes her heart jump. It's what's on the dimmed display of the phone in her hand. She presses a key and the backlight activates.

Five missed calls.

The most recent of these was from Norton, just a short while ago. And the others? She doesn't know, but wonders if they could *all* have come in the last twenty minutes. Is that possible, or likely? Of course it is, and as the full significance of this hits her, she also realises that it's too late to do anything about it. Because what she's hearing now, from her left, is the unmistakable sound of an approaching vehicle.

She turns to look, and freezes.

It's a small white van. It comes screeching to a halt next to the Saab. Driver and passenger doors open simultaneously and two guys get out, then a third. They're carrying things – she can't see them clearly, but they look like . . . sticks or bats.

There's no point in Gina's moving or trying to hide – she may be visible here, but these guys are in a hurry and unlikely to look in her direction.

She thinks of using the phone to warn Stack, but there isn't time – this is all happening too fast.

The three men converge on the steel door, kick it open and pile in.

The door remains wide open.

Immediately, from across the yard, and through the wind, she hears voices . . . shouting . . . roars . . . then a loud crack, followed by more shouting, followed by two more loud cracks.

Gina is paralysed, not shivering anymore.

She is barely breathing.

The shouting continues. Then it stops.

There is silence for . . . what . . . ten seconds? Fifteen seconds? She doesn't know, her ability to gauge non-existent. She's about to lean forward and get up when she sees something. There's a shadow at the doorway. It's moving. Remaining still, Gina stares across the yard as one figure, then two, emerge from the warehouse into the orange light. The first figure is limping. The second one is doubled over and clinging to the first one.

'Ow . . . *jaysus* . . . *fuuuuuuck.*'

This comes from the one with the limp. The other one is groaning, or crying.

It takes them a while, but they eventually make it to the passenger side of the van. From the way the van is parked, Gina can't see clearly, but she hears the door being opened. Then she hears the door being slammed shut again. A moment later the first guy comes around, hopping on one foot, and gets in on the driver's side.

The van starts up immediately. It reverses, seems as if it's about to back right in on top of Gina, but then turns suddenly, tyres screeching, and speeds off, heading in the direction of the exit and the main road.

Mark opens his eyes, stirred, it seems, by this awful silence, this rude stillness. Moments before, he was lost in a dream, and an ugly one – hellish, frenetic, noisy, and . . . of course, he's now realising, not actually a dream at all.

Which means those must have been gunshots he heard just now, real ones, and the screams too, and the screeching tyres. As well as the voices he heard earlier – from the open window six feet above him . . .

Talking, shouting, arguing.

Those also must have been real.

He tries to move, responding to the panicky signals coming from his brain, but he can't. The pain is too intense, and all-pervading. Like the freezing cold. It's as if he's set in cement.

But what about Gina?

Is she . . . ?

He parts his lips to say her name – not even to call it out, because he knows *that's* not going to happen – but in the end nothing happens anyway. He makes no sound at all.

What is going on?

He closes his eyes again, squeezes them shut.

Kaleidoscope eyes.

He dragged Gina out here. *He's* responsible for . . .

Newspaper taxis . . . appear on the shore.

This is *his* fault.

Waiting to take her away . . .

Minutes pass before Gina can move, or even take her eyes off the steel door on the far side of the yard. Eventually she looks away. She reaches an arm out and struggles to her feet. She slips Fitz's mobile phone into her pocket. Then she takes a step forward, but stops at once, acutely aware of the sound her own shoes are making on the concrete. She doesn't want to attract any attention. She doesn't want to be seen. But most of all, she doesn't want to see anyone else, and especially not anyone walking out of that door.

She looks around. Apart from the wind, there is absolute silence.

She turns left and starts walking. All she has to do now is *keep* walking, and in ten or fifteen minutes she'll be clear of here, past the roundabout, into one of the housing estates – near a pub, near people.

Safe.

But when she's halfway to the exit, she stops and turns around. She hesitates. Then she starts walking back the way she came.

She can't just *leave*.

She needs to know what happened. She needs to know that there wasn't anything else she could have done. She needs to know – for later – that she didn't walk away.

The steel door to the warehouse is wide open. As she approaches it she sees blood inside, streaked on the floor. She realises that there's blood outside, too – a trail of it on the concrete, leading over to where the white van had been parked.

She swallows, and braces herself.

Incredibly, the first blood drawn here tonight was drawn by *her* – so she doesn't get a pass on this.

She steps inside the door. She has to adjust her eyes for a second to the harsh fluorescent light, a fleeting respite before the full horror materialises in front of her. She did the math walking back . . . two got away, which means there should be four left.

And there are.

On the floor, all of them, evenly spread out, two over here, two over there. But she still has to count them – one, two, three, four – and more than once, as if she doesn't trust herself to get this simple calculation right.

The other thing that hits her is the smell.

It is sharp and overpowering, a combination – she quickly realises, glancing around – of smoke, piss and shit.

Over to the left, in a grey tracksuit, is the third guy from the white van. He's flat on his back and has a bullet hole in his forehead. In his hand he's still clutching what Gina had assumed outside to be a stick or a bat but now sees is a machete.

It is smeared with blood.

A yard farther on from this guy lies Terry Stack. He's slumped on the floor, facing Gina. His eyes are open, but so too is the side of his neck – a clean, deep swipe from the machete, leaving blood everywhere. He has a gun in his hand.

Over to the right, near the pallets, lies Stack's young associate, the hoodie. He's also on his side, but facing away from her. There is a pool of blood forming around his legs. Gina takes a few steps forward and looks at him more closely.

He's still breathing.

She bends over him and sees his chest moving – he's unconscious, but definitely still breathing.

She stands back up. Very slowly she turns around to get a proper look at what previously she only allowed herself a glimpse of – having had to avert her eyes before a coherent image formed.

Martin Fitzgerald is lying on the ground. He's in the same position as earlier, and still tied up, but now his jeans and boxers are bunched down around his ankles. There are small clamps and wires attached to his genitals. The wires are connected to a black rectangular device on the floor next to the toolbox. There is a cable running from the device through an extension over to a socket in the wall. Fitzgerald has soiled himself, and pretty badly – it's seeping out on both sides. He has also vomited, down his neck and all over his chest. In fact, there are still deposits of vomit in his mouth and caked on his chin, and it even looks as if he might have choked on it. Or maybe not. She can't be sure. It hardly matters, though. The expression on his face is startled, terrified . . . and frozen.

The state this man is in – not forgetting, of course, the gash on the side of his head – is the most awful, most appalling, most unforgettably distressing thing Gina has ever seen in her entire life.

She looks away. Her impulse is to throw up as well, or to cry, but not wishing to add to the sum total of excretions and effluvia in here, she steels herself and resolves to get outside before allowing anything like that to happen.

Stepping gingerly around the streams of piss and pools of blood, she makes her way across the warehouse floor. At one point someone's mobile goes off, and she freezes, the frenzied hurdy-gurdy ringtone piercing the silence like a scream. She waits for it to ring out, her heart pounding, but halfway through the sequence someone else's goes off. This time it's the absurd, bombastic theme from some TV series she can't remember the name of.

Eventually, they both stop. In the miraculous silence, Gina gets to the door and staggers out into the cold, fresh air.

Breathing heavily and with arms outstretched, she leans against the wall. She's ready to get sick now, and really wants to, but in the end she can't.

She straightens up.

Through the confusion and turmoil, she then remembers that one of the four men inside is still breathing – or at least he was a couple of minutes ago. She reaches into her pocket and takes out her phone. She's about to dial 999 when something else strikes her. She takes out Fitz's phone instead and uses that. She gets through to the police and gives them the address. She says that three men are dead and one is still alive. She cuts them off before they ask any questions.

She looks at her watch and then over at the Saab.

Which she's assuming is Fitz's.

She considers it but shakes her head.

Vigorously.

It would mean going back inside. It would mean kneeling down next to him again. It would mean rummaging through his pockets for the keys.

Gina is still shaking her head a few minutes later when she gets to the exit of the industrial estate, turns left onto the footpath and starts walking towards the Cherryvale roundabout.

Hearing a sound, Mark opens his eyes and struggles to bring the world around him into focus.

He's been drifting in and out of consciousness for what feels like ages, and has little sense anymore of what is real or imagined. Time, space . . . sound, temperature, pain – these have all come to seem fluid to him, and interchangeable.

Oceanic, ubiquitous, immeasurable . . .

But this is different.

What he's hearing at the moment is concrete, and penetrating, and increasingly real.

In fact, as the sound gets louder, and seems to divide into separate strands, he realises what it is. Of course. It's a medley of approaching sirens, the sirens of what must surely be multiple police cars and – more important right now, as far as Mark is concerned – an ambulance . . .

Seven

1

The next morning there is saturation coverage in the media, with newspaper headlines ranging from the hysterical – BLOODBATH! – to the soberly informative – THREE DEAD, TWO INJURED, IN GANGLAND FEUD. On one of the radio breakfast shows the Minister for Justice declares all-out war on the city's criminals and drug barons. Among commentators a consensus about what happened quickly emerges: it was a dispute between a senior gangland figure and an ex-paramilitary activist, with its roots possibly going back many years. It was also quite clearly an incident that got way out of hand. Live reports from the scene of the discovery – the result, it appears, of an anonymous tip-off to Gardaí – are shocking enough, but as usual it's in the tabloids that the truly gruesome stuff is to be found.

The dead men are named as Terry Stack, Martin Fitzgerald and Eugene Joyce. One of the injured men – both of whom are still in intensive care – is named as Shay Moynihan. The other one has yet to be identified.

Investigations are ongoing.

'I mean, *hon*estly,' Miriam says, flicking off the radio with one hand and pouring freshly brewed coffee into her husband's cup with the other, 'what *are* these people anyway, savages?'

'Yes,' Norton says, 'they are, they're animals, pure and simple.'

He and Miriam's rapprochement started late last night and he doesn't want to do or say anything now to endanger it – such as disagreeing with her, or pointing out to her that one of these savages may actually have been in this kitchen once, may have sat where she's sitting, may even have drunk from the very cup she's holding in her hand.

Norton stares into his coffee.

Since first hearing the news this morning – and on the radio like everyone else, though probably earlier than most – he's been trying to visualise the scene, to conjure it up in all its graphic horror. But he can't. More sober calculations keep getting in the way.

He raises his coffee cup and takes a sip. Miriam is concentrating on peeling an orange.

These two men in intensive care, for instance – he can only assume that the unidentified one is Mark Griffin . . . in which case he can only hope that the little fucker doesn't make it. Terry Stack's being out of the way, however, is a major plus, his involvement even breathing new life into Norton's original strategy of trying to make the whole thing seem gang-related. Fitz himself – who clearly couldn't organise a piss-up in a brewery – wasn't much of a threat, but he *was* the one direct link between Norton and pretty much everything that's happened recently.

There are variables, of course. Knowns and unknowns. What happens if Mark Griffin *does* make it? And what kind of a trail did Fitz leave behind him at High King? Documents? Recordings? Transcripts? Probably. But Norton's not too worried, because it would hardly be in High King's interests to compromise the confidentiality of their single most important client.

No, the biggest variable in all of this, the least predictable one – the great *un*known known – is Gina Rafferty. She wasn't mentioned in any of the radio reports, so . . . where *is* she? Weighed down at the bottom of a river somewhere? Hidden in the boot of a car? Would that be too much to hope for?

Miriam places a few segments of orange before him on a plate. 'There you are,' she says. 'Vitamin C.'

'Thank you, darling.'

What kick-started the rapprochement last night was an email from their daughter in Chicago. At the very end of it, and almost as an afterthought, she mentioned that she'd be home for Christmas. This was great news, and enough to alter Miriam's entire mood, taking her in seconds flat from chilly to warm, from clipped monosyllables to a torrent of chatter. Patricia's last visit over two years ago hadn't gone at all well, and here would be a rare chance for mother and daughter to regain some lost ground.

For his part, Norton was – and still is – relieved. But he knows from experience that this will now become a major project for Miriam – doing up rooms that don't need to be done up, organising lunches and drinks parties, as well as endless shopping. He knows her propensity to obsess. He also knows from experience that ten minutes off the plane and Patricia will be choking on all the attention. Ten minutes inside the house and she'll be on the phone to see if she can't bring the date of her return flight forward.

But at least it means that for the moment Miriam will no longer be giving a shit about *him* and his supposed dependency on prescription painkillers.

Vitamin C?

Thanks a lot.

Half an hour later he's in the car on Pembroke Road – but instead of going straight on to Baggot Street, to the office, he turns right at the canal and heads down towards the quays.

He phones his secretary and tells her he's going to be late.

'But not *too* late, I hope,' she says, 'because you have –'

'I know, I *know*.'

He has an eleven o'clock meeting with the Amcan people to iron out the final details of the tenancy contract. He gave in to Ray Sullivan last night on the question of the additional security measures, and there's no reason now why they can't close the deal, and soon – the beginning of next week or maybe even as early as tomorrow.

'I'll be all right,' he says, glancing at his watch. 'I've plenty of time.'

It's a crisp late-autumn morning, calm and clear after the high winds of last night. As he moves along South Lotts Road, Norton glances to the left. Dominating the city skyline, defining it, is Richmond Plaza. Then he looks to the right. It used to be that wherever you happened to find yourself in Dublin, you could pretty much rely on the red-and-white-striped twin chimneys of the Poolbeg power station to find *you*. Situated in the bay, these were a sentimental reference point for many people – they defined the city, they were the first thing you saw, through mist and cloud, on the flight path into Dublin Airport. But that has all changed. Because what immediately catches the eye these days is the considerably taller glass and steel structure rising up out of the docklands. It's a more appropriate structure *anyway*, in Norton's opinion. Better to have office and retail space, a hotel, condominiums – he thinks – than a brace of ugly industrial smokestacks.

Stopped at a red light on Pearse Street a few minutes later, he reaches into his pocket and takes out his Nalprox. He wasn't sure about these yesterday. Compared to the Narolet they seemed weaker somehow, but at the same time . . . stronger? Is that possible? Differently calibrated? He doesn't get it. They're all he's got, though. He pops two of them into his mouth, hesitates briefly, and then pops a third one in as well. For good measure.

The traffic moves and he turns right onto Tara Street. They crawl along and stop at another red light. He reaches over with his left hand and opens the glove compartment. He waits a moment and then looks. There it is, the grey barrel sticking out from under his pouch of AA documents. Before leaving the house earlier, he got this from the safe in his dressing room. He's never used it, nor does he have a licence for it – but he's always liked the idea of having a gun. Fitz got it for him some years back after there'd been a spate of burglaries in the neighbourhood.

Apparently it can't be traced.

The light changes. Norton flips the glove compartment closed.

He crosses the river and turns right onto Custom House Quay.

Gina Rafferty has an apartment down around here somewhere – that's what she told him the day they met – and he's guessing it's in one of these new complexes.

Fitz would have been able to give him the exact address.

But even *with* the address – and assuming she's still alive – how likely is it that he'll just see her here, spot her walking along the pavement or coming out of her building?

Not very.

In any case, the traffic is moving at quite a clip, and in seconds he has already gone too far. He cruises past Richmond Plaza. At the end he takes a right and goes over the toll bridge. He'll loop around through Ringsend, make his way back to the other end of the quays and start again.

At this point, he doesn't know what else to do.

As Larry Bolger steps into the shower, he wonders if this delay isn't going to scupper everything. If the moment isn't going to pass.

Bracing himself, he turns on the water and lets it run cold for a while.

The plan was hatched late last night in a fug of nervous exhaustion – with Bolger himself and a few others working the phones to drum up support. But then, at the last minute, there was a complication.

Isn't there always?

Just after 2 a.m. news broke of a horrific gangland massacre in the west of the city, three dead apparently – so they decided at once to abort. There was no point in going head to head with a story like *that*. It would dominate the news cycle and upstage any other story, especially a political one, for at least twenty-four hours.

He adjusts the temperature of the water and reaches for the soap.

But in a way he's relieved – because although he's been working up to this for years, now that it's within his grasp he feels deeply uneasy about it. Over these last two days he hasn't had a chance to make any enquiries into the circumstances surrounding his brother's death, but he's determined to rectify that. What he'd really like to do, in fact, is to visit the old man out in the nursing home in Wicklow – and today, if possible. When else is he going to be able to do it? This may be the last chance he gets for a while.

He'll have a look at his schedule.

As he scrubs away the anxiety and tension of a long night, it occurs to Bolger that there's something else he should be relieved about, too – the ease with which he appears to have seen off this recent so-called scandal. The affair part of it was a non-starter – in post-Catholic Ireland no one had the stomach to get into *that*. And as for the gambling debts, well, they were eventually seen as just a personal-finance issue, nothing that could be spun as improper 'contributions' or that involved any obvious conflict of interest. So although the media gorged themselves on the story and wanted more, the opposition parties folded quickly.

He puts the soap back in the dish, turns, closes his eyes and lets the jet of hot water massage the back of his neck.

Besides, as often happens in politics, the story moved on all by itself, in this case mutating over the space of forty-eight hours into a full-blown backbench revolt. The thing is, while the Taoiseach's spineless performance in the Dáil on Tuesday may not have been enough to trigger the long-anticipated leadership crisis, an imminent leak to the media revealing the source of the *original* Bolger story almost certainly will be.

He turns off the water, steps out of the shower and puts on his towelling robe.

An official in the Taoiseach's own department? The irony is too rich.

Bolger looks at himself in the mirror.

So, a plan was hatched.

The idea was that once this new angle on the story got fed to the media – and preferably this morning – senior figures in the party would persuade the Taoiseach to stand down and cede power. To none other than the Minister himself. There'd be no need for a divisive leadership contest.

It was perfect – a bloodless coup.

But then someone decided to turn on the radio.

Bolger picks out a shirt, and as he's putting it on, his phone rings. He looks at the display. Paula. He puts the phone on his shoulder, cocks his head to one side and starts buttoning up his shirt. 'Paula, yeah, what is it? I'm tired.'

In the brief moment before she answers, Bolger can picture Paula rolling her eyes and thinking, Jesus, Larry, we're *all* tired.

'Have you heard any of the details of this *thing*?'

'What, the shooting?'

'Shoot-*out* more like. Bloody OK Corral stuff. And fifty euro says at least *one* subeditor sticks that in a headline somewhere.'

'Do they know who's involved?' All Bolger heard on the early bulletin was the body count. No names had been released at that stage.

'Yeah, the main players seem to be Terry Stack and someone else called . . . er . . . Martin Fitzgerald.'

Bolger stops, hands poised to do up the top button of his shirt. He looks at himself in the mirror again. These two names . . . there's a resonance here, an echo . . .

'Larry?'

'Is that the Martin Fitzgerald who owns High King Security?'

'I think so,' Paula says. 'But they're playing up a paramilitary angle. I don't know, ex-INLA, some crap like that. Two scumbag smack dealers blowing each other away obviously isn't sexy enough for them.'

Bolger doesn't quite know what to make of this.

'But I'll tell you *one* thing,' Paula goes on, 'we were right to hold off, because it's going to be wall to wall today, the law-and-order agenda for breakfast, dinner and *bloody* tea.'

'Yeah, I know,' Bolger says, doing up the button. 'But anyway, listen.' He slips the phone from his shoulder into his hand. 'This little delay actually suits me. Because there's something I need to do this afternoon.'

'Oh.' Suspicious. 'What's that?'

He tells her about how he intends going out to the nursing home in Wicklow to see his father. But as he speaks – still staring at himself in the mirror – his unease deepens.

What's he expecting to find when he gets out there?

He doesn't know. Maybe nothing. Clarification. If he's lucky. Answers.

Though how much he thinks the old man will be able to tell him – in fact how much he thinks the old man will be able to *remember*, and about anything – well, that's another matter altogether.

When Gina wakes up, it takes her a moment to remember where she is. Leaning on one elbow, she raises herself up a little in the bed and looks around.

She's in the spare room of Sophie's new apartment.

But . . .

Oh *God*. Of course.

She throws the duvet back and swings her legs out.

After what happened last night, she can't believe she actually *slept*.

Sitting on the edge of the bed now, she runs her hands through her hair and tries to pull everything into focus. But there's really only one point to consider here, one central fact: no Mark Griffin. The warehouse, Fitz, Terry Stack, those other guys who came, the awful carnage that ensued . . .

But where the hell was *Mark* through all of it?

Where is he now? She's got to –

Then a stab of panic hits her as she registers the morning sunlight and realises that hours must have passed – six, seven, *eight* hours – since she left the warehouse.

She looks at her watch.

A quarter past nine.

Jesus, how did she sleep so –

What did Sophie *give* her?

She stands up but feels weak, her movements sluggish, her limbs heavy.

She sits back on the bed and closes her eyes.

Once beyond the roundabout last night she hailed a cab and came directly out here – because there was no way she could face going back to her own place. But she needed somewhere to regroup, to *think*, to work out a strategy. Once inside the door, though, she made it plain that she didn't want to answer any questions, and Soph went along with that. She offered Gina a drink, which Gina didn't want, and then offered her a Valium.

Gina opens her eyes.

Maybe that explains why she's still so groggy, why she was able to *sleep*. She just took what Sophie gave her and didn't check its strength. But it's obvious now that it wasn't a tranquilliser; it was a bloody sleeping pill.

She looks down. She's still in her clothes, black jeans and a sweater. Her leather jacket is on the end of the bed, folded neatly.

She looks around.

Where are her shoes?

She has to get out of here. She has to find out where Mark is and what happened to him.

She stands up and walks over to the door in her bare feet. The door opens directly onto the living room, and there, sitting on a leather couch, dressed for work, looking up at her a little nervously, is Sophie.

'Hi.'

'Hi,' Gina says back, and shrugs. 'What the hell was that you gave me, Soph? It knocked me out.'

'You *asked* for something. Do you know how upset you were when you got here last night? You were . . .'

Gina shakes her head. 'I don't really remember, not in any detail, but look, I . . . I have to get out of here. I've got –'

'You were bordering on hysterical,' Sophie says, leaning forward on the couch. 'But you wouldn't *talk* to me, you –'

'I'm sorry, Soph, I didn't mean to put you through that. You were the only pers–'

'I didn't *mind*, you idiot. But I was worried. I figured that maybe you'd . . .' She stops here and stands up. 'Look Gina,' she says, as though about to make a formal announcement. 'There was something on the news this morning.'

Gina looks at her. Oh God. Of course there was. Media coverage. It had never occurred to her.

But then something *else* occurs to her, and she looks over at the main door of the apartment. What kind of a trail did she leave behind her last night?

She swallows.

Should she even be here? Is it safe for Sophie? Is it safe –

'Gina.'

She looks back. 'What?'

'On the news. There's been this, I don't know, gangland *thing*. In a warehouse somewhere. Three people are dead, including that guy who was at your nephew's funeral.'

Gina stares at her, nods. 'Three? You sure?'

'Yeah.'

The hoodie must have made it.

'Anything else?'

'Anything *else*? Christ, Gina, didn't you hear what I just said?'

'Yeah, Soph, I heard. Now what else was there?'

'OK, *OK*. Let me think.' She shifts her weight from one foot to the other. 'They also said there are two guys in intensive care.'

Gina looks at her.

'*Two?*'

'Yeah, one of them was stabbed and the other one was shot. I can't believe I'm even saying this. The one who was shot they found in an alleyway or something. Nearby.'

Mark.

It has to be.

Gina feels simultaneously sick and relieved.

Then Sophie takes a step towards her and says, 'You were there, weren't you, last night?'

Gina doesn't answer.

'I mean, come on,' Sophie continues. 'The time you got

here, the state you were in.' She pauses. 'The blood on your shoes.'

Gina's eyes widen.

Sophie points. 'They're over there on the kitchen floor. I cleaned them.'

Gina nods, and then sits on the edge of the sofa. After a long silence, she says, 'Shouldn't you be at work?'

'Don't worry. I called in sick.'

Sophie takes off her jacket and places it over the back of a chair. She turns the chair to face the sofa and sits in it. 'I didn't like leaving, and then when I stuck my head in the door to check up on you before heading out, I noticed your shoes.' She shrugs. 'And *well*, on top of what I'd just heard on the radio . . .'

Gina nods again. Then she does her best to explain. She goes through it in detail, and in sequence – from her earliest suspicions on that awful Tuesday morning to everything she endured, and witnessed, last night.

Sophie is pale by the end of it.

'Holy God, Gina. Jesus Christ. You've got to go to the Guards.'

'I can't. I –'

'But you're still –'

'Look, I brought Terry Stack *in* on it, I called him, I encouraged him to . . . to *interrogate* that guy. I mean, *listen* to me.'

Sophie leans forward. 'But Gina, you're still . . . it sounds to me like you're still in danger.'

'Yeah. I suppose I am.' She shrugs. 'Yeah. But listen . . . do you have any coffee?'

Sophie nods. She gets up at once, heads over to the kitchen and with all the focus of a staff nurse preparing to dress a wound or give an insulin injection, she gets busy filling the kettle and then her cafetière.

Gina stands up and walks back over to the spare room. She sits on the end of the bed and picks up her jacket. She goes through the pockets and extracts whatever doesn't belong to her. Mark Griffin's mobile. Fitz's mobile. Fitz's *gun*. The three photographs.

She spreads all of these items out on the bed.

She glides a hand over the photos.

I finally saw them today. For the first time. Saw what they looked like. My family. I'm looking at them now. Lucy was so small, she –

Gina turns away, and stares at the floor.

Jesus. Poor Mark. Seeing these . . . these faces, after so many years, and then . . .

Then whatever happened to him. Getting shot . . .

Though she wonders now when exactly *that* happened, and where. Because something occurs to her. Mark sounded very weird on the phone. Out of it. Delirious almost. So could he actually have been shot *before* they spoke?

Then something else occurs to her. Sophie is right. Gina herself is still in danger. This isn't going to stop just because Fitz is no longer around. And if she keeps on asking questions the way she has been, she's probably going to wind up seriously injured – or even dead – herself.

Unless she gets some real answers first.

'I'm stunned.'

Gina looks up. Sophie is leaning against the doorjamb with her arms folded.

'Sorry?'

Sophie exhales. 'I'm in total shock, Gina. At *all* of this.'

'I know. I know. Me too.'

Gina tugs the jacket towards her to cover the items on the bed.

Out in the kitchen, the kettle whistles to a boil and then clicks off. Sophie steps away from the door. 'So,' she says over her shoulder as she moves off, 'what are you going to do?'

Gina flips the jacket back. She looks down at the charcoal-grey gun lying on the bed. It is dense and angular, and radiates an undeniable seriousness. Next to it, the mobile phones, metallic and shiny, look like trinkets. She picks the gun up, holds it in her hand, feels it.

'I don't know,' she says, her voice a notch or two louder, 'but I think I'm going to continue doing what I've been doing all along.'

'What's that?'

Closing one eye, Gina raises the gun and points it at the wall. 'Asking questions.'

2

Norton feels a little dizzy as he steps out of the elevator onto the third floor. His secretary greets him with a list of calls he absolutely *must* return, but when he gets to his desk the first call he makes is to Dr Walsh's surgery.

But Dr Walsh won't talk to him.

Prick.

Norton then looks at the list of names his secretary gave him, stares at it. He has no interest in returning any of these calls. He looks at his watch. Twenty minutes to go before the Amcan meeting. He's finding it hard to drum up any interest in that either. What he really wants to do is to reach into his pocket and take out his pills. He wants that sensation, that little ritual, with its attendant promise of . . .

But he's *done* it already, that's the problem – less than an hour ago he took three of the bloody things. He can feel them in his system all right, just not in the way he's used to. It's very frustrating.

No less frustrating was his attempt to find Gina Rafferty. He cruised along by the quays *four* times, then parked and walked around for fifteen minutes. But he didn't see any sign of her.

The Amcan meeting passes in a blur. He pretty much agrees to everything on the agenda and proposes that the contract be signed tomorrow. He can see that the chief negotiator, a forty-ish RFK wannabe from Boston, is a little perplexed – but Norton doesn't care. Besides, this is what he wants, and where's the point in breaking their balls just for the sake of it? With Amcan on board, and the name of the building officially changed to reflect this, the project's success isn't exactly guaranteed, but it stands a pretty good chance. And all those people who predicted that thirty or forty floors would remain unoccupied, thus making a mockery of Norton's ambitions . . . well, they can now go and fuck themselves.

Soon after the meeting concludes, Norton gets a call from Ray Sullivan in Vienna. He'll be back in Dublin tomorrow for the signing.

Norton welcomes the news.

'. . . and what's more, my friend,' Sullivan goes on, 'get a load of *this*. Mr V. is in London at the moment, so he's going to fly over, too. All informal, of course, and strictly private. He'd just like to have a look around. Do the tour.'

When he hears this, Norton bucks up a little in spite of

himself. James Vaughan? In person? Of *course* he'll keep it informal and strictly private – though that won't stop him from making damn sure the right people hear about it all the same . . .

Norton savours the moment. But it doesn't take long for the excitement to abate. Because where the bloody hell, it occurs to him, is Gina Rafferty? Running scared? Waiting in the long grass? He tunes in to Newstalk at 12.30 and listens to the headlines. There are no developments.

Then, as he's considering his options, a courier arrives with a package from High King Security. Norton rips open the envelope and empties its contents onto his desk.

He can only imagine the panic they're in over there, but he's glad they decided not to destroy these documents, because within less than a minute he has in front of him Gina Rafferty's full address and telephone number.

He's still not sure what to do, though.

He thinks calling her up might be the wrong move. It might frighten *her* into making a wrong move. He'll go down by the quays again later, go to her building, confront her in person, and find out what he can.

He wishes now that he hadn't been so bloody self-controlled that day up on the forty-eighth floor of Richmond Plaza. He could easily have got away with it, spun some story. *She was upset, I suppose, about her brother – depressed you might even say. Anyway, I got alarmed and stepped forward . . . I tried to grab her, but . . .*

It strikes him as extraordinary now that if he *had*, all of this could have been avoided.

At one o'clock he switches on the radio again – to a breaking news story. An exclusive RTÉ report is claiming that the source last Wednesday for the original leak to the media about Larry Bolger's private life *was someone in the Taoiseach's office.* Hardly an exciting development next to the multiple killings in Cherryvale, but to any self-respecting news junkie the story's significance is unmissable.

Norton reaches for the phone and tries Bolger's mobile, but it goes straight into voicemail. He tries the Department but is told the Minister is unavailable. Then he tries a number he has for Paula Duff.

'Mr Norton.'

'Paula, how are you? I'm trying to reach Larry. Do you know where he is?'

She sighs loudly. 'Oh, don't ask. He's gone AWOL for the afternoon.'

'What do you mean? I thought with all this —'

'I know, I know, tell me about it. We were trying to keep the story on hold until tomorrow but somehow it got out. A bloody leaked leak about a leak, can you believe it? Anyway, Larry chooses *this afternoon,* God knows why, to go off and bond with his old man.' She pauses. 'Out in Wicklow somewhere.'

'He's going out to the *nursing home?*'

'Yeah. I suppose that's it. I don't really —'

'*Why?* What did he say?'

'He didn't say anything, Mr Norton.' She pauses. 'But for the last few days he's been in the weirdest mood. I don't know if it's —'

Norton cuts her off. 'Soon as you hear from him, get him to call me, would you?'

'Of course.'

He puts the phone down, slowly, onto his desk.

He leans back and takes a couple of deep, calming breaths.

*

After coffee and a shower, Gina phones BCM. She talks to the receptionist for a few minutes, mainly about Noel, and then asks if she can get a number for Dermot Flynn's widow.

'Of course, Gina, no problem. I have it here somewhere.'

'Thanks. What's her name?'

'Claire. She's lovely. The poor *thing*. The removal is tomorrow, by the way.'

'Right.'

'Here it is. I'm sure she'll appreciate the call.'

'Yeah.'

But Gina waits a while before actually making the call. She and Sophie sit together and drink more coffee. They talk things through but end up going around in circles – so when Gina picks up the phone again it's nearly eleven o'clock. As the phone rings, she gazes out the window. The day is starting to cloud over.

'Hello?'

'Claire? Hi. My name is Gina Rafferty. Er . . . my brother and your husband both worked –'

'Yes, I know,' Claire interrupts. 'Hello.'

'Hello.'

'*Gina*, did you say?'

'Yes. I hope I'm not . . . intruding.'

'No. *Well.*' She clears her throat. 'What is it? What can I do for you?'

'I'd like to meet up with you, if that's possible. Soon. I need to ask you something. It's important. I realise this is not –'

'Ask me what?'

Gina closes her eyes. 'I know this is going to sound pretty

blunt, but I don't believe my brother's death was an accident, and I'm wondering if you have reason to believe . . . anything similar. About your husband's death I mean.' She opens her eyes, stares at the floor, waits.

Ten seconds pass, maybe fifteen – it's hard to tell. Then Claire Flynn releases a slow, whispered *'Jesus Christ.'*

Gina waits for more. In vain. Eventually, she says, 'Claire?'

'Hhmm.'

'Can we meet?'

'Yes.'

'Now?' Another long pause. 'Later today maybe?'

'OK. This afternoon. I have to, er . . .'

'That's fine. Whatever.'

'Three thirty, four? Here?'

'Yeah. The –'

'Forty-seven Ashleaf Drive. Sandymount.'

Gina is about to say something else, but Claire has already hung up.

At midday Gina goes out to get an early edition *Evening Herald*. On her way back to the apartment, she makes a detour into Blackrock Park, where she sits at a bench by the pond and reads through the paper's coverage. The only thing of significance they can add to what she's already heard on the radio is the fact that the second man in intensive care, whose name they're still not releasing, is the owner of the warehouse where the incident took place.

Which amounts – as far as Gina is concerned – to a confirmation of his identity.

His condition, on the other hand, remains critical – though what exactly *that* means Gina isn't sure at all. But shouldn't she be doing something to find out? At the very least contacting the hospital to make enquiries? Probably. But something is holding her back, a reluctance, an awful feeling of guilt.

She gazes out over the pond.

If she hadn't dragged Mark into this, he most likely wouldn't be in the ICU right now, fighting for his life. So chances are the last person he's going to want to hear from is *her*.

And who could blame him?

Gina puts the newspaper away.

After a while, to distract herself, she takes out the two mobile phones. She examines them. There are three numbers for Paddy Norton on Fitz's phone, and she finds her own number on Mark Griffin's. But nothing else she comes across means anything to her. Then, as she's leaving the park a few minutes later, she drops Fitz's phone discreetly into the pond. Because these things can be detected, can't they? And located?

As for the other one, she decides . . . well, if there's any chance at all, she'd like to return it in person.

Back at the apartment, and at Sophie's insistence, Gina finally gets around to ingesting something other than black coffee. She has half an orange, followed by a poached egg and a slice of toast.

She turns on the radio and listens to the one o'clock news – and as she does so can't help feeling increasingly dislocated from reality. Because even though the bulletin presents the two main stories separately, *she* knows that in some crucial way they are connected. Later on, heading in towards Sandymount on the DART, it occurs to her how like a classic symptom of clinical paranoia this is – seeing a pattern that no one else is seeing, reinterpreting the *news*, twisting it so it conforms to some personal context or scheme of grievances.

But she doesn't care anymore, not after last night. She knows what she knows. And besides, she's not alone. Claire Flynn, the woman she's about to visit, seems to know something, too.

As they pull into the driveway leading up to the Glenalba Nursing Home, Bolger realises that he hasn't been out here for over three years. He *has* seen the old man in that time, of course – at his sister Una's house. She lives in Bray and takes him for Christmas and birthdays and whatnot. Larry lives in Deansgrange, but with the extra distance, and the old man's condition . . . well, it never made much sense to do it any other way.

Besides, he and the old man have never really got on. Larry was always second best, and he was certainly the second choice when it came to a career in politics. After Frank died, the old man pushed Larry hard, schooled him, moulded him, and even though Larry did well, *very* well, there was always a tension between them. Larry resented how he was being manipulated, and the old man could never *really* forgive Larry for not being Frank. But by the time Larry made it to the cabinet, the old man's influence in the party had long since waned, as had his interest – even to the extent that Larry felt he was barely showing up on the old man's radar screen anymore.

And Bolger can't help resenting *that*. Which he knows is absurd, because apart from anything else, the old man is in the clutches of some form of dementia these days, not quite Alzheimer's, but not quite anything else they seem willing to name either. He floats in and out of focus. One minute he's the acerbic old bollocks he's always been, cutting you down to size, and the next he's slumped in a chair and staring vacantly at the wall, or worse, at *you* – decades of the unspoken, and the unthinkable, suspended terrifyingly in mid-air between you.

When Bolger gets out of the car he is greeted by the director of the home, Mrs Curran, a severe matronly type in her mid-fifties. They exchange a few words on the steps. When they go inside, the first thing that hits Bolger is the smell: a combination of permanently on heating, cooking odours, carpets and – there's no other way of saying it – old people.

Mrs Curran leads him down a corridor to the lounge. This is a large room with perhaps a dozen sofas and armchairs spread about. There is a fireplace, a TV mounted on a high shelf and a sectioned-off area with four card tables in it.

Mrs Curran indicates an armchair on the far side of the room.

The old man is sitting alone, facing a window that looks out onto a rolling lawn and the nearby hills.

Having engaged in small talk up to this point, Mrs Curran lobs a curve ball at Bolger. 'I should warn you . . . Liam is in a very, shall we say, *isolated* place of late. He's fine really, and seems quite tranquil in fact, but he has very much retreated into himself.'

Bolger acknowledges this with a silent grimace.

He makes his way through the maze of sofas, half of which are occupied. He greets people as he passes, but is unsure if anyone is noticing him – and not *who* he is, but at all. When he gets to the window, his father looks up and nods a *hello*, as though they'd last seen each other half an hour ago.

Liam Bolger is in his late seventies and suddenly looks it. As always he's wearing a suit and tie, but today this old, familiar suit looks too big for him. He seems small in it, shrunken, even since the last time they actually did see each other, which was what . . . about two or three months ago? At Una's. A birthday?

Bolger pulls an armchair over and angles it so that he's half facing the old man and half facing the view. He sits down.

'How *are* you, Dad?'

There is no reply.

Bolger glances out the window. It's an oppressive afternoon, dull and overcast. The autumnal view is lovely, but it needs a few shafts of sunlight to animate it. And that's not going to happen today.

'I spoke to Una last week,' he says, and immediately feels stupid for saying this, as though speaking to his sister were an actual piece of news.

It's not even true.

The old man turns to him and their eyes meet.

In the next couple of seconds, Bolger feels a rapid succession of things: he feels accused, rebuked, ridiculed even. He wants to say, *'What?'*

'They're in the cupboard,' the old man whispers.

Bolger leans forward, as though he's been thrown a lifeline, something he can work with.

'The cupboard? What's in the cupboard, Dad?'

The old man's watery eyes widen, revealing crimson rims. He doesn't look tranquil at all. He looks terrified.

'That'd be telling you.' He shakes his head. 'Do you think I'm a fool? That's what *they* want.'

Bolger swallows. He's lost here. He says nothing. He studies the old man's face and sees flickers of himself, flickers of Frank. He thinks of the questions he came out here to ask . . . and all of a sudden asking them seems about as plausible as asking a two-year-old to explain string theory.

But he decides to ask them anyway, to throw a curve ball of his own. Maybe it's a brutal thing to do, but he figures he might be able to shock the old man up onto some higher level of awareness.

'Dad,' he says, hunching forward, 'I want to ask you something. The night . . . the night Frank died, was *he* responsible for what happened? Did *he* cause the accident?'

There.

He remains hunched forward, tense, waiting for a response.

The old man stares at him.

Bolger feels strangely liberated. They've never talked about this before. In fact, all they've *ever* talked about over the years is constituency stuff, or the North, or Gaelic football.

But as the seconds tick past, Bolger begins to suspect that nothing is going to happen here, that the grenade words *Frank* and *accident* might still be lying on the floor of his father's mind, undetonated.

'Dad?'

'They're in the *cupboard,* you eejit. I *told* you.'

Bolger sighs. He leans back in the armchair, resigned, impatient.

'*What* are, Dad?'

The old man bends forward.

'The *paratroopers.*'

The word is delivered in a loud whisper, and with such urgency and desperation that Bolger is alarmed. But what can he do?

After another twenty minutes or so, most of which passes in silence, he stands up. He says goodbye, trying hard to make leaving like this seem normal. He avoids eye contact with anyone as he crosses the lounge area.

Walking back to reception, along the corridor, he is upset and distracted, and has to make a huge effort to compose himself when he hears someone calling out his name.

'Hello Gina, come in.'

Claire Flynn holds the door open and Gina steps into a narrow hallway. The two women proceed through a door on the left into the living room. Claire takes Gina's jacket, invites her to sit down, offers her something to drink – coffee, tea. It's all very formal and awkward. Gina can hear voices from another part of the house – young voices. The girls?

'I've been drinking coffee all day,' Gina says, 'so maybe just a glass of water?'

'Fine.'

Claire retreats. Gina sits down in an armchair and looks around. It's an attractive room, with wooden floors, an old-fashioned fireplace, a coffee table and a very comfortable three-piece leather suite. It's also very much a family room. There are a couple of beanbags, bookshelves in an alcove and a home cinema system in the corner. From what she can see the DVD collection is dominated by Disney and Pixar titles.

There are double doors leading to another room, but these are closed.

Claire returns carrying a glass of water in one hand and a mug of tea in the other. Gina reaches up and takes her water. Claire steps backwards and sits on the sofa, nestling in at one end, resting her mug on the edge.

'So,' she says.

Gina nods and half smiles. She takes a sip of water from her glass. This is the first chance she's had to focus, to get a proper look at Claire Flynn, who's probably about the same age as Gina is, but seems slightly older. Is this because of that extra little touch of seriousness and maturity that comes – Gina *imagines* – from being a married woman and a mother? And now a widow? Maybe. She's a redhead in any case, pale, with freckles and green eyes. It's a very particular look – and Gina's prepared to bet that if she gets to see either of the daughters, it's a look she'll see replicated. Dermot Flynn, as she remembers – a little uncomfortably now – was fairly nondescript-looking, featureless.

'Thanks for agreeing to see me,' she says.

'I didn't have a choice, really. After what you said.'

Gina nods. 'I'm sorry about your husband. You have my sympathies.'

This is something she hates saying, and hates hearing, but it's a formula and a necessary hurdle to get over.

'Thank you.'

'How are your girls?'

'OK. They don't really understand yet. I'm trying to keep things as normal as possible for them, at least until the removal tomorrow. And then the funeral.' She shakes her head. 'After that, I don't know. It's going to be hard.'

'Of course.'

There is an awkward pause.

Claire says, 'I'm sorry about your brother.'

Gina looks into her glass. 'Thanks. I haven't come to terms with it yet. I haven't even started. The thing is, since it happened I've been in the grip of this awful *suspicion* I mentioned to you on the phone. Though it's more than a suspicion now, a lot more, which is why I wanted to talk to you.' She looks up. 'But I'm getting ahead of myself. Let me try and explain.'

Claire nods. She takes her mug of tea, wraps her hands around it, and holds it in front of her.

Gina unconsciously does the same thing with her glass of water, then notices and shifts position again.

She starts talking.

It's an edited version of what she told Sophie, with a slight change of emphasis. She leaves out Mark Griffin and Paddy Norton. She leaves out most of last night. She concentrates on Terry Stack, on the two Noels, on Fitz, on BCM – the essentials, context.

'So look, Claire,' she says, finishing up. 'I don't know. If you have any grounds for suspicion, any grounds *at* all, it should be possible to get to the bottom of this.'

Claire stretches forward and puts her mug, untouched, onto the coffee table. As she's leaning back, tears come into her eyes. She makes a sound, a sort of primal whimper, and all of a sudden she's crying.

Gina watches. She feels awful, but at the same time knows there's nothing she can do. She demonstrates her understanding, in fact, precisely *by* doing nothing – by not moving, by not resorting to the false comfort of easy words. The impulse to join in, to cry herself, is immense, but she resists. Instead, she drinks the water in her glass, finishes it in one go, and then stretches forward to put the empty glass onto the coffee table.

Eventually, the tears subside. Claire extracts a tissue from the sleeve of her sweater and blows her nose. When she has finished, she looks at Gina.

'What you're saying is . . . it's *horrible.*'

'I know.'

'I mean, does stuff like this really go on?' There's still a tremor in her voice and she's doing her best to suppress it.

'Because I'm as capable of being cynical as the next person, I really am, but I mean . . . *Christ.*'

Gina shrugs, as if to say *I know, me too.*

'But Claire,' she then says, leaning slightly forward, nowhere left to go with this. 'Your husband's death? Is there anything that makes you think it wasn't an accident?'

'There is *now*,' Claire says at once. 'Absolutely.' Her eyes widen. 'In the context of what you've just told me. I mean, I just thought I was . . . well, I didn't know what I thought. But I've kept it to myself. I haven't told anyone.'

'Haven't told anyone what?'

'In the two weeks before the accident, before the . . . the . . .' – she waves it away – 'before he *died*, Dermot was not himself, he was acting weird, he was hyper, he was distant, he was evasive, I even thought he was . . . I even thought he was' – the second time she utters the phrase, her voice cracks slightly – '*having an affair*. Which was ridiculous.' She emits a quick, mirthless laugh to show just *how* ridiculous. 'I loved Dermot, Gina, but he wasn't the type. Women scared him. He wouldn't have known where to begin. But anyway, looking back, I think he was freaked out about something, and that breaks my heart. That I couldn't help him. That he couldn't *tell* me, because we told each other everything –'

'Freaked out about what?' Gina says, jumping in here, trying to pre-empt the next surge of emotion.

'I don't know. Jesus. If I *knew*. But –'

'Yeah?'

'The other weird thing, and I'm only connecting it up now, is that there was some . . .' – she seems barely able to say the word – '. . . *cash*. Hidden in a box at the bottom of the wardrobe. *Ninety-something thousand euro.*' She pauses. 'I found it yesterday. I also found some jewellery, earrings and a gold chain. Still with the receipt. Worth over two grand.'

They leave that hanging. Gina tries to square it up in her mind with everything she knows.

But can't.

'What about the way he died,' she then says, 'the actual . . . the . . .'

'Again, that's weird,' Claire says. 'On the face of it he was crossing the road and was run over. But I'm sorry. What was he doing there in the first place? In that laneway? It's not a route he would ever take. Coming out onto Bristol Terrace? *On his way home?* It makes no sense.'

'Any witnesses?'

'No. Just the driver. Who said Dermot was running.' She pauses. 'But why would he be *running*? He never had occasion to run. He wasn't the running *type*.'

'What about work? BCM? Did he mention anything unusual going on there?'

'No. He didn't talk that much about work. It was very technical what he did, so it wasn't stuff we chatted about. But still . . .'

'What?'

'In the last month or so he seemed to be doing a lot of extra work. And not at the office. At home.' She points at the closed double doors. 'In there.'

She gets up off the sofa, walks over and opens the doors. Gina gets up as well.

'This was originally a dining room,' Claire says. 'But we made it into a study. For Dermot.'

They go in.

The room is small and cluttered. It is lined with books and there are piles of magazines on the floor. There is a desk – an old-fashioned escritoire – above which there is a poster for some kind of design exhibition.

Lying on the desk is a laptop.

Gina stares at it. *'That,'* she says to Claire, pointing. 'His laptop, have you . . . checked it out?'

Claire gives a quick shake to her head. She is obviously very uncomfortable standing here.

'In that case,' Gina says, 'would it be OK if *I* took a look?'

Claire turns to her, brow furrowed. 'Why?'

'There was something going on at BCM, Claire. It's what links them, Noel and Dermot. It's the key to this. I don't know. Maybe I can find something . . . a clue, relevant information.' She shrugs. 'I know my way around computers. I work in software.'

Claire considers this, and nods. She holds a hand out. 'Please.'

Then she turns around abruptly and leaves the room.

Gina hesitates. She feels a bit like an intruder, but she goes over to the desk all the same, sits down and opens the laptop.

Bolger looks around.

Coming towards him along the corridor of the nursing home is a man in an electronic wheelchair.

'I'm right,' the man says, 'amn't I? It's Larry Bolger?'

Bolger nods, ever the politician, and extends a hand. It's only at that point that he recognises who this is.

'Romy?'

The man in the wheelchair shakes Bolger's hand vigorously

and then refuses to let it go. 'Jesus, Larry,' he says, smiling. 'Look at you. Come a long way, what?'

Jerome Mulcahy. Contemporary of the old man's.

Bolger smiles, too. 'Yeah', he says, 'it's been a long road, right enough.'

'I just heard the news,' Romy says. 'At lunchtime. It's looking good for you.' His smile disappears and is replaced by a frown. 'But it's a pity,' he says, flicking his head in the direction Bolger has just come from, 'it's a pity that His Nibs is in no condition to appreciate it.'

'Indeed.'

Bolger tries, but fails, to retrieve his hand.

'You see, the thing is,' Romy goes on, 'physically, I'm fucked, but I'm grand mentally. *He's* the opposite. Cruel, isn't it?'

'It is, yeah, but I have to say, that's quite a grip you have there.'

The smile returns. The hand is released.

'*He* can walk and eat and go to the jacks, but he couldn't tell you his own name. *I'm* stuck in this yoke, all I can eat is puréed vegetables, and I've got a bag attached to my arse. But I could repeat to you conversations I had twenty years ago, and practically fucking verbatim.'

Bolger stares at him. 'How about twenty-five years ago?'

'Try me.'

Bolger had forgotten, but this place, the Glenalba, was a sort of unofficial rest home for party members of a certain vintage, mainly the old Talbot Road gang. Quite a few of them had passed through here and he imagines that Romy and his father must be among the last. He remembers the two of them, along with a few others, and his uncles – even from when he was a kid . . . meetings at the house, summers in Lahinch, Paddy's

Day parades, All Ireland finals. They really *were* a gang. And later on, when he came back from Boston, they really *were*, at least at a local level, the party machine, too.

'Is there somewhere else we can go, Romy?' Bolger asks, glancing up and down the corridor.

'Over here,' Romy says, whirring his wheelchair around and heading for a door to Bolger's right. 'This used to be the *smoking* room. That's a laugh.' They enter what looks like a waiting room in a dentist's surgery. 'They've done nothing with it since the ban. It's like a shagging mausoleum.'

Bolger looks around. There are a couple of low tables in the middle of the room with empty ashtrays on them. He walks past these and sits down in a hard plastic chair, one of several lined up against the back wall. Romy follows and positions himself directly in front of Bolger. Despite his obvious frailty and limited mobility, this pale, stick insect of a man is restless and full of nervous energy.

'So,' he says with a smirk, his eyes like tiny caged animals. 'What do you want to know, *Taoiseach*?'

Bolger gives the barest nod of acknowledgement to this, liking the sound of it – at any rate allowing himself for half a second, in the safe confines of this private room, to like the sound of it.

He clears his throat.

'The night Frank died,' he then says, jumping right in – and knowing he doesn't have to say much more than that. 'Er . . .'

'What about it?'

In the pause that follows, Romy's demeanour changes. Proximity to power, this unexpected blast from the past, the little bit of company – whatever it was that was animating him a moment before is now gone.

Alan Glynn

Bolger speaks very quietly. 'I was never really told what happened.'

'You never asked.'

'I *did*, and *was* told, but I don't think I was told the truth.'

Romy makes a face. 'The *truth*? Would you fuck off, would you?'

'Romy, *you* were around at the time. *I* wasn't.' He leans forward. 'Did Frank cause that accident? Was all that talk about the other fella being drunk just a . . . just a –'

'Jesus Christ, are you out of your mind?'

Bolger shakes his head. 'Romy –'

'What are you asking me this for? And today of all days? We may not have had spin doctors back in my time, Larry, but even *I* can tell you that asking a question like *that* . . .'

'I'm asking *you*, Romy, not some journalist.' He waves an arm around, indicating the empty room, the empty chairs. 'I'm not posting this on the bloody Internet. I wanted to ask my father . . . but it seems . . .'

Romy studies him for a moment, then says, 'What difference does it make anyway?'

'Well, who knows, but maybe there could have –'

'No, no, Larry, no. It doesn't make *any* difference. And let me tell you why. I don't know what happened, I really don't, I wasn't at the actual scene, you'd have to look up the, the what's it, the toxicology reports for that, but even if Frank *was* the one who was drunk, it wouldn't bring anyone back, it wouldn't change a fucking thing.'

'*I* mightn't have got elected.'

'There you go.'

'But would that have been so bad?'

'Ah, for –' Romy jerks his head backwards in a gesture

of disbelief. 'I think *you're* the one who's fucking drunk now.'

Bolger takes a deep breath. 'Listen, I know it broke Dad's heart when Frank died. I know all his *real* hopes, his ideals, died with Frank, and that I was only –'

It's the look on Romy's face that stops him.

'*What?*'

Romy shakes his head. 'What are you talking about?'

Bolger pauses, unsure of himself now. 'I thought –'

'Of course it broke his heart,' Romy says. 'Jesus Christ, his *son* died.' He hesitates. 'But the fact of the matter is, Larry . . . Frank broke your old man's heart a *long* time before that . . .'

After about fifteen minutes, Gina turns the laptop off and closes it. She unplugs its various cables, lifts it up and carries it into the living room. There's no one there. She goes out to the hallway and there's no one there either. But she can still hear voices coming from the back of the house. She walks along the hallway to a door, which is ajar, and nudges it open.

Sitting at a long table, huddled over colouring books, are two small . . . replicas of Claire. They look up. One smiles, the other doesn't. Claire herself is standing behind them, leaning back against a counter. Standing next to Claire is yet another replica – though this one's hair is grey rather than red.

'Hi,' Gina says, waving at everyone. 'Claire?'

As Gina retreats into the hallway, she notices the older girl eyeing her suspiciously, and then hears her whispering, '*That's my daddy's computer*,' and the grandmother saying, 'Ssshh, pet, it's OK.'

When Claire appears, Gina gets straight into it – both of them standing there in the hallway. She holds up the laptop.

'Lots of technical stuff, like you said. Papers, drafts of papers, articles. Going way back. But the thing is, I checked out the activity logs and he . . . he didn't throw much stuff out, did he? Tended to hang on to –'

'To everything, emails, letters, *magazines,* total magpie. You saw the floor there in the study.'

'Yeah, so, the day after Noel died . . . Dermot seems to have deleted some stuff.'

'Oh.'

'Well, a couple of files anyway. *And* some emails. Maybe it's nothing, but . . . the timing *is* strange.'

'Yes.'

Gina hesitates, and then says, 'Claire, if you let me take this away, I can probably retrieve the stuff he deleted.'

'Really?'

'Yes.'

She won't actually be able to do it herself. She'll have to get one of the guys in the back room to do it. But that isn't anything Claire needs to know.

'It's what the company I work for *does,*' she goes on. 'And it's actually pretty straightforward. We have software back at the office, applications that can –'

'OK. Take it.'

Gina looks at her. 'You sure?'

'Yes. If there's something there . . . well.' Her eyes are glistening. 'We need to *find* it, don't we?'

'Yes. We do.'

Up close like this, Gina can see that Claire is barely keeping it together. She reaches over, places a hand on her arm and gives it a gentle squeeze.

On the DART into town, she phones the office and talks to

one of the guys in the back – Steve, her favourite, a lanky, laconic programmer from Cork. She asks him if he could do her a favour. 'OK,' he says, a little cagey, 'I suppose, yeah. What is it?' Looking out at a sombre, overcast Ringsend and clutching the laptop to her chest, Gina says she'll see him in twenty minutes and will explain it to him then.

'*How?*' Bolger says, after a long pause. 'I don't understand what you mean. Broke his heart *how?*'

'Well . . .' Romy exhales. 'You know. It was a long time ago now, and maybe –'

'No, no, tell me. *Explain* what you mean.'

Romy shifts his position slightly in the wheelchair, wincing as he does so. The move looks uncomfortable but is clearly a delaying tactic.

Eventually, he says, 'Our party stands for certain things, right? You embody those things. Frank didn't. It's that simple. He started out OK, and he was a natural, he had charm, he appealed to people, but pretty quickly he became an embarrassment to the party. He started shifting his position on things. He took up, what'll we call them, *inconvenient* causes. He was using the word *environment* a lot. Back then that was bordering on the radical. I don't know *what* he was reading or who he was talking to, but I can tell you one thing, if he'd survived he wouldn't have got renominated, to say nothing of getting re-elected. And if he was alive today . . . well, more than likely he'd be wearing a woolly jumper and canvassing for the bloody Greens.'

Bolger looks past Romy now, to the wall on the far side of the room.

What he's hearing here flatly contradicts what he has always understood, but he doesn't dispute what he's hearing either, not for a second – because there's something in Romy's voice, a weary, resigned authority, a convincing absence of the need anymore to lie or dissemble. And in a weird way it even accords with Bolger's own memory of Frank as a kid. He was a contrary little fucker. He'd twist everything around until it was on his own terms. But he got away with it because he was also a star.

'Look,' Romy says, 'when you came back from the States, right, you were wet behind the ears, you were bloody clueless – and I don't mind telling you that now, because this time tomorrow you're going to be the fucking Taoiseach – but you had no *idea* what'd been going on here, and in fairness you had no time to find out either. Because it was all about moving forward. You were thrown straight into the campaign, knocking on doors, tramping through housing estates in the rain.' He pauses. 'That must have been quite a shock to the system after Boston.'

Bolger nods, still not looking Romy in the eye, still not speaking.

'Anyway,' Romy goes on, 'in those last couple of weeks before the accident things were chaotic here. Frank got into a row about the rezoning of a piece of land out beyond the airport. He started making threats, saying he'd expose the voting records of a few of the councillors who were in favour of the re-zoning – the implication being, of course, that they were on the take.' He rolls his eyes. 'After more than ten years of the planning tribunal up in Dublin Castle I think we all know how that one goes, but back then you simply *didn't talk about it*. There was consternation in the party. These were councillors your old man *sat* with, people he'd known for twenty, thirty years.'

Bolger is white now.

'And he was mortified. Because there was nothing he could do about it.' Romy pauses, and sighs. He looks exhausted all of a sudden, his skin virtually translucent, like rice paper. 'So if you have issues with your old man, as they say nowadays . . . I think it might be less about anything *you* ever did or didn't do, and more about the fact that *he* has issues with himself.'

Bolger finally turns his head. 'What do you mean?'

'Look, this is difficult,' Romy says, speaking in a whisper now. 'Liam suffered a lot of guilt because . . . he *adored* Frank, you're right about that, but he also had to live with the knowledge that a small part of him was actually relieved when he heard the news that Frank had died. He was saved any further embarrassments in the party. That's how he felt. I know it. I was with him. I saw it in his face. And I saw him try to bury it. But he never succeeded. And *that* tormented him for the rest of his life.'

Bolger gets up out of the chair and walks across the room. He stands motionless, staring at the beige wall, trying to process what he has just heard, trying to steady his nerves, his heartbeat, the ripple of chemical reactions in his brain.

After a few moments, Romy says, 'Your old man thought the world of *you*, too, you know. He did. He was just never able to say it. He was probably afraid to. Afraid how it'd sound, to *himself*. Afraid that putting it into words might be another act of betrayal.'

Bolger exhales loudly and then turns around.

'My God,' he says, shaking his head, 'we all think we know what's going on, but we haven't a bloody clue, have we?'

'Not really, no.' Romy shifts his wheelchair so that he's facing Bolger again. 'Listen, Larry. That all just came spilling out there. I'm sorry. Ten minutes ago I was trying to decide whether I preferred turnips or parsnips. I'm not used to adult company anymore.'

Bolger shakes his head. 'I shouldn't have put you on the spot like that. *I'm* sorry.'

Romy shrugs.

Bolger then takes a deep breath. He hesitates before speaking. 'Three other people died that night, Romy.'

'I know. It was awful. And there was that kid who survived.'

Bolger stares at him, remembering, making the connection. 'Yes, yes . . . of course.'

'There was a whip-around done for him, you know. In the party. Some sort of fund was set up. He was looked after. It was actually your old man who organised it.'

Bolger nods.

After a while, he looks at his watch. 'Look, I have to go,' he says, his voice a little shaky. 'Thanks for talking to me.'

'You're welcome,' Romy says. 'And good luck.' There is an awkward pause. 'Keep the head, won't you?'

'I'll try.' Bolger walks towards the door, but stops halfway. 'As a matter of interest,' he says, still facing the door, 'that land you mentioned, the land that was up for rezoning?'

'Yeah?'

'What happened to it?'

Romy snorts. 'Well, Taoiseach, what do *you* think?'

'Right.' Bolger turns around. 'And where's this you said it was again?'

Romy narrows his eyes. 'Beyond the airport somewhere. It was one of those old ascendancy piles. On a few hundred acres. It's probably a bloody golf course now, or an estate.'

Bolger narrows *his* eyes. 'Hang on a second,' he says, staring at Romy. 'You're not talking about Dunbrogan House, are you?'

'Er . . . yes.'

Bolger immediately sees it on Romy's face, the merest hint of confusion, a flicker of doubt, as though he's just given something away but doesn't quite know what – and the feeling seems to be as unfamiliar to him as it is unwelcome.

Bolger's pulse quickens.

'Yes,' Romy repeats, in a smaller voice now, 'Dunbrogan House, that was it.'

3

The programmer from Cork is one of those geeky obsessives who can sit at a computer terminal for hours on end and seem to move only the muscles in his eyeballs and fingertips. It's a level of concentration that Gina envies. She watches from the other room, through the open doors, and wonders how he doesn't need to fidget, squirm, stretch, yawn – all things she's been doing non-stop herself since she sat down here.

She looks around. Everyone else has left, and the place is eerily quiet.

It's already dark outside.

Gina was a little self-conscious walking into the office with a laptop under her arm, given that she's effectively been using her bereavement to justify not coming to work, but she didn't have any choice. She got a bewildered, slightly frosty reception from Siobhan, and was relieved to discover that P.J. was in Belfast for the day. She went straight through to the back and over to Steve's workstation. When she apologised for taking him away from whatever he was working on, he shrugged and said, 'Same difference sure' – the implication no doubt being that it didn't matter what he was working on since the company was going down the tubes anyway. Which was maybe true, but Gina didn't want to get into it. She handed him the laptop and explained what she needed. At first he was reluctant; then he started to focus – as she knew he would – and before long he was totally absorbed.

Gina tried to get busy at her own desk, organising work stuff and answering emails, but she couldn't concentrate and after a while fell into idly monitoring Steve through the open doors.

She looks at her watch now, and something occurs to her.

She reaches back over the chair to one of the pockets of her jacket. She pulls out the three photographs she found in the warehouse and puts them on her desk. She switches on her printer and scans the photos. Then she puts them together in a file and emails the file to her own address as an attachment.

After that, she leans back in the chair and looks over at Steve. 'So, how're we doing?'

'Yeah.' He doesn't look up. 'We're getting there.'

'I've never seen him like this before,' Paula says, and chews her lower lip for a second. 'I think he's getting cold feet. Or something.'

'No, he'll be fine,' Norton says. 'He's probably just tired.'

'Well, he should get some caffeine into his system then, and plenty of it, because the next couple of hours are going to be crucial.'

Norton has a headache and is finding Paula's voice grating. They are in the corridor outside Bolger's offices in Government Buildings. There are two people ahead of them, with three others already inside, camped in the Private Secretary's office. Behind them, and all along the corridor, little groups are huddled – whispering, texting, shuffling, *waiting*. Everyone is hoping for five minutes with the Minister.

The atmosphere around Government Buildings this evening – and around Leinster House, and even out on Kildare Street – is electric. Speculation is rife that a major development is imminent.

The Taoiseach is isolated. The numbers stack up. The prize is there for the taking.

So what's wrong?

Alarm bells rang for Norton when he got the message, through Paula, that Bolger wanted to see him in his office – and this evening, straightaway, A-S-A-fucking-P. Because that isn't how it works between them. Larry doesn't *summon* Norton. Though maybe he's trying to mark out his new turf, establish a new set of ground rules. *Maybe*. But Norton doubts it. He suspects it has more to do with this trip Bolger made out to Wicklow earlier.

The door of the Secretary's office opens and a current of expectancy ripples down the corridor.

Bolger himself appears. His shirtsleeves are rolled up and his tie is loose. He looks frazzled. He points at Paddy and indicates *inside* with his head. Gritting his teeth, Paddy follows Bolger into the Secretary's office and then through to the inner sanctum. They pass anxious-looking party officials and civil servants. At the door, Bolger turns. He allows Norton in but puts a hand up to block Paula.

'Ten minutes,' he says, not looking at her, and shuts the door.

Bolger's office is spacious, all mahogany panels and red

leather. Norton has been in here only a couple of times – because again, if they have business to do, it tends to be on Norton's terms, and on Norton's turf.

'Jesus,' Bolger says, pacing up and down in front of his desk, 'I don't know if I can handle this. They're like fucking vultures out there.'

'Come on,' Norton says, forcing a smile, 'you can tell your grandchildren about it someday.'

Bolger ignores this.

The smile drops from Norton's face. His head is pounding. He's about to say something when Bolger stops moving and turns to face him. 'Paddy, I was out in Glenalba this afternoon.'

'So I gather. How is he?'

'Shite. Awful. He didn't know who I was. He's . . . he's gone.'

'Really?'

'Yes.'

Norton wasn't aware that the old man's condition was as bad as all that, and he shakes his head. At the same time, he's mildly relieved at the news. It's one more thing out of the way, one more little dose of closure.

But Bolger doesn't seem to be finished. He takes a step forward.

'I ran into someone else, though.'

'Oh, you did? Who was that?'

'Romy Mulcahy.'

Norton releases a barely audible groan.

Bolger says, 'You remember him then?'

'Yeah. I do. Very much.' Norton pauses. 'So. The old bollocks hasn't kicked it yet?'

'No. In fact, he's very much alive.' Bolger points a finger at the side of his head. 'Upstairs, anyway. We were raking over some ancient history.'

'I see.'

Romy Mulcahy and Liam Bolger. That whole crowd. Norton shakes his head again. They were among the first people he ever had dealings with in his business career, and the strange truth of it is, in some ways he's *still* dealing with them.

'He had a couple of interesting things to say, Paddy.'

'Yeah?'

'Yeah. A couple of *very* interesting things.'

Bolger lets that hang in the air for a moment. But Norton snaps. He's had enough.

'OK, Larry,' he says, 'get to the fucking point, would you? I don't appreciate being dragged in here like this. You're not the only one who's busy, so come on, what *is* it?'

'It's Frank,' Bolger says, getting red in the face now. 'It's Dunbrogan House. It's *you*.'

'What are you talking about?'

'I've been on the phone,' Bolger says, and points at his desk. 'I've been talking to people, checking some *facts*. Dunbrogan House and estate, that was the site Frank didn't think should be rezoned, wasn't it? It was the site that he kicked up a stink over.' He pauses. 'That he became a right pain in the arse over.' He pauses again. 'The hundred-and-fifty-acre site that *you* owned.'

Norton rolls his eyes.

Bolger holds up a finger. 'No, no, Paddy, not so fast. You bought it off Miriam's old man for a few thousand quid and then sold it after it was rezoned for a quarter of a fucking *million*. It was the deal that made your fortune. It set you up, it —'

'*So fucking what?*' Norton roars.

'It was –'

'*It was perfectly legitimate is what it was.* A bloody land deal. I've made hundreds of them. What's so –'

'Frank dies in a car crash *days* before a county-council meeting on the issue, a meeting he's declared he's going to disrupt? Come *on.*'

'Ah, would you fuck off, Larry. Really. You're losing the run of yourself here.' Norton's head is ready to burst.

'I'm not,' Bolger says. 'I'm *not.*' He turns and slaps the palm of his hand down on the desk. 'Something weird went on back then, Paddy, and there's something weird going on now, too. Because that young fella the other day in Buswell's Hotel? I know who he was. He was the kid who survived the crash. He was Mark Griffin. He *had* to be. I thought he was just some journalist looking for a story, but a couple of hours ago –' he motions back at his desk again, at the phone, 'I get a call, and do you know what? The Guards have identified that second guy who's in intensive care out in St Felim's, from last night, from that thing in Cherryvale. It's going to be on the news at nine o'clock.' He pauses to let that sink in. 'And do you know who it is? They said he's in a bad way and mightn't make it, but it's *him,* Paddy. Mark Griffin.' He holds up his hands. 'Explain *that* to me.'

Norton stares at Bolger for a long time.

'What are the Guards saying?' he says eventually.

Bolger stares back. He hesitates, but then says, 'That it was his warehouse. That he's a local businessman. They're saying it might just be that he was unlucky. In the wrong place at the wrong time.'

'What, like a random victim?'

Bolger nods. 'That sort of thing.'

'But no reference to . . . *who* he is, to . . .'

'No.'

'OK,' Norton says, considering this, looking at the floor. 'And of course why would there be? It was a long time ago? If he dies, who's going to make the connection, right?'

'Ah, now hold on, Paddy, hold on . . . for the love of Christ, what are you saying to me here?'

Norton continues staring at the floor. 'But even if someone did make the connection,' he says, almost to himself now, 'even if some industrious hack dug it up, so what? It'd just be a curious fact, with a nice tabloid ring to it.' He pauses. 'But it wouldn't *mean* anything, it wouldn't have any further resonance . . . unless . . .'

Norton hears a gentle tap on the door behind him, a creaking sound, and then an obsequious male voice, 'Er . . . Minister, excuse me, but –'

'*GET OUT!*'

Norton then hears the creaking sound in reverse.

Visibly trembling, Bolger takes a couple of steps backwards and leans on his desk. 'Unless what?'

'Calm down, Larry.'

'Unless *what*?'

Norton sighs. 'Unless *you* keep asking questions about Frank.'

Silence fills the room, spreading out like a toxic vapour, finding every corner.

'But Paddy,' Bolger eventually manages to say, leaning forward, pleading, 'he was my *brother*.'

Norton winces and raises a hand to his head. Without saying anything, he then walks across the room. He goes in behind Bolger's desk and starts pulling at the various drawers, opening one after the other and rummaging through them.

Bolger turns, still at the front of the desk, and says, 'Paddy, what are you doing?'

'I need something for this headache,' Norton says, 'I need . . .'

He pulls a packet of Advil from one of the drawers and holds it up. On a shelf behind him there is a tray with glasses on it and half a dozen bottles of Ballygowan. He opens one of the bottles. He fiddles with the packet of Advil and knocks four of the tablets back in one go, followed by a long slug of water. He puts the bottle down and rolls his neck a couple of times. When he is ready, he walks back into the middle of the room, turns and faces Bolger.

'Right,' he says, closing his eyes for a moment and then opening them again. 'You have a simple choice here. You can either pursue this and keep asking questions – what happened that night, was he drunk, was he pushed, blah, blah. You can go down that road, resurrect shit from two and a half decades ago and feed it to the media on a platter.' He pauses. '*Or* you can go out that door over there and embrace your destiny. You can take power and run this country for five, maybe even ten years. You can change things, make a difference, fix the Health Service, build infrastructure. You can have access to Downing Street, to Brussels, you can sit on the UN Security Council, you can eat dinner at the fucking White House, *whatever*. But believe me, Larry . . .' – he holds up a finger and shakes it – '. . . you can't do both.'

Bolger stares back at him, deflated. The silence is excruciating and goes on for nearly a minute.

Norton is the one who breaks it.

'I'm going to leave now,' he says in a quiet, measured voice.

He turns and heads for the door. 'By the way,' he adds, over his shoulder, 'I'm having lunch tomorrow with James Vaughan. He's flying in from London. I'm sure you'll be busy, but maybe you could fit us in?'

He stops at the door and looks around.

Bolger hasn't moved.

'Jesus, Larry,' Norton says. 'Look at the bloody state of you. Straighten your tie up at least, would you? Christ.'

Shaking his head, he turns back to the door, opens it and leaves.

'Still with us, yeah?'

Gina hops up from her desk. Only half awake, she was lost, eyes closed, in a Technicolor re-enactment of what had happened the previous night.

At his workstation, Steve is leaning back in his chair, arms outstretched. 'Got it,' he says.

This is the jolt that Gina needs. It wakes her up.

'Excellent,' she says. 'You're a genius.' She pauses. 'So what is it?'

'I've no idea. Two PDF files, one long, the other one not so long, and five emails. I've copied them and sent them over to you.' He nods in the direction of her desk.

'Thanks. I really appreciate this.'

He shrugs. 'Who do I bill for the time?'

'Oh God, Steve, look, I know things are –'

'*Gina,*' he says, holding a hand up. 'Don't. I was only messing.' He turns and grabs a jacket from the back of his chair. 'Buy me a drink sometime.'

'OK. Thanks.'

After he leaves, Gina makes herself some coffee, turns out most of the lights and sits at her desk again. She is just about to open one of the PDF files when her mobile rings. She picks it up.

New number.

'Hello?'

Silence.

'*Hello?*'

More silence, then, 'Gina?'

'Yes.'

A click and it goes dead. She looks at the phone, *stares* at it for a few moments, as though expecting it to talk up, to explain itself. With an unpleasant churning in her stomach, she then goes to Options and presses Reply. It rings. No one answers. There's no voicemail. It rings out.

Gina swallows.

She runs a hand through her hair, and sighs.

After a few moments, she turns back to the computer.

So she *is* alive.

Norton stands in the phone box with his hand on the receiver. He hasn't been inside one of these things in ten or fifteen years, not since the days when most of the damn things were permanently out of order.

He slides his hand off the receiver and backs out through the glass door.

Anyway, she's alive. And answering her phone.

He looks around. He's on the Long Mile Road. When he got back to his car on Baggot Street, the Advil were only just kicking in, so he decided he'd drive around for a while and give them a chance to work. Besides, he had no desire to go home. And in any case after about half an hour Paula phoned – on Bolger's instructions. The choreography had been set in motion. Three senior ministers were in with the Taoiseach at the moment, and assuming he didn't put up a fight, which no one expected him to do, his office would shortly be releasing a statement announcing his resignation – after which a statement from party HQ would be released. It should all be wrapped up within the hour, Paula said. So was he coming back in? There'd be celebrations. Champagne.

Norton declined. He was relieved to hear the news, but what he couldn't tell Paula was that *nothing* would be wrapped up until a separate, and hopefully final, piece of business had been taken care of.

Something that would have to start with a phone call.

It was another fifteen minutes, however, before he could bring himself to make the call, and it was only at the *last* minute that it struck him how stupid it would be to make it on his mobile.

So he pulled over as soon as he spotted a phone box.

Inside the box, he fumbled for the piece of paper he'd written her number on. He fumbled for coins. Eventually he got through, and when he said her name he tried to disguise his voice. There was no disguising *hers*, though. He didn't hear enough to gauge what state of mind she was in, but she was alive, and that was all he needed to know.

As he steps away from the box now, the phone inside it rings. He turns and walks off, the sound receding into the general din of the traffic. His car is parked on the other side of the road. He waits for an opportunity and crosses.

He unlocks his car from ten yards.

She's alive.

Fuck it.

*

Bolger can see it in their faces, the merest flicker of it. He wouldn't call it panic, not yet, but that's where it's headed. It's as if they've woken from a dream and are looking around in bewilderment, not quite sure of anything anymore – of who they are, of where they are, of what they've done.

For his part, Bolger finds it liberating.

In his office, sitting opposite him, are the Ministers for Finance, Transport and Education. Already being dubbed the Gang of Three, these men are here for a quick strategy powwow before Bolger gives a press conference.

Outside everyone is waiting. The corridors are jammed, there is a media scrum on the steps of Leinster House and RTÉ is on standby to broadcast a news flash.

For his part, the Taoiseach-designate is in no hurry.

In those first few moments after Paddy Norton left his office, Bolger just stood there, immobile, the various implications of what Norton *hadn't* said going off inside his head like a series of controlled explosions. And then, as the door opened, unleashing a tidal wave of handlers, advisers, mandarins, functionaries, hangers-on, the awful truth sank in. He actually did have to choose. He *couldn't* do both.

Though the decision, in a certain sense, made itself – since it was all pretty clear-cut when you looked at it, morally, ethically, every bloody way. And he came close a couple of times to articulating this – but only in his head, as it turns out, because at no point did he actually *say* anything, to anyone, about any of it. Instead, he allowed Paula to stand in front of him and straighten his tie. He accepted a sheaf of papers from his private secretary. He nodded when he was told that so-and-so was outside to see him. He put on his jacket. He went behind his desk and poured himself a glass of water. In all of this he had an air about him that was unfamiliar and slightly self-conscious, an air of calmness, of quiet authority. In fact, with each passing second, with each move and gesture he made, he could feel himself morphing into someone different, into someone new.

And what he is beginning to discover now, having just casually lobbed the words *cabinet* and *reshuffle* at the three men sitting in front of him, is a little something about who that person might be.

'*Well*,' the Minister for Finance is saying, 'I don't know, maybe we should take it one step at a time.'

'Of course,' Bolger says. 'But I'll definitely be making changes.'

I'll be.

In the absence of a contest, and once the announcement has been made, the ratification process will be a mere formality, but still – he has to be careful.

'OK,' he adds, 'you're right, the press conference is important.' He pauses. 'But you *know* it'll be one of the things they ask about.'

The Minister for Transport is squirming. It's obvious that he's dying to know what changes Bolger intends making, but is afraid to push it. The Minister for Education, as usual, is stony-faced, but Bolger can tell he's furious that the subject has come up so soon.

'We can't let the media dictate our agenda,' the Minister for Finance goes on. 'And I really –'

'A cabinet reshuffle is what's expected,' Bolger says. 'It's what people want, and it's what they're going to get. Besides, a reshuffle formalises the honeymoon. Ministers get to throw a few shapes and look good in front of the cameras.' He shrugs.

'It's pretty much win-win all around. *We're* happy. Louis Copeland is happy. Everyone is happy.'

It's amazing how the dynamic in the room has shifted: a few minutes earlier, these four men were fellow conspirators, co-equal plotters, and now they are divided – *they're* the king-makers and *he's* the king. And there's nothing any of them can do about it. It's the nature of the process.

Bolger stands up and buttons his jacket. 'Let me just be clear about this. A show of unity is what's required out there. At the press conference *and* talking to journalists afterwards. That's the script and we stick to it. Absolute, unconditional, one hundred per cent.' He looks across the room, over their heads, at the door. 'Anyone displays anything less and there'll be blood on the walls. *Tonight.*'

Ten minutes later, as he sits at another table, in another room, looking out at the assembled media, waiting for the hail of camera flashes to subside, Bolger realises something. Despite what has happened this evening, despite his impressive command of the situation, he doesn't feel any sense of triumph or achievement. He doesn't feel nervous or excited or even pleased. What he does feel, all he feels – as he glances down at his prepared statement, and at his gold cufflinks, and at his soft, manicured politician's hands – is tired, and empty, and numb.

The bigger of the two PDF files is fifty-four pages long, has no title or table of contents, and from a quick glance looks to be about as incomprehensibly technical as most of the other stuff Gina saw on Flynn's laptop. She reads a paragraph here and there, but the prose is dense with unfamiliar terminology and her mind quickly glazes over. Throughout the document, too, there are diagrams, charts, figures and equations. Despite the complexity, however, Gina has a general enough idea of what she's looking at – it seems to be something, a study or report, about *some* aspect of the structural design of Richmond Plaza. But should this come as any surprise? It's what Dermot Flynn was working on, after all.

It was his job.

The shorter file is very similar and appears to be no more than a draft version of the longer one.

Discouraged and tired, Gina looks out across the empty, semi-darkened office, at the windows, at the orange wash now coming in from the lights out on Harcourt Street.

Then something occurs to her.

She turns back to the screen.

Claire said that in recent weeks Dermot had been doing a lot of extra work – at home, in his study. Is *this* what he was working on? If so, she thinks, fine, why not? Except that Richmond Plaza is almost finished. She herself was up on the forty-eighth floor – the *top* floor. Why at such a late stage in the construction *process* would he be working on an aspect of the building's structural *design*?

It makes no sense.

Unless something was wrong.

Gina feels her insides turning.

This is what Noel was talking about that night. He said it to her: *You don't want to know, believe me . . . it's engineering stuff, an unholy bloody mess . . .*

She takes a deep breath and clicks on the first of the emails. It's from Noel, and was sent on Wednesday, 24 October.

> *Hi Dermot, Got your message. I'm still looking at your report. I'll see you when I get back to the office later in the*

p.m. Please keep this to yourself until we've had a chance to discuss fully. N.

Gina immediately clicks on the second message. It's from Dermot. Two days later.

Noel, Given the nature of the situation, shouldn't we be doing something, showing this to someone? I'm very anxious. Please let me know what's happening. Dermot.

The next one is a reply from Noel. Same day.

Dermot, I've already shown it to someone – just this morning – so please, bear with me. We can't afford to let this get out there – not unless we're 100% certain of our facts. I'll talk to you later. N.

But let *what* get out, exactly? It's clear that Gina has hit paydirt here, and she's excited, but she's also frustrated, because she isn't sure what any of it means.

She clicks on the fourth email. It's from Dermot. It was sent after the weekend, on the Monday – *that* Monday.

Noel, I didn't see you in the office on Friday, or this morning. I've left several messages on your voicemail. I can't help but question the wisdom of – if not yet the motive for – this delay in taking action. And surely the longer we hold off, the harder it's going to be to explain? Dermot.

Noel's last email, sent that afternoon, is very different in tone from his others. It is, in effect, a memo.

Dermot, Please be advised that I have scheduled a conference call for 10 a.m. tomorrow morning with Yves Baladur in Paris. The purpose of this call is to make an official

presentation of the findings in your report. I have scheduled
a further conference call for 2 p.m. with Daniel Lazar. N.R.

Yves Baladur? Gina isn't sure, but she thinks this is the head
of BCM. There's no doubt in her mind, however, about the
second name, Daniel Lazar – he's the architect who designed
Richmond Plaza. She closes her eyes. So. Dermot Flynn gave
this report he'd compiled to Noel, and expected him to pass it
on, to pass it *up*. To head office in Paris. To the architect. To
someone. Noel dragged his feet on it for a while, made excuses,
but then he capitulated.

And that's what sealed his fate.

Gina opens her eyes.

Because there was someone who didn't want the report
to be seen – the same person, she assumes, who Noel said in
his email he'd already shown it to. And it's pretty obvious to
her now who *that* is. Even though there's still nothing concrete
she can point to, nothing she can adduce, no evidence, no
demonstrable link . . .

But then she looks at the screen again, at that final email,
and she sees it.

She didn't spot this the first time, but she's definitely seeing
it now.

It's the last field in the message header, right there along
with the others, with the sender and the receiver, with the date
and the subject line . . .

Digital, ineradicable.

Cc: *Paddy Norton.*

He is parked along the quays, not far from her building, close
enough to see her coming out or going in.

He looks at his watch.

Maybe he should try phoning her again. But what would he say this time if she answered? He doesn't want to scare her off.

Outside, it's cold and blustery, and there's hardly anyone about, the odd pedestrian maybe, *some* traffic, but not much. An articulated truck rumbles by.

He switches to another station. There'll be a news bulletin on in five minutes.

He rubs his chest.

Ten minutes ago, he got out of the car and walked up to the entrance of her building. He found her name and rang the bell. He waited, but there was no answer.

He came back to the car.

He looks around again now. Then he looks at his watch again.

Gina's brother was that dangerous animal, a man of principle – so Norton wonders what *she* is like. He knows she's stubborn and determined, but is she smart? Will she listen to reason?

On reflection, he doesn't think she will. He's been turning this over in his mind all day. He knows from what Fitz said that her software company is in financial difficulty and it occurred to him that he could offer to bail her out – he could provide some capital investment, or just *give* her the money he'd promised to pay Fitz.

But somehow he doesn't see it.

What if he talks to her tonight and makes her an offer, and she accepts, but then in the morning she changes her mind?

There's too much happening right now to justify that level of risk.

The news bulletin comes on. The reporting – live from Leinster House – is breathless, almost hysterical. He listens, but any sense of satisfaction or achievement he might have expected to feel is muted. In 'other news', it is reported that Gardaí have established the identity of the last victim of last night's gangland shootout. He is thirty-year-old Dubliner Mark Griffin. Gardaí, however, don't believe that the local businessman, who is still in a critical condition, has any criminal connections, and they are operating on the assumption that he may simply – and tragically – have been in the wrong place at the wrong time.

Norton groans.

How is Gina Rafferty going to react when she hears *that*?

He looks around, checks out the street, ahead and behind. The place is deserted. It would be so perfect if she were to turn up now.

He reaches across to the passenger seat, to where he impatiently tossed the gun when he got back into the car a few minutes earlier.

He picks it up, turns it, studies it, rests it in his lap.

Where the bloody hell *is* she?

From O'Connell Bridge the taxi makes a right onto Eden Quay.

Gina's main reason for going back to her apartment is that she needs a change of clothes. Sophie tried to convince her to stay another night at her place, but it seems intolerable to Gina – as well as absurd – that she should be denied access to her own wardrobe.

It's clear from the anonymous call she received that someone is keeping tabs on her. They have her mobile number, and no doubt have her home address as well. But Gina refuses to be intimidated.

She has Fitz's gun in her pocket.

The taxi passes under Butt Bridge and along by the Custom House. A moment later, they stop at a traffic light, and the driver says, 'That's a blustery one.'

'Yeah,' Gina responds, distracted, and then adds, '*awful night.*'

'Not a bad one for your man Larry Bolger, though.'

'Sorry?'

'You didn't hear? It was on the news there. He's going to be taking over. A palace coup, they're calling it.'

Gina is stunned. This was expected, but somehow it doesn't feel that way. Pressing back against the leather of the car seat, she senses new, subterranean levels of activity in all of this, like little tremors, previously undetected, but now growing stronger.

She puts her hand into her jacket pocket. 'Listen,' she says, leaning forward, 'there wasn't anything else on the news, was there, about that thing in Cherryvale?'

The taxi driver whistles. 'Jaysus, that was shocking, wasn't it?' A nanosecond before the light turns green, he accelerates. 'Anyway, they've named your man, the one in hospital, the last one. Seems he's in a bad way. Internal bleeding, organ failure, what have you.'

'You don't happen to remember the name, do you?'

Gina is keenly aware of having asked this same question not so long ago.

'*Owhhh,*' the driver says, as though in pain, 'come here, what was it . . . *Mark* something, I think. Yeah, that was it.'

Gina closes her eyes.

'Apparently, he had nothing to do with it,' the driver goes on. 'They said he was just unlucky to be there.' He laughs. 'I lost a hundred euros on the gee-gees last weekend. *That* was unlucky, but I mean your *man*? A bullet in the back? For *fuck's* sake.'

Gina opens her eyes.

The reality of this hits her hard, as does an inescapable corollary: the bullet concerned almost certainly – well, very probably – came from the gun she's now holding tightly in her hand.

The taxi begins to slow down. 'So, here on the left somewhere, is it, love, yeah?'

Gina looks around her and out of the window. She sees her building up ahead. As usual at this time of night the place is more or less deserted – a pedestrian or two, a few parked cars, but that's it.

'Er . . . yeah,' she says, releasing her grip on the gun. 'But you know what? Keep going. If you don't mind. Change of plan.'

'No problem,' he says, picking up speed again.

They cruise past her building.

'So,' the driver says. 'Where to?'

Gina feels foolish, and even considers getting him to turn around and go back, but what she eventually says is, 'Take the toll bridge, would you? Thanks. Then head for Blackrock.'

4

The sight of the parsley-flecked potatoes, the poached salmon, the yellowish sauce, it's all making him a little sick – as is everything else on this large round table in front of him . . . the silverware, the curlicued edges of the condiment sets and serving tureens, not to mention the wider room's busy, crimsony, five-star decor . . .

There is a mildly hallucinatory aspect to everything.

James Vaughan, sitting opposite him, concentratedly guiding his fork towards his mouth, looks like a wizened, hundred-year-old baby. Ray Sullivan, in his shiny grey suit and silver hair, reminds him of the Tin Man.

Norton is exhausted. From lack of sleep, and possibly from not having eaten for . . . at least since breakfast yesterday, now that he thinks of it.

In fact, did he eat at all yesterday? He can't remember.

Last night he stayed outside Gina Rafferty's building until 2 a.m., to no avail, and when he finally got home to bed he couldn't sleep. Not for ages anyway – though he must have dozed off at some point, because when the alarm clock went off at 6.30 he woke up. From a muddled dream. And with a blinding headache.

He immediately took three Nalprox tablets – his new standard dose.

'And what about the press,' Vaughan says, taking a breather from his food. 'What kind of a ride do you think they'll give him?'

'I haven't looked at the papers today,' Norton says. 'But they did their best to crucify him recently, and failed, so I'd say they might just go all out and canonise the man this time.'

'It's been quite a turnaround.'

'Yeah, but Larry's a survivor. He's got the human factor as well, vulnerability, people tend to like that. The thing is, he never really lost public support, which I think is crucial.'

Norton is waffling here. He wishes he could just go somewhere and lie down.

'Ray, old sport,' Vaughan then says, dabbing his lips with his napkin. 'Pour me some more wine there, would you?'

Sullivan obliges, and Norton idly watches as the golden liquid passes, glugging loudly, from bottle to glass.

Norton could probably do with some coffee or something, but doesn't think he'd be able to hold it down.

'Sure you won't have something to eat, Paddy?'

'No, no, I'm fine. Thanks.'

He's about to pat his stomach and say something moronic like *Watching my figure*, but he manages to restrain himself.

It's going to be a long afternoon. After they leave the hotel here, they're heading down to the site for a quick tour and then Norton and Sullivan will be officially signing the tenancy contract. They'll hang around the newly named Amcan Building for a while, and then Vaughan and Sullivan want to play some golf, so it'll be out to the K Club.

Norton is their host for the afternoon, and won't have time for anything else.

He's about to ask Vaughan a question when he detects some kind of a commotion behind him.

'*Ahh,*' Vaughan says, raising an arm, 'here he is, the man of the moment.'

Norton turns around in his seat. Entering the dining room with his entourage, like a Roman emperor, is Larry Bolger. When he gets to the table, he stretches out his arm and shakes hands with Vaughan and Sullivan in turn. He nods at Norton but doesn't look him in the eye.

A waiter pulls out a chair and Bolger sits down. His entourage – Paula Duff and various others, secretaries, advisers – hover in the background and look busy with their PDAs and mobile phones.

'It's great to see you again, James,' Bolger says. 'Everything is to your satisfaction, I hope?'

James.

Jesus.

Norton knows for a fact that people call Vaughan either *Mr* Vaughan or Jimmy. There is no James.

'Oh, excellent, Taoiseach, excellent. But tell me, how are *you*?'

'I'm fine, but let's not jump the gun. There *is* a ratification process to be gone through.'

Vaughan waves this away.

Norton leans back in his chair and exhales. He barely listens to the ensuing conversation, but he can tell from the body language that it's all good-humoured banter – skilful and professional. Norton's in a foul mood, OK, but he can't deny that Bolger is carrying himself very well here. He also has to remember that this is what they've both been working towards, in one way or another, for many, many years. The thought helps to elevate Norton's mood a bit, and he even allows himself, fleetingly, to speculate that Gina Rafferty poses no real threat . . . that she knows nothing of substance, or is too stupid to act on what she does know – or too frightened.

After about ten minutes, Bolger rises, as do Vaughan and Sullivan, and there is another flurry of formal handshakes. The imperial party then sweeps out of the dining room.

Vaughan remains standing. He picks up his napkin, wipes his mouth with it and then throws it back down.

'OK, fellas,' he says, 'let's get this show on the road.'

They move out of the dining room and into the lobby, where Sullivan stops by a marble pillar to take a call on his mobile. Norton and Vaughan stand and wait. Near the reception desk, by a large potted plant, a burly man in a grey suit and dark glasses is flicking through a brochure or guidebook. Ostensibly. This is Jimmy Vaughan's bodyguard. The lobby is quite busy. At the reception desk, there are a few obvious stragglers from the media, hovering, trying to pick up crumbs of information in the wake of Bolger's brief visit.

'I have to hand it to you, Paddy,' Vaughan says. 'You've done a good job here. I only wish things were this easy over in London.'

'Yeah?'

'*Oh.*' Vaughan's face contorts briefly. 'Please. Dealing with the Brits? It's hard work, believe me. Same language, OK, but you still need an interpreter, and I'm not talking differences in vocabulary – elevator, lift, that kind of thing, cell, mobile.' He taps the side of his head. 'It's approach I'm talking about. In this country I feel we understand each other.'

Norton nods in agreement. He can't help feeling pleased at this, and encouraged. 'Absolutely,' he says. 'Fifty-first state and all that. Now if we could just do something about the weather.'

'Yeah.' Vaughan laughs. 'That'd be something. But you know what? I remember Jack Kennedy once telling me that if you . . .'

He stops.

'Paddy?'

Norton is staring across the lobby, the spike in his mood reversing rapidly. Standing at the entrance to the hotel, glancing around, is Gina Rafferty. Behind her, the revolving door is still in motion. Slowly, like a roulette wheel, it comes to rest.

She spots him.

Before he can do anything, she's on her way over.

*

As she gets closer, Gina sees that the man beside Paddy Norton is elderly. He is small and slightly stooped. She'd prefer it if Norton were alone, but for the moment this'll have to do. What she wanted was to take him by surprise, and she can see from the expression on his face that she has accomplished that.

'My dear,' Norton says as she arrives, 'how lovely to see you.'

The smile is clearly forced. It doesn't make it to his eyes. The elderly man is smiling, too – but *his* eyes are sparkling.

'Mr Norton,' Gina says, not smiling at all, 'I need to talk to you.'

'*Paddy*. Please. Call me Paddy.'

She has already decided on a policy. She's going to remain calm and take this in stages.

'*Paddy*,' she says. 'I need to talk to you.'

'Yes, of course, but –'

'I need to talk to you *now*.'

'Fine, fine. But . . . how did you track me down?'

'I've just been to Baggot Street. They told me you'd be here.'

'I see.'

He doesn't like this.

'So, er . . .'

The elderly man, who is standing to Gina's right, clears his throat. She turns to look at him. He extends a hand in her direction.

'Jimmy Vaughan,' he says. 'Enchanted, I'm sure.'

Gina shakes his hand.

'Er . . .' She's distracted now, not certain that she's heard this right. Did he just say *enchanted*? '. . . Gina Rafferty.'

His hand is soft, like silk.

'Er . . . Gina here,' Norton says, addressing the old man, 'she's the sister of our, er . . .' – this is an awkward way of phrasing it, and he isn't comfortable – '. . . er . . . she's the sister of our chief structural engineer, Noel Rafferty –'

'Oh?'

'– who, who died unfortunately, a couple of weeks ago, in a car accident.'

'Oh my goodness,' Vaughan says, turning back to Gina. 'That's dreadful. I'm *very* sorry to hear that. You have my deepest sympathies.'

He's American.

'Thank you.'

'Gina, may I ask how old your brother was?'

'Yes. He was forty-eight.'

'Oh, that's just terrible.' He shakes his head. 'You know, I had a brother who died, *many* years ago now, in Korea actually, but it's not something you ever really get over, is it, the death of a sibling? I mean in the sense that it affects your identity, it . . . it redefines you in a way.' He reaches across and pats her gently on the arm. 'I hope I haven't spoken out of turn.'

'No, not at all,' Gina says. 'That's very perceptive actually.'

She feels slightly snookered here. Who *is* this old guy? He has a courtly and at the same time quite commanding presence. She needs to refocus.

'Paddy?'

She turns back to Norton, but he's looking off to his right. In the next moment, he is joined by someone else, a tall silver-haired man in a grey suit.

'Paddy,' this man says, taking Norton by the arm, 'come here, I need to ask you something . . .'

'Er . . .' Norton turns back to Gina and Vaughan. 'I'll just . . . er –'

'Go,' the old man says, 'go. Allow me to have the pleasure of this charming young lady's company for a few minutes.' He beams at her.

Moving off with the other man, Norton glances over his shoulder. Gina can see that he's extremely agitated. She isn't sure what to do and considers just going after him. But then it occurs to her that maybe the reason he's so agitated – in part, at least – is because he's had to leave her alone with this old guy.

Gina turns back to Vaughan, who is still beaming at her. 'Hi,' she says, and smiles.

'Hi.'

'So. Tell me. Who *are* you?'

'Who am I? Oh *my.*' He breathes in sharply, as though the challenge of answering such a question by close of business today might be beyond him. 'Well, for starters, I suppose, I'm the chairman of a private-equity firm called the Oberon Capital Group.'

Oberon?

Gina's heard of it – usually in lists, along with other names such as Carlyle, Halliburton, Bechtel, Chipco. She can see the old man trying to gauge how impressed she is.

'*Wow.*'

'Yes, I have many interests, many *lives,* you might say. I advise governments. I broker deals.'

She nods along silently.

'In the early eighties,' he goes on, gazing into her eyes, 'I was Deputy Director of the CIA. Before that, among other things, I was Assistant Treasury Secretary under Jack Kennedy.'

'Really?'

'Oh yes.'

This is bizarre. He *is* trying to impress her. He must be nearly eighty – though he does have, she has to admit it, a certain charisma.

'Interesting times *they* were, I can tell you.'

'I'm sure.'

There are questions she could ask him about this, but now is hardly the time.

'So what are you doing here?' she says. 'How do you know Paddy?'

'Oh, well, yes.' He pokes a finger in her direction, as though he knows she'll find *this* interesting. 'Richmond Plaza. I have a sizeable stake in it . . .' – turns out he's right – '. . . and I'm just here, basically, to have a look.'

'I see.'

'We're heading down there now, actually.'

Gina glances over at Norton, who is standing about thirty feet away, still listening to the man in the grey suit but staring directly at her.

'I've been up it,' she says, turning back to Vaughan. 'Only once. But it's certainly impressive. I know my brother was very proud to have worked on it.'

As she says this her voice cracks a little – which may, at some level, be deliberate. Or not. She can't really tell. She's nervous, and confused, but also aware of a certain element of gameplay here.

'Listen,' Vaughan says, 'I don't know if you're free, but . . . would you care to join us?'

She seems to consider this for a moment. But given the circumstances there's nothing really to consider.

'Yes, Mr Vaughan. I would. Thank you.'

'*Mr?* Oh come now, Gina,' the old man says, tilting his head in Norton's direction. 'If *he's* Paddy then I'm Jimmy. I insist.'

'OK. Jimmy.'

'Wonderful.' He smiles again. 'So, let's go. There's a car waiting outside.'

He extends an arm, which Gina takes.

'Now, young lady,' he says, 'you must tell me all about yourself.'

'Oh sure. Well, where to begin? I ran the State Department under FDR . . .'

Vaughan laughs at this, and as they start to move towards the exit, Gina glances over at Norton.

'What's the matter, Paddy? You're not listening to me.'

'I am, Ray, but come *on*, let's go.'

'Yeah, yeah,' Sullivan says. 'In a minute. Now take it easy, will you?'

Norton watches as Vaughan whispers something to his minder and then disappears with Gina through the revolving doors.

The minder walks over, informs Sullivan that Mr Vaughan will meet them at Richmond Dock in twenty minutes.

'OK, Phil,' Sullivan says, 'thanks.'

The minder turns and leaves.

'Yeah, so, er . . . it's two per cent, or two and a half, three tops, but the point is it's doable.'

'Whatever, Ray. Can we *go* now?'

'Take it easy. We're going.'

Outside, as they climb into the back of a silver Merc, Sullivan asks about the girl.

'She's just . . . the sister of a . . . a colleague,' Norton says. He doesn't want to get into it.

Though he is going to have to do something here.

Sullivan laughs, and Norton looks at him. 'What?'

'Jimmy. He's fucking incorrigible. Chasing skirt at his age? He can't resist a pretty face. The man's had four wives, and who knows how many affairs.'

They're on Nassau Street.

Norton stares out the window. The other car can't be too far ahead.

What could they possibly be talking about?

As the Merc glides onto College Green, Norton begins to feel a thumping in his chest and stomach. He's used to feelings of anxiety, but this is a level – almost of panic – that he's unfamiliar with.

'Look, Ray,' he says, staring straight ahead, unsure what he's about to say next – and surprised when he hears the words coming out of his mouth – 'I think she might be dangerous.'

'Oh, that's the kind he likes. He comes over all old-school, but believe me, deep down he's really –'

'No, no, I mean *dangerous*, a threat, security-wise. I'm not sure that she's quite . . . stable.' Once he starts he can't stop. 'She has a history. She . . . she's been sort of, well, more or less *stalking* me, and making claims, outrageous stuff.'

'*What?* Jesus Christ,' Sullivan says. He pulls out his mobile phone. 'Is she a psycho? Who the fuck *is* she?'

Norton explains. He mentions about Noel, and adds that she's possibly delusional, paranoid, deranged with grief. This is the best he can manage by way of a pre-emptive strike.

Sullivan has the phone up to his ear. 'Phil? Yeah. Woman

you've got there in the car with you? Keep an eye on her. When you arrive, don't let them out of your sight. Stick close by the old man. We'll be there a few minutes after you.'

He closes the phone.

'Jesus, Paddy,' he says. 'If this bitch pulls anything, I swear I'll . . .' He sighs. '*Christ*. How did you let this happen?'

'*You* took me aside,' Norton says. '*You* distracted me. And anyway, *I'm* the one she has the problem with, and I don't think . . .'

But Sullivan isn't listening. 'Hey, driver,' he's saying, 'step on it there, would you?'

They turn onto Custom House Quay.

Norton wonders if this Phil in the car up ahead is armed.

'. . . so we're in this hotel suite, at the Plaza I think, and *I'm* left standing there waiting. Bobby's in front of me, shirtsleeves rolled up, on the phone. He's pacing back and forth. Behind him, at a table, five or six aides are sorting through campaign leaflets. One of them is working a telex machine. TV's on in the corner.'

Gina nods along, finding this more than a little bizarre. In 1960, her parents had just moved to Dolanstown, part of the city's new suburban frontier. Noel was still a baby, with no sisters. She herself – his fourth sister – wouldn't be born for another fifteen years.

'On the far side of the room,' Vaughan continues, 'there's a closed door. It opens, just slightly, and *Jack appears*. He lingers in the doorway and straightens his tie. He looks as if he's still talking to someone in the room he's just come out of. Then Bobby goes over to him, holding the receiver to his chest, and as they're speaking the door opens a little further, and who do

I catch a glimpse of? Sitting at a vanity table? Looking into the mirror, applying lipstick?' Vaughan laughs. 'My goddamned *wife* is who.'

'Wow.'

'My *first* wife, that is,' he says, shaking his head. 'Though not for long, of course.'

Gina stares at Vaughan, intrigued, but also wondering if she's going to get a word in edgeways, and what it will be if she does.

'Anyway, the penny soon drops and all of a sudden Bobby starts waving his arms about. Then in seconds flat the door is slammed shut and I'm being scuttled out of the room.' He laughs again. 'Six months later I'm at the Treasury.'

'Incredible.'

'Yeah, I laugh about it now, but at the time . . . *boy*.'

Her opportunity comes a couple of moments later when the building looms into view.

'So,' she says, pointing ahead, 'how big a stake?'

'I'm sorry?'

'You said you have a stake in Richmond Plaza. How big is it?'

Vaughan stiffens. She can see that he's a little taken aback by the directness of this. He turns to look at her, and hesitates, holding her gaze, as though trying to calculate something.

Gina is nervous now, and acutely aware of the two men up front.

But it seems to be OK.

'Fifteen per cent,' Vaughan says eventually, still holding her gaze. 'Of course, we have Amcan, too, as the anchor tenant.'

'I see.'

'It's going to be their European headquarters.' He pauses.

'Ray Sullivan? Tall guy back at the hotel? He's their CEO. Good man.'

'I see,' she says again, nodding her head.

'And I don't know if you know it,' Vaughan continues, almost in a whisper now, as though telling her something intimate, 'but we're changing the name as well.'

'Oh?' she says, matching his whisper. 'I didn't know. What to?'

He whisks a hand through the air in front of her, conjures it up. 'The Amcan Building.'

'Of course,' Gina says. 'The Amcan Building, what else?'

She is suddenly irritated, and unable to hide it.

Vaughan stiffens again. 'Well, it *was* a strategic decision –'

'Oh, I've no doubt,' she interrupts him. 'None at all. But the thing is, Jimmy, what's happening *now*? I mean, *you're* here, and this Ray Sullivan is here.'

'So?'

She shrugs. 'The big guns are in town.'

It's as if she's thinking out loud.

'Well, I don't know about that, Gina. I wouldn't exactly –'

'And everyone's on their best behaviour. Or supposed to be.'

Vaughan furrows his brow. *He's* irritated now, too – she can see it. He's confused by her tone, and at the same time put out that their flirty little exchange has gone flat.

She needs to be more careful.

What's to stop Vaughan from having her thrown out of the car before they hook up again with Paddy Norton?

'I'm just sorry,' she then says, turning to him, 'that my brother can't be here.'

She feels her face going red.

'Of course, of course.'

It's funny, Gina thinks, how you can be lying to someone and telling them the truth at the same time.

The car pulls up at Richmond Plaza.

Before the second car – the silver Merc – has come to a complete stop alongside the kerb, Ray Sullivan is reaching over to get the door open.

He climbs out.

Norton waits. From where he is, he can see Gina Rafferty and Jimmy Vaughan standing in the middle of the concourse at the foot of the building. Phil is a few feet behind them. Vaughan is pointing upwards and Gina is nodding. They seem to be having a reasonable, normal sort of conversation. It's just not obvious what they are saying exactly, what *she* is saying.

Norton slides across the seat to the open door of the car. He gets out. The driver closes the door behind him.

It's cold today and quite breezy, but not unpleasantly so. As he stands on the pavement, Norton watches Ray Sullivan hurry over to join the little grouping in the middle of the concourse.

Waiting on the far side of it, at the entranceway to Richmond Plaza, there is a second little grouping – two men and a woman. This is the reception committee he has organised for the visit. It consists of the project manager, Norton's own director of development and his senior operations manager. They are all wearing yellow hard hats and protective jackets. Over to the left, in front of the wooden hoarding, a few construction workers are standing around watching the scene unfold.

The one incongruous element in all of this, however, the one thing that makes Norton feel like he's in the middle of an anxiety dream – the middle of a *nightmare* – is the presence of Gina Rafferty.

He walks to the centre of the concourse, a little unsteadily, almost as though he's drunk. He doesn't feel as frantic as he did earlier, which is good. But maybe that's because he surreptitiously popped another three Nalprox tablets in the car as they were approaching Richmond Dock, and as Sullivan was occupied with his BlackBerry.

'Ah, Paddy,' Vaughan says, holding an arm out in a gesture of welcome to Norton. 'Come along, come along. I was just saying to Gina here . . . when I was a kid, do you know who my heroes were?'

Norton shakes his head.

'Not Batman, not Superman, not Buck Rogers, no, no, the labourers who built the Empire State, that's who, the "sky boys" they were called.' He waves a hand in mid-air. 'Those young fellas in overalls, you know, the ones who stood on bare girders a thousand feet above the sidewalks of Manhattan.'

'That so?'

'Oh yeah. Man, those guys were incredible.'

Norton nods his head, thinking, *How does this old fucker do it? If I had half his energy . . .*

He glances around.

Standing very close to Vaughan now, right next to him, is Ray Sullivan. Phil has moved in a little closer, too.

Gina is standing there, slightly apart from the others, in her leather jacket – exposed, vulnerable.

He tries to catch her attention, but she won't look him in the eye.

What is she thinking?

'You see a part of the problem,' Vaughan is saying, '*I* think, is that people don't *get* the romance of it anymore, the romance of the skyscraper.'

'No?'

'Not in the States anyway, because we're jaded, we've *done* it already.'

'Done what?' Gina says, her tone hard to gauge.

'Look,' Vaughan says, 'you've got the Woolworth Building, the Wrigley Building.' He checks them off on the fingers of an outstretched hand. 'Tribune Tower, the Chrysler, the Empire State, *on* and *on*, the World Trade, Sears, whatever the next one's going to be. No one cares anymore. But what's happening now in Dublin, with *this*,' he throws an arm upwards, in a voilà flourish, 'well, it makes the whole thing exciting again. It's like a return to those earlier days, it's like . . . what is it Fitzgerald calls it? A fresh, green breast of the new world?'

'Though of course,' Gina says, 'in reverse.'

'Excuse me?'

'Well, it *is* like the frontier, I suppose, except that this time you're heading east, back across the ocean.' She pauses. 'I just hope for *your* sake, Jimmy, that you're not in for too much of a shock.'

Vaughan gives a little shake of his head. 'What's that supposed to mean?'

'Why don't you ask our friend Paddy here?'

Norton's insides turn.

'Ask him *what*? I don't . . .'

He stops.

There is a long tense silence, broken only by the hum of passing traffic, the sound of a distant pneumatic drill, the intermittent whistling of the wind blowing in now from the Irish Sea.

'Please, Gina,' Norton says eventually, 'for God's sake, you shouldn't be out like this –'

'Sorry?'

'You're not well, we know that, and –'

'*What?*'

'Your doctor, he's advised –'

She leans forward. 'Fuck you.'

'OK, OK,' Ray Sullivan says, stepping forward, arm outstretched, 'enough already. Come on, miss, whoever the hell you are.'

Gina recoils. 'Get *away* from me.'

Sullivan stops. 'Phil?' he says, quietly, over his shoulder.

'What's this?' Vaughan asks. 'What's going on?'

Phil steps forward. Sullivan turns and stands in front of Vaughan, blocking his view.

'It's nothing, Jimmy,' he says. 'Let me handle it.'

Norton stares at Gina. 'Don't make a scene,' he says. 'It's not worth it.'

Phil approaches her. 'Come on, lady,' he says, holding out an arm. 'Let's go to the car.'

She pulls away again. 'Don't you *touch* me.'

Norton swallows. Sullivan looks around. They're very exposed here, but –

All very quickly, it happens. Phil lunges for Gina. It's like a rugby tackle. He goes for her waist. He tries to restrain her by binding her arms together inside his own and then lowering her to the ground. But she manages to get one arm free and to wallop him on the side of the head a couple of times. The extra leverage this gives her causes Phil to lose his balance. Locked together in a wrestle, they turn and fall.

Norton looks on in horror.

Still trying to block Vaughan's view, Sullivan catches a glimpse, over his shoulder, of what is happening.

'Paddy,' he says, 'Jesus, *do* something.'

But Norton is paralysed. He watches Phil and Gina struggle on the ground, hears grunting, heavy breathing, is aware, too, on the edge of his vision, of an alarmed stirring – one or two of the construction workers rushing forward, the reception committee in sudden disarray.

Then there is a sharp, loud crack. It is followed by a single, brief yelp of pain. The construction workers pull back, as though reacting to the force of an explosion. The two bodies on the ground prise apart. Phil rolls sideways, remaining on the ground, and clutches the lower part of his left leg. Gina rolls the other way, but faster, with more purpose, and rises to her feet. She takes a few steps backwards, both arms held out.

In her right hand she is holding a gun.

Sullivan is saying, 'Oh Christ, oh Christ.' Vaughan is pale and looks confused.

Norton takes a couple of tentative steps over to where Phil is and bends down as though checking to see if the man is all right. 'Have you got a gun?' he whispers.

Phil nods, his face contorted with pain.

'Then *shoot* her.'

Gina is looking around, and behind her. It's clear to Norton that she has no idea what she is doing.

'In the head,' he says to Phil, 'and *quick*.'

He withdraws.

'Tell me,' Vaughan is saying to Sullivan, '*tell* me . . . what's going on?'

'I don't know, Jimmy, I don't know. Let's just get you back to the car.'

Slowly, Sullivan starts manoeuvring Vaughan around.

'*Don't move,*' Gina shouts.

They stop.

Out of the corner of his eye, Norton sees Phil struggling to get something out of his pocket, then turning and raising his arm.

But in that same moment, Gina rushes over and flicks her leg up. She manages to kick the gun out of Phil's hand and send it flying across the concourse.

Phil yelps in pain once more and collapses back onto the ground.

Gina then grabs Vaughan by the arm and sticks the gun into his side. Ray Sullivan steps backwards, arms up.

'No,' he says. 'For Christ's sake.'

Norton steps away as well. He can't believe what's happening. He's right there, watching it, but feels detached from it.

The two construction workers in the distance remain frozen – undecided, terrified, useless.

Gina moves, taking Vaughan with her.

'You, too,' she says to Paddy. 'Come on, let's go.'

'*What?*'

'Come *on.*'

'Where?'

'Inside.'

Norton follows.

They walk across the concourse towards the building. Vaughan is an old man, so progress is slow and tense. As they approach the arched glass entranceway, the reception committee disperses, left and right. Norton is aware of the others behind him, following at a discreet distance. He glances over and sees one of the construction workers talking on his mobile.

They go through automatic doors, along the entranceway and into the vast atrium.

Still pale and a little shaky, Vaughan nevertheless seems to be OK. He stares ahead, very intently, and remains silent. Gina has a drawn, anxious look to her, as if she knows that this act of stupidity and desperation can only end badly for her.

Which, of course, it *will.*

Because soon enough the Special Branch and Emergency Response Units will be here, and they'll all be armed, and seeing as how she's already shot someone and taken two hostages, one a frail old man – what kind of a chance does she stand?

Norton only hopes that it's quick and efficient – and final.

They move across the vast atrium, which has been cleaned up since he was last here. Shimmering, pristine, the place is ready for occupation by an army of consumers and office workers – but right now it feels eerie and uninviting.

Gina stops and looks around. 'Those over there,' she says to Norton, pointing to a bank of six elevators. 'Are they working?'

'Gina, look, this is insane. What do you –'

'*Are* they working?'

He is struck, and a little disturbed, by how calm she sounds. 'Yes.'

'OK.'

They move towards the elevators.

Norton looks over his shoulder and across the atrium. There are five people standing just inside the entranceway now – three construction workers, Ray Sullivan, and Norton's director of development, Leo Spillane.

No one is moving or speaking.

Gina looks quickly at the elevator cars. Norton can see at once that she's confused. Each car has a touch-screen terminal in front of it and operates on a digital control system that depends on traffic patterns, but since these patterns have yet to be established, the system hasn't been fully programmed. She steps forward to one of the terminals and enters a number, but nothing happens. She's about to get annoyed, and turn to Norton, when she sees that the last car doesn't have a terminal in front of it. On the wall to the side, there is a plain silver push-button marked 'Express.'

She steps over and presses it.

The door opens immediately.

Norton's heart sinks. This could get very complicated.

'*GINA!*'

Norton looks around.

Leo Spillane is stepping forward. He worked closely with Noel and would have met Gina at the funeral.

'*Gina,*' he says, 'please . . . whatever this is –'

'*Stay back.*'

Spillane stops.

Gina shunts Vaughan and Norton into the elevator car. She leans her back against the door to hold it open. Standing half inside the car and half out, she raises a hand up into the air – the one with the gun in it.

'Pass this message on to the police,' she says, speaking directly to Spillane – and again Norton is alarmed by how composed she sounds. 'Tell them I want to speak with Jackie Merrigan. Detective Superintendent Jackie Merrigan.'

Then she withdraws into the elevator car. The door automatically whispers shut.

She presses a button.

Vaughan clears his throat. 'Gina,' he says, 'I don't und–'

'*Shut up.*'

Vaughan hesitates, looks as if he's about to continue, but thinks the better of it.

Norton's heart is racing. His palms are sweaty. As the car starts its rapid, hushed ascent, he closes his eyes.

When they step out of the elevator car into the middle of Level 48, Gina looks around and tries to get her bearings. The tower's main elevator shafts are located in its central core. But the last time she was up here – with Norton, two weeks ago – they used a service elevator that was located at the end of the building, and the *back* end, the one facing north.

Behind where they are now.

She waves the gun at Vaughan and Norton, directing them to move forward.

Vaughan hesitates.

'I'm not sure,' he says, turning to her, 'that you fully appreciate who I *am*.'

Gina raises her arm and points the gun at his head. 'I told you to shut up. Now *move*.'

'OK.' He holds a weary hand up. 'OK.'

As she follows the two men, she looks around – left, right, ahead, behind. There doesn't seem to be anyone else up here. She notices, too, that a great deal of work has been done since that last visit. All the windows, floors and ceiling panels have been fitted, and the place no longer looks like a building site. It's still an open space, but it's a lot closer to becoming the teeming ecosystem of reception areas, office suites and con-ference rooms the architect no doubt intended it to be.

At the end they stop next to a tall stack of what look

like prefabricated wall or partition units. The windows are floor-to-ceiling, and the view, as before, is spectacular.

But also a distraction.

Gina turns around. She leans her head back onto the glass and immediately starts wondering how thick it is, and how easy it would be for a trained marksman perched outside on the jib section of the crane to pick her off. Then again – she thinks – someone in here could probably do the job just as easily. They'd come up in the service elevator and position themselves on either side of the central core, or behind any one of the nearby supporting columns.

All of which means one thing: she doesn't have much time.

'Right,' she says, turning to Vaughan. 'Where were we?'

Norton glares at her.

Vaughan sighs peevishly. 'I don't remember.'

'Well then,' Gina says, 'let me remind you.' She taps the floor with her right foot. 'This building you have such a big stake in, that you're here to inspect? I was saying I hope you don't get too much of a *shock* when you do.'

Vaughan looks at Norton and shrugs.

'What's she talking about?'

'I don't know, Jimmy. She's deranged. Look at her. I feel sorry for the bitch.'

Gina says nothing. There is a long pause.

'Oh, what *is* this?' Vaughan says eventually. 'Listen, I'm not a well man. I have a blood condition.' He looks at his watch, and then at Gina. 'I have meds to take. Can we cut to the chase here, *please*?'

'Sure,' she says, nodding her head in Norton's direction. 'But it has to come from *him*.'

'Paddy?'

Norton shakes his head. 'I told you, Jimmy, she's disturbed. She can't come to terms with her brother's death. She's been making these wild allegations. It's . . . it's all bullshit.'

'What kind of allegations?'

'I don't know. She thinks someone had her brother killed, but –'

'Why?'

Norton pauses. 'Sorry, what . . . *why* does she think –'

'No. Why would someone want to kill her brother?'

'But that's the thing, you see, she –'

'No, no, wait a second. He was the chief engineer on this, right? So if there was a reason for someone to want to *kill* the man, I think we should know about it, don't you?'

Gina is about to say something when she hears a siren in the distance. She freezes, afraid to look, but does it anyway. She turns to the window and peers down. Three police cars, blue lights flashing, speeding along the quays.

From up here they appear tiny.

She turns back.

Neither of the two men has moved.

Vaughan is old and frail, but Norton? He could easily have lunged at her, twisted her arm back and wrenched the gun from her. So why didn't he? Maybe he was unwilling to take the risk. Or maybe he's assuming, *hoping*, that the Emergency Response Unit guys, when they get here, will waste no time and simply take her out with a clean shot to the head.

'Paddy,' she says, looking behind him, 'why don't you tell him about the report?'

There is movement up ahead, behind the core section that

houses the elevator shaft and stairwells – one person at least, possibly more.

But it won't be the police, not yet.

She looks Norton in the eye, and sees a flicker of panic.

'I don't know what you're talking about,' he says.

'Fine,' Gina says, 'whatever.' She looks past his shoulder again, just for a second, and then turns to Vaughan. 'Listen carefully because here it is, *Mr* Vaughan. A man named Dermot Flynn who worked with my brother at BCM wrote a report about this building we're in. He showed the report to my brother, who showed it to *him*.' She waves the gun in Norton's direction. 'Now I don't know what's in the report exactly – it was too technical, I couldn't understand it – but for some reason *Mr* Norton didn't want anyone else to see it. And now, as a consequence, my brother is dead and Dermot Flynn is dead.'

'This is nonsense,' Norton says. 'I told you she was crazy. They both died in accidents. There *is* no report.'

The sirens have stopped.

Vaughan is staring at her. It's clear that he doesn't know what to think.

'Would you like to see it?' she says.

'What?'

'The *report*.'

'Jesus, Jimmy –'

'Shut up, Paddy.'

Gina reaches into her jacket pocket and takes out her mobile phone.

'What's your email address?' she says.

There is a pause. Vaughan tells her. She keys it in.

'Gina,' Norton says, a hint of desperation entering his voice, 'what are you doing?'

She hesitates. Her stomach is jumping. 'I'm emailing him a copy of the report,' she says. 'Just like I emailed it this morning to Yves Baladur and Daniel Lazar.'

'*What?*'

'I retrieved it yesterday from Dermot Flynn's laptop –'

'*Jesus Christ.*'

'– and stored it in my email account.'

She waves the phone at him.

He glares back.

She looks at the display for a moment and then says to Vaughan, 'Yep. There. It's gone. Now *you* have it too.'

As Vaughan turns to Norton, he takes out his own mobile. 'What the hell's this all about, Paddy?'

Norton says nothing.

Vaughan looks at the phone, squints at it, presses something and waits.

Over his shoulder, Gina can see Ray Sullivan now – in the distance. He's standing in full view, near the elevator. There is someone else behind him.

She turns to the window again and glances down to check out what's happening at street level. Traffic has been halted and is backed up along the quays. People are gathering everywhere in little clusters. Some appear to be pointing up, others to be talking on their phones.

The jumping in her stomach is relentless.

She turns around again.

Norton is standing very still, staring at the floor.

'Yep,' Vaughan says. 'I got it.'

He folds his phone shut and puts it away.

Gina holds hers down by her side.

'I don't know, Paddy,' Vaughan says, shaking his head, 'but it seems to me that she's got you by the balls here.' He pauses. 'So you want to tell me what's *in* this report?' Sensing the activity behind him, he half looks over his shoulder. 'And you might want to hurry.'

Gina watches as Ray Sullivan moves out of view and a uniformed guard takes his place. A second guard appears, and then a third.

She moves her own position, just slightly – closer to the stack of partition units.

'*Paddy,*' Vaughan snaps. 'Are you going to make me *read* this damn thing? Or have me hear about it from someone else?'

Norton looks up. He is pale. He shakes his head.

'It was purely theoretical,' he says slowly, almost in a whisper. 'He'd made these ridiculous calculations based on a set of *theoretical* conditions. Believe me, you'll see.'

'What do you mean, conditions?' Vaughan says impatiently. 'What conditions? *Weather* conditions?'

'Yes.'

'So we're talking, what . . . *wind*?'

'Yes. But quartering winds, tropical winds, stuff that doesn't apply here, stuff that isn't relevant.'

'Shit,' Vaughan says. 'I don't like the sound of this.'

Gina looks at him.

'*What?*'

'It's *the* most significant calculation you have to make. How much wind stress a building can absorb. Testing is exhaustive. It's done in controlled tunnels. Everything is computer simulated, checked a thousand times.' He turns to Norton. 'Jesus, what are you telling me, there's a *mistake* somewhere?'

'Not exactly.'

'Then *what*?'

Norton exhales, struggling. 'Noel's design for the wind-bracing system included a series of diagonal steel girders, and for some reason it came to Flynn's notice, don't ask me how, that the joints of these girders were bolted together, and not welded, as Noel had specified –'

'Jesus –'

'No, no, bolting them together was fine. Welded joints would have been stronger all right, but the contractor decided, and legitimately, that welding them was too expensive, too time-consuming and, in fact, *un*necessary. For *here*. But Flynn went ahead anyway and did all these additional load-bearing calculations, extrapolating this, that and the other – what'd happen if we had a tropical cyclone or a hurricane. Wild stuff. It was pure speculation. So don't be under any illusion, the building *complies* with all required codes and regulations –'

'But?'

Norton swallows, looks around, exhales loudly.

Gina is crouched down now – phone in her hand resting on one thigh, gun on the other – looking up at the two men. With the stack of partition units in the way, she can no longer see what the guards are up to, but nor can they see her.

'What he found was that the increase in stress to the building in the switch from welding to bolts was negligible for local weather conditions ... but not when you took quartering winds into consideration.'

'What are quartering winds?' Gina says.

Vaughan looks down at her. 'They're winds that come in at a forty-five-degree angle and hit two sides of the building at once.'

She nods, barely understanding any of the words in isolation, let alone the complete sentence.

'In that scenario,' Norton goes on, 'the difference is marked, and from then on . . . it's exponential.'

Vaughan closes his eyes.

'A simple increase of twelve or fifteen per cent could translate into an increase of . . . more than a hundred and thirty, a hundred and forty percent.'

'*Jesus* –'

'But only in conditions that are *never going to happen*, that's the whole point. It's like removing a safety net you don't need in the first place. He fed in all this speculative data that was based on *projected* climate-change scenarios and the *possible* long-term consequences of global warming. It was ridiculous.'

Gina looks up, glares at him. 'You're like a fucking *child*, do you know that? Trying to talk your way out of trouble. If the report was so ridiculous, then what was the problem? Why bury it?'

Norton shrugs. 'It was . . . not a problem as such, I mean, you couldn't really –'

'*Look*,' Gina says, holding up the gun, '*enough*.' She points it directly at him. 'Do you want me to shoot *you*, too? In the fucking *head*?'

'OK, OK. There *was* a problem. It was with his conclusion. He recommended that repairs be done immediately, that steel reinforcements be welded onto each of the building's three hundred joints.'

Vaughan whistles. '*That* would be expensive.'

'Yes. Very.'

'And best-case scenario you'd be looking at a . . . what, a six to nine-month delay?'

'Easily, and with huge knock-on penalties for going over

agreed completion dates. Plus, we'd miss the tax-incentive deadline.'

'Not to mention what a PR catastrophe it'd be.'

There is silence for a moment.

'And if the repairs aren't done?' Gina then says.

Norton stares down at her now with naked contempt. 'You're not going to let it go, are you? You're like a dog after a bone. Like Flynn, like your brother.' He pauses. 'What is it you want, the bottom line in all of this, is that it?'

She nods.

'Right. Fine.' He takes a deep breath and holds it in for a moment. 'According to these calculations, *without* the repairs, and in storm conditions so rare you might only see them in this country once every hundred years, the building has a fifty per cent chance of, let's say . . . of *withstanding* the pressure.'

Gina shakes her head. 'No.'

'What?'

'Let's *not* say that. Let's say it another way. Let's be as explicit as we can, shall we?'

She gives the gun a little shake.

Norton rolls his eyes and breathes out sharply.

'OK, yeah, let's. In certain extreme weather conditions, this building, Richmond Plaza, has a fifty per cent chance of *collapsing*. Are you happy now?'

'Fifty per cent?'

'According to these calculations, yes.'

'And given the potential for loss of life and damage to surrounding property, you think that's an acceptable level of risk?'

'Absolutely. *I'm* not worried at all.' He pauses. 'Because what

I *don't* accept is the data he was working with. I just don't believe it would ever happen. But none of that would matter if the report got out, you see. Perception would be everything.'

'*Perception?*'

'Of course. The sound bite. *Fifty per cent chance of collapsing?* You think anyone's going to see beyond that?'

Gina presses her head back against the glass. 'And that justifies having people killed? For completion dates, for *tax* purposes, for fucking *PR*?'

Norton throws his hands up, as though in exasperation or despair.

'There you go again with this crap,' he says. 'I didn't have anyone killed. What do you take me for?' He turns to Vaughan. 'Jimmy, look –'

'Save it, Paddy. I'm not interested.'

'What?'

'This is . . . I'm having a hard time believing this is actually happening. I just . . .' He looks at his watch. 'I just want to get on the next goddamned plane out of here.'

'But what about –'

Vaughan holds up an admonitory hand.

Norton stops, his frustration palpable.

As the two men stand there in silence, Gina checks something on her phone. Then she looks up at Vaughan. She waves the gun at him.

'Go.'

'What?'

'Go. *Now.* Get your meds. Catch your flight.'

Five minutes after Vaughan has left, Gina's mobile rings.

'Yeah?'

'Gina? Are you all right there?' A Kerry accent, the voice soft and instantly reassuring. Whoever this is has been trained in the subtle art of hostage negotiation. 'Listen, can we maybe –'

'I *said*. I want to talk to Jackie Merrigan. In person.'

'Yeah, Gina, we were looking for him, but he's on his way now. So, I don't know, in the meantime –'

She cuts him off.

Norton sighs impatiently.

She looks up at him. '*What?*'

'You're a very stupid girl, do you know that?'

'I'm not a *girl*, Paddy. And we'll see who's stupid.'

Hunkered down at the window, facing the partition units, she doesn't have a direct view of the rest of Level 48 and can't tell what is going on. Norton can, and keeps looking around. At one point she catches him trying to gesture or signal to someone.

'Face the window,' she says. '*Now.*'

He does.

'There's a whole bloody *army* back there,' he says. 'They've got flak jackets, machine guns, the works.'

'I can hear them, but I've got *this.*' She points the gun directly at him. 'I've used it once. I'll use it again.'

Norton says nothing. After a while, he asks if he can take something out of his pocket.

'What?'

'Tablets.'

'You as well? Go on.'

He takes out a packet, fumbles with it and swallows two – maybe three – tablets.

'What are they for?'

He looks at her. 'What do you care?'

She sighs. 'You're right. I don't.'

She starts keying something into her mobile.

'You know, Gina,' Norton then says, 'this is not going to end well for you. It can't.' He clears his throat. 'Any credibility you might have had before, you cashed in by doing *this*. So no one's going to listen to you. And if you think sending that report to Baladur and Lazar is some kind of a trump card, you're wrong. They'll close ranks now, everyone will, Vaughan, the contractors, everyone. The spin merchants will be out in force. Coming from Noel, the report might have carried some weight. It was his design. People would have had to listen. But not anymore. *No one* will endorse it now.'

She looks up at him. 'What, no one will admit what you just admitted a few minutes ago?'

'Of course not. And no one has to. No codes or regulations have been broken. The arguments in the report can be torn to shreds in five minutes, and they will be. Because no one's going to want to be associated with *this* carry-on.'

She shrugs, and goes back to what she was doing on her mobile.

'The media won't take it seriously either,' Norton continues. 'They won't understand it for one thing. And if you persist in making those claims about how I had something to do with your brother's death I'll have a restraining order slapped on you so fast you won't know what hit you.' He shakes his head. 'Believe me. I'll come down on you like a ton of bricks. I'll tie you up in legal knots for years.' He laughs. 'But sure that won't matter anyway, because you'll be in *prison*.'

Gina ignores him.

Behind her, faint at first, but growing louder, is the sound of a helicopter.

'You see, *you're* going to be the story in all of this, Gina, not some stupid fucking report. What *they'll* be interested in' – he nods his head forward, indicating the helicopter – 'is the crazy lady who shot some poor innocent bastard in the leg and then took two hostages. You'll be tabloid fodder for days, *weeks*.' He laughs again. 'You see, like I said, it's all about perception.'

'Jesus, Paddy,' she says, not looking up from her mobile. 'Would you ever *shut* up?'

Fifteen minutes later, her mobile rings again.

'Yeah?'

'Gina? It's Jackie Merrigan.'

'Where are you?'

'I'm here. Over at the elevator. Do you want me to approach?'

'Yes. *Alone*.'

Pressing back against the window, she eases herself up into a standing position. Over the stack of partition units she sees Merrigan walking slowly towards her. ERU personnel are positioned everywhere.

She glances over her shoulder and down at street level. There is no traffic at all now. Parked alongside the concourse are squad cars and police vans. There are also several large trucks. These are probably Outside Broadcast Units. A couple of hundred yards down the quays barriers have been set up, behind which a sizeable crowd appears to have gathered.

The helicopter is still out there, cruising a wide area. Every now and again it comes in close and circles the building. When it does, the sound is almost deafening.

She turns back around.

Norton is standing a few feet away from her, staring straight ahead.

Merrigan comes to a stop in front of the partition units. 'Hello, Gina.'

She nods.

He is as she remembers, tall, stooped, white hair. He's got a heavy overcoat on. From where he's standing she can't see his hands. But he was a close friend of Noel's. She's not expecting him to pull out a gun and shoot her.

'Thanks for coming.'

Norton turns around. Merrigan looks at him.

'Are you OK?'

'Well what do *you* think? I've got this deranged bitch –'

Gina raises her hand. 'Shut *up*.'

'Take it easy, Gina,' Merrigan says. 'Let's all stay calm, yeah?'

It's only then that Gina sees it. Merrigan is nervous. And of course why wouldn't he be? This is a volatile situation, and probably not the sort of thing he's ever had to deal with before. Besides, he doesn't really know her . . .

'Look,' she says in a hurry, 'I don't want to drag this out. I just . . . I need some assurances from you.'

He nods.

'One, I saw security cameras on the way in here. At the entrance. One of them was trained on the concourse out front. I don't know if they're working, but if they are you'll see that I was attacked first. The shot I fired was in response to that, to being assaulted. Anyway, there were witnesses, a couple of builders, I think.'

'Fine. Of course. We'll check it out.'

'Second, I want you to look into Noel's death. The circumstances. His mobile-phone records. Where he went after he left Catherine's. Check the brakes on his car.'

Merrigan hesitates. 'OK, Gina. I'll . . . I'll do my best.'

'Third thing.'

She holds up the gun. Merrigan flinches.

'*This?*' she says. 'I'm telling you in advance: it isn't mine.'

Merrigan swallows. 'I didn't imagine it was.'

'No, but I'll bet you don't know whose it is.'

He shakes his head.

'It belonged to Martin Fitzgerald.'

Merrigan's eyes widen. '*That* Martin Fitzgerald?'

She nods, and brings her hand down. 'I'm not sure, but I think it might be the gun he used to shoot Mark Griffin with.'

'*What?*'

Merrigan stops, and for the first time the focus of his attention shifts. Gina can see it in his face, in his eyes.

He is making connections.

'The thing is,' she says, 'I want *you* to know, before I'm arrested, that this is a complicated situation. I need to know that I'll be listened to.'

'You *will* be.'

'Oh, don't worry,' Norton says, 'there'll be no shortage of sound bites if that's what you're after.'

She looks at him. 'And what about you?'

'What *about* me, love? I'm not the one with the gun.'

'No, but . . .'

She stares at him for a moment in silence, then looks back at Merrigan. 'Last thing. I've got an email I need to send.' She holds her phone up to him. 'Yeah?'

He nods.

'It has an attachment,' she says. 'I'm sending it to RTÉ and to Sky News. And to YouTube.'

She presses a key on the phone and waits for a few moments. 'OK. Gone.'

'What was that?' Norton says, glaring at the phone.

'It's very short, only about ten seconds. I hope it's enough of a sound bite for you.'

She holds the phone up high, so they can all see the display. The view is of Norton, from a low angle. Gina's voice is heard first. The sound is tinny.

Let's be as explicit as we can, shall we?

After a pause, Norton's voice is heard.

OK, yeah, let's. In certain extreme weather conditions, this building, Richmond Plaza, has a fifty per cent chance of collapsing. Are you happy now?

Shock registers on Merrigan's face.

Fifty per cent?

According to these calculations, yes.

'Oh my God . . .'

And given the potential for loss of life and damage to surrounding property, you think that's an acceptable level of risk?

Absolutely. I'm not worried at all.

Gina flicks the phone closed and brings her hand down.

Norton lunges forward. '*Jesus, I'll –*'

Merrigan's arm shoots out. He holds it against Norton's chest to block him.

'*Easy.*'

Norton resists for a second and then backs off, shaking his head. He turns around and moves away, along by the window.

Gina looks at Merrigan. She feels relieved, but also – she can admit it now, if only to herself – a little insane, a little psychotic. Every muscle in her body is rigid. Every thought in her head is conditional. It's as if she's been holding her breath non-stop for the last three weeks.

She hands him the gun.

Within seconds armed police officers have swarmed the area and taken full control.

Gina leans her head back against the glass, and breathes out slowly.

At the same time, several miles away, in an isolated ward of the intensive care unit of St Felim's Hospital, Mark Griffin is breathing slowly, too.

Sixteen times a minute, in fact.

Unconscious but stable, the thirty-year-old victim of the city's latest gangland shooting is hooked up to a ventilator. A second machine monitors his heart rate and blood pressure. He also has three IV tubes attached to a strip on his neck. These provide medication for pain control, fluids to keep him hydrated and sedation to prevent him from making any extreme involuntary movements.

When he was brought in on Wednesday night the first thing they did was give him an X-ray. This showed he had a single perforating wound caused by a bullet that is now lodged in his abdomen. He was then rushed to an operating theatre for an exploratory incision, the results of which showed extensive damage to his liver. Next, they stanched the internal bleeding and stabilised his BP.

Since then he has had two further operations, one to repair essential organ functions, the other to close the entry wound. And although doctors are concerned about the possibility of his contracting an infection, by this afternoon most of his vital signs seem to be showing a marked improvement.

Mark's aunt Lilly spent all of yesterday and several hours this morning at his bedside, but the whole thing has proved so stressful for her, and so exhausting, that one of the doctors took a look at her and recommended that she go home to her own bed – unless she wanted to end up in one of theirs.

After lunch, the nurse on duty phoned Lilly and reassured her that there was no change, and that Mark was stable. A ten-year veteran of the ICU, this nurse has always found that the word 'stable' has a remarkably stabilising effect on those who hear it.

In any case, she prefers it when there are no visitors – because they get in the way. It's not called *intensive* care for nothing.

Staring at Mark now, she wonders if he is aware of her presence. His eyelids flutter on occasion, but they don't open, so she can't be sure. It's one of the recurring mysteries of her job.

She chooses, nevertheless, to talk to him.

'It's me again,' she says. 'Helen. How are you? I'm going to take your temperature now, if that's all right.'

It seems to be.

Outside the room, sitting on a bench in the corridor, a full-time guard is on duty. He is listening to a news update on his small pocket radio.

He stares at the floor.

There's a breaking story.

After a moment, he looks up, takes in the calm, anodyne surroundings of the hospital, and sighs.

He can't believe this.

He's stuck here and right now, in that new skyscraper down on the quays – apparently, according to the bulletin – there's a full-blown hostage crisis unfolding . . .

5

And in the twenty-four hours following this so-called crisis, the clip of an Irish property developer's breathtaking admission – caught on a camera phone *during* the crisis – has been viewed all over the world, on computers, on mobile phones and on TV news bulletins. The incident is seen as the latest example of how digital technology is driving the definition, generation and delivery of today's news content. Outside of Ireland, the story has a kind of train-wreck fascination, and proves irresistible to cartoonists and joke writers. But at home the whole business is seen as something altogether more urgent – because as far as the public at large is concerned, and despite numerous assurances to the contrary, this shiny new forty-eight-storey glass box is, in the words of one vox pop contributor, 'just sitting there waiting to keel over'.

So it's no surprise that action is taken quickly. On Saturday afternoon, the tower and surrounding area are evacuated and cordoned off. Emergency meetings are held. The nature and cost of the repairs are discussed and hammered out. Schedules are drawn up, with work to start almost immediately.

Then on Sunday morning, in the papers and on blogs and radio phone-ins, the affair is parsed endlessly for its cultural and sociological significance. It becomes a kind of template for everything that is wrong with the country, a forum for self-important investigations of national identity, a vessel for people's moral outrage, for their feelings of powerlessness and disenfranchisement.

On the lunchtime news, Taoiseach-in-waiting Larry Bolger says that although he's been personally assured there's no immediate danger, he nevertheless regards it as appalling and unconscionable that such a thing could have been allowed to happen in the first place.

The individual involved, he says, *must* be held accountable.

And naturally enough, it is on this 'individual' that most of the media attention is now heaped. Who *is* he? What other buildings has he put up? Where does he live? How rich is he?

The degree of media attention Gina receives, by contrast, is surprisingly limited. In all, the 'hostage crisis' lasted less than an hour, so the story didn't have time to breathe. No sooner had coverage started than the whole thing came to a head – only to be superseded by the business with the camera phone.

Legally, she's not in as much trouble as she expected to be either. She learns on Sunday evening that for some reason Paddy Norton is refusing to press charges, and that the same goes for Phil Mangione. It turns out that Mangione, whose injury was not serious – the bullet just grazed his shin – has already left the country, accompanied by James Vaughan and Ray Sullivan. So the only thing Gina is charged with in court on Monday morning is illegal possession of a firearm.

She is then released on bail.

Outside the courthouse, flanked by Yvonne and Michelle, she manages to get away and down the street without having to stop and talk to any reporters. The three sisters go to the lounge of a city-centre hotel, where Gina does her best to give a clear account of what happened. But it's not easy. Yvonne and

Michelle are sceptical. They're also, to some extent, embarrassed. It reminds Gina of when she was a teenager and they were in their twenties.

Except it's different.

Except it's *not*.

Leaving the hotel after about an hour – frustrated and tired – Gina gets a call on her mobile. It's from Jackie Merrigan. Where is she? Can they meet? Can they talk? She says she needs to go back to her apartment, that she hasn't changed her clothes in more than four days – but that yes, they can meet.

How about later? Early afternoon?

They make an arrangement for two o'clock.

Over in Government Buildings, at around the same time, Larry Bolger is preparing for a meeting of the parliamentary party at which it is expected his colleagues will choose him as their new leader. This will automatically qualify him to become Taoiseach. He will then travel to Áras an Uachtaráin in the Phoenix Park and receive his seal of office from the President.

Sitting at his desk, in his best suit, he feels the way he remembers feeling when he was about to make his First Holy Communion – stirred by the promise of plenty, and yet uneasy about it all, vaguely humiliated somehow.

He'd love a drink.

His secretary buzzes in to say he has a call from Paddy Norton on line one. Bolger hesitates and then says he'll take it – unlike all the other calls from Norton he's declined to take since Friday.

He has to speak to the man *some*time.

He picks up the phone. 'Paddy?'

'The individual involved? The fucking *individual involved*? Is that what I am now?'

Bolger throws his eyes up. 'Hold on there, Paddy, what did you expect?'

'What did I expect? A bit of *loyalty*, that's what.'

'Oh come on, be realistic. With all this *stuff* going on, and all these questions being asked . . . no public representative in his right mind would –'

'And what does *held accountable* mean?'

Bolger stares at a folder on his desk.

'I think that's pretty obvious, Paddy, isn't it? There's a lot of hysteria at the moment, a lot of anger, and even if it *is* all bullshit, there's an election coming in the next twelve to eighteen months. People need to see some action, you know? They're not going to let this slide.'

'So you're going to give them *my* head on a plate, is that it?'

'It's not me.' Bolger laughs. 'I think you've taken care of *that* yourself.'

There's a pause.

'Fuck you, Larry.'

Bolger says nothing.

'You're a two-faced *bastard*, do you know that?'

'Right.'

'If it wasn't for . . . Jesus, *I* put you where you are today.'

'Of course.' Bolger clears his throat. 'Listen, I have to go. I have a meeting, a pretty important one, as it happens.'

'Grand, keep your distance, don't answer my calls, cut me off, *be* a prick, fine, but I can ruin you, Larry. There's all that financial stuff, going way back, the loans, the dig-outs. And that's just for starters.' He pauses. 'I can, and I *will*.'

Bolger swivels his chair from side to side.

'You know what, Paddy?' he says. 'I couldn't care less. Do what you have to do. I'm going to be the leader of this country in about an hour's time and no one can take that away from me. My name will be entered into the history books. So whatever happens afterwards . . . scandals, enquiries, tribunals . . .' He shrugs. 'I don't *care*. These days that stuff is almost par for the course anyway. It comes with the territory.' He pauses. 'So . . . whatever. I'll be seeing you, Paddy.'

He puts the phone down.

'Minister?'

He looks up. His secretary is standing in the doorway. She's pointing at her watch.

'Er, yeah.'

Bolger gets up from the desk. He gives a quick shimmy to his suit, gets it into shape. He straightens his tie. He clears his throat.

'OK,' he says, 'I'm coming.'

He heads for the door.

About an hour later, in the ICU ward of St Felim's, Mark Griffin opens his eyes.

His mind is blank, and it remains that way for several seconds.

Then . . . *bed*.

I'm in a bed.

He concentrates.

In a hospital . . . and that's a nurse.

She's at the foot of his bed, filling in a chart, concentrating herself.

He stares at her. She glances up and gets a start.

'Oh,' she says. '*Mark.*'

She reattaches the chart to the end of the bed and comes around to the side.

He follows her with his gaze.

She then leans in closely and examines his eyes with a penlight – first the left one, then the right.

She stands back.

'It's Helen,' she says. '*I'm* Helen. How are you feeling?'

He gives a slight nod to his head, and then frowns.

He's confused.

'You're under sedation,' she says, apparently reading his confusion. 'Movement will be slow. For a time. Don't worry about it.'

He opens his lips to speak, but nothing comes out. He nods again, still confused.

'It's Monday,' she says. 'Monday afternoon. You've been here for more than four days.'

His mind goes blank again.

Four days? Is that what she said? Fine. Whatever.

Then it hits him.

Four days?

It's like getting whacked on the head with a baseball bat.

Evidently, the panic shows.

'Look,' the nurse says, 'I'll . . . I'll call one of the consultants. They'll want to have a look at you anyway.'

He watches her leaving and then stares at the door.

Four days?

Was that . . . the alleyway, the warehouse, and then earlier . . . *was all of that four days ago?*

Jesus.

What's happened since then?

He looks around the room, struggling to focus. Fighting the narcotic sludge. There are machines next to the bed, humming and beeping. There's a wall-mounted TV.

No windows.

What happened?

Fear pulses through his system. He looks over at the door again.

What's happening now?

'You know . . . you're a *very* lucky girl.'

Gina bites her lip, holds back. She's exhausted. She's been awake, more or less, since she got up on Friday morning in Sophie's apartment. Over the weekend, while in garda custody, she lay down a few times and closed her eyes, but she never sank far below the threshold of consciousness.

'I don't feel it,' she says eventually.

Merrigan lifts his coffee cup and holds it in front of his mouth. 'Believe me, you could have faced charges a lot more serious than illegal possession of a firearm.'

He takes a sip from the coffee, blows on it and then takes another sip.

'I know,' she says. 'But I really don't think luck comes into it.'

'What do you mean?'

She glances around. They're in Neary's on Chatham Street, at a table towards the back. The place is almost empty. Halfway along the bar two burly middle-aged guys are nursing pints and talking. Every now and again a word or phrase from their conversation breaks loose and carries down the room, *director's cut, salad dressing, gigabytes.*

'Well,' Gina says quietly, 'for one thing, *he* should be facing charges, not me.'

'What he *will* be facing is litigation, and plenty of it.'

'Yeah, but that's not –'

'Gina, *listen*.' He puts his cup down and sits back in the chair. 'You've destroyed the man's reputation. You've held him up to ridicule. His career is finished. He'll never get another project off the ground. Literally. But that other stuff? The emails you showed us? The phone calls? His association with Martin Fitzgerald? What Terry Stack said? It's all circumstantial.'

'What about –'

'Noel's SUV was a total write-off. Nothing's going to come out of that either. There's *no* evidence.'

She looks at him. 'What do *you* think?'

He exhales loudly. 'I've investigated a good few murders in my time. You learn to be pretty resigned about it. If you haven't got the evidence, you move on. You can't go by what something *looks* like. Not if it's *all* you've got. Not if you're unsure there's even *been* a murder.'

She nods, eyes focused now on the low table between them, on the arrangement of objects on it – the coffeepot, her own untouched cup, his cup, the milk jug, the sugar bowl. After a few seconds, and in her exhausted state, it takes on the character of a weird, phantasmagoric arrangement of chess pieces.

'You also learn to be dispassionate,' Merrigan goes on. 'Though having said *that*, Noel was a good friend of mine. I knew him for nearly twenty years and I hate the idea that . . . that . . .'

He waves a hand in the air, dismissing the thought, banishing it.

She looks back over at him. 'No, say it, go on, you hate

the idea that he might have been murdered. Is that what you actually *think*?'

He is silent for a moment. Then he says, 'OK, I'll admit it . . . it doesn't look good.'

'He just gets away with it then?'

'Well, not technically.' Merrigan drums his fingers on the side of the chair. 'Because technically, you see, *legally*, the man hasn't done anything to get away *with*. He hasn't been –'

'Oh come on.'

'Look, I don't like this any more than you do, Gina, but I can't ignore my professional training, my –'

'Fine, but that's not something *I* have to struggle with –'

'Oh I know.' He pauses. 'That's what has me worried.'

'What do you mean?'

Merrigan sighs. He seems exhausted, too – though not from lack of sleep. His face is lined. He looks drained, weary, ready to retire.

'I think you're a lot like Noel,' he says. 'You're tenacious. You don't give up easily. But you're also very foolhardy, you've shown that already, and if you push this any further you could get into serious trouble, more trouble than you're in now.'

'But if he's guilty –'

'Even if he *isn't*, Gina, there are libel laws in this country. You can't just go around making accusations against people like that. This is a wealthy man we're talking about. He could make life very difficult for you.'

'So his wealth protects him? Is that it? This fat murdering *bastard*?'

She looks away, shaking her head.

Merrigan takes in a long, deep breath.

He leans forward in his chair. 'Suppose for a moment he

is guilty, and that everything you say is true. Think how dangerous that makes him. Then think how much you've pissed him off already. What is there to protect you from him?'

'Nothing.'

'Exactly. *I* can't protect you. The Gardaí can't protect you. Not without reasonable cause. You'd be on your own.'

'I've been on my own all along.'

Merrigan sits back and shrugs his shoulders. 'Norton has taken a *very* serious hit here, and where it hurts. Why can't you be satisfied with that?'

'Because it's nothing compared to the damage *he* has caused.' She sighs. 'Paddy Norton has destroyed people's lives. I mean, apart from the others . . . look at Mark Griffin, on a bloody ventilator.' She pauses. 'And you know, to be honest, I don't even know what happened there, or why, the background, the *history* . . . but Norton's prints are all over *that*, too.' She pauses again. 'I should have asked him about it when I had the chance.'

Merrigan holds her gaze. 'I can see this becoming an obsession with you, Gina, do you know that? I can also see it destroying *your* life.' He pauses. 'So I'm asking you – in fact, as a senior police officer, I'm telling you – leave this alone. Don't ever go near Paddy Norton again, or make contact with him. Yeah?'

Gina's impulse here is to push it, but what's the point? It would be futile. She knows the arguments. She doesn't want to hear them from him. She doesn't want to hear them from *herself.*

Nothing would change.

He is staring at her.

'*Yeah*?' he repeats.

After a few moments, she nods her head.

'Anyway,' she then says, and smiles – her first in quite some time – 'you knew Noel for twenty years?'

'Yes.'

She is almost alarmed to see the effect her smile has on Merrigan. The reaction is instant. He moves, shifts his position in the chair, all but wriggles.

She smiles again. She can't help it.

It's like administering a small jolt of electricity.

'*Yes*,' he repeats, nodding vigorously, 'I did.'

'So,' she says. '*Talk* to me about him.'

Norton turns right onto the Dual Carriageway from Eglinton Road. He's been driving around for a while, an hour or two, and doesn't want to stop – or go home, or go *anywhere* – but he's tired and definitely getting a little woozy.

He went into the office this morning but stayed only twenty minutes. Then he turned his mobile phone off. It was after that conversation with Larry Bolger. But he was getting too many calls from people he didn't want to talk to anyway – Daniel Lazar, Yves Baladur, Ray Sullivan, someone from the Department of the Environment, someone from the bank, various investors, journalists . . . Miriam . . .

He passes the RTÉ studios at Montrose.

Those bastards in there have been running the same identifying clip of him in all their news bulletins since Friday. It shows him, some months back, entering the Fairleigh Clinic, taking the front steps two at a time – but over and over again. The repetition of the clip has become something of a joke, with one smart-arse on the radio today even remarking that after so much exercise Mr Norton should probably expect to lose at least a *little* weight.

It's humiliating.

The box and torn packaging on the passenger seat beside him is what's left of the Nalprox. He's been popping them indiscriminately all weekend and is going to have to arrange a repeat scrip soon.

He flicks on the CD player.

Jarring, dissonant brass and a demented string section. He goes on to the next track. It's more soothing, some clarinet thing, but after a minute he flicks it off anyway.

He keeps replaying Friday in his head.

He just didn't see it coming, not like that.

He didn't have her pegged for such a scheming, devious *bitch*.

Stopped at lights, he reaches over and opens the glove compartment. If he'd had this bloody gun with him on Friday, he would have used it and dealt with the consequences later.

But he didn't. It was sitting here in his car, gathering dust.

He'd still like to use it, though – and will, if he ever gets the chance.

If she ever comes near him again . . .

A few minutes later, as he's pulling into the gravel driveway of his house, he has a momentary lapse of concentration – or maybe even of consciousness – and swerves a bit to the left. He scrapes the side of his car against the iron gate and then mounts a rock-bordered flower bed, crushing a row of crocuses. It takes him a few awkward moments to manoeuvre the car off the flower bed and park it properly.

When he gets out of the car, he stands for a moment on the

gravel and takes a couple of deep breaths. He looks up at the sky, which is grey and overcast. Then he inspects the side of the car, swears under his breath, shakes his head. Turning to go into the house, he notices two men standing at the gates.

One of them has a camera.

'*Fuck off!*' he shouts, and raises his fist in the air.

He hadn't noticed them on the way in.

Miriam is waiting at the bottom of the stairs. For the last three days she has been struggling to maintain some kind of equilibrium. But conflicting forces have made this very difficult. One side of her wants to be loyal and supportive to her husband. The other side, it appears, wants to insult and belittle him.

The best she can manage is a sort of tense neutrality – severe, clipped.

No make-up.

'Where have you *been*?'

'Out. Driving around.'

'I see. Why didn't you answer your phone?'

'I didn't feel like it.'

'Did you check your messages?'

'Oh *Jesus*, Miriam.'

He walks across the hall and into the main reception room. He goes over to the drinks cabinet and pours himself a large Bushmills.

Then he stands, looking at nothing in particular, and sips the drink. He has his back to the door and doesn't know if Miriam is there or not.

But she doesn't have to speak. He can hear her voice in his head.

Whiskey? For goodness' sake, Paddy, it's four o'clock in the afternoon.

He turns around.

She isn't there.

Keeping a close eye on the door, Mark tries to piece everything together in his mind – but the pieces keep shifting position and changing shape. At the end there, in the warehouse, something happened, it's just that he doesn't know *what* exactly. Because he wasn't in any condition to take it in. What he does know is that Gina was supposed to show up, but someone else was there, someone who knew *he'd* be there . . . and then, after a while, seemingly, all hell broke loose . . .

But what happened to Gina? Where is she now? *How* is she now?

One way or another he's going to have to find out. He's going to have to ask the nurse if she knows anything, or if she can arrange to buy him a phone, or get him a newspaper – or, at the very least, turn on the TV.

Assuming he can trust her, that is. Assuming he can trust anyone.

Because there was that guy at the warehouse, and the guy earlier, the one in the car park, the one who shot him.

So presumably there'll be others.

Mark's stomach turns.

Not to mention the police. The police will definitely want to interview him. But given that he almost tried to *kill* a government minister, well . . . the police are probably the very *last* people he should trust.

Then, as if on cue, the door of the room flies open and a tall man in a blue suit barges in.

Mark flinches and turns his head to the side, expecting the worst.

'So, Mr Griffin,' the man says in a booming voice, 'Nurse here tells me that you've decided to rejoin us.'

Mark looks up.

The man in the suit is about fifty and has the air of an ex-rugby player.

The nurse is standing behind him.

'Henry Dillon,' the man says, producing a penlight from his breast pocket and clicking it. 'Shall we?'

He then proceeds to examine Mark thoroughly, prodding, probing, moving him on his side, testing his reflexes.

He makes adjustments to the various IV drips.

Mark remains anxious, but at the same time – for the moment, at least – he's relieved.

'So,' the consultant says, folding his arms, 'that bullet? Looks like it had your name on it all right.'

Mark's eyes widen. 'What do you mean?'

'Oh, just that you may have it for life. We can't take it out. Well we *could*, but it wouldn't be worth the extra damage the operation would cause. But you'll be fine. It's more common than you might think. People leave hospitals with foreign objects in their bodies all the time.'

Mark stares at him, unsure what to think. Foreign objects? Is this some kind of code? Is he being threatened here? Or *warned*?

He remains silent.

'Well, you seem to be making a remarkable recovery,' the consultant says, heading for the door. 'We'll probably move you to a step-down unit later today or tomorrow. By the way, there are some people who want to have a word with you and

I'm going to go ahead and authorise them to pop in for a chat. Is that OK?'

Mark swallows.

Some people? A chat?

'Yeah, but . . . what people?'

Halfway out the door, the consultant glances back.

'Why, the police, of course.'

As Gina walks down Grafton Street, around College Green and onto the quays, she hears Merrigan's words in her head.

I can see this becoming an obsession. I can see it destroying your life.

She doesn't think he's wrong.

She knows she's under the influence of a compulsion that she doesn't understand or currently have the energy to resist. She thought after Friday that it would dissipate, that she could settle for how things had turned out, for a lesser form of justice.

But it only intensified.

And hearing last night that Norton was refusing to press charges actually made it worse. Something crystallised for her in that moment. It was the realisation that *she* needs to press some form of charges against *him*.

But now, in the cold light of day, that seems like a remote possibility. Because how does she pursue this? How does she even approach him after everything that has happened?

Walking along by the river, Gina looks up at Richmond Plaza and finds it hard to believe that she's not still up there, not still holding a loaded gun in her hand, not still pointing it at Norton's head, because compared to the intensity of *that* experience, everything else seems unreal to her, pallid and insubstantial.

But at the same time she can't give up.

That's not an option.

So when she arrives at her building, gets upstairs and through the door of her apartment, she walks straight over to the desk in the corner. She takes off her jacket. She puts down keys, wallet, phone.

And stares for a while, first at the wall, then at the keyboard of her computer.

She could call him on his mobile.

But that might be too direct. What if he doesn't answer? What if he decides to alert the guards?

She needs something that will give him pause, something to provoke him.

Sitting down, Gina pictures Mark Griffin lying in an ICU ward, on life support, and it occurs to her again that *his* involvement in all of this is something she has never challenged Norton on. It's actually the one aspect of the whole business that doesn't fit, that she doesn't understand.

So with the queasy self-awareness of a compulsive gambler about to place one more – one *last* – bet, she taps the centre of the keyboard and activates her computer. She opens the file. She turns on the printer.

She looks at her watch: 4.25.

I can see this becoming an obsession. I can see it destroying your life.

Then she picks up her mobile and calls a local courier service.

When Mark mentions Gina Rafferty's name to the nurse, she recognises it immediately and is able to inform him that not only is Gina all right, she's been in the news and has made quite a splash . . .

Mark finds this alarming, and then confusing. It just doesn't make sense.

Richmond Plaza? Paddy Norton?

He is relieved to find out that Gina is OK, that she's *alive,* but he doesn't get what she is up to, he doesn't –

Which is when the nurse suggests that she might try and get a hold of one of yesterday's newspapers for him, an *Independent* or a *Tribune.* There was plenty of coverage in all the Sunday papers, and at least one of the patients in the next ward along is sure to have something left over.

She'll go and have a scout around when she gets a chance.

But maybe in the meantime Mark might like to watch some TV?

'There'll be news on in a while.'

'Yes,' he says. 'Fine. Thanks.'

The nurse switches on the TV and hands him the remote.

'Er, Nurse,' Mark then says, 'look, there isn't any chance I could get my hands on a mobile phone, is there?'

'Yes, I suppose so. You could borrow mine if you really need to make a call . . . or –'

'Do they sell them downstairs, at reception? Is there a shop? Could –'

She nods. 'Yes, don't worry about it. I'll arrange something.'

After she leaves, Mark stares up at the screen for a while but is unable to focus on anything.

He keeps glancing over at the door.

When are the police going to show up? And what are they going to ask him when they do?

He exhales loudly.

But let's face it, are they really going to bother asking him anything at all? Because in whose interest is it to hear what *he* has to say?

It's in *his* interest. And in no one else's.

Mark may no longer be a threat to anyone physically, but he *is* still a threat, just of a very different kind. The mere fact that he's alive and has a story to tell not only threatens Bolger's advancement in the party, it may also seriously threaten the reputation and stability of the great party itself.

Mark feels as though he's emerging from a dense fog, which he puts down to a combination of the adjustments the doctor made to his IV drips and what he imagines to be a natural surge in his own adrenaline levels. But the result is that he's now extremely agitated and doesn't know how much longer he's going to be able to just *lie* here like this.

Doing nothing, waiting for . . .

For what?

He looks at the door, and then up at the TV again.

The news is coming on.

The programme's signature tune rises portentously, and fades.

He tries to focus.

The doorbell rings.

Norton doesn't move.

He has no intention of answering it, given that it's probably a journalist out at the front gate. They've tried this on a few times over the past three days.

He's been drinking coffee and his heart is racing. The whiskey earlier made him sick. For the first half an hour he felt fine, even a little exhilarated – which was probably due to the mix with the pills – but then he got nauseous and threw up.

The switch to coffee was fine at first, too – but now he feels jittery and anxious and has a tightness in his chest.

He should eat something, but . . . maybe later.

The TV is on. He's not focused on it, though.

Then the phone rings. In the hall.

He has no intention of answering that either.

It can ring out. Or Miriam upstairs will answer it. There were several calls earlier, which he's assuming she did answer. But if so, she never passed on any messages. And some of the calls had to have been for him, because he hasn't been getting back to people. Voicemail, text messages, emails – he's been ignoring them all.

He's not in the mood.

A few moments later, he hears Miriam coming down the stairs.

He tenses, not in the mood for her either.

She opens the hall door. He hears her stepping out onto the gravel.

He waits, listens.

What is she doing?

She'd better not be going out to talk to a journalist, because that'd be really stupid. Though on reflection it's not something he can see Miriam doing. With her it'd almost be like breaking a religious taboo.

She comes back in and slams the front door shut. Then she comes into the living room. Without saying anything, she walks over to the sofa where Norton is sitting. She has a large brown envelope in her hand. She drops it in his lap.

'What's this?'

'I don't know, Paddy. I'm not in the habit of opening other people's packages.'

She turns and leaves.

Norton looks at the envelope for a moment and then tosses it down beside him on the sofa.

He turns back to the TV. The six o'clock news has just come on, and guess what – for the first time since Friday evening Norton is not the lead story.

Larry Bolger is.

Norton grunts. He wants to turn the TV off or switch to another channel, but he can't. He stares at the screen – fascinated, mesmerised, but also disgusted. It's not so much that he thinks he should be there, in the background, basking in the reflected glory – of *course* he should – it's more that Larry's arrogance is so breathtaking, his casual assumption that he can cut old ties so . . . so *deluded*.

They show clips of Bolger leaving Áras an Uachtaráin, then arriving back at Leinster House, and then – at which point Norton presses the Mute button on his remote – addressing the chamber. After that, in a quick résumé of his career, various photos appear on the screen: a schoolboy in front of a grey institutional building, Liam Bolger flanked by his two teenage sons, the mangled car, a campaign poster . . . then Larry wearing an election rosette, Larry sitting at the cabinet table, Larry standing in front of the main stage at an Árd Fheis . . . on and on, the young man Norton first knew, slim and with an implausibly bushy head of jet-black hair, morphing into the greying, stocky middle-aged *bollocks* he is today.

Taoiseach Larry Bolger.

Give me a *fucking* break.

Whatever it is Mark is expecting to see on the news, it's not what he gets, because the lead story isn't about Gina Rafferty or Richmond Plaza – though it was hardly likely to be – it's about Larry Bolger and how he has taken over as . . .

Taoiseach?

But –

How could this have happened so fast? Last Wednesday the man was just a minister, getting over a personal scandal. There was talk all right, speculation, but –

Gazing at the screen, Mark feels as if some kind of cosmic trick is being played on him.

His stomach is jumping.

He feels like Rip van *fucking* Winkle.

In utter disbelief, he watches as they show footage of Bolger leaving Áras an Uachtaráin, returning to Leinster House and addressing the chamber, after which they go back over his career and show photos from the archives, old black-and-white ones . . . of a small child in a school uniform, of Bolger's father flanked by his teenage sons, and then –

Mark flinches, rears back in horror.

– of a crushed and mangled car by the side of a country road.

He grabs the remote and turns the TV off.

Holy fuck.

Holy *fuck*.

He takes a few deep breaths, and then, unwilling to linger on the image in his mind's eye – *unable* to linger – he flicks the TV back on.

Bolger at a press conference, flanked by senior ministers.

Mark can't believe it.

Can't believe any of it.

And as he stares at the man on the screen he is seized by this awful, queasy sense of himself as an inconvenience, as a piece of someone else's unfinished business. Twenty-five years ago his family was wiped out, taken from him physically, which was bad enough, but then they were taken from him emotionally as well – and now the person responsible for that is trying to wipe *him* out, too? And why? Because he's apparently looking for . . . what? Some kind of *closure*?

Well, so be it.

Mark pulls back the covers of the bed.

So be it.

He moves his legs to the edge, slides them over and manoeuvres himself into a sitting position.

If he wants closure, then he can fucking well have it.

But it's only at that point that Mark realises he has a catheter attached to him, and that the catheter is, in turn, attached to a drainage bag hanging from the side of the bed. What does he do? Yank it off? He then tugs at the lumen strip on his neck from which the various IV drips connect to bags mounted on a mobile unit next to the monitors. Does he yank this off, too?

He should try and stand first.

He glances up at the TV. They're in a studio now, dull voices droning on about momentous events, the big day, history.

He eases his feet down onto the floor, aware for the first time in a while of a dull pain in his back – a pain that seems to be rapidly intensifying.

He raises his hand up to his neck and is about to tear the strip loose when suddenly his eyes well up with tears.

What does he think he's doing? Is he *insane*? What's his plan here, to breach government security wearing a hospital gown and then strangle the new prime minister with his catheter tube?

It's beyond pathetic.

He leans back against the bed and groans, the pain getting worse.

Across the room, the door opens.

The nurse is backing in with a trolley, but she stops halfway and addresses someone outside, maybe the guard, maybe another nurse.

'Ah go *on*, he's not, is he?'

Mark lifts himself up onto the edge of the bed. He turns, wincing, and eases himself into position again.

'Listen, don't believe everything you hear.'

He pulls up the covers, leans his head back against the raised pillows and closes his eyes.

'See ya.'

He listens as the nurse wheels the trolley in through the door and across the room.

His heart pounding, his eyes stinging.

After a moment, the nurse comes over to the bed, picks up the remote control and turns off the TV.

Mark then feels her tossing something onto the end of the bed.

A while later, when she has left the room once more, he opens his eyes.

At the end of the bed there is a copy of the *Sunday Tribune*.

To distract himself from what's on the TV, Norton picks up the envelope beside him on the sofa and examines it. He doesn't recognise the handwriting. He tears the envelope along the top. Inside it there is a single page of glossy photo paper. Printed on the page are three photographs.

One each of a man, a woman and a small girl.

At first he is puzzled. He looks inside the envelope again and sees a business card. He takes this out and examines it.

The name on the card is Gina Rafferty.

His heart lurches.

If she ever comes near me again . . .

He looks back at the photographs and . . .

Of course.

Jesus, she has a nerve. But what is she up to? Is this meant to be some sort of coded message – a veiled threat? He thought that by not pressing charges he'd at least be eliminating *her* from the equation. He thought she'd go away and leave him to deal with the fallout, with all the shit she'd stirred up . . . but now *this* . . .

He reaches forward, straining to breathe, and places the page of photos on the coffee table. He picks up his mobile and flops back. He switches the phone on, enters his PIN and waits.

Then he looks for her number, finds it, calls it.

It rings.

There is an ad on the TV, a silver car speeding across a desolate moonscape.

'Yes?'

'This is harassment. I could get the Guards to have you –'

'Then go ahead. Call them. They know where I live.'

He pauses, glances at the photographs again – at the three faces, with their alien, remote expressions.

'What am I supposed to do with these pictures?' he says. 'What's your point?'

'My point?' She almost laughs. 'That no one has made the connection yet.' She pauses. 'But they will, sooner or later, and probably sooner.'

'What connection?'

'Oh come *on*. All it takes is one journalist to see it, to remember the name from the other night. Or one phone call.'

He grinds his teeth. He stands up. 'I don't know what you're talking about.'

This sounds weak, even to him.

'No?'

'No.'

He waits. She doesn't respond. The silence goes on for quite a while. During it, he walks across the room and stands at the window. The curtains are half open. It's dark outside, except for the security lights on the front lawn, and the streetlights in the distance, and *all* the lights of the city, thrown up, reflected, falling back like snow.

'Listen,' Gina says eventually, 'those three people died unnecessarily. And it wasn't *his* fault, Tony Griffin's, like everyone said it was at the time. Now, *I* can't prove it, of course, what was going on. No one can. Mark couldn't. But maybe it's time that someone bloody well *admitted* it, yeah?'

'*Jesus.* What was *going on*? I don't . . .' He is barely able to suppress his rage. 'Meaning *what* exactly? Dunbrogan House? Is that it?'

She says nothing.

'Been doing your homework, have you? You *bitch.*' He puts a hand up to his chest and rubs it. 'Very well,' he goes on, wincing, 'you want to talk about this, yeah? About Frank and Larry? About the accident? Let's talk about it then.'

'Yes . . . *let's.*'

'But not over the phone.' His voice is hard now, and controlled, almost a whisper. 'Somewhere outside. Somewhere neutral. And right now.'

If she ever comes near me again . . .

'Fine,' Gina says without hesitation. 'Tell me where.'

*

The main story on the front page of the *Sunday Tribune* is about Larry Bolger and his imminent coronation. However, there is a piece at the bottom – and two more inside, on page 8 – about Richmond Plaza.

Mark reads these, a little impatiently at first, but then with growing interest.

It is not stated explicitly – nothing is, presumably because of the country's strict libel laws – but with the report by that engineer, what Gina seems to have uncovered here, theoretically, reading between the lines, is a motive for the murder of her brother.

Or what *she* sees as the murder of her brother.

And this Paddy Norton, the developer, is the focus of all her attention. She seems to have pursued the man with a ferocious determination, and . . .

Mark puts the paper down for a moment, and as he gazes at the wall opposite, and listens to the monotonous beeping of the monitors, a thought occurs to him.

She was going to tell him something.

It was their last conversation. The one on the phone. She was talking and he interrupted her.

What had she been going to say?

He tries to remember. He was . . .

I think I'm maybe on the wrong track.

That was it.

About Bolger.

He closes his eyes.

I think I'm maybe on the wrong track, about Bolger. I mean, it doesn't seem –

He opens his eyes again.

But what? It doesn't seem *what*?

It doesn't seem that Bolger . . .

He's confused. He takes up the paper again and scans the final paragraphs of the article he was reading.

Paddy Norton . . . Paddy Norton . . .

He's barely able to focus on the words.

. . . started out over twenty-five years ago . . . web of business and political connections . . . soon established as a leading . . . party affiliations . . . the Bolger brothers . . .

Mark feels dizzy.

But what does this mean? Has he been wrong all along? *All his life?*

He goes back a few pages, to another article, one about Bolger and scans that.

. . . called back from Boston . . . funeral arrangements already in place . . . reluctant to run . . .

Mark closes his eyes.

It hits him now with the force of a religious revelation.

Bolger wasn't even in the country when the accident happened . . .

By the time he got back from America, everything had been taken care of, everything had been set in train.

Jesus Christ.

He has always just assumed . . .

The name . . . it was always the name, Larry Bolger, looming like a dark cloud over everything he ever did.

Larry Bolger . . . Larry Bolger . . .

But he never questioned it, never talked to anyone about it. No one ever talked to *him* about it . . .

He shakes his head, a surge of anger now rising through him.

He needs to know.

He needs to know.

Paddy Norton.

Billionaire property developer.

The name is familiar, of course, but Mark can't put a face to it. Then it occurs to him that given how the construction industry works here, he might actually have *met* Norton at some point, or at least have seen him at functions, trade fairs.

And he definitely knows people who *have* met him. Just a while back, in fact – there was that developer from Cork. Didn't he say he'd been 'talking to' Norton?

Jesus.

How many degrees of separation? Never too many in this fucking town, that's for sure.

Never *enough*.

As a politician, Bolger had always seemed a distant figure to Mark – in a numb, mediated sort of way. But *this*? This is too close to the bone.

Way too close . . .

They might have shaken hands.

Through his anger, and now revulsion, Mark steels himself, does his best to concentrate, to focus.

Winterland Properties. Their head office is on Baggot Street. But Norton himself . . . he has that huge spread out in . . .

He's read about it.

Foxrock.

It shouldn't be too hard to get his number. It might even be listed.

When the nurse comes back, before she's even through the door, Mark calls out to her.

Startled by the urgency in his voice, she comes straight over to his bedside.

'Yes, love, what is it?'

'That phone?'

'Oh yes, I haven't . . . er, I'll –'

'Can I borrow yours then? You said I could borrow yours. Can I? It's just for minute. It's just . . . *Can* I? It's important.'

Gina stands at the door of her apartment and looks back in. She switches off the light and steps out into the hallway. She closes the door, locks it. She takes the stairs, just to be moving.

What is she up to? Is she insane?

Don't ever go near Paddy Norton again . . .

But she needs to know.

She needs to hear him *say* it, and if she can get him talking, and keep him talking, then maybe he will.

Down on the street, it's cold and forbidding, a mid-November evening. They've arranged to meet on the seafront at Sandymount. On a bench. Somewhere neutral, somewhere outside. But also somewhere potentially – in *this* weather – quite isolated . . . a person here or there, but only maybe, and walking their dog, huddled into their overcoat, shivering, staring straight ahead, distracted . . .

She doesn't care, though.

If Norton is prepared to talk about Larry Bolger and *his* brother, then maybe he'll talk about *hers*.

She takes her mobile out of her jeans pocket, checks it, switches it to vibrate and then puts it back.

She looks up and down the quays. With this traffic diversion in place, it's not so easy to get a cab anymore.

She starts walking back towards town, towards the IFSC.

It'll be easier up there.

Standing in the hall, Norton puts on his Crombie coat. He folds up the page with the photographs on it and slips it into his pocket.

He also puts on a scarf and gloves.

He looks at himself in the mirror. His face has a greyish pallor.

He was stupid on the phone. He shouldn't have mentioned Dunbrogan House. He knew the moment he said it that she had no idea what he was talking about.

But what was the point of the photographs then? Were they a taunt? Some sort of sentimental plea? All along he's been saying she knows nothing, and all along he's been right.

But she refuses to go away.

Norton reaches his hand towards the door and is about to open it when the house phone rings.

As before, he has no intention of answering it, but something makes him stop and listen all the same. The ringtone continues for a bit and then cuts off.

Miriam.

Again, something holds him back, gives him pause.

He turns around.

Miriam appears at the top of the stairs. She's holding the phone in her hand.

She looks at him strangely – and he guesses it's not just because he's leaving the house without having said a word. Her reproach of the past hours and days, her contempt, seem to have fallen away and been replaced by something else, something that goes much deeper, something he's finding it difficult to read.

She comes down a few steps and holds the phone out.

Quietly, almost in a whisper, she says, 'It's Mark Griffin.'

'Hello?'

Mark draws in a deep breath.

It's as though he's been waiting all his life to draw in this particular breath, and he holds on to it. The words are ready – in whatever combination they may see fit to arrange themselves, they always have been – but there's something unique, and mysterious, about the brief moment of silence before they take over.

It is a bridge, already in flames, between his past and his future.

'It was *you*,' Mark says eventually, his voice, when it comes, sounding strange to him, almost like someone else's. 'Wasn't it?'

And then, as he waits for a response, afraid he might miss something, a phrase, a word, even a syllable, he presses the phone tightly against his ear.

He stares at the door.

His heart is pounding.

For his part, Norton is standing in the hallway, at the foot of the stairs, barely able to comprehend what is happening – not least the banality of it, how the simple, physical act of taking a telephone into his hand can belie the enormity, the significance, of what he's about to do.

Which is talk to Mark Griffin.

Little Mark *bloody* Griffin.

But what does he say? How does he respond? In the circumstances, words seem not only inadequate and puny, but also potentially dangerous, because he mightn't be able to control them. If he starts in here – even with a rational, innocuous *Excuse me* or *I beg your pardon* – who's to say what torrent of less innocuous words might follow? He's acutely aware, too, of Miriam, who's still halfway up the stairs, and staring at him, *listening*, but for what? Some formula of words as well? The answer to a question from twenty-five years ago? A question that she never asked? A question that has *remained* unasked, and unarticulated, and in the air between them all this time, like interference, like a dense wall of radioactive dust particles, sometimes visible, sometimes not?

He *could* just hang up here, tell her it was some tabloid scumbag fishing for a quote, but –

'Wasn't it, Norton?'

The option recedes.

Quickly, he moves across the hall and back into the living room. With his foot, he nudges the door closed behind him.

Words, words . . .

He's always been good at using them, to negotiate, to obfuscate, to deny, to bludgeon.

'Sorry . . . *what* did you say your name was again?'

'Oh *Jesus.*' Mark, in his overheated, airless hospital room, shakes his head. 'Let's not do *this*, Norton,' he whispers, and glances up at the ceiling, '*please.*'

But Mark's mind is almost blank now, a hundred different ways to proceed fanning out bewilderingly before him.

Rage his only constant.

'Because you *know* who I am.' He swallows. 'You fucking *made* me who I am.'

'OK, calm down there. Just take it easy. I . . . I thought you were in intensive care. I read –'

'Oh, I *am*, you needn't worry about that.' Mark moves his neck slightly and feels the tug of the various IV tubes. 'But the point here is . . . I always thought it was *him*, all these years, but it wasn't, was it? It was *you*.'

'It was me *what*?'

'*Jesus*.' Mark leans forward in the bed. He almost wants to laugh at this point, but knows if he does it won't sound anything remotely *like* a laugh. 'It was you who covered it up that night,' he says, 'and it's you who's trying to cover it up again now. Because it's come back at you. And you're freaking out.'

'That's ridiculous.'

Norton stops in the middle of the living room, faces the TV screen on the wall above the fireplace, sees his reflection in the grey darkness – this prosperous middle-aged man in an overcoat and scarf, talking on the phone.

Business as usual.

'I didn't cover *anything* up.'

But he *is* beginning to feel rattled. And a little flushed. The novelty wearing off. He taps at his coat pocket with his free hand, fumbles for the pack of Nalprox.

A part of Norton wishes this weren't happening over the phone, that they were face to face, that he could at least *picture* the young man on the other end of the line. But he can't. All he's got are images left over from long ago, images assembled from reports, from scraps of conversation, from dreams.

Images of a five-year-old boy with a bloodied face, and puzzled, vacant eyes, walking over shattered glass . . . and walking towards *him*, towards Norton . . .

Who wasn't even there.

'You may think I'm some kind of fucking idiot,' Mark is saying, 'and that's fine, but let me tell you *this*.'

Mark has no idea what *this* is, what it is he's supposedly going to say next, but he can't stop it, any more than he could stop a surge of reflux rising up from his stomach.

'I've survived this far, OK? The crash, getting shot, whatever, and I'll go on surviving, because sooner or later I intend to make *you* pay for what you did to my family . . . what you've gone *on* doing to them.' He gets a flash of the three photographs he found and wonders where they are now. 'But that's all finished,' he continues. 'It's over. I'm not taking any more of it. I'm *here*, Norton, I'm here *now*, and I'm not going away.'

He's pressing the phone so hard against the side of his head that it hurts.

He holds up his other hand. It's shaking.

Norton remains silent, but as fascination gives way to impatience, and guilt to indignation, he has to make a conscious effort not to lose it.

Because how *dare* this little bastard talk to him like that? How dare he even call him in the first place, and *at home*?

It's outrageous.

Norton manages to pop one of the pills from the blister, but it slips from his hand and falls to the carpet.

Shit.

From his bed, Mark strains to hear, to interpret the silence – but is unable to match it.

'So if you send anyone near me again,' he says, 'in here to the hospital, a cop, some visitor, whoever . . .' He pauses, keenly aware of the absurdity of what he's about to say next, but again, unable not to say it. 'I'll kill them with my bare *fucking* hands, is that clear? And then I'll come after *you* myself.'

Norton tries to bend down to get the pill from the carpet, but gives up. Out of breath, wheezing, he fumbles with the blister again for a replacement.

Don't say anything. Don't say anything.

'*Look,*' Mark goes on, forcing himself to concede a little, but still desperately struggling to deliver a killer blow, 'maybe . . . maybe I can't do anything to get you now, realistically, maybe it's too late . . . but we both know I'm not the only one out there. And if you're thinking, well, *this* clown will eventually give up, do you really think *she* will?' He pauses, waiting, eyes wide open. 'No,' he then says, '*I* don't either, and I hope she *doesn't*, I sincerely hope she fucking *crucifies you.*'

As Norton raises his hand with the pill in it to his mouth, he knows that that's it, any appeal to willpower, to self-discipline, is futile now – he's going to let go, he can feel it inside.

It's like a loose bowel movement about to explode . . .

But that's fine. He doesn't mind. He almost welcomes it.

He places the pill on his tongue and swallows.

'You know what, you little prick?' he then says. 'You're absolutely right. And I'm not going to let that happen. Because I think I've taken enough shit from her already, don't you?' Deliberate implication here being, of course, that he's not in the market for any from *him*. Which is maybe a little too subtle for this . . . this what? This child? But the person he's talking to is no longer a child, not by a stretch – and in any case, *fuck* subtlety. 'I mean, Jesus Christ, Mark,' he says, and clears his throat. 'Come on. Let's face it. Why the hell do you think I'm heading out the door right now to meet her?'

Mark flinches. '*What?*'

His brain automatically rescans the last few seconds. Then it short-circuits, scrambles, cuts for a moment to white noise.

Norton unassailable now.

'Yeah, to discuss who might be in the new cabinet? I don't *think* so.'

Oh God . . .

And with that, every solid object around Mark seems to start moving – the bed he's in, the drip stand, the walls, the very room itself – all of them, like tectonic plates, shifting, sliding in different directions . . .

Why did he have to mention her? Why did he have to bring her into it?

He closes his eyes to block it all out, but the sudden, frenetic darkness is worse, coloured patterns flickering and multiplying in a queasy kaleidoscope.

Why did he have to open his fucking mouth?

Which he tries to do again now, but his voice catches.

'I'll –'

It's as if having used all his energy and resolve to cross this bridge before it collapses, he inexplicably finds himself turning around and rushing headlong *back through the flames* . . . back to the other side, to the past, to that desolate, all-too-familiar landscape of guilt and shame and self-loathing.

'I'm sorry?' Norton says, looking at his watch now, and over at the door. 'You'll what? You'll do *what*? I didn't hear you.' He starts walking. 'But anyway, Mark, let me remind you of something, yeah? Little detail.' He pauses. 'You're in the *hospital*.'

He doesn't say anything else.

For Mark, the silence that follows is awful. It becomes worse with each passing second.

It becomes unbearable.

He opens his eyes.

He is two or three words into a last, desperate attempt at a sentence when he realises that Norton has already hung up.

Let's talk about it?

Gina crosses the street and takes the boardwalk.

But talk about *what*? Dunbrogan House? She has no idea what that refers to. Saying she couldn't prove what was going on implied she knew *something* was going on. But she didn't really.

She was bluffing.

The river is dark and glistening, and moving at speed. Clouds reflected in the water ripple past.

Back in the apartment she considered taking something with her, just in case, a weapon of some sort, a carving knife, a pair of scissors, a skewer – but she felt foolish, standing there in the kitchen, staring into an open cutlery drawer.

What did she imagine was going to happen?

At the last minute, however, picking up her keys and phone from the desk in the corner, she also picked up a glass paperweight that she's had for years. It's in the shape of a star, with a millefiori design. It's made of Venetian crystal. It's solid, and heavy, and has sharp angles.

She dropped it into the pocket of her leather jacket.

At Matt Talbot Bridge she sees a passing taxi. She hails it. The taxi stops. She gets in.

Her stomach is churning.

'Sandymount, please. The seafront.'

The car pulls away.

'That's a chilly one to be –'

'*Please,*' she says, clutching the paperweight in her pocket. 'No talking.'

She looks out of the window.

As soon as Norton puts the phone down he leaves the house. He gets in the car, turns it on the gravel driveway, activates the electronic gates and flies out onto the main road.

Moments later he's turning at the light and joining the Dual Carriageway.

Thinking, for *fuck's* sake.

Mark Griffin.

But also thinking, calculating, and quickly coming to the conclusion that Mark Griffin knows nothing, poses no real threat and is clearly deranged – not to say hysterical, not to say out of his *fucking* mind.

Going by *that* performance, at any rate.

But he's not a threat.

No one will listen to him. In fact, if anything, Mark Griffin resurfacing in the public consciousness after all this time will only get people wondering about Larry Bolger, asking questions about *him,* speculating – the way Griffin himself obviously was.

But that's not something Norton cares about anymore.

Because no one knows the truth. No one knows what really happened that night.

Only he does. And he's not telling.

He taps his fingers on the steering wheel.

Of course it's true what he said on the phone. He *didn't* cover anything up. He had nothing to *do* with it. Larry's old man, Romy Mulcahy, the party hacks – as far as he knows, *they* were the ones who did it.

It wouldn't have been his style anyway.

And yet . . . and yet . . .

There was one thing Griffin said that *was* right.

It may be irrational, it may be illogical, but Norton feels that if anyone could tease it out of him – what he did do that night – if anyone could pick at it, worry it apart, conjure the whole thing up out of smoke, Gina Rafferty could. And now that he's given her Dunbrogan House as well, she'll never leave him alone.

She *will* fucking crucify him.

He glances over at the glove compartment.

So what choice does he have?

There is a wide curve in the road ahead. As he takes it, the sparkling city, spread out below, reveals itself. There in the distance, in the bay, imposing, magnificent, like a flourish – like a *signature* – is Richmond Plaza.

Norton feels an unexpected rush of pride, and it strikes him that maybe all hope is *not* lost. OK, Amcan is pulling out, other clients have already pulled out, and the building may well stand empty for a considerable period of time. But when the hysteria dies down, and the repairs are done, when further studies prove that *there* was *never any danger in the first place,* and when the economy picks up again – people will come around. The building will get a second chance. *He'll* get a second chance. He'll be able to rebuild his reputation, and to end his career on a high.

He stops at a red light.

But again, not if *she* starts tugging at the other end of it . . .

With his left hand he picks up the blister of Nalprox tablets from where he tossed it on the passenger seat. There are five left. He quickly takes three, swallows them dry. Then he turns on the CD player – that clarinet thing . . . or is it an oboe? Or a *cor anglais*? He stares at the dashboard, listening.

The car behind beeps its horn.

Norton looks up. The light has turned green. He's in the middle lane, traffic on either side already surging forward.

Shit.

He accelerates, his heart racing.

What he's doing tonight . . .

His mind wandering.

What he did that night . . .

The thing is, there on the stairs, when Miriam handed him the phone, Norton felt the weirdest mix of emotions – irritation, but with a tinge of curiosity . . . fear, but with this undeniable *throb* of longing . . .

The Stillorgan Park Hotel flits past on the right.

It was almost like a homecoming.

Soon he's approaching Booterstown Avenue.

Sort of in the way *this* is . . .

He indicates, and turns. Then, before he knows it he's on the Rock Road, heading for Merrion Gates.

His insides lurch.

There's no way around it, is there?

He glances over at the glove compartment again.

She was depressed . . . unhinged really. She should have been in therapy, or on medication . . .

He tries to imagine how it will be . . . Gina there beside him on the bench, talking . . . it's windy and cold, traffic rumbles past in the background. There aren't that many people about, almost no one in fact. The sea is in front of them – shadowy, vast, heaving. He looks around, chooses his moment, turns to her, puts the gun right up against the side of her head and pulls the trigger.

Then he steadies her as best he can, settles her on the bench, puts the gun into her right hand, and walks away.

It's not exactly how he wants it, but *what choice does he have?*

At the end of Booterstown Avenue, he turns left, onto the Rock Road, his mind in turmoil now, spinning, flipping . . . forwards, backwards, conjuring it all up . . .

What he's going to do tonight.

What he did that night . . .

Mark pulls the covers back, moves his legs to the edge of the bed again and slides them over. He shunts up into a sitting position and eases himself off the bed. He picks the mobile phone up and slips it into the pocket of his gown. Then, without giving it a second's thought, he yanks off the catheter tube from below. There is immediate and considerable pain involved in this, but Mark does his best to absorb it. He then takes a hold of the mobile drip stand and starts moving across the room with it, wheeling it slowly, focusing all his attention on getting as far as the door.

When he's almost there, he notices that there are spots of blood on the floor and on his feet.

But he has to keep moving, because . . .

How could he have been so fucking stupid?

He opens the door.

The guard, who is on the bench draining a mug of tea or coffee, sees him and is immediately up on his feet.

'*Whoa!*'

He puts the mug down and reaches out in support.

'Jesus, what are you doing there?' He looks around. *'Nurse!'*

Mark takes the support for a moment, then pulls away.

The alarm on the guard's face is curiously reassuring. At least, Mark feels, it's not going to be *him*.

Up and down the corridor there is a ripple effect as people take notice and react – but after the guard, the closest person, and quickest on the move, is his own nurse.

What did she say her name was?

Helen?

'Mark, my God, what are you doing?'

She moves in front of the guard and takes Mark by the elbow. She guides him to the bench, making sure to keep the drip stand, with its various dangling bags of fluid, in position. She sits down next to him. Then, noticing the splats of blood on the floor, she takes a couple of deep breaths.

'OK, OK,' she says slowly, 'we have to get you back inside. We –'

'No.'

'What?'

'No.'

He looks up. The guard and some others, a nurse, a doctor or two, are standing around watching.

'I need to get a number, a mobile number,' he says, in a half whisper, and wincing now from the pain. 'I need –'

'Yes, yes, we'll get whatever you want, Mark, but you have to get back inside, into *bed* –'

'*No*, I said.'

The guard takes a couple of tentative steps forward. 'Easy on there, pal, all right? There's no problem here. There's no problem.'

Mark watches him, feeling dizzy suddenly, and weak.

'In a few minutes,' the guard goes on, 'the detectives will be here to see you. They're on their way . . .' – he waves his walkie-talkie – '. . . and we can sort it out then, whatever it is –'

The detectives . . .

Mark shoots a look up and down the corridor.

Everyone is watching. No one is moving. The light is harsh and uncomfortable, the atmosphere unnaturally still.

'*NO,*' he says.

Lifting his hand – and almost before he knows what he's doing – he takes a hold of the strip on the side of his neck and starts trying to rip it off.

'My God, *STOP!*' the nurse screams, and grabs him by the wrist. 'What are you doing? Jesus. That's . . . that's your *jugular.*'

Mark pauses, allowing her to hold his wrist. She's leaning in close now, their faces inches apart.

'You can't just . . .' She hesitates.

He looks into her eyes. 'What?'

'Those tubes,' she says. 'You can't just remove them like that. You'll bleed. You're bleeding now. You could give yourself an embolism. You could *die.*'

He nods.

He can already feel a trickle of blood on his neck.

'Well, Helen,' he whispers, 'it's either that, or you get me the number.'

'*Mark,*' she pleads, tightening her grip on his wrist, 'this is crazy –'

'No,' he says, 'it isn't,' and with his free hand he reaches around her and punches one of the bags of fluid on the drip stand. The bag bursts and its contents splat loudly onto the floor.

There is a general gasp of disbelief.

The nurse, in shock, releases her grip on Mark's wrist and pulls away. But as she's doing this Mark reaches along the bench and grabs the mug. Taking it by the handle, he swings it around and smashes it into the wall behind him. Pieces fly everywhere. Then he brings what's left – a jagged shard of ceramic earthenware – up to the side of his neck.

'*Get away . . . move.*'

Slowly, reluctantly, people comply. The nurse does too, but looks appalled, her arms held out in a desperate appeal to reason.

'*Mark, you can't –*'

'*MOVE.*' He jerks his head sideways. '*I'll tear right into the vein.*'

She nods quickly and takes another few steps back.

'*You,*' Mark then says, addressing the guard, '*stay.*'

The guard freezes.

Apart from the constant drip-drip to the floor of what remains from the infusion bag, there is now an eerie silence all along the corridor.

Mark leans his head back against the wall. There are spots of blood on the front of his gown.

'OK,' he says, nodding at the guard, at his walkie-talkie. 'You're going to get me that number, and *right now.*'

When they get to Strand Road, Gina asks the taxi driver to pull over. Her hands are shaking as she pays him. She wonders if he'll remember her later.

Yeah, that stuck-up bitch who didn't want to talk.

She gets out and starts walking along by the low stone wall. It's freezing cold, the wind cutting through her like a knife. To her right, cars stream past in a steady flow. To her left, the bay seems shrouded in a murky orange darkness. There is a lot of cloud, a gathering mist, and no moon. The tide is in. The lights of Howth and Dun Laoghaire are just about visible.

She is sick to her stomach.

She comes to the end of the stone wall. She goes through the small parking area – which is almost empty – and onto the promenade.

An elderly man with a dog approaches, nods, passes.

There is no one sitting on any of the first few benches.

She can't tell if she's shaking from nerves or shivering from the cold.

Why is this so different from Friday? She was extremely nervous then, too, and even had a gun in her pocket. But she still managed to stay calm. There was no *plan* of course, and that was it – everything just happened, unfolded, second by second, none of it anticipated.

This evening is different. She has a sense of foreboding. She also has a sense of purpose, an almost visceral need to engage head-on with this, and to close it down, even if it means *bashing* someone's head in – his, her own, it barely seems to matter anymore.

She approaches a bench that has four or five teenagers on it. They are huddled together, smoking and laughing.

She goes by, half hearing a comment one of them directs at her.

The next few benches are empty. Then there is the Martello Tower. On the other side of it the promenade continues, and although they didn't say where they'd meet exactly, or at which bench, that's probably where she'll find him. It makes sense. It's the direction he'll be coming from.

She keeps moving.

Towards him, into his orbit.

Earlier, Jackie Merrigan asked why she couldn't be satisfied with having destroyed Paddy Norton's reputation, and she said because it was nothing compared to the damage *he* had caused to others.

It's only now that Gina is beginning to see how she herself is one of these others, how Norton is like a virus she has contracted, or a toxic substance in her system she may never be able to eliminate. With each step, it becomes a little clearer . . . how he has influenced her behaviour, twisted her emotions, choked her sense of who she is . . . how he has turned her into the crazy lady, the mad bitch who can't be stopped . . .

But what Gina is most afraid of now, as she pushes on against the wind, past the Martello Tower, is that Norton is pulling her towards something else again, something awful – a confession she doesn't want to hear, a revelation she doesn't need to know about. She's afraid that he is pulling her towards a place from which there can be no route back, that he is pulling her towards annihilation.

She looks ahead, along the remaining stretch of promenade, and thinks of the two Noels. She thinks of Dermot Flynn, of Mark Griffin's parents and sister. She thinks of all their lost, stolen futures.

Then she thinks of Mark himself, of his uncertain future, and of her own future, the reality and promise of each diminishing, slipping away with the passing hours, and as a plea, almost as a prayer, she gazes up and asks out loud what it will take, if anything, to save them.

*

What he did that night . . .

As Norton approaches the level crossing, the light turns red and the gates come down.

He waits, feeling overwhelmed all of a sudden – exhausted, short of breath.

What he did that night barely seems real to him anymore. It was so long ago now, and seems less like a sequence of concrete actions than a fragment from a dream – and a half-remembered, *mis*remembered one at that.

He stares through the gates, over to Strand Road.

But he was only doing what had to be done . . . to protect his interests, his family, his business. Just like tonight. Just like that other night, a while back, with Fitz.

In a sudden burst, the DART train, an illuminated streak of green, hurtles past along the railway line, click-clacking, click-clacking, the force of it seeming to correspond to – seeming to be commensurate with – the sudden force now pressing in on Norton's chest.

He closes his eyes, and the pain subsides.

Frank Bolger came to the house that night. The house on Griffith Avenue. He was on his way to a meeting in Drogheda and stopped by to have a quick word with Norton about the proposed rezoning of the Dunbrogan estate. Standing at the front door, he said he wanted to clarify his position – and face to face, man to man, not through the usual, twisted, sniping back channels that were so typical of local politics. He felt that Norton was a reasonable man and would respect Frank's position if it was presented to him in a proper and honest fashion. Norton invited him in. He was alone in the house. Miriam was out for the evening, at the theatre. They went through to the kitchen and sat down.

Frank was nervous, but coming here like this showed he had balls.

Norton actually admired him.

Click-clack, click-clack . . .

No compromise was going to be possible between them, though – because there was nothing new in Frank's much-vaunted 'position'. Dunbrogan House was a part of our heritage, he argued, and taking the wrecking ball to it would be nothing less than a tragedy. Blah, blah, blah. He then added – his voice a little shaky, but desperately earnest – that he wasn't going to be bullied or intimidated. He knew his old man wasn't happy about the stand he was taking either, but this was a matter of principle for him. So not only did he intend lobbying further against the rezoning, *and* speaking out about the dubious voting records of certain councillors, he also intended to publicly berate Miriam's father for selling off the property in the first place. And he made no apology for the fact.

Norton stared at him in disbelief.

Click-clack, click-clack . . .

'I don't know whether to laugh or cry,' he remembers saying.

Frank was the one who laughed, but nervously. Then he looked at his watch.

'OK,' he said, 'I just wanted to get that straight, put it on the record.' He cleared his throat and made a move to get up. 'Right. I'd better be going. I don't want to be late.'

Norton waved a dismissive hand at this.

'You'll be fine,' he said. 'The roads will be quiet at this hour. You'll fly up.'

It was in that moment – panic rising in his throat, like bile – that it came to him.

Click-clack, click-clack . . .

What he could do.

'Listen,' he said, 'I'm not going to argue with you, Frank. I can see there's no point. But I want to thank you for coming, I respect you for it.' He paused. 'Anyway, you'll have a drop for the road? Call it a peace offering.'

Frank hesitated, and then said, 'Sure, why not?'

'Good. I'll . . . just be a minute.'

Click-clack, click-clack . . .

Norton left the kitchen. The drinks cabinet was in the living room. But he went upstairs first, and into the bedroom. He went over to Miriam's bedside table. He picked up her bottle of sleeping pills. He opened it and shook one out into the palm of his hand. He went back downstairs. In the living room he poured out two drinks, whiskey with a splash of soda water. He crushed the pill between his thumb and forefinger and sprinkled it into the glass for Frank. He watched it dissolve. He had no real idea what he was doing, if it would work or not, or what effect it would have – but it was *something,* and he was desperate, because although Frank Bolger was earnest and naive, he was popular, he had that sheen to him, people listened, they paid attention . . .

Click-clack, click-clack . . .

Norton brought the glasses into the kitchen, handed one to Frank and raised his own.

'Your health.'

'Cheers.'

A few minutes later, Frank Bolger left. Got into his car. Took the airport road.

Click-clack, click-clack . . .

Drove north. Then came, at one point – drowsy, dreamy, seeing double – to a sharp bend in the road, where another . . .

Click-clack, click-clack . . .

Norton opens his eyes.

As suddenly as it appeared, the DART train is gone . . . and he's staring through the gates again at Strand Road.

But staring vacantly, distractedly.

Because it's a long time since he's done *that*, recalled it in sequence, recalled it whole. It's a long time since he's even thought about it at all.

But then, as the gates lift, the pain in his chest returns . . .

How easy it would be, Mark thinks, to surrender here, to drift off, to lose consciousness . . .

Which he probably *would* do, if it weren't for the incredible tension in his right arm and wrist, and the effort it's taking to hold this sharp-edged piece of ceramic tightly against the side of his neck.

A few feet away, leaning against the opposite wall, the guard is chewing his lip, jigging his right leg, waiting.

After he'd frantically fed Mark's instructions into his walkie-talkie and then listened for a moment, he'd held the walkie-talkie up and said, 'Couple of minutes. Two or three. *Tops.*'

But a hundred and eighty seconds?

That's an eternity.

And it's already been longer than that.

Farther down the hall, people are hovering, watching. Mark can't see them clearly.

He can't see anything clearly.

At his feet, the trickle of blood is inching forward and will soon be making contact with the pool of clear fluid from the burst infusion bag.

Mark glares at the guard.

'*Tell them to hurry up.*'

This time the pain is in Norton's shoulder, too, and all down his left arm.

He struggles to release the handbrake. Then he struggles to get a firm grip on the gearstick. When the bastard in the car behind beeps him several times in rapid succession, Norton rallies briefly and somehow manages to shunt the car forward – over the tracks and around to the left.

But once he is on this short tree-lined stretch of road that leads to the seafront, the pain intensifies, and is so severe for a couple of seconds that all he can see is a blinding flash of white light.

But he rallies again.

He spots a parking space on the right, in front of a large grey house, and on the spur of the moment – but awkwardly, without indicating – swerves over and pulls into it.

The car behind beeps him once more as it passes.

Closing his eyes, Norton heaves a long, nervous sigh.

At the end of the promenade, Gina turns around and starts walking back towards the Martello Tower. Behind it, looming in the distance, is that other tower, Richmond Plaza. Glimmering through the mist, white points of light dotted here and there, the building looks ghostly and insubstantial – though Gina understands that teams of welders are already in place, busily working around the clock to make headway on the repairs.

She looks away, a little queasy at the thought of her direct involvement in all of this. It's like an anxiety dream, one in which she has somehow – improbably, and with disastrous consequences – got mixed up in her brother's affairs.

She glances out across the bay, and then looks at her watch.

But it's not a dream, is it?

She stops at a bench and sits down.

In the background, she hears a car horn – a quick, impatient series of beeps.

She takes the glass paperweight out of her pocket, holds it in her lap, looks at it.

Millefiori.

A thousand flowers. What's she going to do? Hit him over the head with a thousand flowers?

Oh *God*, she suddenly thinks.

This is hopeless. It's insanity.

She gazes out into the heaving darkness.

Then she gets up, replaces the paperweight in her pocket, walks back towards the end of the promenade and passes over to the pavement running along by the main road.

Norton opens his eyes, tries to focus.

A few feet ahead of him there is another parked car, and several more beyond that. Farther on again, he can see the promenade.

But he can also –

He leans forward and stares for a second.

He can also see . . . *Gina* . . .

She's maybe a hundred yards away, at the end of the promenade, and walking in this direction.

He's pretty sure it's her.

Jesus.

He reaches across to the glove compartment and opens it.

With any luck he mightn't even have to get out of the car. He could be gone from here in minutes, before anyone . . .

He presses the button for the window. It hums open.

He looks ahead. She's getting closer, but slowly.

He puts a hand up to his chest.

Jesus, woman, come *on*.

There is a crackle of static and the guard holds the walkie-talkie up to his ear.

'Yeah?'

Mark leans forward on the bench, straining to hear, every nerve end in his body alert now.

The guard fumbles in his breast pocket for a notebook and pen.

Mark takes a deep breath.

He glances down the corridor.

There is some activity at the far end, through a set of double doors, but he can't make out what's going on.

He looks back at the guard.

'Come *on*.'

The guard tears a page from his notebook and steps forward, nervously, arm outstretched, as though feeding a lion through the bars of a cage.

Mark grabs the piece of paper with his free hand and puts it down beside him on the bench.

With the same hand he fishes the mobile phone out of his gown pocket. He glances around and then quickly starts punching in the number.

*

Where the hell is Norton?

This is the direction he should be coming from.

She keeps moving.

Up ahead there are some parked cars, but somehow she doesn't feel good about this.

After another few paces her mobile starts vibrating in the pocket of her jeans.

She slows down.

Maybe it's Norton.

She stops, extracts the phone.

Looks at the display. New number.

Shit.

She hesitates. Not *now*. But still brings the phone up to her ear.

'Hello?'

'*Gina?*'

It takes her a second.

'*Mark?*' She spins around to face the sea again, something inside her also turning. 'Thank God. You're OK.'

Grinding the nurse's phone into the side of his skull, Mark wonders if this is true, if he *is* OK, because he doesn't feel it, doesn't feel he has the strength to go on.

But all he has said so far is her name.

And that's not enough.

'*Listen* to me,' he then says, each syllable on its own taking so much effort he can't even be sure they're coming out in a logical sequence. '*Stay away from Paddy Norton. Don't go to meet him.*'

Gina is taken aback by this – not so much by the fact that Mark seems to know where she's going, but by his tone. It's a command, and for weeks that's all she's been hearing, commands, and negative ones, don't do this, don't do that . . .

Not something she responds well to.

And yet . . . and yet . . .

Isn't there something different about this one? Isn't he someone, of all people, she *should* listen to?

For his part, Mark – hanging on by a thread, waiting for some kind of reaction from Gina – can't help suspecting that he might be seriously deluded here, or insane, or just *too late* – a feeling that is compounded when he suddenly hears, down the phone line, a dull thud . . . followed by shattering glass and the sound of an alarm . . .

He freezes.

Waits.

Is she there? *Please.* Let her still be there, let her *say* it –

'*Gina?*' he whispers, unable to bear it any longer. '*What was that?*'

Then, for what feels like ages, but can be only a few seconds, there is silence, nothing, just the muted, filtered wailing of the alarm.

He is about to erupt when Gina speaks, her voice muffled and quiet.

'I don't know,' she says.

And it's true.

She has turned around again, and is in shock. Whatever that was is just up ahead.

She hesitates, trying to make sense of it.

'But look,' she says, starting to move. 'I'm OK, Mark. Really. Give me a few minutes and I'll call you back on this number.'

Slumped over the wheel now, Norton can't feel a thing.

He can't move.

It's all very weird – one second she's approaching, coming within range, and the next she's . . . what?

Slowing down? *Stopping?*

She's fucking turning around?

*Un*believable, he thinks.

So he loses it, starts rocking back and forth in his seat, banging his fists against the steering wheel, shouting, '*Move, move, MOVE*' – but it turns out he mustn't have put the hand brake on, because suddenly the car itself is moving, sliding forward, only a few feet, but knocking into the car in front, smashing its rear lights and triggering the alarm.

Triggering the pain again, too, it seems, and the white light . . . the pain even more severe than earlier, the light even more blinding . . .

But it's OK now. He doesn't *feel* the pain.

Not anymore.

Except, of course, that he *does*.

Because as everyone knows, there are different kinds of pain.

Like the pain of remembering.

Because back then, you see, he *did* know what he was doing – it's just that nothing was ever confirmed about it afterwards, nothing was ever said, no one ever used the words *autopsy* or *toxicology*. In those days there was no such thing as the Serious Accident Unit, and in any case the party handlers, for their own reasons, weren't slow in putting it about that the other man was to blame – so it wasn't long before Norton was able to convince himself that what *he'd* done . . . well, that maybe the two things, the pill and the crash, weren't directly connected after all . . .

The pill and the crash.

Alan Glynn

There's always been a part of his brain that has resisted joining *those* particular dots . . .

But not anymore.

The pill and the crash, the pill and the crash . . . the pill . . . the *crash* . . . the pill, the *crash,* the pill, the *crash* . . .

In his head, these words and the shrill, piercing tone of the alarm fall into alignment, merge, and become something new, a sound with a certain feel of permanence to it, a sound that might never ease, that might never subside . . .

On the edges of his vision, he can just about detect movement, flitting shapes, patterns. Is someone there? Maybe he could ask them to make the sound stop, or at least to turn it down, just a bit, just a *little* . . .

He tries to speak, tries with all his might, tries to utter even a single syllable, but in the end it is useless.

In the end no sound comes from his mouth.

Mark leans his head back against the wall, relaxes his arm and slowly lowers his hand from his neck.

He drops the fragment of the mug and it falls to the floor.

His hand is smeared with blood.

The guard, hovering at a discreet distance, seems reluctant to tackle Mark, but is probably already suspecting that when he's talking about this later in the pub he'll regret *not* having tackled him.

Or maybe, Mark thinks, he was ordered not to.

Like everyone else here, it seems.

Turning his head now to the left, weary beyond measure, struggling to focus, Mark sees them approaching – two men, striding with purpose, parting the ways. Doctors, nurses, admin staff, the guard . . . they all stand aside.

Mark then glances downwards and sees that the pool of clear fluid on the floor has become infused with the blood, and that streaks and rivulets of red are spreading outwards and making their way across the floor to the opposite wall.

Streaks and rivulets of *his* blood.

It'll make it easier for them, he thinks, easier in whatever way they have it in mind to finish him off.

A hurried struggle, some use of necessary force, a bullet even.

He starts to reduce, to shrink into himself.

He did his best. At least he tried.

Head down, he waits, listens.

Closes his eyes. Senses them standing there now.

Come on. Get it over with.

'Mark? Are you OK there? Mark?' The voice is calm, solicitous. '*Mark?* Look at me.'

He looks up.

Standing directly in front of him is a tall man with a stoop and silvery white hair.

'Mark,' the man says, 'I think we need to talk. I'm a detective superintendent. My name is Jackie Merrigan.'

Gina recognises the car at once.

It's *his*.

She walks slowly, approaching the scene with caution.

The alarm is still wailing, but in the strong east wind it sounds a little wobbly, a little plaintive. There are already people about – from the surrounding houses, from the line of cars now backed up to the level crossing.

Norton's car – however it happened – is lodged into the back of the car parked in front.

As she gets nearer, Gina sees a man coming out of a house on the left. His arm is outstretched and he is pointing something at the parked car.

The alarm stops ringing.

The silence that follows, at least for a few seconds, seems vast and dense with significance.

But this doesn't last.

More and more people appear, and by the time Gina gets right up to Norton's car, it is surrounded and she can't see a thing.

But she can hear the comments.

'*Yeah, he's dead,*' someone says, '*for sure . . . must have been a heart attack . . .*'

She leans against the garden railings behind her and glances around.

When the ambulance appears a few minutes later, and is inching its way down from the level crossing, she hears another comment. It comes from one of two young men who are taking turns peering in through the window of Norton's car.

'*Oh my God,*' she hears him say, '*What's that in his hand? Jesus, I think . . . I think it's a gun . . .*'

This piece of information passes like a lick of flame out of the window and spreads, almost visibly, from person to person, until the whole scene is engulfed with it.

A gun . . . a gun . . . a gun . . .

Gina swallows.

She sways from side to side now, gently, rhythmically, waiting for the ambulance to get as far as the car and stop.

When it does, the onlookers quickly disperse, and from where she's standing Gina catches a glimpse of the body.

It's a really strange scene, simultaneously pathetic and eerie. Norton is just slumped over the wheel. Everything is drenched in a wash of orange and blue, a combination of the streetlights and the slowly rotating beacons on top of the ambulance.

Gina wonders if he has the photographs on him, or in the car somewhere. Not that it matters anymore. Though if they *are* found, and identified, who knows what may yet transpire?

That's something she'll have to tell Mark about. It mightn't be easy to explain, but at least she now has the chance to try.

One of the paramedics opens the door of the car, and it's not long before Gina hears the first mention of Paddy Norton's name. She's not sure who says it; the words just seem to be floating on the air.

'Isn't that . . . I think . . . isn't that your man . . . it is . . . Paddy Norton . . .'

Then someone mentions Richmond Plaza.

At this, Gina immediately leans back against the railings, as far as she can, and looks to the right. There's a curve in the road, and from the angle she's standing at the building is just about visible in the crook of the bay. As she gazes at it now a tiny flash of light, a Roman candle effect – what at this distance she can only assume is a gush of welding sparks – seems to shoot off the side of it and into the night-time mist.

It's as though the building, like a wounded organism, is busy renewing itself, carrying out its own repairs, determined to survive.

Reverting – of *course* – to Noel's original specs.

And with this dawning realisation comes an acute sense of relief. Because among other things it means that she can stop now, finally – she can *stop*.

And maybe even carry out some repairs, engage in a renewal process of her own.

She closes her eyes for a moment.

When she opens them again, a garda squad car is approaching from the seafront section of Strand Road.

Before it pulls up, Gina takes off – and without a further glance at the building, at Norton's car, or at Norton himself. She passes through the crowd of assembled bystanders and walks along the pavement towards the level crossing.

As she moves, she reaches into her pocket to get the phone out. Her hand is shaking a little. She looks for the number and presses Call, and as she waits, in the background, from over the houses to her left, she can hear seagulls squawking and the faint sound of the tide lapping up onto Sandymount Strand.

Read on for an excerpt from
Alan Glynn's next thriller,

BLOODLAND

Coming Winter 2012
in trade paperback from Picador

The way his heart is beating is unreal, the rate, the intensity – it's like a jackhammer drilling into rock. He puts a hand up to his chest, and waits, gauges. This has to be close to some upper limit of what his or anyone else's heart is capable of enduring, because it's only an organ after all, a pump, a piece of meat, dark, red, wet – and incessant, naturally . . . but not imperishable, not indestructible.

You can push it, but only so far.

Weird thing is, however, he's not actually doing anything right now – he's not on a treadmill, or on top of some girl, he's not running from anyone or engaged in direct combat. What he's doing is sitting in the passenger seat of an SUV next to the most chilled-out motherfucker he's ever met in his entire life. They're both former servicemen, he and this other guy, and are virtual clones to look at – the buzz cuts, the pumped-up muscles, the armored vests, the mirrored shades – but Ray Kroner is prepared to lay even money that whereas he is ramped up to the max, his dial straining at eleven, Tom Szymanski here is barely a notch or two above clinically dead.

OK, Ray has got 600 milligrams of Provigil in his system, but that's not what this is. Big in the military, and even bigger now in the PMCs, Provigil will keep you awake for days on end, but it's not speed, it's not even coffee, it's just like an off switch right next to the sleep option in your brain – press it and one thing you won't have to worry about anymore is getting tired.

Ray looks out at the passing terrain.

This two-mile dirt track they're on runs from the compound to the landing strip. The SUV he and Szymanski are in is the last in a convoy of three, with the 'package' just up ahead, and it's a safe route, they do it all the time, no need for armored personnel carriers or anything.

So that's not what this is about either.

Could it be the heat then? Because man, it's hot here, and not dry hot like Iraq, or even Phoenix; it's humid, sweltering, you can't breathe – four in the morning and you're like a beached fucking whale. It's unbearable. Pretty much like everything else in this shithole of a country.

Except of course that he can bear it, because he's trained to, and he's experienced – and if hot weather really was a problem for him, he wouldn't be here in the first place, would he? So what is his problem?

Why is his heart racing like this?

Is it the choices he's made? Quitting work last spring? Walking out on Janice? Selling the car, the computer, even Pop's old vinyls? Scraping enough money together to pay for the six-week training course? And all so he could do this again, hold a Bushmaster M4 in his hands? In his arms? Cradle it? Stroke it? The hard chrome, the matte black finish, the coated steel and aluminum?

Nah.

Those choices were inevitable, pre-ordained. The six months he spent at home after his tour in Iraq were a disaster, and when the momentum started building in his head after he read that magazine article about Gideon Global, he just knew where it was leading and he went with it, didn't resist, let it envelop him. Janice was pretty much an alien by this stage anyway, with all that delusional new-age self-help shit she'd been gorging on while he was away, not that he's blaming her or anything, he just couldn't listen to it, the gossamer-light optimism, the breezy promises . . . not after what he'd seen.

And wanted to see again.

He closes his eyes.

Wants to see again.

But strangely enough still hasn't.

Because what's ironic is that this country is ten times more of a catastrophe than Iraq ever was, or ever will be, with millions dead, literally, and the kind of barbarism going on every day that even a sick fuck like him would be hard-pressed to imagine.

On top of which, as a private contractor, he's getting paid ten times more for being here.

It's weird.

He opens his eyes again, and looks around.

In Baghdad he often went on convoy runs like this one, from the Green Zone to the airport, but along what was essentially a six-mile shooting gallery of snipers and car bombers, a flat, sunbaked road with endless blackened auto husks and rotting corpses strewn on either side of it.

Here on this route it's just, well . . . countryside, scrubland, lush green hills, faraway mountain peaks, and one roadside village – up ahead a bit now – which is little more than a cluster of wooden huts with aluminum roofs and a single-story concrete structure, dusty and shell-like, that has a faded Coca-Cola sign hanging off the front of it.

A village.

With never too much going on.

Which is the exact opposite of what it was like in Baghdad, where something was happening all the time – a guy pretending to repair his stalled car over here, a vehicle suddenly cutting across the median over there, and people just standing around, random pedestrians, old men, raggedy kids, spooky-looking women in black chadors, everyone gazing up at you with suspicion or even hatred in their eyes . . .

It meant you were permanently on edge, coiled tight, ready to respond at any second.

Which is something about here, actually, that he misses.

But then, curiously, in that very moment – and unlike his heartbeat – the convoy starts to slow down.

'What the fuck,' Szymanski says under his breath.

They're approaching the edge of the village, where something seems to be happening.

They both crane forward, and sideways a bit, to try and get a better view.

Then the radio crackles to life.

'Deep Six, stand by, some kind of bullshit here.'

Szymanski is Deep Six. His radio call sign. The guy up ahead, in the lead vehicle – Peter Lutz, their unit commander – is Tube.

Ray is Ashes. As in rising from. And Phoenix. His hometown.

After another few seconds, the convoy – flush now with a cluster of huts on the right and the concrete structure on the left – comes to a complete halt.

'Man,' Szymanski says, with a weary sigh, and leans forward over the steering wheel.

Ray stares out of the window.

The village, he thinks – half in wonder, half in disgust – the village. What is a fucking village anyway? Do they even have them anymore, outside of fairy tales, and Europe, and Vietnam, and godforsaken shit-holes like this one?

The village.

Against all protocol, he suddenly turns, opens the door of the SUV and gets out.

'The fuck, man,' Szymanski says.

The door remains open.

'Ashes, what are you doing?' an alarmed Tube adds, over the radio.

Ignoring them both, and with a firm grip on his M4, Ray steps away from the convoy to get a proper view of what is going on.

'Get back in, man. Jesus.'

In the second car, the package – some grey-suited fuck from New York or Washington – has his window down and is looking over at the wooden huts, clearly nervous.

Up ahead, Ray sees what is wrong – there's a pile of vegetables or some shit spilled in the middle of the road, and two women are frantically loading whatever it is back into a large wicker basket.

Behind them, playing, are three small children.

Ray glances across at the wooden huts and thinks he detects some-thing . . . inside one of them, movement . . . someone . . . moving. Then he turns in the other direction and looks towards the concrete structure, only a sliver of which he can actually see, due to the position of the two SUVs. But framed there in the space between them is a tall man leaning against the wall, staring right back at him.

The man's face is long and drawn, his expression intense, his eyes bloodshot.

He seems restive, restless . . . shifty.

Ray hears the crackle of another radio communication from inside the car, but he can't make out what is being said.

He looks around again, rapidly – at the huts, between the SUVs, up ahead – only difference this time being that the two women have stopped doing what they were doing.

Perfectly still now, crouched on the ground, they too are staring directly at him.

And that's when it dawns on Ray what's going on, what this is – it's not fear, not anxiety, not regret, it's anticipation . . . a sickly, pounding realization of what might happen here, of what he might do, of what he might be capable of doing, and while there's no way he could have known in advance they were going to stop in this village, not consciously anyway, it's as if his body knew, as if every nerve ending in his system knew, recognized the signals, picked up on them, so that now, as he raises his weapon a little higher, he feels the rhythm of his heartbeat falling into sync with the rhythm of this unfolding situation. . . .

He directs the muzzle of the gun at the huts, then at the women and children.

'Kroner, Jesus, are you fucking crazy?'

Ray glances back at the car, Deep Six more animated than he has ever seen him.

In the middle car, the package is still staring out of the window, a look of horror forming on his face. It's as though the anticipation has spread, as though it's a virus, or a stain, alive somehow, crimson and thirsty.

Ray swallows.

He's thirsty himself, the feeling in his veins now, inexorable, like a dark, slowly uncoiling sexual desire that senses imminent release.

He puts his finger on the trigger.

A few feet away, the door of the lead car opens slightly, just a crack.

'RAY.'

This is shouted.

Ray exerts a tiny amount of pressure on the trigger.

'Tube,' he shouts back.

'DON'T.'

The car door clicks shut again.

Ray re-focuses, taking everything in.

But there's no longer any movement he can detect from inside the huts. And the man at the concrete wall is inert now, frozen – like a splash of detail from some busy urban mural.

The women ahead are frozen too, and still staring at him – though the children in the background seem oblivious, unaware. . . .

Hopping, dancing. Licks of flames.

In the oppressive heat, Ray shivers.

He really doesn't have any idea what he is doing, or why, but one thing he does know – there is nothing on earth, nothing on the vast continent of Africa, nothing in the even greater interior vastness of Congo itself, that can stop him now from doing it.